GHOST OF THE TON

Misfits of the Ton
Book Ten

by
Emily Royal

ARE YOU SIGNED UP FOR DRAGONBLADE'S BLOG?

You'll get the latest news and information on exclusive giveaways, exclusive excerpts, coming releases, sales, free books, cover reveals and more.

Check out our complete list of authors, too!

No spam, no junk. That's a promise!

Sign Up Here

www.dragonbladepublishing.com

Dearest Reader;

Thank you for your support of a small press. At Dragonblade Publishing, we strive to bring you the highest quality Historical Romance from some of the best authors in the business. Without your support, there is no 'us', so we sincerely hope you adore these stories and find some new favorite authors along the way.

Happy Reading!

CEO, Dragonblade Publishing

Additional Dragonblade books by Author Emily Royal

Misfits of the Ton
Tomboy of the Ton (Book 1)
Ruined by the Ton (Book 2)
Thief of the Ton (Book 3)
Oddity of the Ton (Book 4)
Harpy of the Ton (Book 5)
Heartbreaker of the Ton (Book 6)
Doxy for the Ton (Book 7)
Duelist for the Ton (Book 8)
Taciturn in the Ton (Book 9)
Ghost of the Ton (Book 10)
The Taming of the Duke (Novella)

Headstrong Harts
What the Hart Wants (Book 1)
Queen of my Hart (Book 2)
Hidden Hart (Book 3)
The Prizefighter's Hart (Book 4)
All I Want for Christmas is My Hart (Novella)
Haunted Hart (Novella)

London Libertines
Henry's Bride (Book 1)
Hawthorne's Wife (Book 2)
Roderick's Widow (Book 3)
A Libertine's Christmas Miracle (Novella)

The Lyon's Den Series
A Lyon's Pride
Lyon of the Highlands
Lyon of the Ton
The Lyon and the Unicorn

PROLOGUE

Glenblath Chapel, Scotland

"THE STATE OF holy matrimony is not to be taken lightly, wantonly, nor for the pursuit of carnal pleasure."

Hamish glanced at the woman standing beside him at the altar.

Nae worries about the pursuit of carnal pleasure, vicar: There's more chance of a flock of grouse flying out of my arse.

Almost as if she'd heard, the bride turned toward him. The veil concealed her face, but Hamish could picture her expression, the haughty disdain that had soured her features the moment they met. Pretty enough—many would say beautiful, with her chestnut tresses and aquamarine eyes. But the contempt gleaming from those orbs, the pointed nose wrinkled in disgust, not to mention the permanent sneer on those fair lips...the sight of them was imprinted into his mind, like an indelible shit stain on a man's britches.

That's unfair, son.

Hamish winced as his ma's voice whispered in his mind, repeating the admonishment she'd doled out many times since the Honorable Aurora Young had been presented to him.

He glanced at his mother in the front pew. Once hailed as the Beauty of the Highlands, her eyes now carried the burden of years gone by—an unhappy marriage, innumerable harsh winters, influenza...

...and the reduction of the Glenblath estate to near penury that necessitated Hamish's marriage today.

But, as Ma endured a loveless marriage, so must I.

"Ahem."

Hamish resumed his attention on the minister—the man who'd be responsible for securing the marriage manacles around Hamish's ankles.

Reverend Sutherland arched an eyebrow and Hamish could almost hear the man's voice in his mind, sharp and stern.

Pray tell me when yer mind has returned from its feverish wanderings so that I might continue with this sacred ceremony for which ye seem to harbor little reverence.

A small huff of impatience came from behind the bride's veil.

Perhaps the minister should have included a prayer to protect the groom from a henpecking harpy. For it was universally known that a woman's gentleness of character was in exact inverse proportion to her beauty. And the Honorable Aurora Young was the epitome of that rule, in that she was a very beautiful woman indeed.

Unlike…

No.

There was little merit in dwelling on she who had been merely a means to an end—the woman who no longer lived. The Honorable Aurora was his bride. She would, in time, adapt to her role as Lady of Glenblath.

Perhaps a kind soul lay beneath Aurora's cold exterior.

Very far beneath.

Hamish's late father had said that if a man were to understand what the wife he chose would be like, he only need look at her mother. The Honorable Aurora had no mother, but her father stood across the aisle like a spider waiting to suck the life out of his prey.

Might the Honorable Aurora suck the life out of me?

But perhaps, once she were free from her father's menacing influence, Aurora might blossom into a flower rather than sharpen into a thorn. It hadn't escaped Hamish's notice that Lord Young had looked upon his daughter with disgust as he propelled her along the aisle, his skeletal fingers gripping her upper arm and leaving an indent in the fabric of her bridal gown. Doubtless, Hamish would reveal a bruise when he succumbed to duty tonight and disrobed her.

Perhaps, when she realized that Hamish was not an advocate of punishing a woman into filial or marital obedience, she might nurture a spark of gratitude, which, though unlikely to blossom into love, might, with a little luck and a following wind, grow into some kind of regard for him.

If all else failed her dowry would, at least, ensure the survival of Glenblath.

That was how Hamish viewed his bride. She was merely a means to ensure that the long-overdue repairs to the estate buildings could begin, that finer fare could grace the tables at Glenblath, and, more importantly, that his ma could, once again, seek the services of a reputable doctor. Any physician would be better than the charlatan from the next village who seemed to think that leeches were the answer to every ailment—a leech on the chest for a chill, leeches along the arms to soothe aching bones after a day's work in the fields, and, no doubt, a leech on Hamish's cock if his seed failed to strike root in the Honorable Aurora's belly.

"Laird MacLennan?"

Shit. He'd done it again—let his mind drift from the vicar's monotones and the unsavory prospect of lifting the Honorable Aurora's skirts.

"Pray continue, Reverend Sutherland," Hamish said.

The minister dipped his head until he was staring at Hamish over the top of his spectacles.

"Ye're *too* kind. Laird MacLennan."

The minister resumed his attention on the open book in his hands.

"I therefore charge every soul here today," he said, "in full understanding of the dreadful day of judgment that comes upon us all when the truth shall be revealed, even that which we seek to hide in this mortal life, though such reckless concealment should result in a descent into the pits of hell…"

Holy ballocks—did the man have to sound as if he enjoyed threatening damnation upon his flock with such relish?

The minister licked his lips before continuing.

That'll be an aye, then.

"…that if any of ye here today know of any just cause and impediment why the two souls before ye today should not be joined in holy matrimony, then ye must declare it here and now, or forever suffer the dreadful wrath of…"

The minister paused as the door rattled, followed by the metallic clink of the door handle and the creak of the hinges, as if the door groaned in protest at being opened at such a solemn moment.

Then footsteps—too light to be a man's—clicked on the flagstones.

Hamish allowed himself a smile. In all likelihood it was Maisie. She'd promised to attend the wedding, to slip into a pew at the back once the ceremony had started and be gone long before the congregation departed for the wedding breakfast. As she had told him when he'd ridden her last week as a parting gift ahead of a lifetime of monogamy, it was not the done thing for the local whore to remind the company too rudely of her existence. Half the men sitting in the chapel had paid for Maisie's services and would have to conceal their lust for fear of having their wives chew their ballocks off.

The footsteps came to a halt. The minister cleared his throat, then continued.

"I ask that if any of ye know of any impediment why—"

"I do," a female voice said.

Hamish glanced at the veiled creature next to him. Was she that eager to wed him that she uttered her vows before being asked?

But it wasn't the bride who'd spoken.

The minister lifted his chin and looked over Hamish's shoulder.

"I beg pardon, Miss…?"

"I know of a…" The voice hesitated. "I mean…there is an impediment."

Whispers threaded through the congregation and Hamish turned toward the owner of the voice.

Standing halfway along the aisle was a woman. She wore a veil, but there ended the resemblance to a bride. Instead of a white gown, she wore a coat the color of charcoal, beneath which peeked the hem of a dark-orange skirt, and she carried a valise rather than a bridal bouquet. Her veil was not the pure bone-white lace of the bride's. It was dark blue, but fine enough in texture to discern a pair of eyes gleaming from behind the fabric.

"I beg pardon?" the minister said.

"I said there's an impediment," the woman replied. "This man is already married."

The minister cleared his throat. "I'm afraid ye're mistaken."

The woman gestured toward Hamish. "You are Hamish MacLennan?" she said. "Hamish Alastair Jamie MacLennan?"

Holy fuck.

A cold knot of dread curled in Hamish's gut.

"Aye," he whispered.

"In which case, I'm *not* mistaken," the woman said. "You are already married."

"To whom?" the minister asked.

She tilted her head to one side and Hamish caught the hard-ened expression in her eyes as she removed all doubt, and with it, his hopes.

"To me."

CHAPTER ONE

Gracechurch Street, London, three months earlier

"MISS LUCAS, WE buried your father today."

The voice, though gentle, hammered against Mia's senses, joining the constant throb of pain that swelled and receded with each rattling breath she drew.

"D-Doctor McIver, I-I…"

"Hush, lass, dinnae speak if it pains ye." A shadow moved, an indistinct form looming over her against the backdrop of a blurred world, as if Death had come to claim her so that she might join Papa. But, instead, she felt a soft coolness on her forehead.

Footsteps approached, followed by the creaking of a door.

"Ye cannae enter, Mr. Sullivan," the doctor said.

"You cannot deny me. I'm her cousin, her only living relative."

And the sole beneficiary if she dies unmarried.

Though the last words were left unsaid, Mia heard them in her cousin's tone, the nasal whine she recalled from when she'd first encountered him as a child—lazy, selfish, with soft, fleshy fingers that were all too likely to dip into drawers, caskets, and desks to appropriate that which didn't belong to him.

"Yer cousin's too ill to see anyone," Dr. McIver said.

"Yet she'll see *you*."

"I'm her doctor."

"And, no doubt, looking for a tidy sum to charge in lieu of your services. Her fortune may be small, but she has no right to fritter it away."

"Whereas ye have?" the doctor said, an edge to his voice. "Ye visiting yer cousin will not expedite her departure from the world in order for ye to claim yer inheritance, which, I presume, is the only reason ye've come to see her."

"How dare—"

"However," the doctor interrupted, "it might bring about yer demise. Smallpox is highly contagious."

Had the act of breathing not brought about a spasm of pain, Mia might have laughed at her cousin's yelp of fear.

"P-perhaps I'll visit another time," her cousin said, fear tightening his voice. "Do you know the identity of my uncle's lawyer?"

"Yer uncle's will has already been read, Mr. Sullivan."

"Very well, my cousin's lawyer."

Mia inhaled, shuddering.

"I-I'm not dead yet, cousin," she croaked. "I'm…"

Her throat tightened in a spasm of pain and a wave of heat rippled through her veins. The doctor placed a light hand on her shoulder.

"Dinnae speak, lass, for yer own sake." Then his voice hardened. "Mr. Sullivan, I'd advise ye to leave. The greatest service ye can do is to let yer cousin die in peace."

Mia closed her eyes.

"So, she'll not survive?" her cousin said.

"The chances are slight," the doctor said. "The chances of yer survival are diminishing with every moment ye spend in this room."

"Then I'll bid you good day, Dr. McIver. I trust you'll inform my lawyers when she—"

He broke off with a yelp. Mia heard a scuffle, followed by two sets of footsteps receding. Then a door slammed in the distance. She resumed her attention on the looming darkness, letting her body sink into the bed, which seemed to drift in and out of the mortal world.

The chances are slight.

Most of Dr. McIver's patients would have preferred him to coat his diagnoses in honey, or utter falsehoods to peddle hope in lieu of a fee. But the straight-talking Scot was never a man to embellish his words with poetry or tales best confined to the nursery.

If only he had been my father, rather than...

Then Mia admonished herself. Papa had loved her, in his own way. He now lay cold in his grave and she hadn't been able to bid him farewell.

The footsteps returned, a single set this time, and Mia caught the unmistakable scent of lavender.

"Dr. McIver, i-is he...?"

"Yer cousin won't be visiting ye any more, lass. I've told Gertie not to admit him again."

Mia opened her eyes and the doctor's concerned face swam into view, blurred by pain and tears.

"I-I'm sorry, I..."

"Hush, lass. Here—take this. It'll ease yer pain."

Something cold and unyielding was pressed to her lips. Obediently she parted them and liquid slipped onto her tongue, filling her mouth with its bitter taste.

"H-how long...?"

He placed a hand on her shoulder. "How long have ye got? The crisis should come within three or four days, after which..." His voice cracked a little before he continued. "I'll make sure ye're comfortable, lass. And Gertie will remain with ye until the end."

"Three or four days?"

"A week, at most. Now, is there anything ye want?"

Mia nodded, then winced at the stab of pain in her neck. "I want to see Mr. Stockton. I wish to settle my affairs before—"

She broke off, unwilling to voice what must be inevitable, though she lauded the doctor for voicing it.

"Yer affairs are already settled, lass," he replied. "That vile cousin of yers—if ye'll permit me to speak so freely—is to inherit under rules of the entailment. There's no way to prevent it."

"There's one way," Mia whispered. She blinked, clearing her vision for a moment, and winced against the bright backdrop of sunlight from the window that silhouetted the doctor's frame.

Then the doctor, displaying the intelligence and insight that set him apart from the rest of his profession—nay, the rest of his sex—drew a sharp intake of breath.

"Ye dinnae mean…"

"Yes, Dr. McIver," Mia said, ignoring the agony in her throat as she voiced what was to be her last wish. "I want a husband. I wish to marry before I die."

CHAPTER TWO

"I'M AFRAID I'VE exhausted every path, Lord MacLennan. I cannot secure you credit from any of the London banks."

Hamish clasped his hands together as the lawyer delivered the news. "Not even the Hart Bank, Mr. Stockton?"

"*Especially* not the Hart Bank. Mr. Hart has a keen understanding of business risk and is therefore very particular about whom he accepts as a client."

Fucking Sassenachs.

The solicitor's clear gray eyes glittered with disapproval, almost as if he'd heard the insult.

"Lord MacLennan, if you're about to accuse Mr. Hart of harboring prejudice based on nationality, I'd counsel you to first consider the prejudice *you* harbor against the English. Such outmoded attitudes hamper a man's ability to flourish in business."

Pompous arse!

"I'm sure I can find another solicitor more easily than a creditor, Mr. Stockton," Hamish said.

"You're at liberty to try, Lord MacLennan. But you must settle your account with us before attempting to engage the services of another. Until you do, I cannot in all conscience recommend another firm to you—nor vice versa. I only agreed to take you on as a client because your solicitor in Edinburgh, Mr. McSwain, confirmed that you had settled all your accounts to date. You'll find that lawyers are less inclined to take risks with their finances than bankers."

Hamish sighed. "But I cannae…" His voice trailed off and he shook his head. This venture was proving to be an utter disaster. The funds expended in coming to London were only a worthwhile investment if he could, among the London bankers, secure credit that those situated in Edinburgh no longer extended. But bankers had an annoying habit of talking to each other, even across the border between Scotland and England. The MacLennan name, rather than serving as a key to unlock Society's doors, instead served as a warning to creditors not wishing to take on an unacceptable degree of risk, and fathers not wishing to hand their daughters' dowries over to a wastrel.

Unacceptable degree of risk. That was the phrase that almost every London banker had tossed at him.

He slumped back in his chair and sighed, letting the mask slip for a heartbeat. Then he gritted his teeth, sat up, bringing his big body to its full height as much as he could, and leaned toward the older man. Any other man, when faced with a sight such as he—a wild beast of a Highlander, built for savagery, his eyes flashing with determination and teeth ready to tear into the neck of his prey—would have crumpled. But the little solicitor, with his quiet self-assurance and calm dignity, did more to break Hamish's resolve than the most hardened clansman, bloody and mud spattered, readying himself for battle.

Clearly, battles were fought differently in the drawing rooms of London. Funds couldn't be gained by standing half a head taller than a prospective creditor, and wives couldn't be procured by tossing a woman over his shoulder and carrying her back to his lair.

What he wouldn't give to return to the days of Medieval savagery, when life was simpler and a man could simply take what he wanted!

The solicitor regarded Hamish with an intelligence he couldn't hope to match, able to see the desperate man beneath

Hamish's Highland brawn.

"Is there nothing I can do, Mr. Stockton?" Hamish said. "I've no wish to lose my home. Many souls depend on the survival of Glenblath. I cannae see them suffer as a result of my inability to remain solvent."

Or rather, his forebears' inability. But there was little point in wasting time blaming others. Like it or not, the burden of rectification lay upon him.

As if in acknowledgment of Hamish, at last, revealing his desperation, the solicitor smiled. He reached for the decanter on his desk, shook a measure into a beveled glass, and pushed it toward Hamish before pouring a second glass for himself. Hamish lifted his glass and took a sip.

"I applaud your honesty," the solicitor said. "Most of my clients never reveal their true wishes. Instead, they ask for that which they believe will help to accomplish what they desire."

Now he was talking in riddles—like all lawyers who issued salvo after salvo of incomprehensible phrases, often in Latin, which only their fellow lawyers could hope to understand. A ploy to perpetuate their businesses, given that their unsuspecting clients had no hope of understanding them.

Still, at least he kept a decent brandy.

"I think," the solicitor said, setting his glass aside, "I might have a solution to your problem. Well, not a *solution*, but a respite."

"Respite?"

The solicitor nodded. "It's a little unconventional. You'd have to act quickly, but out of all my clients, I consider you the most worthy."

Worthy? What the devil did he mean?

"Though Mr. McSwain gave me this list of your creditors," the solicitor continued as he held up a piece of paper, a very *long* piece of paper, "he said that you're an honest man whose financial situation is not of your doing."

"Worthy of what, Mr. Stockton?" Hamish said.

"A little good fortune."

"Are ye about to present me with a fortune?"

"Only a small fortune, to be acquired in a most unusual fashion."

"Ye mean it comes with a condition attached," Hamish said.

"Yes, but sadly that condition will be short-lived."

For a moment, the solicitor's expression slipped, revealing a flicker of sorrow.

"As will the benefactor," he said, more quietly.

So that was it.

Hamish leaned back in his chair. "Ye have a dying client wishing to act as benefactor."

"After a fashion," Stockton replied.

"And the client wishes me to meet him to demonstrate my worth?"

The lawyer shook his head.

"I'll do anything he wishes," Hamish said.

"The client's a young woman."

"What does she want?" Hamish lifted the glass to his lips for another sip.

"You must marry her."

Hamish caught his breath as he swallowed a mouthful of brandy. The liquid exploded on his tongue, sending fire through his throat, and he spasmed into a cough as he spluttered droplets onto the papers before him.

The solicitor raised his eyebrows. "I thought you'd be surprised. The marriage will need to take place within the next few days. I've already secured leave for a special license."

Hamish wiped his mouth then set his glass aside. "So soon? If I'm to marry, I should at least get to know the lass."

"That won't be possible. My client's gravely ill and isn't expected to survive more than a week, at most."

Sweet Lord Almighty! "Y-ye said she's a young woman?"

The solicitor nodded, a grave expression in his eyes. "She's been struck down with smallpox. Her father passed two days ago and the poor girl was too ill to attend the ceremony."

"Then why…" Hamish made a random gesture in the air.

"She wants her fortune to pass to a better man than her cousin, who, under the terms of the entail, is the sole beneficiary. If she marries, her fortune passes to her husband."

The solicitor paused, waiting for the obvious question. But Hamish didn't have the heart to ask it.

"The fortune's a little over one thousand," he said. "Not enough to repay all your debts, but it should clear those attracting the highest rates of interest, thereby easing the burden on your estate enough to enable you to clear the remainder of the debts over"—he eyed the papers in front of him—"over the next year. Quicker if you employ thrift."

"It seems a little callous," Hamish said.

"Your concern does you credit, Lord MacLennan. But the young woman asked me to find a suitable man and I presented your case to her." Stockton raised his hand as Hamish leaned forward to respond. "Naturally, I refrained from divulging your name in case you weren't in agreement. I merely told her that I'd found a young man with some debts in need of settling." He gave a wry smile. "In that respect, you're in a similar predicament to her cousin. However, his debts have been incurred through drinking, gaming and"—for the first time, the solicitor's cheeks colored—"indulging in the baser amusements that London offers a young man who cares only for his own pleasure. You, Lord MacLennan, strike me as a man who, though he may indulge in pleasure himself, does not do so to the detriment of those who depend on him."

Which was the lawyer's way of saying, in his pompous, businesslike language, that he was expecting Hamish to spend the funds on his estate, whereas the woman's cousin would piss, gamble, and fuck it away in London's dens of iniquity.

"Very well," Hamish said. "I'm ashamed to say my circumstances are such that I'm obliged to accept such an offer. But what if the young woman…"

What if she survives?

No—he couldn't bring himself to ask such a question.

"Miss Lucas is already near death," Stockton said, his voice almost a whisper. "We may already be too late, but she's determined to survive until her hand, and her fortune, is secured with another. I understand that the prospect may be unsavory to you. But rest assured that marrying Miss Lucas on her deathbed is the greatest service that any man can perform. You'll have the satisfaction of knowing that you granted a dying woman her final wish."

Miss Lucas.

Hearing her name on the lawyer's lips brought the circumstances from behind the fog of supposition, to the stark forefront of reality.

The solicitor sighed. "Were she to survive, you'd be a fortunate man to have her for a wife. I would rather she *did* survive, but I'm instructed to act in a manner which anticipates that outcome not happening."

Hamish paused, then nodded. "What do ye know of her?"

"Her name is Euphramia Mary Lucas."

Euphramia…

Hamish played with the name in his mind, imagining how it might sound on his lips.

"She's the only daughter of Dr. Lucas," the solicitor continued. "An intelligent young woman with ambitions herself to become a doctor that were thwarted not only because of her sex but because of her father's insistence that she restrict herself to the pursuits of a woman."

"Yet she is near death?"

"Not even doctors are protected from the onset of disease, Lord MacLennan, particularly when they refuse to administer modern treatment." The lawyer's tone hardened. "The poor girl tried to persuade her father to agree to them both taking this new smallpox vaccine. But Dr. Lucas refused. That refusal cost him his life, and will soon cost that of his daughter."

Poor lass, to have her life curtailed by the man who believed he owned her! But it was a fate that many women shared. Hamish had seen the toll on his ma, whom his da had considered to be his rightful property—his to own, to sap her strength and spirit.

Perhaps, if Hamish agreed to marry Miss Lucas, he could take comfort in thwarting the ambitions of a man who believed he owned her. He would give her his name, then honor hers by praying for her each day so that her spirit might survive, even if her body did not.

"Very well, Mr. Stockton," he said, at length. "I agree. Tell Miss Lucas that I offer my hand willingly and gratefully. I'll present myself as soon as required—today, if necessary."

The solicitor nodded his approval, then stood and extended his hand. Hamish took it and the older man held his hand in a surprisingly firm grip. Then he summoned a clerk to usher Hamish out of the building with a promise that he'd send a message to take him to his bride forthwith.

Not the most conventional of courtships, but Hamish had never wished to fritter away his soul and funds trotting about London wooing a brittle, haughty debutante.

And, by the time he returned to Glenblath, he'd be solvent— or at least, a little *more* solvent—and widowed, neither of which he'd expected when entered London.

But then, the winds of Fate never blew as a man expected.

CHAPTER THREE

THE CLOAK OF oblivion seemed to hover merely inches above Mia's body, waiting to descend and claim her at last. But she held it at bay, willing Death to be patient.

Only a few hours more, then you can take me.

A slow, steady drumbeat echoed in her mind—as if to herald her departure. At first it was thick and low, in unison with her heartbeat, vibrating through her bones. Then she heard footsteps.

Perhaps it was an angel, or a demon, come to ascertain whether her soul was virtuous enough to ascend into heaven?

But she was not virtuous. She had sinned. In the eyes of the Almighty she'd displayed filial disobedience and defiance rather than the meekness expected of a dutiful daughter. And her strength was fading—she could feel it draining from her mind and body.

A hand touched her shoulder.

"N-not yet," she croaked. "I'm not ready."

She creaked her eyes open and groaned at the intensity of the light. Then a veil was placed over her face and gentle hands took her by the arms and pulled her upright.

"It's time, miss," a voice whispered.

"Time for my death, Gertie?" Mia whispered. "Do you place the shroud over me in preparation?"

"No, sweet girl," Gertie said, her voice filled with the rich warmth of a kind soul dedicated to the service of others. "It's time for your wedding. This is your bridal veil."

"M-my…?"

Then Mia recalled the previous day, when Mr. Stockton had presented her with the details of a young man in need of funds. A good, whole-hearted man dedicated to improving the lot of others. Not a Society gentleman who'd fritter away her fortune at the gaming tables, but a Highlander, raised in the mountains, among fresh air and clear skies. A man who worked the land. A little roughened around the edges, the lawyer had said. But beauty and gentility rarely went hand in hand with true goodness.

There was a knock on the door, and three figures entered. Mia could discern the familiar shape of Dr. McIver, who approached the bed, his frame obscuring the others. He placed his hand on her arm.

"Ye're burning up, lass."

Mia shook her head as a shiver rippled over her skin. "It's cold…so cold."

Gentle hands pushed her forward, then a shawl was wrapped around her shoulders and she was pushed back onto the pillows.

"There!" Gertie said. "You look like a proper bride. Beautiful."

Mia's eyes stung with tears as she recalled the image of the sores on her arms and how the doctor had refused to hand her a mirror so that she might see those on her face—sores that burned and itched despite the lotions Gertie applied.

"Have ye given her anything, Gertie?"

"No, Dr. McIver, sir. I-I thought it best to leave the laudanum until after the ceremony, in case she—"

"Just so," the doctor interrupted.

In case she does not wake.

"Forgive me," Gertie said. Then she leaned close and whispered in Mia's ear. "Your bridegroom's here. He's as fine a young man as I ever saw."

Dr. McIver stepped aside and Mia saw two blurred shapes in the doorway.

"Reverend Staines, we should proceed," the doctor said. "Miss Lucas is very weak and I have no wish to overtax her."

Reverend *Staines*?

"No…"

Mia turned her face aside with shame. Not one week earlier she had accompanied Reverend Staines—or rather, *Lord* Staines— to Olivia Whitcombe's wedding, thereby placing the entire congregation at risk of infection. How he must hate her!

She let out a whimper. "Forgive me, Lord Staines, I-I…"

A warm hand took hers. "There's naught to forgive, Miss Lucas."

"B-but you could be infected. I-I…" She tried to withdraw her hand, but he held it firm.

"Be assured, sweet girl, that I and my family are well. We were fortunate enough to have taken the vaccine. None of the wedding guests have fallen ill. You've nothing to reproach yourself for."

"Why are you…" She trailed off as her throat tightened in pain.

He patted her hand. "I went to school with the archbishop's eldest son, which enabled the expedition of the license. And I cannot have you married by a stranger when you've friends in London. My Juliette would have attended had she not been in the country. She'll be most sorry that she was unable to arrive in time…"

"In time to see me still alive?"

"Perhaps the Almighty will be merciful and spare you."

"Lord Staines," Dr. McIver warned, "ye mustn't give her false hope."

"Your profession is based on evidence and facts, doctor," Staines said. "Mine is built upon the foundation of faith. The worst sin we can commit is to destroy someone's faith." He turned toward the huge, blurred figure waiting in the doorway. "Lord MacLennan, if you wish to proceed, the time is now."

"H-he's a lord?" Mia whispered.

The figure moved and Mia caught the faint scent of wood, earth, and smoke—so unlike the sickly sweet scents that had thickened the atmosphere of the sickroom. Then he spoke.

"Does the lass not know the name of the man she's to wed?"

His voice seemed to resonate through her bones. Rich and warm, it carried a Scottish brogue that gave him a musical air. It was a voice that brought forth a vivid image of a deep river bubbling and dancing over the granite rocks of the Highlands—a land that she would never live to see.

Her soul cried out as his voice filled her mind. Steeped in promise and honor, it was the voice of a good man, an honorable man.

Exactly the sort of man who could have made her happy, and yet also exactly the sort of man who would never have looked twice at her.

The shape moved closer, the masculine aroma intensifying, and Mia shrank back.

"Please..." she whispered. "*No.*"

"Is the lass unwilling?" the bridegroom said. "Or perhaps changed her mind now she's to wed a Scot?"

Mia shook her head and let out a groan of pain. "I-infection," she whispered. "I-I have no wish..."

"Devil's ballocks!" the bridegroom muttered, stepping back.

"The risk is negligible providing you don't touch her, Lord MacLennan," Staines said, an edge to his voice.

"Aye, I understand that," came the reply, and Mia's eyes filled with tears once more at the kindness in his voice. "Miss Lucas"—he hesitated—"or I should say 'Euphramia,' seeing as we're to be wed. I cannae thank ye enough for yer kind offer, and for yer consideration in wanting to protect me from the pox. If ye're still willing to wed this blundering oaf who stands before ye, then I'm willing to wed the lass whose selflessness surpasses that of any other living soul."

He dipped into a bow, and Mia caught a flash of two emerald eyes twinkling in the afternoon light.

"Hamish MacLennan of Glenblath, at yer service," he said. "It would fill my heart with joy to have ye as my wife."

"Then I suggest we proceed with all haste, so that Miss Lucas might take her rest," Dr. McIver said. "Reverend Staines, when ye're ready."

The vicar cleared his throat, then the ceremony began. Mia gripped Gertie's hand, taking comfort from the older woman's solidity, while the world drifted in and out of focus as Lord Staines delivered the words.

"I therefore charge ye both, as ye shall stand before the Almighty on the day of judgment, that if either of ye know of any just cause why ye shall not be legally wed, then ye must declare it."

The pause seemed to extend into forever, the silence punctuated only by the ticking of the longcase clock in the hallway outside and the steady breathing of the groom. Would he retreat at the brink?

No. He remained, steadfast, voicing his vows in that rich voice—a voice that any woman with half a soul would fall in love with. Mia herself might have fallen under its spell had she lived.

When the ceremony came to the exchanging of the rings, Mia closed her eyes and turned her head away. But a large hand took hers and, ignoring her protests, the groom slipped a cool metal band onto her third finger.

"Sir, I beg you not to—"

"Hush, lass," he said. "What sort of a man would I be if I didnae give my bride a ring on our wedding day? I can risk a little infection to do right by ye."

Oh, heaven! Would that he were a profligate, or some spendthrift stranger she could care nothing for! But this man—this kind, brave man—had nothing to gain from giving her a ring.

What might her life have been like had she survived? But the question was futile, for she'd only offered marriage—and he'd only accepted—on the basis that she had no chance of survival.

The ceremony concluded, Lord Staines closed his Bible with a snap.

"I now pronounce you man and wife."

The groom leaned close and caught Mia's veil. Then he began to lift it and she cried out.

"Can I not kiss my bride?"

Mia shook her head.

"I'm not afraid of infection, lass. Ye're my wife, and I wish to kiss ye."

"P-please, you cannot look at me."

"Och, lass, do ye think I fear a few pockmarks? To me, ye'll always be beautiful. Not for yer appearance, but for yer selfless act of kindness. Now…may I kiss ye?"

Mia's heart ached at his gentle plea. There was nothing in the world that she wanted more than to be kissed by him. But, fine though his words were, she was not so naïve as to believe that he wouldn't shrink away from her. The sight of her pockmarked face—so hideous that Gertie refused to let Mia look at it in the mirror—would disgust him, no matter how valiantly he tried to disguise it.

Tears again stung her eyes as he lifted the bottom of her veil to his lips, then let it fall.

"Thank ye, lass," he said. "I'll not forget yer kindness. And I'll ensure that yer name will live on in the hearts and souls of the people of my home."

"Will you make me a promise?" Mia asked.

"Gladly, lass." Her heart ached at the warmth and kindness in his voice.

"Do not mourn me…Hamish." Her throat tightened as she uttered his name. "Be happy. Find another wife. Be happy with her."

She heard a sharp intake of breath, then he sighed. "Aye, lass, if it be yer wish, then I will. But know this: Every soul at Glenblath will pray for ye and remember ye—Euphramia."

"M-Mia," she whispered, but her voice was almost inaudible and he rose from the bed. "M-my name is…" She broke off as a spasm of coughs racked her body.

Gertie took her hand. "I think Miss Lucas…I mean, Lady MacLennan needs her rest, now."

Lady MacLennan.

A title that was, like Mia, destined to be short-lived.

The groom bowed, then he exited the chamber.

"My wife and I will pray for you, Lady MacLennan," Lord Staines said. "When the time comes, I will of course preside over—"

He broke off, and Mia allowed herself a smile. So many grown men who considered themselves the stronger and braver sex, yet they were unable to complete a sentence that referred to her impending death and the funeral that would follow.

After he left, Gertie removed the veil and settled Mia back into a prone position in the bed.

Dr. McIver approached with the familiar phial, then he uncorked it and shook a few drops out onto a spoon before holding it to her lips. She parted them in eagerness, relishing the anticipated release from pain.

"Is there anything else you wish for?" Gertie asked.

Mia shook her head. The nurse placed another cool cloth on her forehead, then stroked her cheek.

"Sweet girl."

Mia let Gertie's soft voice caress her senses—the soothing words of love, hitching occasionally as the nurse caught her breath—and waited for the inevitable to claim her.

CHAPTER FOUR

HAMISH HELD HIS breath at the familiar silhouette of Glenblath Castle. The building dominated everything around it save for the peak of Beinn Blath, which stretched to the sky and disappeared behind the thick white clouds that clung to the summit.

His heart swelled with love. Was there ever a greater sight for a man to behold than his beloved home? Twelve days he'd been on the road—two of which he'd wasted at some cursed inn waiting for the next carriage. No amount of counting the hours and days away made time run faster.

Then he checked himself as his conscience stabbed at him.

Time was a commodity he'd spent the past fortnight wishing away. But in London, another would have clung to the few precious hours that she had left.

He lifted his gaze to the clouds, behind which the sun struggled—and failed—to penetrate, and uttered a small prayer of thanks.

"Euphramia Mary Lucas…"

The carriage drew to a halt and Hamish climbed out, stretching his body that had grown cramped in the carriage.

"Hamish, my son!" a voice cried out, filled with love.

His mother stood at the castle entrance, leaning on a stick. By her side stood Hamish's sister Iona, together with his friends Murdoch and Robbie. Robbie's wife Shona was by his side, her gaze fixed on Iona, but of Murdoch's wife there was no sign. Behind, the servants lined up in a row, from Ailsa, Murdoch's eldest, who'd joined the kitchens last year, to Brodie the groom, who stared at Iona with slavish devotion, and finally Mr. and Mrs. Bron standing at the end.

Ma shuffled forward and Hamish embraced her. His heart ached at how frail she was, completely engulfed by his embrace.

"I've missed ye, Ma," he said, releasing her and stepping back. "Ye're looking unwell. Has Iona not been looking after ye?"

His sister let out a huff and folded her arms. "Can ye never find anything kind to say of me, brother?"

"Iona's taken good care of me," his mother said. "Haven't ye, my love?"

Iona at least had the grace to blush. Doubtless she'd been spending Hamish's absence wandering about the hills and causing mischief. She'd always been a wild lass, so unlike his gentle mother that he'd often thought she were a changeling left by the kelpies.

Ma gestured toward the carriage. "I take it yer trip to London was successful?"

"Partly," Hamish said.

"If ye're married, it's most uncivil to leave yer bride waiting in the carriage."

"I'm not married," Hamish replied. "Not anymore."

Murdoch let out a laugh. "Ye talk in riddles. Is there a wench in there or not? Or perhaps she's an ugly woman and ye're ashamed of her?"

Robbie chuckled but was silenced as Shona gave him a sharp nudge.

"She no longer lives," Hamish said. "I was widowed within days of the wedding."

"Oh, Hamish!" his mother cried. "I'm so…"

"It's all right, Ma. It was expected. I'm not grieving, only thankful for what the lass did for us."

"What do ye mean? What lass?"

"Mr. Stockton presented me with a girl on her deathbed who wished to marry a man so that he might claim her fortune."

"Well!" Murdoch said. "I've never heard the like. How much did ye get?"

"A little over a thousand pounds," Hamish said. "It's cleared some of the debts, and should enable us to service the rest."

"A thousand?" Robbie said. "Easy work if ye can get it." He glanced at Iona. "Perhaps ye can make a similar arrangement for this wee one here—find her a man on his deathbed. Old man Stewart two valleys over must be sitting on a tidy sum, he's such a miser. He cannae have long left and might be willing to part with cash if yer sister parts her—"

"Robbie!" Shona cried as Murdoch laughed. "Leave her be."

"I dinnae need *ye* to speak for me," Iona said, glaring at Shona. "Ye're nothing but a whore who—"

"Sister, that's enough!" Hamish roared. "Do ye want the strap?"

"Ye'd never dare."

"Care to test me on that?" Hamish said. "I'm disappointed to have returned while working hard for the benefit of Glenblath to find ye've not improved one jot. In fact, ye're worse than ever."

His sister's body stiffened, and for a moment, he thought she might strike him. Then, her eyes glistening with unshed tears, she whirled around and sprinted across the drive, slipping between two outbuildings.

Holy cock—that was all he needed, another dose of his sister's histrionics. With a sigh, he moved to follow her, but his mother caught his arm.

"Leave her be, son. She'll come to her senses after a good dose of fresh air."

"She needs a good dose of the strap," Murdoch said with a growl.

Hamish winced. His late father had often taken a strap to Iona, but though it tempered her wayward ways, Hamish could never bring himself to adopt the same form of discipline now he'd succeeded as laird, no matter the provocation. No man could call himself a *true* man if he used violence to keep his women in order.

Iona needed a husband, and the sooner Hamish could hand over responsibility for her to another, the better. But he wanted her to marry for love, not necessity.

"If my Ailsa spoke to me like that," Murdoch said, "I'd leather her arse so hard she'd not be able to sit down for a twelvemonth."

The maidservant at the end of the line blushed and shuffled from one foot to the other.

"Ye need to beat the wildness out of yer sister," Murdoch continued. "'Tis the only way to teach a woman her place, is that not so, Robbie?"

"Aye," Robbie replied. Then he glanced at Shona and flinched.

"Ha!" Murdoch laughed. "Ruled by yer cock, ye are, Robbie." He gestured to the young man standing beside Ailsa. "Mark my words, Brodie, if ye wish for a quiet life not plagued by a woman's henpecking and yammering, ye must show her who's in command, like ye would taming any mare."

Brodie nodded his head, coloring. His gaze flicked to the path Iona had taken, then he lowered it to the ground.

Poor, lovesick lad. But that little wildcat would wither his cock. She needed a firmer hand—a man prepared to place a bit and bridle over her head and keep her on a short rein. Brodie needed to find his ballocks before he began courting.

Ma ordered the servants to return to the castle, then she slipped her arm through Hamish's and he led her into the building.

"Has Iona been troublesome in my absence?" he said.

"No more than usual, son. The next time ye venture to London, ye must bring back a wife. I'm sure the company of a woman near Iona's age will settle her. An English lady might be a good influence on her and show her the rewards of good and virtuous behavior. But perhaps ye wish to wait awhile before finding another wife. Ye must tell me of that poor lassie ye married."

"Her name was Euphramia," Hamish said. "A doctor's daughter who wished to keep her fortune from a wastrel cousin."

"Did she say that?"

"Her lawyer did."

"What did *she* say?"

"She gave me her blessing to marry again," Hamish said, recalling the softly spoken words from the woman behind the veil whose features were indistinct, save a pair of bright eyes that looked upon him as if he were her savior. "It was the last thing she said—her dying wish."

"Poor lass," his mother said. "To think: how unhappy her life must have been to have done such a thing! If only she'd lived and ye could have brought her home. But I daresay ye'll find another wife. Must ye marry for convenience still?"

"Aye, I must," he said.

"A pity," she said, sighing. "What might seem a noble gesture at the altar is a decision that will remain with ye forever."

He lifted his mother's hand to his lips. "If ye were prepared to make such a sacrifice when ye married, Ma, why may I not be permitted to do the same? I'll do it gladly for the sake of the souls here."

And to honor Euphramia's memory.

CHAPTER FIVE

A LOW, STEADY hum vibrated through Mia's body, which rocked from side to side, as if she were riding a ship across an ocean in a storm. Though darkness surrounded her, the pain that gripped her body refused to fade.

Perhaps Reverend Staines had spoken an untruth when he said that all pain ceased the moment a soul entered heaven.

Or perhaps she was destined for hell…

The hum separated into a multitude of voices, perhaps demons ready to claim her.

"She stirs."

A voice spoke, gentle and feminine, in contrast to the harsh cackles she'd expected. But perhaps that was how demons ensnared unwary souls, promising softness before delivering retributions for the sins committed in the mortal life.

"Ma'am?"

A hand touched her cheek.

Mia whimpered and opened her eyes. But rather than the fires of Hades, a bright white light filled her vision.

"A-am I in heaven?" she whispered.

A blurred shape appeared. Mia blinked, her eyes stinging with moisture, until the shape came into focus to reveal a young girl dressed in a neat, plain pale-blue gown and apron. From beneath a starched white cap, wisps of pale-blonde hair peeked out, forming curls that seemed to glow in the sunlight. She leaned forward to reveal a face with soft blue eyes and elfin features.

It was the face of a girl.

"Wh-who…" Mia's throat caught, and she coughed.

A light hand caressed her forehead. "There, there, ma'am, be steady now. Here—take this."

Something cold and hard was pressed against Mia's lips and she jerked back.

"It's just a little water," the girl said, her voice a gentle caress.

Mia took a sip, letting the cool liquid trickle down her throat. "Where am I?"

"The hospital at Wolseley Heath," the girl replied. "We're all right glad you're here. We thought you were destined for the—"

"Hush, Tilly!" another voice said. "That's enough. The young lady doesn't need to hear it."

Another face appeared, wrinkled and lined with age, from which steel-gray eyes twinkled with kindness.

"Sorry, Mrs. Ford," the girl said.

"I told Dr. McIver you were a strong 'un," Mrs. Ford continued, "but he wouldn't believe it, fond of you though he is. He'll be right glad to see you when we give him the news."

"I-I'm alive?" Mia croaked. She tried to move, but her arms lacked any strength.

"Tilly," the older woman said, her voice carrying an air of authority.

The younger girl wrapped her arm around Mia's shoulders and lifted her to a sitting position, while the older women plumped up the pillows behind her. Mia cast her gaze about. Her neck ached as she moved her head, but she had to see—had to know whether the world around her was real, that the women spoke the truth.

She was in a small chamber. Though it contained three beds, only hers was occupied. Other than a table beside each bed and a chest of drawers beside the door, there was no other furniture in the room. The wall opposite was white and plain, save for a nail, below which she could discern a faint rectangular outline, as if a picture had been removed after residing there for years. She inhaled and caught a pungent odor of vinegar and herbs.

"Am I alone here?"

"We have no other patients with smallpox," Tilly said, "not since Miss Merrill were laid to rest. Dr. McIver's ever so particular about the risk of infection."

No doubt he was, given that the odor in the bedchamber was strong enough to ward off the Grim Reaper himself.

The older woman took Mia's hand. "How are you feeling, my dear? Could you take some water? Or soup? We've some broth in the kitchen. It's very light so shouldn't overwhelm you. You can't have eaten for days."

Mia glanced at the window. "H-how long…?"

"How long have you been here? Ten days, at least. You were in such a state of fever when you arrived that I told Dr. McIver he shouldn't have tried to move you, but it seemed as if you had to leave London, so he brought you here. It's a miracle you survived the journey—there was a right downpour the day you arrived. You were soaked through, but the coachman refused to help move you, fool that he was. Luckily Tilly here's a strong girl, aren't you, Tilly love? Dr. McIver would have carried you himself if it weren't for his rheumatism that always plays up in the wet weather. I'll say that he's the most…"

She rattled on, and Mia sank back into the pillows and closed her eyes, relishing the sound of the woman's voice.

I'm alive…

She smiled and let out a sigh.

"Bless me!" the woman cried. "Here's me prattling on and you're needing that soup. Tilly, run along to Mrs. Miggs and ask her to set aside a bowl for the lady."

Lady? I'm no lady.

But Mia had neither the strength nor the inclination to respond. Any such argument seemed insignificant compared to the knowledge that she had cheated the Grim Reaper.

Tilly bobbed a curtsy, then exited the chamber.

Mrs. Ford gave Mia's hand a reassuring pat. Mia lowered her gaze and caught her breath. The back of her hand was covered with marks of varying colors ranging from angry red to pale pink.

"Don't you be fretting about those," Mrs. Ford said in the stern, professional tones of the accomplished nurse. "We've a salve for that. Tilly's been applying it ever since you arrived."

Mia lifted her hand and inhaled the aroma of lavender and chamomile.

"The marks will fade in time, though they might never disappear completely…" Mrs. Ford's voice trailed off as she lifted her gaze to Mia's face. Then her eyes narrowed as if it pained her to have given offense, and Mia caught a flicker of pity in them.

She lifted her hand to her face, and Mrs. Ford caught her wrist.

"No, my dear. Leave it a week or two, when things have improved."

Mia lowered her hand. "Fetch me a mirror, Mrs. Ford."

"I don't think that's—"

"*Please.*"

A sheen of moisture gleamed in the nurse's eyes. "Are you certain?"

Mia nodded. "I count myself fortunate to be alive," she said. "I was never a beauty. My ambition was to become a doctor. As far as I'm aware, one doesn't need to be beautiful to treat the sick."

"Very well."

Mrs. Ford rose and approached the chest of drawers. She opened the topmost drawer and pulled out something wrapped in a cloth. Then she unwrapped it to reveal a mirror the same size and shape as the mark on the wall, a thin chain suspended along the back. The mirror facing toward her chest, she approached the bed and paused, then placed it in Mia's hands.

Aware of the pity in Mrs. Ford's eyes, Mia turned the mirror, slowly, until her reflection came into view.

The face that looked back was thinner than when she'd last

seen it. And paler. Perhaps that was why the marks that adorned her skin were so prominent. She turned her head to one side and back, taking in every sore, every scab. Almost as soon as her gaze fell upon each one, it burned and itched, and she fought the yearning to tear at them with her fingernails.

The resignation in the face threatened to dissolve, and Mia set the mirror aside before the first glimmer of despair became visible.

Mrs. Ford returned the mirror to the drawer, then pulled out a shawl and draped it over Mia's shoulders.

"Right," she said, in the manner of a general rallying troops on a battlefield, "I'll go and see where that soup's got to. Tilly's such a chatter-mouth, I'll wager she's gossiping in the kitchens just now, telling them all about your recovery. But we can forgive her, can't we? It's not every day a patient recovers from smallpox. Oh, you cannot imagine how delighted Dr. McIver will be! He'll want to visit you himself."

Mia smiled at the older woman's joy. "Thank you, Mrs. Ford."

"It's no trouble, Lady MacLennan."

Mia's stomach clenched at the woman's address. "I-I beg pardon?"

"I said it's no trouble, Your Ladyship." Mrs. Ford dipped into a curtsy. "I'll leave you in peace, now, and will send Tilly in with your soup."

Before Mia could respond, Mrs. Ford exited the chamber, closing the door behind her.

Lady MacLennan...

A voice—the same voice that had faded in and out while she'd waited for Death to claim her—pushed itself to the forefront of Mia's mind. Deep and rich, it echoed through her bones.

Thank ye, lass. I'll not forget what ye did for me. And I'll ensure that yer name will live on in the hearts and souls of the people of my home.

She lowered her gaze to her hands once more, and her breath hitched as she caught sight of the thin gold band at the base of the third finger of her left hand. She lifted her hand to get a closer look, turning it one way, then another. Then she clasped the ring between the thumb and forefinger of her right hand and rotated it. She closed her eyes, and two emerald pinpoints flickered in her mind—two bright eyes staring at her through a thin white muslin veil.

Sweet heaven!

Not only was she alive…

…she was married.

CHAPTER SIX

Glenblath Chapel, Scotland, two months later

"Y OU ARE ALREADY married…to me."

Hamish stared at the cloaked figure, his stomach knotting.

It cannot be.

Perhaps Iona was playing a trick?

But no—Hamish's sister sat beside his mother in the front pew, a look of astonishment on her face to match his own.

"MacLennan, this is most unseemly," a harsh voice said, and Hamish recognized the nasal tones of his soon-to-be father-in-law.

Or perhaps not quite so *soon-to-be.*

"Papa, I—" the Honorable Aurora began, before her father interrupted.

"Silence, girl!"

Lord Young drew alongside Hamish and gestured toward the veiled figure. "What are you about, woman?" he sneered. "Are you a whore seeking to disturb my daughter's marriage out of envy? If you think you're entitled to him merely because you've spread your legs, you—"

"Lord Young, let me deal with this," Hamish interrupted. He stepped closer to the veiled woman, whose knuckles whitened as she tightened the grip on her valise. "Madam, I dinnae know what brought ye here," he said, "but I'm not married. I was, but she died from smallpox nearly three months ago."

A murmur of voices rippled through the congregation. When it faded, the veiled woman spoke.

"No." She set her valise down. "I survived."

Then she lifted her veil.

Hamish couldn't suppress the shudder. Were it not for the marks on her face, she might have been pretty—beautiful, even—with her bright hazel eyes framed by soft brown hair, heart-shaped face, and full, round lips. But her skin was covered in scars, some a pale pink, almost white, others a deeper pink. The more he looked, the more he could discern.

Sweet heaven, how she must have suffered!

She regarded him, her eyes showing no anger, only sorrow. He caught a flicker of shame in them before she blinked and it was gone, replaced by determination as she tilted her chin up, bringing her face more into the light, as if to challenge the world to deride her.

A collective intake of breath filled the chapel, followed by a series of mutterings.

"Dear Lord!"

"How horrible!"

"Just *look* at her!"

The young woman's forehead creased, but her jaw tightened as if she gritted her teeth, striving not to be cowed by the disgust of those around her.

Brave lass.

Somewhere a child burst into tears and was quickly shushed. Then the bride let out a scream.

"Decorum, daughter!" Lord Young snapped, before he approached Hamish, his boots clicking angrily on the flagstones. "What manner of horror is this?" he demanded. "You signed a marriage contract, in exchange, I'll add, for a very tidy sum. Are you playing me false, MacLennan?"

Hamish shook his head. "I signed the contract in good faith, Lord Young."

"So this, this"—Lord Young wrinkled his nose and gestured toward the newcomer—"this *ghoulish creature* cannot have a prior claim on you." He addressed the newcomer. "Have you nothing to say for yourself, girl, after coming here uninvited to ruin my daughter's prospects? I ought to have you publicly disgraced, sued for breach of contract. Just look at yourself! I've never seen such a monstrous—"

"Have a care, Lord Young," Hamish growled, as another child in the congregation burst into tears. "Ye're upsetting the guests."

"I rather think *she's* upsetting the guests," Lord Young said. He gestured to the woman. "Cover yourself up, for God's sake. We shouldn't have to look at you."

The woman picked up her valise, then reached for her veil to lower it. She paused as Hamish raised his hand.

"Dinnae move, lass," he said. "Lord Young, ye're not master here. *I* am. This woman will leave only if I wish it."

He approached her and lifted his hand. She flinched and stepped back. Though her jaw was still firm, tilted upward in defiance, he could discern a faint gleam in her eyes of unshed tears. "Tell me yer name, lass," he said.

"D-don't you know it?" she replied, a faint tremor in her voice.

"Tell me," he growled.

"M-my name is Euphramia."

She stepped back, holding her valise to her chest as if she wished to shield herself against that which might harm her— Hamish's horror, Lord Young's hatred, the Honorable Aurora's screams…or the fear and revulsion of the congregation.

"E-Euphramia Mary…" She blinked, slowly, and her throat bobbed as she swallowed, before she held up her left hand to reveal the plain gold band he'd placed on the third finger in that dreary little bedchamber in London. "…MacLennan."

Hamish's mother rose, trembling. "Son—is it true?"

A hush fell over the congregation, as if the world awaited his response, praying that it was merely a jape and that the beautiful and wealthy Miss Young would become Lady MacLennan and her dowry would save the estate.

Hamish nodded, slowly. "Aye, Ma. It is."

"No!" The Honorable Aurora let out another scream. Lord Young grasped her by the arms and she dissolved into sobs.

"Desist, girl!" he snarled. "Would you disgrace my name by acting in such an indecorous manner before these savages?"

Savages, eh?

"*You* wanted me to marry that savage, Papa," Aurora cried. "I had no wish to—Oh!" She screamed again as her father backhanded her across the face.

"Silence, slut! I arranged this marriage because no other would have you after your disgraceful behavior. But you're not even good enough for *them*."

"Lord Young," Hamish began, "there's no need to—"

"There's every need, MacLennan," Lord Young snarled. "Rest assured, you'll pay for the insult."

"I heard it on good faith that this woman was dead."

"Then my misfortune is also yours, MacLennan."

Lord Young wrinkled his nose and glared at Euphramia, who stood as still as a statue, save a slight tremor in her skirts.

"I wish you joy of her," he continued. "She'll be your misfortune, but I have every intention of seeking recompense for mine."

"I'll reimburse ye for any expenditure incurred in bringing yer daughter here, Lord Young," Hamish said, his voice a low growl, despite the turmoil in his heart. "Would twenty pounds suffice?"

"The wedding gown alone cost—"

"Fifty, then," Hamish said, "provided ye leave forthwith and release me of any obligation toward yerself and yer daughter."

"But…"

"It's fifty or nothing."

"Very well." Lord Young grasped his daughter's shoulder and steered her along the aisle, her feet tripping as she tried to keep pace.

Hamish ought to have spared some sympathy for the girl, but despite her father's contempt, she at least had a future ahead of her—marriage with another, and a dowry large enough to ensure financial security.

Whereas I find myself not only with no dowry, but an increase to my debts.

How the bloody hell was the estate going to survive when, in his mind, he'd already spent half of the Honorable Aurora's dowry?

"Ahem." The vicar cleared his throat, a habit that now made Hamish's fists itch with the urge to plant them squarely on the man's nose.

"Forgive me, Reverend Sutherland," Hamish said. "It seems, unfortunately, that I have a wife still living."

Unfortunately…

As he uttered that cruel word, unable to confine his bitterness, the newcomer—no, like it or not, he must think of her as his wife—flinched, as if he'd struck her. Then, with quiet dignity, she lowered her veil, turned, and walked, alone, to the chapel door. It creaked open then shut with a clang.

Whispers broke out among the congregation and Hamish gave vent to his anger.

"Be quiet!" he roared. "Go to yer homes and leave me be. Ye've no reason to remain here. There will be no wedding here today."

The guests dispersed. Some approached Hamish to offer their condolences; others scuttled past him, unwilling to meet his gaze. Iona let out a laugh, which was quickly silenced. Hamish's mother paused and remained by his side until the chapel was empty.

"Hamish, son, what will ye do?"

"Other than arrange passage for Lord Young and his daughter to Edinburgh, I know not," he said. "I've no wish to think on what will befall me after today."

"But ye must, son." She gestured toward the chapel doors. "They all depend on ye—family, servants, tenants, and…and…*her*."

He placed his head in his hands. "I know, Ma, but all I want at this moment is to not be the laird, for everyone to leave me be."

She placed a kiss on his cheek. "Aye, son, I ken that. I'll leave ye to collect yer thoughts. But eventually ye'll have to face yer responsibilities, and that lass ye married."

"I will," Hamish said. "But not today."

⤜⤜⤜✸⤛⤛⤛

THE HISSES AND cries of the congregation swirled in Mia's mind as she ran from the chapel doors toward the long drive along which she'd traveled moments before. But there was no sign of the carriage that had brought her here from the inn.

Not that it would have made a difference. She'd exhausted the last of her funds on the final stage of the journey and had nothing save the clothes in her valise and a shilling in her reticule. And that shilling was, by rights, the property of Dr. McIver, who'd given her five pounds for the journey—which, despite his protests, she'd promised to repay as soon as she was able.

The castle that had towered above the tree line from the moment the carriage emerged from the forest now engulfed Mia with its shadow. She shivered and drew her cloak about her. On the path toward the mountain in the distance, she could discern the edge of the shadow, the shape of battlements on the ground, and beyond, a squat gray rock that glistened in the sunlight as if it contained a thousand tiny diamonds. She set off toward the rock, pausing halfway to catch her breath. Dr. McIver had tried to persuade her to remain in Surrey for another month to regain her strength, but she hadn't wanted to trespass on his charity any longer. She'd argued that the fresh air of the Highlands would revive her, as well as the company of a kind and loving husband. At night, since her recovery, she had lain awake, dreaming of the man with the kind eyes and rich voice who had thanked her so beautifully for her kindness. He'd promised to never forget her, to honor her gift for eternity.

She reached the rock and leaned against it. At close quarters she could discern a rainbow of colors—not only within the rock itself, where she could discern soft blues and purples among the gray, but the patches of lichen added yellows, greens, and a tint of red to the mix, completing the palette.

Dr. McIver was right about the Highlands—it was the most beautiful place to behold. And it was her home.

Or she'd believed it to be.

She turned her face to the sun, letting its warmth caress her face.

It seems, unfortunately, that I have a wife still living.

So short a sentence. Each word on its own had little significance. She'd used them all on numerous occasions. But the order in which he uttered them…

At first, her mind had refused to accept he'd said them. They must be a figment of her imagination, brought about by the demon who sat on her shoulder. That invisible little creature had emerged the first day she'd set eyes on her pockmarked reflection. Each time he came to the fore, he told her that she was no longer fit to live, let alone be seen. He had grown from the stares of the other inmates at the convalescent hospital. Then, when she'd ventured further afield, the sneers of contempt and disgust in the wider world gave him an almost solid form until she could hear his laughing in her ear.

And what had she focused on to conquer that little demon? She had steered her soul toward the man who'd promised to honor her forever. Throughout the journey to the Highlands, while she'd endured the looks of horror from the coachmen, innkeepers, and her fellow travelers, she had brought forth the image of *him*. Of Hamish MacLennan—her husband.

She had pictured a man with strong, smooth features and soft green eyes filled with love and tenderness. But the reality far surpassed her dreams. The man who'd turned to face her in the chapel was larger, handsomer, stronger, and more virile than the limit of her imagination of masculinity.

And he'd scorned her before a chapel filled with his family and friends.

She inhaled, taking in a lungful of the sweet, pure air, and listened to the sounds of the Highlands—the rush of the wind in the trees, a distant waterfall tumbling over rocks, and the faint cry of a bird of prey. Opening her eyes, she tipped her face upward, searching the sky until she saw it, an eagle circling far above, calling to his mate. Then she heard an answer, as the bird was joined by another in a dance of courtship.

"What am I to do?" she cried.

But the eagles did not respond. Instead, they spiraled upward until they disappeared out of sight, leaving her alone.

And, for the first time in her life, she *was* alone, totally alone, friendless and destitute in a strange land.

Hamish MacLennan had spoken the truth. It was a misfortune—his, and hers. It would have been better for everyone if she had died.

CHAPTER SEVEN

AFTER GIVING VENT to her despair, Mia wiped her eyes and admonished herself.

What an ungrateful fool I am.

Hundreds—no, *thousands*—had died in agony of smallpox and countless other diseases. The Almighty had chosen to spare her, yet, rather than reflect on her good fortune, she was sobbing on a rock in one of the most beautiful places she'd ever seen.

How Dr. McIver would have chastised her! He had bestowed upon her his knowledge of medicine, taught her almost everything he knew. He'd even emptied his purse to fund her journey to the Highlands. How ungrateful she was to set aside her good fortune and ignore the feelings of others.

In all honesty, could she blame Lord MacLennan for his reaction? Believing that she had died, he'd done what any self-respecting man would do—what she herself had charged him to do. He'd moved on for the benefit of his estate and found another bride. And a beautiful bride at that. Mia knew of the Honorable Aurora Young. A haughty and unpleasant creature. Olivia Whitcombe, or Lady Devereaux as she was now, loathed her. But Aurora had every right to think well of herself, for she had the face of an angel. Quite what had happened to result in her marrying an impoverished Highlander rather than a wealthy London lord, Mia couldn't fathom. But they would have made a handsome couple, Hamish with his rugged, masculine good looks and Aurora with her porcelain beauty.

No wonder Hamish was angry! His hopes were dashed when Mia arrived at the chapel, a ghost in solid form, of whom no exorcism could rid him.

But she could not weather that anger, nor make her home where she was not wanted. Neither could she spend the rest of the day hiding among the rocks like a frightened child. She must face the consequences of her arrival—speak to him on equal terms, no matter how much the prospect frightened her.

He couldn't insult her more than he had already.

Mia smoothed her skirts, picked up her valise, and returned to the main building. She spotted a carriage on the driveway and allowed herself a moment of hope. Perhaps she might be granted passage to Edinburgh. As she approached, she saw Lord Young bundle his daughter into the carriage, Hamish by his side, a handful of children watching in wide-eyed wonder.

Aurora tripped and let out a cry.

"Stop your sniveling!" Lord Young snapped. "Wait until we return home, then I'll give you something to snivel about."

"Lord Young, there's no need to—" Hamish started.

"There's every need, MacLennan. She's still my concern, worse luck. You've got your burden to bear with that pock-marked—" Lord Young broke off as he glanced up and met Mia's gaze. "Get yourself in the carriage, Aurora, before you catch the pox." He gestured to Mia. "Stay back, lest you infect us all!"

One of the watching children burst into tears.

"Lord Young, there's no risk of infection," Mia said. "Please may I travel with you?"

"Don't be preposterous!" he said. "We wouldn't travel with one such as you, even if you weren't riddled with the pox."

"I'll sit outside with the footmen, if you prefer."

"You'll do no such thing. I'll not have you come within ten feet of my carriage—"

"*My* carriage," a deep voice said, and Mia's heart fluttered as she turned to see her husband staring directly at her, his eyes like two hard, unyielding emeralds. "I say who does and does not travel in the carriage, Lord Young. Though I agree that the lass will not travel with ye. Now, go. Dinnae test my patience more than ye have already."

"*Your* patience?" Lord Young said. "After the way you've insulted me?"

"For fuck's sake!" Hamish cried, and Mia drew in a sharp breath at the anger in his voice. "Do ye think *I* wanted this?"

Lord Young curled his lip in a sneer. "I wish you joy of her," he snarled. Then he climbed in after his sobbing daughter and closed the door.

"No—wait!" Mia cried, running toward the carriage. "*Please* let me go."

But before she reached it, the huge Highlander blocked her path.

"Ye're going nowhere, lass."

He caught her arm as the carriage set off. No matter how she struggled, his grip remained firm and unyielding. Then, as the carriage disappeared into the trees, he released her. The sound of the horses' hooves faded until all Mia could hear was the steady breathing of her captor, the rush of wind in the trees, and the soft wailing of the crying child.

"Why didn't you let me go?" she asked.

Ignoring her, he strode toward the chapel, where a handful of guests still milled about.

"Did you not hear me"—she hesitated, unwilling to remind him of the contract that bound them—"Lord MacLennan?"

He stopped, then turned to face her. Another child joined in the wailing.

"For fuck's sake!" he cursed, and balled his hands into fists.

"What must I do?" Mia cried.

He lifted his hand to his face, then brushed it across his brow, as if wearied by the weight of the world. Then, at length, he sighed and slumped his shoulders, as if in defeat.

"Cover yerself up and get inside," he said gruffly, gesturing to the castle building. "Ye're frightening the children."

Mia bit her lip to stem a cry of despair. Loathe her he might, but she'd not hide herself away in shame. Clutching her valise, she tilted her chin up, then, with as much dignity as she could feign, approached the huge, arched doorway of the castle building. The guests parted, flowing back like a receding tide as she walked past, almost as if they were welcoming her as a new bride into their home.

But a home was where one was loved, cherished, and wanted—or tolerated at the very least.

Therefore, Mia had no home.

CHAPTER EIGHT

MIA STEPPED THROUGH the castle doors into the hallway. No—a cavern.

The walls, made from huge gray slabs mottled with texture, stretched toward a high beamed ceiling, from which hung a chandelier fashioned from jagged, pointed shapes that wouldn't look out of place in a Medieval torture chamber. Flagstones lined the floor, in differing tones ranging from charcoal to marble white. Though uneven, the stones looked as if they had been polished and worn with use, as if thousands of feet had walked upon them over hundreds of years.

Mia's footsteps echoed as she crossed the floor. How many brides had been carried across it by a loving bridegroom? Perhaps that was what Mia's husband had hoped to do with the beautiful Aurora Young.

What might Aurora have thought of this place? A pampered lady such as her would have expected light, comfort, and warmth. The air in the hallway seemed to shimmer with the cold and the dark. A breeze whispered over Mia's skin and the flames flickered from the candles on sconces, casting dancing shadows across the floor. The place was a haven for ghosts, with dark corners and niches sunk into the walls where the shadows obscured what lay within.

Mia approached one wall where a huge tapestry rippled in the breeze. Unlike the delicately embroidered fire screens that graced the drawing rooms of London, this tapestry was primal, earthy. Instead of soft pastel shades, it had been woven in earthy shades of green, brown, and gray, with the occasional splash of dark red. She drew near and traced the outline of a shape with her finger, then recoiled. The shape was a stag, its legs thrust out at unnatural angles, as if the beast were in the final throes of death. Its mouth was open, teeth bared, and a single white-rimmed eye stared directly at her. A spear protruded from the animal's flank, which was a chestnut brown save for the smears of red where the arrowhead had pierced the flesh.

The scene was set against a backdrop of a huge mountain—the same mountain, perhaps, that towered over this very building. Yes—it was. As Mia let her gaze wander about the scene, she caught sight of the image of a dark-gray building among a forest, its turrets peeking over the tree line—the turrets she'd noticed on her arrival.

How long ago that seemed, though it could not have been more than an hour! Then, she had viewed those turrets with a sense of hope that, though her husband might be surprised to see her, he would, ultimately, be thankful that she lived.

But this was no place for her, nor a debutante such as Aurora. It was harsh, primal, and savage, where men ruled not through wealth or rank, but through pure, unbridled brutality.

Mia glanced back at the image of the stag. Did the animal accept death as she herself once had, or did it kick and scream against the cruelty of the world?

She lifted her gaze and froze. Mounted on the wall was the head of a stag, its fur identical in color to the animal in the tapestry. Two huge antlers protruded from the stag's head, branching out to form sharp, vicious points. Its eyes stared at her with a baleful malevolence, and though Mia retreated, the animal's gaze followed her. The eyes blinked and her stomach fluttered in fear. Then she chided herself. It was a reflection of the flickering candle flames, nothing more, a product of the ever-present breeze.

Mia drew her cloak around herself and shivered. Old buildings were known for harboring the souls of the dead—ghosts for whom no respite could be found.

And I'm just one more ghost.

Voices came from behind a set of doors carved with a pattern of leaves and vines. Creatures were carved among the leaves—birds, a catlike animal, and, in the center, the head of a stag.

Savages the folk here might be, but their craftsmanship surpassed anything Mia had seen, even from London's finest furniture makers.

The doors led to a passageway that opened out into a hall even more cavernous than the one she'd left. An enormous fireplace dominated the far wall like a huge, gaping mouth in which a fire blazed, as if a dragon resided in the castle. In front of the fireplace was a long wooden table, laden with platters of food, and Mia's stomach rumbled at the scent of roasted meats. Similar tables ran along the perimeter, with rows of chairs either side.

Servants milled about, clearing the tables with a clatter of cutlery and the scrape of chairs. A young boy dropped a plate that shattered into shards. An older woman approached him, muttering, and clipped him around the ear. Then he scuttled off and returned with a broom. Mia retreated against the wall and held her breath, unwilling to disturb their toil while they chattered to each other.

"I dinnae care what Mrs. Bron says," a young woman said. "It's a right shame, that's all I have to say."

"Ha!" another woman said. "If that's *all* ye have to say, Ailsa, then I'll eat my arse. Ye've a right tongue on ye when ye get to gossiping. Come and help me with this pie—I cannae carry it on me own."

"Ailsa's right, though," a manservant said as he approached them. "Here—put that down. It's too heavy for a lass. Ye'll drop it and earn yerself a leathering."

"Aye, I'm right, Lachlan," the first girl said. "She were a beautiful creature, that Miss Young. And her name! Aurora—I've never heard anything so pretty. She'd have given the master a dozen bonnie bairns."

"And a sore head," said the second woman. "A right evil tongue on her, she had. Did ye hear how she spoke to Elspeth? She'd have henpecked Master Hamish into next year."

"That's ladies for ye. They're all like that."

"And what would *ye* know?"

"A damned sight more than ye!"

"Stop yer cursing, Ailsa! Do ye want a hiding?"

"I'm only saying what ye're all thinking," Ailsa said. "It's a cursed shame for the master. Did ye *see* her?"

Mia shrank back, her stomach fluttering. There was no need to ask who the girl meant by *her*.

"Dinnae be unkind, Ailsa," the young man said. "Not all lasses are as pretty as ye."

"Her face!" Ailsa continued. "She was right beside me in the chapel when she took her veil off. I've never seen anything the like. Do ye think she'll give us the plague? Or put a curse on us? They say they're the marks of the devil. I think we should…"

As the girl rattled on, Mia lifted her hand to her mouth to stifle a cry. Then another woman approached the little group of servants. Though she was tall, her shoulders were hunched. She clung to her cane, which tap-tapped across the stone floor. Her iron-gray hair was piled atop her head and dotted with tiny purple flowers, and she was dressed in a dark-purple gown trimmed with a plaid sash.

"Ailsa MacLennan," she said, her tone sharp, "how many times have I told ye not to…"

The woman's voice trailed off and her body stiffened as she looked up. Mia backed against the wall, but it made no difference. Clear green eyes widened as they focused on her, the same color and shape as the eyes that had regarded her with such contempt in the chapel.

The servants turned in unison, and a ripple of whispers threaded through the hall. The clatter of crockery ceased, and

Mia's cheeks flamed with humiliation as the company stared at her. Then, gritting her teeth, she took a step forward so that they might see her cursed face in all its devilry.

The woman in the purple gown resumed her attention on the servants.

"As I've told ye enough times, Ailsa," she said, "ye're not to gossip about yer betters. If ye've no kind word to say, then remain silent. Do ye understand?"

Aisla's cheeks turned a deep shade of pink. "Aye, Lady MacLennan," she mumbled. "Sorry, Lady MacLennan."

"It's not *me* ye should apologize to."

Aisla glanced at Mia, then lowered her gaze to the floor. "Sorry, ma'am."

"Use the correct address, Ailsa," the older woman said.

"I-I dinnae ken—"

The older woman let out a sharp sigh. "This woman is my son's wife, as well ye know, given that ye were in the chapel earlier."

"S-sorry, L-Lady MacLennan," the girl said, flicking her gaze up, then stepping back as if she feared Mia might deliver a curse on her—or infect her with the pox.

"That'll do, I suppose," the older woman said. Then she turned and addressed the company. "And that goes for the rest of ye. It matters not what ye believe or wish. This young woman here"—she gestured to Mia—"is my son's wife, the Lady of Glenblath. Ye shall show her the respect that title merits."

A ripple of murmuring filled the room.

"Now, carry on with yer work. I want this room cleared before nightfall."

The woman extended her hand to Mia and spoke more softly. "Will ye come with me?"

Mia shook her head. "I-I don't think I ought to, Your Ladyship. Hamish..." She hesitated, her voice wavering as she recalled the disgust in his eyes. "I mean...y-your son doesn't want me to—"

"Och, I'll set him right, lass. If ye're lawfully married, then this is yer home, is it not? Ye look in a right state, and well ye might, after such a journey and such a greeting. I'd say ye're in need of some good, strong tea, am I right? And dinnae call me 'Yer Ladyship.' Eilidh will do, seeing as ye're family. Or Ma, if ye prefer."

The woman spoke the first kind words Mia had heard since she'd left Surrey twelve days ago, and, unlike every soul she'd encountered on her journey, Lady MacLennan didn't look at Mia with disgust or fear. Such kindness, unlike the taunts she'd learned to withstand, had the power to breach Mia's defenses.

Unwilling to trust herself to speak, she nodded.

"That's settled, then," Lady MacLennan said. "Elspeth, have some tea brought to my chamber, will ye—then make sure we're not disturbed. My daughter-in-law and I have much to discuss."

One of the older servants bobbed a curtsy. Taking Mia's hand, Lady MacLennan led her out of the great hall.

"I TRUST THOSE marks dinnae pain ye."

After ushering Mia to sit on a threadbare sofa, Lady MacLennan—*the* Lady MacLennan, for Mia could not think of herself as such—lowered herself into a seat beside the unlit fireplace.

Mia lifted her gaze from the valise on her lap to see the other woman looking directly at her. Her unflinching gaze wandered over Mia's form, lingering on her hands before settling on her face. Mia reached for her veil to lower it, but Lady MacLennan raised her hand.

"Please don't on my account," she said, "nor on anyone else's. And ye can set that aside." She gestured to the valise.

Mia obediently placed the valise on the floor, then glanced about the chamber. It was enormous, the rear portion dominated by a four-poster bed and the front section furnished like a parlor, which must be Lady MacLennan's living quarters.

The chamber had the same stone walls as the main hallway, but lacked the air of gloom. The tapestries lining the walls were brighter, both in color and the scenes they portrayed. One depicted the mountain in soft blues and purples, towering benevolently over a meadow covered in flowers and grasses in differing shades of green, pink, and yellow. A path wound through the meadow, leading the observer's eye a little to the left of the center of the tapestry, and Mia caught her breath as she spotted the figure of a stag. But unlike the tormented creature she'd seen in the hall, the animal stood proudly on the slopes of the mountain, head tipped upward as it roared at the sky, proclaiming the land as his. Mia couldn't suppress a smile at the vitality portrayed in the image, the sense of joy in belonging to a land more vibrant than any park in London.

"It is rather beautiful, isn't it?"

Mia glanced at Lady MacLennan, who regarded her with a soft smile.

"Dinnae frown, lass. I would see ye smile. It's a happy day."

"I fail to see a reason to be happy," Mia said.

Lady MacLennan frowned and opened her mouth to reply, but the door opened and a maidservant entered bearing a tray.

"Ah, Elspeth, set the tray on the table, please, and if ye'd be so kind as to pour the tea?"

"Yes, Yer Ladyship."

The maidservant placed the tray on a circular table with a thick column at the base that splayed out at the bottom to form three feet, carved into the shape of cloven hooves. The tray, fashioned from a dark-gray metal, bore a silver tea set, two cups, and a plate piled high with pale-brown slabs dotted with sugar.

"How do ye take yer tea, Lady MacLennan?"

Mia resumed her attention on the tapestry, letting her gaze wander over the flowers in the foreground.

"My dear?" her host said, and Mia glanced back to see both women staring at her.

"I beg your pardon?"

"Elspeth means *ye*, lass."

"B-but I'm not…"

"Ye are, Yer Ladyship," the maidservant said, staring at Mia unflinchingly. Then she smiled. "I've brought some milk and sugar in case ye take it, though the mistress has her tea plain. And I hope ye'll take a slice of shortbread. Mrs. McBride bakes the finest shortbread in Scotland."

She picked up the plate and approached Mia, holding it out.

"Yes, do," her hostess said.

Her hand trembling, Mia reached for a slice, and flinched as she lowered her gaze to her hand, the back of which was covered in pockmarks. To her credit, rather than recoil, the maidservant merely widened her eyes before returning to the table.

"Lady MacLennan?" she said, lifting the teapot.

"A little milk and perhaps a spoon of sugar," Mia said. "I don't usually take sugar, but today I feel…" She paused, her cheeks warming.

"I understand, my dear," her hostess said, gently, while Elspeth poured the tea. "Ye've endured a long journey and yer arrival must have been very distressing for ye."

And for everyone else, except perhaps the woman sitting before her now and the elderly maidservant with the kind eyes and gentle voice.

Unable to withstand even the tiniest act of kindness, Mia let long-withheld tears fall. Her hostess leaned forward and took Mia's hand.

"No, Lady MacLennan," Mia said, "you can't touch my hand, it's—"

"I see naught wrong with yer hand," the older woman said. "It bears the marks of yer survival. Ye should therefore be proud of them, aye, Elspeth?"

"Aye," the maidservant said, as she handed a cup to her mistress.

"And I thought I told ye to call me Eilidh…?" Lady MacLennan raised her eyebrows as if expecting a response.

"Eilidh," Mia said quietly.

"Excellent! Of course, as I said, ye can call me Ma, if ye pre-fer—unless yer own mother still lives?"

Mia shook her head. "My mother died when I was a baby, and my father…"

"I know about yer father, lass. My son told me the circum-stances surrounding yer marriage."

Oh, heavens! Mia looked away, her cheeks warming.

"Ye've nothing to be ashamed of," Eilidh said, "and every-thing to be proud of. I know what ye did for my son. I'm the one who's ashamed—that he's not seen fit to express his gratitude."

"He did, the day we married," Mia replied. "He was very kind."

"And was he as kind today?" Eilidh shook her head and sighed. "I trust ye'll forgive him. He was a little surprised, that's all, given that he must have thought he'd seen a ghost. And dinnae we all act a little oddly when distressed?"

"In my experience, it's when distressed, or angry, that we're less able to conceal our true feelings," Mia said, then she regretted her words as Eilidh's eyes clouded with sorrow. "Forgive me, I did not mean to impugn your son's honor," she continued. "What happened was not his fault."

"Neither was it yers, my dear. We must all accept the hand Fate presents us with. My son is yer husband, and ye must think of him as such, even if he does not—" Eilidh broke off and eyed the maidservant. "Elspeth, once ye've served the tea, go and ask Mrs. Bron to have the main guest room ready for my daughter-in-law, would ye? Have Ailsa light a fire so it's all warm for her."

Elspeth bobbed a curtsy then exited the chamber. Eilidh lifted her cup to her lips, and her hand slipped, splashing tea onto her gown. She set the cup aside with a sigh.

"May I help, Lady MacLennan?" Mia said.

The woman arched an eyebrow.

"Eilidh?"

"No, my dear," Eilidh said, resignation in her eyes. "There's naught anyone can do. My hands…"

"Do they pain you?" Mia said. "Forgive me, I couldn't help noticing…" She gestured to the cane propped up against the table.

"It's old age, my dear," Eilidh said, "and as I've come to accept, there's only one real cure for old age. I'm not quite ready for that."

Surely she didn't mean death? Eilidh couldn't be more than fifty at most, the lines around her eyes brought about by pain rather than age.

"Are you in constant pain?" Mia asked. "Or perhaps at particular times?"

"Particular times?"

"Such as on colder days, or when the air is damp."

"Which describes almost every day here at Glenblath," Eilidh said, with a gentle laugh. "But I do feel less pain in the summer, when the weather's warm and I can venture a little further outside. I find the sunlight soothes my aching body, through lately…" She shook her head. "I ought not to speak of myself when ye must be suffering more pain than I."

"I am in no pain," Mia said. "I have a salve that I apply to the marks on my skin, and they've improved greatly over these past weeks. I made it myself—from chamomile and lavender. I flatter myself that I know a little about ailments and medicines."

"Ye do?"

"Before I fell ill, I was studying under the tutelage of…of Dr. McIver. Though, of course, I wasn't able to—" Mia shook her head. "It matters not now."

"I fancy it matters a great deal," Eilidh said. "That's the first time I've seen yer eyes light up. Which is a shame, as they're such pretty eyes. Was Dr. McIver a friend of yer father's? My son said ye were a doctor's daughter. I'm an advocate for education in women—I was never granted that luxury myself, but when I was a lass, things were very different. Yer father is to be commended for furthering yer education."

"Actually he didn't—" Mia broke off again and sighed. Whatever her father had granted—or denied—her, she had no right to disrespect his memory now he was in his grave.

"I see," Eilidh said. "Well, this Dr. McIver is to be commended."

"I owe much to him," Mia said. "He lent me the funds to pay for my passage here."

Eilidh nodded, compassion in her eyes. "I'm sorry that ye were left destitute on account of my son. I'll make arrangements for him to reimburse Dr. McIver. And ye'll be wanting to write to him, let him know ye arrived safely. He'll be concerned for yer welfare."

Another tear splashed onto Mia's hand and she nodded.

"Excellent!" Eilidh said brightly. "That's settled." She reached for her cup and let out a groan as she curled her hand into a fist.

"May I?" Mia said.

Eilidh nodded, and Mia took the older woman's hand in hers and gently uncurled it. Then she ran her fingertips along the hand, pausing as she reached each swollen knuckle where the skin was reddened. Though the bones were sound, they seemed roughened in places, the texture resembling the bark of an oak tree. Eilidh's eyes narrowed and Mia caught a low hiss of breath.

"Are you in much pain?" Mia said.

"Nothing more than I should expect at my age, lass."

"Does your physician recommend any treatment?"

"Dr. Chisholm advised me not to take milk in my tea. When he used to visit, he did a little bloodletting where it pained me. I'm not fond of leeches, but my late husband thought highly of Dr. Chisholm."

Sweet Lord! What barbarism was this? Doubtless this Dr. Chisholm charged a pretty packet for sticking a leech on his patient's finger. Most likely, he understood that it did nothing to serve as a cure, but provided him with an income.

"Ye disapprove?"

Mia glanced up to see a stern expression in the older woman's eyes. "Forgive me, Lady MacLennan," she said, "but for ailments such as yours, Dr. McIver was never an advocate for leeches."

"And this Dr. McIver is to be thought more highly of than Dr. Chisholm? Dr. Chisholm came all the way from Edinburgh."

Doubtless he had—at Eilidh's expense.

Mia released her hand. "I meant no offense, ma'am. And, if you'll take no offense at my question, may I ask whether Dr. Chisholm's treatments gave any relief from your pain?"

"A little."

"Such as a slight loss of sensation where the leech had been placed, after which the pain returned once it was removed?"

Eilidh's eyes widened. "How did ye know that?"

"Because I understand the effect a leech has on the body," Mia said. "They're beneficial in some cases, but with ailments such as yours, they only provide temporary relief. The loss of blood numbs the skin where the leech has been placed, but in most cases it does nothing to treat the underlying ailment."

"Dr. Chisholm was very expensive. Is that not a sign of accomplishment?"

"It's a sign of his ability to earn a good income," Mia said. "My father adopted a similar practice, whereas Dr. McIver was willing to treat many of his patients for no fee at all, other than a small contribution to reflect what they could afford. Dr. McIver was such an advocate of the smallpox vaccine that he treated several of his patients without charge. Whereas my father…"

My father dismissed the vaccine as the work of a charlatan and died for his troubles.

Mia returned to her seat. "Forgive me, Lady MacLennan. I've no right to interfere when I'm nothing to you."

The older woman took Mia's hand. "Perhaps 'tis I who should beg forgiveness, lass. Ye're not nothing to me—ye're my daughter-in-law. Ye speak with such passion and conviction. It is only fair, then, that I listen. What would ye advise?"

"It doesn't—"

"It *does* matter, lass," Eilidh said. "On some days, my body pains me so much that I'd be willing to try anything. My son offered to send for Dr. Chisholm again as soon as his marriage to Miss Young was…" She colored and sighed. "Well, that's not something we can consider now."

"Then let me atone for your not having the funds for an Edinburgh physician," Mia said.

"There's nothing to atone for," came the reply, "but I would hear what ye might suggest."

Mia glanced at the window, from which a thin beam of sunlight strained across the air, picking up swirling dust motes.

"First," she said, "I'd recommend plenty of sunlight and fresh air. Though the winter months are generally darker, even a little sunlight on a daily basis can ease the ache in your bones. As to milk—do you dislike it in your tea?"

"I like it, but Dr. Chisholm suggested I take my tea plain, for my health."

"I would resume taking milk," Mia said.

"Will that lessen my pain?"

"Over time, if taken regularly, it will lessen the cause of your pain. And if I can find the right herbs and plants, I can make you an infusion to lessen the pain, and a salve to massage into your hands."

"I dinnae know…" Eilidh sighed.

"At least let me try," Mia said. "I'll treat anyone here who needs it if there's no physician available. I'm not afraid of hard work."

"Aye, lass, I can see that," came the reply. "Though it's not the done thing for the Lady of Glenblath to—"

"I think we both know, *Lady* MacLennan," Mia said, "that in every aspect that matters, I am not, and never will be, the true lady of this estate. But I would find fulfilment and happiness in making myself useful in the best way that I know how."

Eilidh smiled. "I must say, ye speak very determinedly and have such unusual ideas for a young lady from London."

Mia returned the smile. "Perhaps that's due to my not being a lady," she said, "at least not in any way that matters. In the eyes of those who matter, a doctor's daughter is nobody."

"Ye're not nobody," Eilidh said, "not to me or my son."

Mia's heart fluttered at the reference to…

My husband.

As if her mind sought to torment her further, his voice, deep and rich, filtered into her senses, at first caressing her with its musical tones, before growing harder, the rich warmth turning to cold anger.

"Damn it all to fuck!"

Eilidh stiffened, her gaze fixed on the door.

Then another voice spoke.

"Ha! Brother, it serves ye right for being such an arse."

"Be quiet, Iona, or ye'll feel the back of my hand on *yer* arse."

"Ye wouldnae dare! Ye're a weakling, Hamish MacLennan."

"And *ye're* a hellion!"

Footsteps drew near and stopped outside the door.

"Go to yer room, Iona," the first voice said. "I cannae stand the sight of ye."

"Better that than the sight of yer wife. I may be a hellion, but at least I'm not saddled with a pockmarked witch!"

"That's *my* misfortune to bear, sister, but take care, lest ye find yerself with an equally undesirable man for a husband. There's plenty hereabouts who'd take ye off my hands, and it'd save me a lot of trouble."

"Ye wouldnae dare!"

"Oh, wouldnae I? What would ye prefer—a bloody good leathering or a pockmarked husband? I—" The voice broke off, then resumed. "What the devil do ye want, Elspeth?"

"I've been seeing to Her Ladyship's chamber," a third voice said, "so she might take her rest."

"Is my mother ill?"

"I-I meant yer wife."

The door opened, and a red-faced Elspeth appeared. Then she stepped aside to reveal Mia's husband standing beside a girl who couldn't be much more than sixteen years of age, with brilliant green eyes set in a face framed by flame-red hair tumbling about her shoulders.

Mia picked up her valise, then rose to her feet. The world blurred before her and she blinked to clear the moisture from her eyes, then met her husband's gaze. A flicker of shame shadowed his expression before he turned his attention on his mother, who was rising more slowly from her chair.

"Ma," he said, "I didnae realize ye were"—he hesitated—"that ye had company."

"I gathered that, son," Eilidh replied, frost in her tone.

"Ma, I…" His voice trailed off as Eilidh raised her hand. Then she turned to the maidservant.

"Elspeth, is the guest chamber ready?"

"Aye, ma'am," Elspeth replied. "It's ready for Lady MacLennan."

Hamish flinched, and his forehead creased into a frown. His eyes seemed to darken, their expression hard and unyielding, barely concealing a flicker of fury.

"I-I…" Mia began, then her throat caught as his expression intensified. "I mean, I'll…"

"There's no need to say anything, my dear," Eilidh said. "Elspeth, please show my daughter-in-law to her chamber. I'd like a word with my son."

The young girl let out a snort, which turned into a squeal as Hamish gave her a sharp nudge.

"That's enough of that, Iona MacLennan," Eilidh said. "As for *ye*, Hamish: ye may be laird, but that disnae give ye permission to behave in such an uncivil manner, particularly toward the woman who's yer—"

"*Dinnae* say it, Ma," Hamish growled, and Mia tightened her grip on her valise.

"I'll say it, lad, because it's true," Eilidh said. "Ye're letting the clan down with yer behavior. Would ye have yer wife think so badly of us on the day she arrives?"

He opened his mouth to reply.

"No, son. Dinnae speak. I doubt there's anything ye can say that will give this lass a more favorable opinion of ye. Like it or not, she's yer wife."

The girl let out another snort. "Like it or not! He definitely does *not* like."

"That's enough, daughter," Eilidh said. "Take yerself to the kitchens and tell Mrs. McBride that ye're to scrub the dirty pans. I'll come along later to check up on ye, so no trying to get out of it."

"But Ma…" the girl whined.

"Either that or ye scrub the chamber pots for a week. Be off with ye before I change my mind and have ye do both tasks."

The girl colored and Mia caught a gleam of moisture in her eyes. Then she nodded, her lower lip wobbling, before mumbling, "Yes, Ma," then disappearing.

"Come with me, ma'am," Elspeth said, holding her hand out. Mia approached the doorway, her stomach knotting as she drew near her husband. He fixed his clear, hard gaze on her and she held her breath, awaiting further insults. But he merely inclined his head then stepped aside to make room.

As Mia exited the chamber, the door closed and almost immediately she heard raised voices.

"Come with me, lass," Elspeth said. "There's naught to be gained from hearing what others have to say about us behind closed doors."

"What else can he have to say that would insult me more than he already has?" Mia said.

"Best not to find out, ma'am."

Mia nodded, then followed the maidservant to a staircase that spiraled upward to another passageway. Elspeth opened the door at the end, leading into a room decorated in a similar fashion to Eilidh's living quarters. Two maidservants were tending to the bed, plumping the pillows and smoothing over a thick plaid blanket, and in the hearth, a fire crackled and spat.

"That's enough, girls," Elspeth said. "Her Ladyship wishes to take her rest."

The maids turned and Mia recognized the pretty young girl who'd declared such a strong aversion to her earlier.

"Close yer mouth, Ailsa," Elspeth said sharply, "or Mrs. Bron will hear of it."

Mumbling, the maids curtsied, then slipped out of the chamber, whispering.

"And none of yer chatter!" Elspeth said.

The whispering stopped and the maids' footsteps faded into the distance.

"Let's get ye settled," Elspeth said, eyeing Mia's valise. "Shall I unpack yer belongings? Or perhaps ye've a trunk that's arriving later?"

Mia lowered her gaze to her valise. "This is all I have."

The maid nodded, sympathy in her eyes, then she spoke more brightly. "Well! I always say that when entering a new home, it's best to make a fresh start with new things. We can run up a gown or two for ye. Some of the finest wool in the Highlands, we have here, which will keep the cold out. I daresay ye're not used to the cold, being from London."

She chattered on, ushering Mia toward a chair beside the fireplace, then she tossed two logs on the fire and poked at it.

"That'll keep ye warm, and I'll come back later to check it's still alight for ye."

"I can tend to the fire, Elspeth," Mia said. "But thank you for your kindness."

"Och, it's not kindness when it's a pleasure, is it, lass?" the woman said, smiling. "And dinnae ye take notice of anything Master Hamish says. He has his da's temper, all right, but there's no malice with it. Now—I daresay ye're hungry. I'll bring up a bite of supper."

"Please don't trouble yourself on my account," Mia said.

"It's no trouble. There's plenty going, what with the wedding feast having been—" Elspeth broke off. "No matter. I can bring ye a bite of venison and some tatties, then I'll leave ye in peace and tend to ye in the morning. Would ye like that?"

Mia nodded. The fatigue she'd kept at bay threatened to overwhelm her, and she lowered herself into a seat and held out her hands to the fire, letting the warmth soak into her palms.

"Yes, Elspeth, I'd like that very much," she said quietly.

The older woman placed a light hand on Mia's shoulder and gave her an affectionate pat. "Good lass," she said. "And may I be so bold as to welcome ye to Glenblath and wish ye joy?"

Mia caught her breath to stem the swell of sorrow, and managed to thank Elspeth in a tight voice. The maid curtsied, then slipped out of the chamber, closing the door softly behind her.

When the footsteps had faded into the distance, leaving only the faint ripple of the breeze flowing around the castle, Mia leaned forward, placed her head in her hands, and surrendered to the tears.

CHAPTER NINE

"SIT DOWN, SON."

Hamish's mother gestured to the seat that…*she* had just vacated.

He folded his arms and shook his head.

"I said, sit *down*, God damn ye!"

He startled as his mother slammed her hand on the table and leaped to her feet. The teacups rattled and one toppled over. Hamish darted forward to catch it, but it fell to the floor.

His mother let out a groan and sank into her seat, eyes squeezed shut, forehead wrinkled.

"Are ye in pain, Ma?"

"Aye."

She opened her eyes and he was met by the force of her gaze. Her body may be weak, but her will—the core of steel forged from her Highland ancestors—was as strong as ever.

Hamish retrieved the fallen cup. "It's fortunate this fell on the rug," he said, "or it would have shattered."

She rolled her eyes. "Is that all ye have to say to me, Hamish MacLennan?"

Not *Hamish*, or *son*, but *Hamish MacLennan*.

"What have I done wrong?" he asked, wincing as his conscience needled at his soul.

"If ye have to ask, then I'll not waste my breath telling ye."

She fixed her gaze on him. For as long as Hamish could recall, his mother had reserved a very specific stare for when he or his sister behaved particularly badly. It was a stare with the specific purpose of compelling a wayward boy into confessing his sins. A stare that could open a portcullis at fifty paces and set dry logs ablaze in the absence of a tinderbox.

Then she blinked and looked away.

"I've no wish to admonish ye," she said, "but ye cannae be surprised that I'm disappointed at what happened today."

"Aye, Ma, so am I."

She muttered something to herself that sounded very much like *cursed boy*, then leaned forward. "I daresay we're disappointed for different reasons, Hamish. Have ye never stopped to think how that poor lass may be feeling?"

"I doubt if the Honorable Miss Young will care whether—"

"Ugh!" His mother let out a snort. "Are ye deliberately trying to vex me? I meant yer wife! That poor lass rose from her deathbed, left England with nothing to her name, save what she could carry in her valise. She borrowed the funds for her passage, endured the stares of her fellow travelers for a fortnight, to reach the only place she could call home—in a land of strangers. And what did she find? The man she'd married and given every penny she owned to, on the brink of marrying another and not in the least pleased to discover that she lived…"

She raised her hand as Hamish opened his mouth. "No, dinnae interrupt me. I will have my say, then ye can go to yer chamber and think on yer behavior."

Devil's ballocks—was she about to make him stand in the corner, or go to bed without any supper?

"That young lass heard every word ye said to Iona," she continued. "Doubtless the whole household heard it."

"It was Iona who called her a pockmarked witch."

"And there ye go," she said. "Just like when ye were a lad, blaming everything on yer sister. She knows no better, but ye're the man of the house. I didnae hear ye say aught in the lass's defense. In fact, ye said it was yer misfortune to bear."

He winced as he recalled his words. "We all speak more harshly of others when we dinnae expect to be overheard," he said. "Anyone who eavesdrops should expect to hear no good of themselves."

She arched an eyebrow in the manner of a disappointed schoolmistress.

"Devil's cock, Ma!" he cried. "If I heard everything Iona said about me behind my back, I'd thrash her black and blue on a nightly basis."

"Does that give ye the right to tell that poor lass that her face is frightening the children?"

Fuck. So Ma had heard that.

Ye're an utter bastard, Hamish Alastair Jamie MacLennan.

Hamish winced at the scolding from his conscience. But he had to set that aside. The future of Glenblath was at stake.

"My anger today was nothing to do with the lass's face," he said.

"At least call her by her name."

"Euphramia."

Hamish's tongue curled over the syllables of the name he'd whispered in his prayers when giving thanks for her generosity.

He lifted his hand to his forehead and wiped his brow, but the ache throbbing behind his eyes that had grown steadily from the moment he'd set eyes on...Euphramia...in the chapel showed no sign of relenting.

"I'm not angry at her," he said. "I'm angry—nay, *concerned*—about the estate. Miss Young's dowry was to pay off our remaining creditors. We'd have finally been free of debt after years of Da's—"

"There's no need to remind me of yer da's excesses," his mother said. "I knew more than anyone of the vices he indulged in. But *ye're* the laird now. Ye must take responsibility. Yer da's been gone two years."

"I know, Ma," he said. "Dinnae ye understand that's why I agreed to wed Miss Young? But now..."

"Now it will take a little more time to clear the debts," she said. "Is that such a tragedy? Isn't it better to learn how to be responsible for yerself rather than rely on some lass's fortune? Ye'd be less likely to get into debt again if ye can learn how to get out of it."

"I'm not some lad learning how to manage his allowance, Ma," Hamish huffed.

"Then stop behaving like one."

He met her gaze, but was unable to reply. After all, she'd spoken the truth.

"Speak to her," Ma said. "Ye may find her a useful helpmate. A lass without fortune may have other qualities."

"Such as?"

"If ye cannae see her qualities, then I'll regret yer union even more than ye."

"Ye would?"

"Aye. But for *her* sake, not yers."

"Then"—he hesitated, bracing himself for the blow that he was about to earn—"ye wouldnae object if I asked the lass for an annulment? The marriage was never consummated."

His mother remained still. The only indication that she'd heard was a slight whitening of her knuckles as she tightened her hold on her cane.

The warm crackle of the fire filled the air, but it lacked the usual aura of comfort that he took on entering his mother's chamber.

"Ye must do as ye see fit, son," she said, after a pause. "I'm just yer ma and have no right to tell ye what to do for the benefit of Glenblath."

"*Everything* I do is for the benefit of Glenblath," he replied. "If I cannae take care of our people, then what purpose do I serve?"

"The first step toward saving the world, son, is to save a single soul. This lass may have been sent here by the Almighty for a purpose—to make ye happy, perhaps."

He let out a bitter laugh. "I've long since surrendered any

hope of being *happy*. I must do what I think is right. If I disappoint ye, that's a price I must pay."

She let out a sigh.

"Ye women have it easy," he said, tempering his irritation. "Ye dinnae have to shoulder responsibility, make difficult decisions, or be hard when hardness is required."

"Och, Hamish," she said. "Ye've much to learn about women."

"Such as?"

"Ye must discover that for yerself. Now, I wish to rest."

Considering himself dismissed, Hamish rose.

"Ye might ignore the advice of a woman," she said, "and an old one at that. But I would beg ye to speak to yer wife."

"Now?" he said, wincing at his tone, which sounded like that of a petulant child objecting to being told to apologize for a petty transgression.

"Leave her be tonight. She's had an ordeal."

She offered her hand and he kissed it. As he approached the door, she called after him.

"Son."

"Yes, Ma?"

"As yer mother, I had only one objective in life."

"Which was?"

"To raise ye to be a better man than yer father—a better man than any other. But I failed, and for that I'm truly sorry." She let out another sigh and her voice cracked. "Perhaps I have no right to be disappointed in ye. I ought to be disappointed in myself for not teaching ye the one simple lesson that even the strongest, most intelligent man should learn above all else."

"And what lesson is that, Ma?"

"The difference between right and wrong."

Hamish opened his mouth to reply then closed it.

What could he possibly say that would make her less disappointed in him? And what could he say that would make him less disappointed in himself?

There was nothing.

He bowed his head, then exited the chamber, closing the door behind him.

CHAPTER TEN

T HE FOLLOWING MORNING dawned cold and sharp. Frost covered the world in a dusting, as if a great hand had sprinkled sugar over the landscape.

And what a beautiful landscape it was. The view from Mia's window took in the mountain in all its magnificence, its snow-capped peak glistening in the sunlight, set against a clear blue sky with a faint pink haze near the horizon. After donning her gown—which, after a fortnight's traveling, had collected a layer of dirt at the hem that no amount of brushing could remove and a soup stain just below the neckline—Mia settled on the window seat, taking in the view.

What must it be like to call this land home, to spend each day savoring the sweet, fresh air, unencumbered by the demands of London life?

But, in all likelihood, the lot of a woman here was the same as in London. And like it or not…

Mia permitted herself a wry smile at the memory of the words spoken last night:

Like it or not, this woman is yer wife.

Like it or not! He definitely does not like.

Like it or not, she was the property of another. She had vowed to obey him. And though she may have believed that vow, and her life, were only to last a few days, she'd still uttered it, before Reverend Staines, before witnesses—and before the

Almighty.

Her life was no longer hers to dictate.

It was *his*.

She sighed, letting her breath mist on the windowpane. Then she drew the outline of a heart with her fingertip before wiping it away.

Last night, he'd come to her in her dreams. But rather than envelop her in his huge arms and speak soft words of love, he had condemned her, calling her a demon, marked by the devil himself, to be thrown into a fiery pit, and…

Mia startled at a knock on the door. She called out and a woman entered. Her hair, black with streaks of gray, was scraped back into a severe style. Her dress was neat and plain and she wore a chain about her waist, from which hung a set of keys.

Mia retreated from the window and the woman frowned.

"Are ye unwell, lass?" Then the woman sighed and shook her head. "Forgive me, Lady MacLennan. I quite forgot."

She dipped into a curtsy, then approached Mia and took her hands.

"Och, ye're freezing! Curse that Ailsa! I told her to light the fire for ye before dawn. What must ye think of us?"

Mia couldn't think of anything to say in response.

The woman sighed. "Better if ye dinnae say what ye think of us after yesterday. But, as I always say to Mr. Bron, a new day brings with it a clear head, a forgiving heart, and the chance to begin again."

"Mr. Bron?" Mia said.

"My husband. He's the butler and served the old laird before Master Hamish. I'm Mrs. Bron."

Mia raised her eyebrows.

"The housekeeper," the woman continued. She cast her gaze over Mia's gown. "Did yer maid not travel with ye?"

"I have no maid, Mrs. Bron."

"Well, I daresay Elspeth could take care of ye if ye wish. Och, lass—ye should have asked her to tend to ye last night, at least to help ye change into yer nightgown."

"I don't need a maid to do that, Mrs. Bron."

"Then why are ye wearing the same gown ye had on yesterday?"

Mia lowered her gaze, swallowing her shame. Then a hand took hers, the fingers gnarled with callouses.

"Perhaps I'm mistaken," Mrs. Bron said. "I know nothing of ladies' gowns—one looks the same as any other. But with a gown that flimsy, ye'll catch yer death. Once ye've seen Master Hamish, I'll ask Elspeth to fit ye out with something better suited to our climate."

Mia didn't know which was worse—the fact that the housekeeper realized that she had only one gown in the world or the woman's kindness in refraining from mentioning it outright.

"Thank you, that would be..." Mia hesitated. "Forgive me...once I've seen Master Hamish?"

"He's sent for ye," Mrs. Bron said. "Best be quick—he disnae like to be kept waiting." She cast her gaze over Mia's gown. "Do ye have a shawl? Ye should see him looking yer best." She flinched as her gaze flicked over Mia's face. "I meant yer *gown* looking its best. I hope I didnae give offense."

"No offense was taken," Mia said with as much dignity as she could summon. "Besides, I've heard worse from..." She shook her head. "It doesn't matter."

Now wasn't the time to wallow in self-pity.

"I understand," came the reply. "Rest assured, ye'll hear none of that from me—or the rest of the household, if I have my way. Be sure to tell me if anyone fails to give ye the respect ye deserve."

At that moment, a clock struck somewhere in the distance, nine times.

"Bless me, where does the time go!" The housekeeper scuttled across the floor toward a wooden trunk and opened it. She pulled out a plaid shawl, nodded, then shook it, sneezing at a puff of dust. "One of Her Ladyship's old shawls," she said. "It'll keep ye warm."

She placed the shawl about Mia's shoulders then secured it with a pin.

"There!" she said. "Ye look very fine. Quick, now—ye dinnae want to keep him waiting."

The housekeeper led Mia through a series of passageways, down a flight of steps, and past a handful of servants who stared open-mouthed at Mia. They reached a thick, dark wooden door in the shape of an arch, with a huge ringed handle fashioned from iron in the shape of twisted rope, and Mrs. Bron knocked three times.

Mia's stomach fluttered as a deep voice called out. The housekeeper opened the door, ushered her inside, then closed it, leaving Mia alone with her husband.

He sat behind a squat wooden desk, decorated with carvings of trees, stags, and other beasts. His chair—more of a throne, given its size and shape—formed the shape of an arch at the back, and was covered in dark metal studs. The chair would have engulfed Mia's frame, but it looked as if it had been made for Hamish, as if they had both been carved from solid, hard wood. But the figure in the chair was a living, breathing man.

The room itself radiated an aura of primal strength. The candle sconces were fashioned from a metal so black that they seemed to absorb the light. The walls were absent of tapestries, bearing instead an array of mounted deer heads, five in total, which stared malevolently at Mia as she stood, awaiting instruction.

The man behind the desk leaned forward, bringing his face into the light, and gestured to the chair in front of the desk.

Her legs threatening to give way, Mia approached the chair and sat, wincing at the scrape of wood against stone.

He remained silent, and Mia studied his face, looking for signs of the kindness that she'd clung to during the long journey to Scotland. But there was none. His face seemed to have been chiseled from granite—a strong, square jaw and a straight nose bearing a slight indent in the middle, as if he'd been engaged in a fight…

Doubtless, his opponent had come off worse, judging by the size of the hands that rested on the top of the desk.

The hands of a warrior.

Clear eyes, the color of hard, unyielding emeralds, focused on Mia, and her stomach clenched in fear. He appeared the kind of warrior who won his battles before they even began, felling his opponents with a single stare.

Well, he wouldn't fell *her*. She had stared Death in the face and survived. This man—the beast sitting before her—couldn't harm her any more than she had been already.

And when a hunted animal has nothing to lose, she stands her ground with a clear conscience. She stares her predator in the face, challenging him to devour her.

Wasn't that what Lady Portia always said?

Mia suppressed a smile at the thought of her friend, who'd faced Death many times, staring at the end of a pistol and reigning triumphant over the male sex—the *weaker* sex. Portia had only faltered once, when she'd faced the man she loved. But Mia was unlikely to love a man—much less likely to be loved by one. Therefore, there was no opponent whom she couldn't face with courage and determination.

She met his gaze. The man across the desk widened his eyes, and Mia caught a glimmer of confusion in them. Perhaps he expected women to cower before him—or dissolve into a puddle of female desire.

Then his expression darkened and she saw, once more, the anger. She clasped her hands together, and he lowered his gaze. Mia caught a flare of surprise in his eyes as his gaze settled on her left hand—specifically, the gold band adorning the third finger.

"Ye'll probably be wondering why I summoned ye," he said at last.

Summoned?

Mia folded her arms. "I thought you'd said everything you

wanted to say to me yesterday."

He frowned and broke the gaze. But the frisson of triumph at making him look away dissolved when he flicked his eyes back at her and she saw the granite-hard frost in his expression.

"I see little point in pandering to the compliments ye'd expect from a London fop, Miss Lucas."

"I assure you, sir, the last thing I expect from *you* is a compliment."

She hesitated, fearing his reaction to her next words. But what did she have to lose?

"And," she continued, "I believe I should be addressed as *Lady MacLennan*."

His lips thinned as her arrow hit home.

Then the corner of his mouth quirked into a smile, though his eyes remained cold.

"Not, perhaps, for much longer."

She caught her breath.

Bastard.

Though she didn't voice the insult, her cheeks warmed at the profanity.

Then he blinked and she caught a glimmer of regret in his eyes.

"Forgive me…" he began.

"There's nothing to forgive," she said, leaning back. "I take it you've been considering how to release yourself of the burden you find yourself under. Given, I would hope, that even *you* wouldn't stoop to murder, I presume you're contemplating an annulment?"

He jerked back as if she'd slapped him. Then he let out a sigh and nodded.

"I've naught against ye personally, lass, but I have the fortunes of Glenblath to consider."

"Fortunes I contributed to."

"Aye," he said, his voice a low growl, "but I never expected our marriage to last."

Mia let out a mirthless laugh. "I suspect I'm more surprised than you that I survived. Certainly I feel the impact to a greater degree than yourself."

He lifted his hand to his face and brushed it across his forehead. Despite her indignation at the cruel words he'd spoken, she couldn't help the swell of compassion at the strain in his eyes brought about by having a large estate to care for, with all the tenants and servants who depended on him. In London, Mr. Stockton had painted a pretty portrait of Hamish MacLennan as an honorable man striving to do what was best for others under dire financial circumstances. And, perhaps, had his anger and revulsion today not been directed toward her, Mia might have loved him for it—as she believed she might have come to love him had he not rejected her so soundly.

"Well," he said, "ye *have* survived. I must therefore decide what to do. Which is why"—he leaned back—"why I wish for an annulment. I dinnae see it as an impossibility, provided that—"

"Provided that I'm in agreement?" Mia said.

"Provided that the marriage has not been consummated. I doubt it would be difficult to prove that ye and I have not"—he made a random gesture between them—"given that..." He lifted his gaze to her face and flinched.

"Given that my looks make it impossible for any man to consider me worthy of bedding?"

"That's not a subject a woman should speak of."

"Not even when she's your wife, which I am at present, even though you wish I weren't?"

"Do ye not also wish for an annulment?"

She paused, letting in the hopes and dreams she'd clung to during the past fortnight. They swirled in her mind, the images of her huge Highlander sweeping her into his strong arms and kissing her into ecstasy. Then she pushed them to the back of her mind, like an old trunk filled with childish toys, to be consigned to the attic to gather dust while she ventured out into the real world.

At length, she nodded, ignoring the shard of pain in her heart at the relief in his eyes. "I agree that it would be more conducive to my happiness to be alone and unmarried rather than married and unwanted."

"Is that a yes?"

How dare he! Did he think to reject her then claim that she welcomed it?

"I have a condition," she said.

His jaw bulged as if he gritted his teeth.

"Be not alarmed, sir, that I wish to remain here forever. You've made it plain that my presence here would be detrimental to your happiness and the welfare of your people. We wouldn't want my face to frighten them again, would we?"

Drawing consolation from the flicker of guilt in his eyes, she continued.

"From what I understand—and forgive the limited understanding of one of my sex—the purpose of an annulment is to render a marriage invalid, as if it had not taken place at all. Yes?"

He tilted his head to one side, then nodded. "Aye."

"Therefore, both parties should be placed in the position in which they found themselves the moment before the marriage took place."

He continued to stare, but she could see no understanding in his expression.

"The same position," she said, "in *every* respect."

He shook his head. "Forgive me—every respect?"

"The same *financial* position."

This time there was no mistaking it. Understanding flooded his expression, followed by a flash of fury. "Ye cannae mean…"

"That would be fair, would it not?" Mia said.

"From *yer* perspective."

"And yours," she retorted. "I assume your purpose in disposing of me is not only to find yourself a wife whose face you can look at without retching, but also one with a dowry large enough to meet your monetary demands." She took his silence as agreement. "It seems only fair, therefore, to return the dowry that you took from me." She arched her eyebrows and tilted her head to one side. "Yes?"

He blinked slowly. "I dinnae have it."

"Then I'll remain here until you do," she said. "Consider your dislike of my presence as an incentive to acquire it." He opened his mouth, most likely to protest, and she raised her hand, tempering the anger simmering in her gut. "I take it you're not so without feeling as to want me to leave here destitute, compelled to use my body to earn a living?"

He shifted in his seat, the first sign of discomfort.

"And," she continued, "you must agree that my prospects of earning a living in such a manner are nonexistent, given I have the face of…what was it?" She placed a finger on her chin. "Yes, that was it…a *pockmarked witch*."

His left eyelid twitched and he lowered his gaze.

"All I ask is that you return what you took from me," she said. "But I won't demand immediate payment."

"That's just as well, lass," he said. "It might take months before I have the means."

"You'll find me a patient woman."

"And then what will ye do?"

She gave a bitter laugh. "Seeing as you're so eager to rid yourself of me, I'll return to England, to train as a doctor. I know a little—"

"Women cannae be doctors."

"That's what most men believe," she huffed. "Fortunately, Dr. McIver has a little more wit than the rest of your sex. He's taught me enough to understand what ails your mother, for example."

"I'll not have ye interfering with Ma's illness," he said. "But if ye are to remain here at my expense"—he held up his hand as she opened her mouth to protest—"ye cannae spend yer days languishing in idleness and frivolity. We've no time for pampered ladies here."

This time her laugh was genuine. "I take it you knew very little of the Honorable Aurora Young."

"She had a dowry," he said. "That's all I needed to know."

"So did I," Mia said.

Heavens! She'd thought her wastrel cousin was the worst of all men, but the giant sitting before her, who seemed intent on insulting her in every manner possible, had earned that title ten times over.

Mia rose to her feet.

"I haven't dismissed ye yet."

"I'm not your servant!" she retorted. "I am your guest until the matter is resolved. But do not fear. I am not afraid of hard work, and I can…"

She paused, recalling the pain in Lady MacLennan's eyes. Hamish's anger was a small price to pay for championing that poor woman.

"Despite what you may think, I *can* alleviate your mother's pain. I know how expensive doctors can be—particularly when they're summoned from Edinburgh at their patient's expense."

He drew in a sharp breath, and she nodded.

"Yes, your mother discussed the matter with me."

"Whatever for?"

"Perhaps because I'm a member of the family by marriage. At least until you dispose of me." She let out a sigh. "I don't wish to quarrel with you, sir. I'll agree to an annulment on the terms already discussed. And, in return for your hospitality while awaiting payment, I'm willing to serve the people of Glenblath in the manner I best know how—as a physician."

He shook his head and she leaned forward, placing her hands on the desk.

"At least let me try," she said. "I'll treat anyone who needs it and will ask for no payment. I can even make arrangements for the people here to be vaccinated."

"To be…*what?*"

Mia gestured to her face. "Wouldn't you want to protect the

people you love against *this?*"

He flinched, and she swallowed her sorrow at his revulsion. Having survived smallpox, she might have gained an immunity against the disease—but would she ever become immune to the disgust of others?

"If you prefer, I can live elsewhere," she said. "I need only a small home and enough room so that I might treat the sick. If I'm not in this castle, you're spared the ordeal of having to look at me. Then you can ready yourself and your household for the arrival of my replacement with a clear conscience."

He blinked again, and she caught something akin to shame in his eyes—shame and defeat. Then she straightened her stance.

"Do we have a deal, sir?"

Slowly, he rose to his feet, scraping the chair back. Then he extended his hand.

For a moment Mia stared at it, then she lowered her gaze to the scars across the back of her own hand.

"Are you quite sure, Lord MacLennan, that you wish to place yourself at risk of infection…or a curse?"

He hesitated, his eyes shining with guilt, then reached forward and took her hand.

A fizz of sensation rippled across her skin and she moved to withdraw, but he tightened his grip, curling his fingers around hers. With the pad of his thumb, he caressed her skin, and she caught her breath at a hot little pulse in her center. A low growl seemed to reverberate in his chest as a spark of gold glittered in the depths of his eyes, like a faint, pulsating star growing brighter with each heartbeat. His nostrils flared and he leaned forward, bringing his face close, and Mia caught the scent of wood, smoke, and peat—the primal scent of man and beast. Her gaze fell to his lips, and she let out a low cry as they parted and his soft, warm breath caressed her face.

"Aye, Lady MacLennan," he said, his voice thick and low. "I am quite sure."

His tongue flicked out and he ran it across his lower lip. Mia's stomach curled with an unfathomable need and something swelled inside her—a knot of primal desire.

No!

Desire was not something she could surrender to—not when no man would ever find her desirable again.

Her cheeks flaming, she broke free and stepped back. But rather than relief in his eyes, she saw disappointment.

CHAPTER ELEVEN

HAMISH CAUGHT HIS breath at the stiffening in his cock.

Devil's ballocks—had the lass not stepped back, he'd have been in danger of kissing her, of claiming those lips.

Why had he not noticed them before, in all their moist, pink sweetness?

Because ye were staring at her scars and griping about yer loss of fortune.

Brave lass, she hid her distress well, but her eyes—those wide, expressive hazel eyes—were now bright with moisture. During their exchange, they had flashed with spirit, myriad green and brown hues with a shimmer of dark gold. Framed with dark lashes, they were extraordinarily beautiful. Not in the conventional way of lasses, but in the determination in their gaze and the undercurrent of steel.

Not once had she dissolved into tears or thrown the tantrum expected of ladies who did not get their own way—the Honorable Aurora being no exception, as Hamish had discovered not long after their first introduction when she complained about a smudge of mud on her gown.

In contrast, Euphramia had acted with a quiet dignity that set her far above the Honorable Aurora. And, come to that, above any other woman of his acquaintance, save, perhaps, his mother.

What a pity, then, that their marriage must come to an end. But she wanted it dissolved as much as he—didn't she?

She lifted her hand, stared at the pockmarked skin as if in disbelief. Hot needles of guilt stabbed at him as he recalled her words. Her quiet request as to whether he feared the touch of her skin might curse him was not voiced as an admonishment, or a plea. It was a simple statement, based, no doubt, on the opinion of the world around her. And she didn't voice anything that he'd not heard. Or said himself. Murdoch had referred to her last night as a *filthy, pox-ridden Sassenach*. And though Hamish had admonished his friend for his words, doubtless the lass had heard worse, and would do so again.

Would he have borne it with the same fortitude?

"Lass," he said quietly, "I must beg forgiveness for—"

"It matters not," she said, her tone businesslike. "And now, if you require nothing more from me, I'll speak to Mrs. Bron about the arrangements."

"Arrangements?"

"To find somewhere else to live. With your permission, of course."

"Ye have it."

She nodded, then moved toward the door. But he had no wish for her to leave still believing him to be the very worst of men.

"Lass."

She turned and regarded him with her clear gaze. "Yes?"

He gestured toward her. "Did ye suffer much?"

"Only at first," she said. "But when I resigned myself to…" She smiled. "It's not of import. What matters is that I survived. I intend to make the best of that."

"Ye do?"

She nodded. "For one thing, I am no longer in danger if I treat others infected with smallpox."

"How so?"

"Because I am immune."

He raised his eyebrows in inquiry. She smiled, and his stomach tightened at the expression in her eyes. The faintest glimmer of joy rendered them more beautiful than any he had ever seen—certainly in sharp contrast to the spiteful expression of expectation and entitlement in the Honorable Aurora's eyes.

Perhaps in interrupting his marriage to Aurora, the Almighty had spared Hamish a lifetime of trouble.

"For many diseases," Euphramia said, "those who recover are at less, and sometimes no, risk of being infected again."

"I dinnae understand."

"It's like training for a battle, or a fight."

"A fight?"

She curled her lip in amusement. "Surely you've indulged in fights? Though I have no doubt, given that at your current size you could fell twenty warriors without so much as a scratch, you must have sustained injuries while learning how to beat another man to the ground with your fists."

The beast lurking at the back of his mind let out a low growl of satisfaction. So…she'd observed his physique and concluded it to be superior to at least twenty other men.

She continued, "Having survived smallpox, my body is now capable of defense against further infection."

"And ye know this, how?"

"Through Dr. McIver's tutelage. He was willing to sponsor my application to train, but it was denied me."

"How so?"

"Had I been born a boy, I would have been permitted to study medicine. But Papa—may God rest his soul—could never forgive me for being a girl."

His heart ached at the pain in her eyes, which she tried to hide with a smile. Poor lass. From the moment she'd entered the world, she was a disappointment to the men who owned her. First her father, and now her husband…

Then her smile resumed. "I oughtn't be ungrateful. Papa was no different to any father who's not blessed with a son."

"Aye," Hamish couldn't help saying, recalling his own father's disappointment when Iona was born. Da had wanted a second son and had blamed Ma for her inability to give him one, cursing his lot on his deathbed for leaving Glenblath bereft of what it needed.

How different Hamish's father had been compared to the brave, kind lass standing before him now, who, on her deathbed, had given him everything she had.

And look how ye've repaid her!

"I would like to think that when I'm a father, I…" Hamish trailed off with shame. Perhaps, if Fate had dealt him a different hand, the woman standing before him could have given him children.

Her cheeks reddened and, for the first time, she looked as if she might burst into tears.

"I shouldn't have spoken with such disrespect toward my father," she said, her voice tight. "He only wished that I'd been born a boy. At least he didn't wish that I were dead."

Her arrow hit home. But he welcomed it.

Then she shook her head. "Forgive me, Lord MacLennan, I spoke out of turn. Rest assured that I'll not trespass on your life here any more than is absolutely necessary. I'm truly sorry for the turn of events and the impact it's had on you."

She withdrew to the door. As she touched the handle, he called out after her.

"Euphramia."

She stiffened at his use of her name and turned.

But what could he say to her? That he was the worst of all cads? That, despite his feelings now, he couldn't deny that he had not only wished that she had died, but he had voiced that wish to others? What purpose would that serve, other than to destroy her more than he had already done?

"I'm sorry for what has befallen ye, lass."

A wholly inadequate speech to convey his regret. It was as well that they were to part, for she deserved a better man than him.

"There's no need for apology," she said, "not if, after we've concluded our business, we both end up with what we want. Perhaps, rather than regret what has befallen us or what we have said and done, we should forget the past and look to the future and to our dearest wish—even if our wishes are not the same."

Before he could respond, she exited the chamber, leaving him with his conscience.

CHAPTER TWELVE

AS SOON AS she closed the door, Mia's resolve threatened to crumble and the tears she'd fought to keep at bay swelled and stung her eyes.

Do not falter now.

She fisted her hands, digging the nails into her palms, letting the pain serve as a distraction.

I'll be damned if I let him see me cry.

She allowed her mind to wander to happier times—lessons from Dr. McIver in applying bandages and manipulating bones…

…and the time she'd tended to Lady Portia's bullet wound. Granted, not a joyous occasion, but Mia could never forget the spark of professional pride in being the one person Portia's maid had sought out to tend to her mistress. Then there was the time Mia had assisted Dr. McIver in resetting Captain Floret's broken leg. Rather than dismiss her as a weak-bellied woman, the doctor had issued firm instructions to her as his helpmate. Afterward, he'd provided her with a study text on tending to broken and dislocated bones in the manner of a tutor who rewarded an able pupil not with fatuous praise, but with more challenging tasks.

That was what she needed to focus on during the months ahead—that and her end objective. There was little point in crying over what might have been, over a love she could never have hoped to have experienced.

She lifted her sleeve and gave her eyes an angry wipe. She

was not some feeble woman to be indulged or bullied. And she'd prove it to...*him*. The expression on his face when she'd set out her demands was almost comical. But, given that she had not a penny to her name, she had nothing to lose. And when a person had nothing to lose, they were at their most dangerous.

For the moment, she needed to return to her chamber, where she could give vent to her emotions in privacy before composing herself for the next challenge.

She slipped along the passageway, her footsteps echoing off the granite walls, then paused at the end as it forked into two. Should she go right, or left?

Footsteps approached from behind. Unwilling to endure a further encounter, she took the right fork and, at length, reached a staircase. It led down rather than up, but, with the footsteps getting closer, she had no wish to retrace her steps, and pressed on.

The other footsteps, curse them, seemed to be following. Mia hurried her pace and found herself once more in the entrance hall with the tapestry depicting its gruesome scene. But in the morning light that stretched across the hallway, illuminating the woven fibers, the scene lost some of its malevolence and instead seemed to pulse with a primal vitality.

She moved closer to the tapestry and her gaze fell upon the man brandishing the spear that pierced the stag. No, not a man. A giant: broad-shouldered, wearing a plaid in muted colors, but with a thick mop of red hair. Mouth open in a roar of triumph, he was looking over his shoulder, directly outward from the tapestry.

At her.

She reached toward him, then withdrew, her heart fluttering. Such vitality, such primal strength—it seemed almost sinful to even be looking at him, let alone touching...

"The likeness is remarkable, is it not, ma'am?"

Mia turned to see the housekeeper standing beside her.

"M-Mrs. Bron," she stammered, "forgive me for..."

"For what, lass? For looking at the likeness of yer husband?"

Mia's cheeks warmed as she resumed her attention on the man in the tapestry.

"Of course, it's *not* Master Hamish, seeing as it was woven nigh on a century ago," the housekeeper said. "It's his grandfather's grandfather, Hamish Malcolm Alastair McCallum. A fine man, by all accounts." She gestured to the mounted stag's head high up on the wall. "*Awld Hamish*, he called him. An eighteen-pointer."

"A what?" Mia said.

"I've never seen one in all the Highlands," the housekeeper continued. "There was a rumor that the MacKenzies had one, but it turned out to be false. Not even Master Hamish has felled an eighteen-pointer. The best he's managed is fourteen. I daresay ye noticed it when ye were in his study?"

"Forgive me…an *eighteen-pointer*?"

"Och!" Mrs. Bron let out a laugh. "Of course, ye Sassenachs know nothing of stags, do ye?" She gestured again toward the mounted head. "See his antlers? There's eighteen points on them—nine each side. A great stag's the most magnificent sight to behold, early in the morning, through the mist, when ye've heard him roaring. Have ye never seen a stag, ma'am?"

"I've seen deer in the countryside in England, but nothing quite so…" Mia trailed off.

"So Scottish?"

Mia smiled. "Yes. He's very Scottish—wild, free, and filled with life."

Whereas I'm a weakling who does not belong.

As if she'd read Mia's mind, the housekeeper touched her arm. "Ye'll be just like him soon, ma'am, I'm sure," she said. "I've seen it before—when Sassenach lasses come here and marry our men. The land will change ye, grow into yer bones, fill yer lungs with Highland air until ye're one of us."

But I'll never be one of you. I'm not wanted here.

"Och, there's no need to look so sad," Mrs. Bron said. "How

about I ask Rory to take ye with him to see the stag? The one hereabouts this year is a sixteen-pointer, so Rory says. For my part, I think he's spinning a yarn to impress that *hure* he's always fooling about with."

What the devil was a *hure*?

"I wouldn't want you to go to any trouble on my account, Mrs. Bron," Mia said.

"Ye're the Lady of Glenblath. Nothing ye ask is any trouble. Now, ye shouldn't be dawdling about here when there's breakfast to be had. Ye've led me on a merry chase about the place. Come along, now."

Mrs. Bron set off, her crisp, efficient tone brooking no denial, and Mia followed obediently. Rather than take Mia to the huge banqueting hall, the older woman led her past the huge, carved doors and through another series of passageways. Perhaps it was as well that Mia was destined to leave, for she'd never find her way about the castle unattended. The building was a labyrinth—complete with its own flame-haired minotaur.

At length, they reached a door, behind which Mia could hear voices. The housekeeper knocked and the voices stopped, then she opened the door to reveal what must be a dining room, in the center of which was a long wooden table with three occupants. A maid circled the table, carrying a tureen. She stiffened and stared, and Mia recognized her as one of the maids who'd been gossiping about her yesterday. The diners turned to face Mia. Eilidh sat at one side of the table, a gentle smile of welcome on her lips. Her daughter, sitting opposite, scowled at Mia before resuming her attention on the bowl in front of her. And at the end of the table sat Mia's husband.

"I've found her, Master Hamish," Mrs. Bron said.

"So I see," he replied, rising. Then he frowned at the young girl. "Iona," he growled.

She pulled a face. "What?"

"Show some respect and stand for our guest."

"Ye've not asked Ma to stand. Why should I?"

"There's no need to stand on my account," Mia said. "I'm—"

"I didnae ask *ye*," the girl said.

"Iona, that's enough," Eilidh said quietly. "Do as yer brother says."

The girl glared at Hamish, then let out a huff and scraped her chair back. "I'll do it for *ye*, Ma, but no one else."

"Here, Lady MacLennan," Mrs. Bron said, leading Mia toward the place setting at the other end of the table. The girl's eyes widened at the housekeeper's address. She opened her mouth, but Hamish raised his hand.

"Sit, Iona," he said, "and keep yer thoughts to yerself. I'll hear no more from ye today unless ye want to be sent to yer chamber with no breakfast."

The girl spooned a mouthful of food from her bowl, then pulled another face. "I'm not a child," she said, her mouth full.

Hamish let out a snort. "Act like a bairn and I'll treat ye like one."

"Ailsa, some parritch for Lady MacLennan," his mother said. The maid frowned, then she exchanged a glance with Iona before approaching Mia with the tureen, eyebrows raised.

Mia peered into the bowl to see a cream-colored substance resembling thick gruel.

"Is it not good enough for ye?" the maid said, her green eyes glittering with spite.

"I-I've not eaten… I beg pardon, what was it called?"

"Parritch."

"I've not tried parritch before, but I would like some, thank you."

The maid tilted her head to one side, then ladled some of the mixture into Mia's bowl. It spilled over, and Mia let out a cry as some fell into her lap.

"Beg pardon, *Yer Ladyship*," the maid said as Iona stifled a giggle.

"Ailsa!" Eilidh cried. "Fetch a cloth at once. No…return to the kitchen and remain there. Send Elspeth with a cloth, seeing as ye cannae be trusted."

The maid blushed and mumbled, "Yes, Lady MacLennan," then slipped out of the room.

"I'm so sorry, lass," Eilidh said, leaning toward Mia. "Yer poor dress! Go to yer chamber after breakfast and change into a fresh gown, and I'll send Elspeth up. I dinnae know what's come over Ailsa. She's..." She paused as Iona let out a snort. "Was this yer doing, lass?"

Iona's cheeks flushed pink and she shook her head.

"Please, don't trouble yourself or Elspeth," Mia said.

"It's no trouble. Now, eat—there's naught like a good bowl of parritch to set ye up for the day."

Mia took a spoonful. The texture was a little sticky, but she could not deny the flavor. Both creamy and nutty, it was neither sweet nor savory, but warm and welcoming. She swallowed it, letting the warmth radiate through her body.

"It's good, aye?"

Mia paused, the spoon halfway to her lips as her husband spoke, and she glanced up to see him staring at her, his gaze as intense as usual but holding a flicker of emotion, almost as if he sought her approval.

Mia nodded. "It's delicious." She smiled, but he did not return the smile. He merely nodded then resumed eating.

"It'll stick to yer ribs," Eilidh said.

"It'll what?"

Eilidh let out a soft laugh. "It's what we say hereabouts. There's naught like parritch to keep ye warm and satisfied throughout the day. We eat nothing else for breakfast. But if ye'd like anything else, I can ask Mrs. McBride to set something else aside for ye each morning."

"Mrs. McBride has enough work to do, Ma," Iona said. "Ye're always telling me I should help her in the kitchen." She glanced at Mia. "Why should Mrs. McBride have to do more work just because *she's* here?"

"Iona," Hamish growled, "do ye want me to take the strap to

ye? Ye gods, what did I do to deserve being saddled with such a brat for a sister?"

Iona opened her mouth to reply, and Hamish slammed his fist on the table, which vibrated with a clatter of cutlery. She flinched and stared at him with defiance. But Mia caught a flicker of fear in her eyes. The girl resumed eating. Her hand shook, and she looked on the verge of tears. But when she met Mia's gaze, she pulled a face.

Breakfast continued in silence, punctuated by Eilidh's pleasantries, but a thick atmosphere filled the air. The sooner Mia found somewhere else to live, the better. Doubtless her presence was the cause of everyone's discomfort.

Breakfast concluded and Mia rose to clear the bowls.

"My dear, what are ye doing?" Eilidh said. "Ye're our guest, not a servant."

"I-I must learn to take care of myself," Mia said.

"Sweet girl, this is yer home."

"But not forever," Mia said. "I've no wish to appear ungrateful, but I should like to make arrangements to live elsewhere as soon as possible."

"I'm sure we'd all prefer it if ye remained here with us, lass," Eilidh said. "There's no need to leave…is there, son?"

Mia glanced at Hamish. "We made a deal, did we not, sir?"

"What's this?" Eilidh said. "Are ye evicting yer wife?"

"It was her suggestion, Ma," Hamish said. "Riverview Cottage would do for her."

"It's been empty for years!" Eilidh exclaimed. "Old Mrs. MacLennan died in the winter of 1806."

"Then it's time it was occupied again," he said. "And it wasnae 1806. She's only been dead two years."

"It'll not be fit to live in. It's smaller than the lass deserves if she's been used to London houses."

"I grew up in a small home," Mia said. "I just need a bed, a warm fire, and somewhere to treat the sick."

"Treat the sick?" Iona said, a high pitch to her voice. Mia

glanced at the girl, who colored and looked away.

"Riverview Cottage has four rooms, if I recall," Eilidh said. "A bedroom, a kitchen, and two parlors."

"That's more than enough for me," Mia replied.

"Ye must dine with us every night here," Eilidh continued. "I'll not have ye turned out as if ye didnae matter."

"Why is she treating the sick, Ma?" Iona asked. "Nobody will want to go to *her*."

Eilidh sighed. "*She* is in the room, and she has a name. Use it."

"Do ye expect me to call her *sister*?"

"No, child," Eilidh said, "but at the very least I expect ye to be civil."

"But—"

"Iona, that's *enough*!" Hamish said, slamming his spoon on the table. "I dinnae want to hear another word from ye. Get ye to the kitchens and tell Mrs. McBride I said ye were to clean the parritch pot."

"I dinnae know why ye're yelling at *me*, brother," Iona said, rising, her eyes gleaming with moisture, cheeks dark red. "Ye hate her more than I do. Ye said as much!"

"Why ye..." Hamish rose, but Iona fled from the room, toppling her chair with a clatter. He glanced at Mia, then resumed his seat. "That girl needs taking in hand," he said. "She's always been wild, but these past two days..." He glanced up.

Mia's cheeks warmed as he met her gaze.

"Perhaps I should make arrangements to move to the cottage today," she said. "I've no wish to upset your sister further when she's so unhappy."

"Unhappy?" Hamish let out a snort. "She's just spoiled and bad-tempered."

"Och, Hamish, ye shouldn't be so hard on the lass," Eilidh said.

"*Ye're* too soft on her, Ma," Hamish said. "She was never this wild before. Perhaps she's fooling around with some man—I've seen her wandering about at night, and there's plenty of rutting boars hereabouts. That young Brodie, for one. He follows her around like a dog with his cock out."

"Hamish!" Eilidh cried. "Brodie's a good lad—too God-fearing to touch a lass. And ye shouldn't be speaking of such matters in front of yer wife."

He frowned, his eyes darkening, as if the very mention of their marriage enraged him.

"Lady MacLennan, I'm not your son's wife," Mia said. "Or, at least, I soon won't be."

"Is an annulment what ye want, lass?"

"Yes," Mia said, and her heart gave a little cry of despair at the relief in Hamish's eyes.

"Son?" Eilidh said, turning to him.

For a moment, he simply stared at his mother. Then he rose.

"Forgive me, Ma, I've duties to attend to." He nodded toward Mia. "Do ye require my help moving yer belongings?"

"No," she said. "Everything I own is in my valise, and I can carry that. I require no help from you. In any case, it's best if I learn to live independently, to prepare for my future life."

Guilt flickered in his eyes and he opened his mouth to reply. Mia held her breath, awaiting his response. Would he admonish her insolence? Or express regret at her leaving?

Instead, he brushed his hand across his forehead as if alleviating a headache, then bowed and exited the room.

"Forgive my impertinence, Eilidh," Mia said.

"There's naught to forgive, lass," came the reply. "At least, not on *yer* part. While my daughter has much growing up to do, it's my son who has the most to learn. Ye could teach him."

"For what purpose?"

Eilidh leaned forward and took her hand. "Ye dinnae have to agree to this," she said. "My son married ye willing—that must count for something. Glenblath can survive if ye stay. We've weathered worse, and have no need for some fine London lady's dowry. Ye could be happy here."

Mia glanced at the window and the view of the landscape—

the sweeping foothills dotted with lines of fir trees and the mountain towering over all benevolently, like a giant sentinel.

"Perhaps," she said quietly, "but not with him."

"Can ye not forgive him?" Eilidh said.

"There's nothing to forgive," Mia replied. "He's not said anything that I haven't heard from others. I endured far worse on the journey here. But I cannot forget the expression in his eyes in the chapel when he realized who I was." She caught her breath, stifling the sob swelling in her throat. "I would rather be alone than live with someone who looks at me the way he did— someone who said that it would have been better if I'd died."

Eilidh caressed the back of Mia's hand, running her fingertips across the pockmarks, with no sign of revulsion or horror, merely kindness and compassion.

"Such a pity," she whispered.

"That I'm scarred by pockmarks?" Mia said. "There's no need to pity me."

"No, lass, I meant it's a pity that my son cannae see beyond the scars to the lovely young woman that ye are. But—and though I love him dearly, I shall say this—it's his loss, and not yers. It is him I pity."

Eilidh blinked, moisture gleaming in her eyes. Then she gave a bright smile.

"Now, lass, we must get to work if Riverview Cottage is to be made ready for ye. Let me take ye there and ye can take a look at it. But if ye dinnae like it, ye only have to say and I'll find ye somewhere else."

"You're too kind," Mia said.

"Nay, it's ye who are kind. And while ye're at Glenblath, we must make sure that ye're as happy as ye can make ye—even if not as happy as ye deserve."

Eilidh took Mia's hand and together they exited the breakfast room. Though she'd not known her own mother, Mia had often dreamed of what it might be like to have a mother's love. In Eilidh she'd caught a glimpse of that love. But it was a love that would be denied her.

Some other woman—a richer, prettier woman—would be granted that particular gift.

CHAPTER THIRTEEN

AFTER SPENDING THE morning with Murdoch, touring the estate to oversee some of the repairs—repairs that would have to cease now that Miss Young's dowry was not forthcoming—Hamish returned to the castle, the stench of peat, hard toil, and sweat in his nostrils. His deerhound trotting at his heels, he headed straight for the dining hall, where luncheon was already laid out—joints of venison and beef glistening on platters, and a huge game pie decorated with thistles and sprigs of heather.

Devil's ballocks—as if he needed reminding of the wedding that had been interrupted, the celebratory feast that had not taken place! All that food—and the expense of procuring and preparing it. And for what? For nothing.

His mother sat at the dining table—he could almost have believed that she'd not moved since breakfast. Of his sister there was no sign. And…

He glanced at the place at the opposite end of the table. Since his da's passing, after Hamish took over the mantle of laird, the lady's place had been empty, Ma now choosing to sit at the side. But now, a place had been set, with a plate, knife and fork, and wine glass.

Yet it was unoccupied.

Good. He had no desire to set eyes on her again.

Ye're a fool, Hamish MacLennan. Ye were hoping she'd be here.

Ignoring the voice whispering in his mind, Hamish gestured

to the dog at his heels. "Get to yer place beside the fire, Monarch," he growled.

The deerhound's tail twitched, then he obediently trotted toward the fireplace, where a fire crackled and spat. The dog circled on the spot three times, then lowered himself on the rug with a grunt of satisfaction.

Hamish settled into his place, nodding to his mother in greeting. Then he gestured to his sister's place. "Is Iona not joining us for luncheon?"

"I dinnae know," she replied. "I've not seen her all morning."

"Foolish, wayward lass."

Hamish reached for the venison joint and carved a slice. He raised his eyebrows and his mother nodded, then he placed the slice on her plate.

"Another? Or some pie, perhaps?"

Ma shook her head and Hamish cut himself a thick slice of the pie, his stomach growling at its savory aroma.

Devil's balls, he was hungry.

"Perhaps it's time Iona was married," Ma said, pouring herself a glass of wine. "The right husband—a man who loves her—and the responsibility of being a wife, and eventually a mother, might do her good."

"She's young for marriage, Ma."

"She's seventeen—a year older than I was," Ma replied. Then she took a bite of her venison and smiled. "Glenblath venison is as good as it was the first time I tasted it on my wedding day."

"And ye want to see Iona married off to a stranger, like ye were?" Hamish said. "Glenblath's her home."

"What woman of our station can claim that the place of her birth is her home?" she replied. "The home she settles in after marriage is rarely the home she was raised in. And even that home she cannae say is truly hers, for she must defer to her husband in all things—and then to her sons. Only a man can truly call a place his home, for he remains there all his life and can lay claim to it."

Was that why *she* was so eager to leave the castle? Because she knew it could never be her home?

"I notice ye've made no reference to yer wife not being at luncheon," his mother said.

"Ma, it does no good to refer to her as—"

"But she *is*, son. Whether or not ye continue with this annulment, that lovely young woman is yer wife at this moment. Because of that, she should be taking her rightful place at our table."

He glanced at the empty space, picturing his wife there as she had been at breakfast—a shimmer of fear in her eyes that she'd fought to conceal. Those eyes had shown kindness and compassion when she'd looked upon Iona, despite the girl's open hostility. She'd discussed her leaving in such a resigned manner, as if she'd accepted her status as being something unwanted, to be discarded.

A shiver rippled across his skin as he recalled the feel of her little hand in his, the soft fingers that had caressed his skin, the scars on her hand from the disease that she'd survived against the odds. And those lush lips, begging to be tasted.

Had he kissed her, would he have been the first man to do so? Might he have opened her body such that the passion with which she defended herself and spoke of her vocation could be put to much better use—to the furtherment of carnal pleasure?

He would never lose enjoyment of the sight of a woman in a state of need, ready to take his cock. And as his wife, she would have been—nay, she *was*—his by right to claim in his bed, his by right to be the first to awaken her to pleasure.

It was something he'd fisted himself to pleasure over in anticipation of—the awakening of an innocent. But that pleasure had been denied him, having only had his bed warmed by the likes of Maisie—earthy creatures of carnal pleasure who knew how to satisfy a man's body even if they could never touch his soul.

What might *she* look like, her pale face flushed with desire, those hazel eyes widening in surprise as her body rippled around his cock? Or those plump lips parting to receive him while she kneeled before…

"Hamish!"

He drew in a sharp breath and glanced up to see his mother staring at him. Shifting in his seat, he became aware of his erection beneath his plaid.

"Y-yes, Ma?"

She arched an eyebrow, her mouth turned down in disapproval. The look transported him to his boyhood, when, his body awakening to unfathomable sensations, he'd first fisted himself to pleasure on the moors after witnessing the stags in rut. Though he'd feigned innocence, the expression in Ma's eyes then was the same as it was now.

Mothers knew—and saw—everything.

Then the door opened and hope surged within him, which was doused as Iona entered. Face flushed, his sister slumped into her seat.

"Where have ye been?" he asked.

"None of yer business."

Hamish carved a slice of the pie and dropped it onto his sister's plate.

"I dinnae want that," Iona said.

Hamish shrugged his shoulders. "Eat it, or dinnae eat it. I care not. Ye won't be my problem forever."

"What do ye mean?"

"When ye marry, ye'll be yer husband's responsibility."

"And if I dinnae marry?"

"I'll make sure that ye do," he growled. "I'll find a man to keep ye on a tight rein."

Her eyes flared with fear, then she sneered. "Am I to be thrown out and treated like shit in a chamber pot, like yer wife?"

Hamish gritted his teeth. Since when had she grown so crude? But there was little point in rising to her bait. Instead, he regarded her coolly while she stared back in defiance.

"I thought ye didnae like my wife," he said quietly.

Iona pulled a face and began eating. But, after swallowing a mouthful, she drew in a sharp breath, covered her mouth, then rose.

"I haven't excused ye from the—" Hamish began, but, ignoring him, she rushed out of the room, not bothering to close the door behind her, and he heard retching outside.

Devil's ballocks—women were more trouble then they were worth. Judgmental mothers, wayward sisters, and…

…unwanted wives.

"Leave her be," Ma said, as Hamish rose. "Ye'll not do any good. *I'll* see to her. She's suffering from something. Perhaps yer wife would be kind enough to see her. She might know what ails her."

"Iona's just overexcited," Hamish said. "Monarch here used to expel his meals when he got excited—especially when Rory's bitch was in heat." He gestured to the deerhound in front of the fire. As if he understood his master, Monarch opened a solitary amber eye, then closed it again.

"Yer sister's not an animal."

"No, Ma," he replied, cutting another slice of venison. "At least animals are easy to tame."

"Och, ye dinnae know how to tame her, that's all, son. Ye might think she needs a bit and bridle, but if ye threaten her, she'll never learn to accept it."

"Did ye accept the bit and bridle when ye married Da?"

Hamish regretted the words the moment he'd uttered them as a flicker of pain crossed his mother's expression.

"We must all take the bit and bridle when we grow into adulthood," she said. "It's called accepting our duty. Mine as a wife and mother, ye as laird…" She gestured toward the empty space. "Perhaps the only soul who's truly free is that lass ye married."

She resumed eating and silence filled the room, save the crackling of the fire, the snoring coming from the shaggy animal at the hearth, and the scraping of cutlery. As he ate, Hamish's gaze kept drifting to the place opposite, where he tried to imagine his future bride—saying grace at the start of each meal, sharing pleasantries with his mother, listening with firm kindness to Iona, and casting him a look of longing across the table as if she eagerly anticipated a bedding.

But the only face he could see was a delicately featured face with a rosebud mouth, wide hazel eyes, and fair skin dotted with pockmarks, her expression showing no eagerness, fear, or judgment—just acceptance of her lot. And it was that acceptance that clawed at his conscience. She considered herself unworthy, not only due to her sex, but due to the illness she'd endured and conquered. Such strength of will ought to be revered, but instead, all she would elicit would be the disgust of the unenlightened.

And there's none more unenlightened than I.

He finished eating and pushed his plate to one side. The dog let out a low whine, and Hamish tore a piece of meat from the venison joint and tossed it toward the fireplace. The dog snapped the morsel in its jaws, then sat up, ears erect in anticipation of the next. When it was not forthcoming, Monarch settled back down and closed his eyes.

"Why dinnae ye go and see her?" Hamish's mother asked.

He shook his head. "No, Ma, ye're right. Iona won't welcome my—"

"I meant yer wife. She's all alone in that cottage."

"I'm sure she's not," he replied. "Weren't ye going to send Mrs. Bron to help make it habitable?"

She let out a huff. "Ye know what I mean, son. Are ye going to disappoint me by claiming that ye dinnae? That poor lass has no friends here. Having come to Glenblath as a bride over thirty years ago, I know how that feels."

"She's not…"

She let out a huff, but rather than admonish him, she scraped back her chair and stood.

"Are ye not eating anything else, Ma?"

"I'm not hungry, and I should see to Iona. But I daresay yer wife's hungry if she's been busy all morning. Ye might want to take her a slice or two of that pie."

"Is that what ye intend to do now, Ma? Issue me orders?"

"No, son—I'll leave the orders to yer conscience."

She placed her napkin on the table, then exited the dining hall. Hamish glanced at his one remaining companion. The dog opened its eyes and stared at him.

"Are ye going to judge me also, boy?" The deerhound thumped his tail on the hearthrug, and Hamish smiled. "Sometimes I think ye're my only true friend here, Monarch."

Which was better than having no friends at all.

He glanced at the slice of pie on his sister's plate. Then, after wrapping it in his napkin, he exited the dining hall and made his way outside to the path that led toward the river.

⟫⟫⟫✴⟪⟪⟪

HAMISH COULDN'T RECALL the last time he'd visited Riverview Cottage—not since the passing of old Mrs. MacLennan, when she'd been carried from the place of her passing to her final place of rest behind the chapel. Widowed and childless, she'd had few mourners save Hamish, who'd attended as laird. Few ventured near while she was alive, and even fewer since her passing, for fear that her spirit would ensnare the sinful and pull them into the river.

And there's none more sinful than I.

He heard the river before he saw it, swollen from the recent rain, bubbling and chattering in deep, masculine notes. As he ventured along the path, the trees thinned out until he could make out flashes of light between the tree trunks as the water danced and boiled over the granite rocks.

The path descended toward the river, then turned to run parallel with the water's edge, before it veered inward toward the forest. Hamish caught sight of a building of gray stone, set in an elevated position and facing the river. Though bathed in the light of the afternoon sun, the cottage looked forlorn, as if it still mourned the previous occupant. Even the windows stared at him like dark, baleful eyes, the doorway forming a gaping, toothless mouth. The log store beside the cottage was now empty, its wooden roof showing signs of rot. The logs had long since gone, having been scavenged over the years, but old Mrs. MacLennan had no further use for them now.

A white figure materialized in the doorway and emerged from the cottage, seeming to glide over the ground. Hamish's stomach clenched in fear. He stepped back and a twig snapped under his feet.

"Who's there?" a female voice called out.

Hamish cursed his foolishness. It wasn't old Mrs. MacLennan, but a different ghost.

His wife.

He stepped forward, and the woman held up her hand to shield her eyes from the sunlight.

"Oh," she said, her voice tightening. "Lord MacLennan. I-I wasn't expecting you."

"May I come in?" he asked.

"Of course," she replied. "I'm on your land. You've no need to ask."

"I do, lass. It's yer home—at least until…"

He trailed off, and she nodded and beckoned him inside. He crossed the threshold, entered a room, and sneezed.

"I'm afraid this room's very dusty," she said. "Perhaps you'd prefer to return when I've finished cleaning the cottage?"

"No, I'll stay, lass."

She nodded and led him into a chamber that overlooked the river. The room was devoid of furnishings, save a chair beside the fireplace and a threadbare rug, which, no doubt, was crawling with lice. A broom was propped up in a corner next to a wooden pail with a cloth hanging over the side. But the fireplace had been raked out and the windows, rather than covered in the grime acquired through neglect, gave a clear view of the river. A beam of sunlight stretched across the floor, casting four patches of light from the windowpanes.

She clasped her hands together—the same gesture she'd made in his study when he caught the fear and rejection in her eyes. Did she perhaps anticipate his reneging on their agreement and evicting her?

Hamish held out the slice of pie, still wrapped in a cloth. "An offering of peace."

She eyed it, raising her eyebrows.

"Ye were missed at luncheon, so I brought a slice of Mrs. McBride's pie. I thought ye might be hungry."

"I'm not hungry."

Her stomach let out a low growl.

"Yer body says otherwise," he said, "but ye cannae eat it here—the room's empty."

He approached the chair, and she cried out, "Don't sit there!" She colored, and he could swear she cringed as if expecting a blow. "Forgive me for speaking out of turn, but it's got a broken leg, see?" She pointed to a leg that was split along the length and cast her gaze over his body. "It might not hold your…"

She paused, blushing.

"Aye, lass," he said with a chuckle. "I'm a big man, am I not?"

Her eyes widened, and he caught a flicker of pleasure in them.

"I've not heard you laugh before," she said quietly.

"I've had little occasion."

"Of course. I'm sorry." She wiped her hands on her apron, crossed the floor, and picked up the cloth.

"Ye've been cleaning the place?" he said.

She nodded. "I've almost finished this room. I thought it might do for somewhere to treat my patients—that is, if any are willing to come here." Then she stopped and regarded him with a thoughtful stare. "You look surprised," she said. "Surely you didn't expect me to live in the dirt?"

"Of course not, but I didnae expect—"

"You didn't think an Englishwoman capable of cleaning a house?" She gestured to the empty fireplace. "I'm no fine lady. I can even light a fire—there's plenty of wood to be foraged hereabouts."

He cast his gaze over her form, the drab dress the same she'd worn on the day of her arrival, and the apron covered in grime and soot.

Aye, she was no fine lady. But her complexion was ruddy with exertion, her eyes bright with vitality, and she was unafraid of hard work. Which made her better than any fine lady.

"Mrs. Bron lent me the apron," she said. "I'll wash it before I return it."

"There's no need, lass," he said. "I'm sure Mrs. Bron meant for ye to keep it." He glanced about the room, letting his gaze settle on a door leading to another chamber. "Is she here with ye?"

"No, I am alone."

He let out a huff. "She should have sent someone from the castle to help ye."

"She sent a manservant—Lachlan, his name was—to see if I needed any furniture. But I have enough."

"A single broken chair?" he said, raising his eyebrows.

"There's also a table, in the room yonder," she said, gesturing toward a door, "and a bed. They only need a good clean, and Lachlan was kind enough to bring me some blankets in the colors of your plaid. They look very pretty."

"But he didnae stay to help ye clean the place?"

"I've no wish to be a burden, Lord MacLennan. It's—"

"Cannae ye at least call me Hamish?" he said. "I understand why ye'll not call me *husband*."

She looked away, and he cursed himself.

"I-I cannot," she replied. "We're not intimately acquainted, and soon I'll be—"

"I'd *like* ye to call me Hamish," he said, lowering his voice. "If we're not to be husband and wife, can we at least be friends? I'd like ye to leave here having made a friend. Or do ye have so many that ye're in need of no more?"

"I've no friends here," she said, her voice almost inaudible.

"Ye have one right here."

"Perhaps."

He smiled then gestured about the room. "Do ye know aught of the previous occupant?"

"Only what your mother told me. Old Mrs. MacLennan, she called her. I'm sorry that she died."

"She's still here," he replied. "Everyone whose heart is in the Highlands lives on after they pass. We're the sunbeams that warm the crops on a bright day, the breeze that sings through the trees, and"—he gestured to the view from the window—"Old Ma MacLennan was rumored to be a kelpie."

"A *what?*"

"A sprite that takes many forms, for good or mischief—though knowing Ma MacLennan, it'll be for good. I heard tales that she took on the sins of all the folk at Glenblath. Each night she entered the river to melt into the water. Ye could see her— the ripples of light when the moon was full. Then, as the first threads of dawn filled the sky, she rose from the water, taking human form once again, having cleansed herself of the sins of others."

She fixed her gaze on him, her eyes wide with wonder, as if enthralled by the spell of his tale.

"How did she die? Had the burden of everyone's sins become to great?"

"She simply passed due to old age," he said. "She'd seen over eighty summers. She was ancient even when I were a bairn, bouncing me on her knee by that very fireplace, telling me tales of the spirits. Folk hereabouts called her a witch."

His wife blinked and the spell was broken.

"Too many women are labeled as witches by men," she said. "If we're beautiful, men will call us vain and say that we use our beauty to cast spells on them. And if we're not beautiful enough…" She sighed. "I understand my father's regret that I wasn't a boy. Reason tells me that the fault lies with the men who rule the world, who cannot accept a woman for what she is. But when has the world listened to reason?"

She wiped her hands on the cloth, then dropped it in the bucket.

"Do men not realize that if we were witches, we'd not waste our efforts turning men into newts? We'd cast a spell to render a cottage clean at the utterance of a few words, rather than a day's toil."

"In the absence of a spell," Hamish said, "will a foolish man incapable of saying the right thing serve as an alternative?"

She lifted her eyebrows in inquiry.

"I'll grant that we men sometimes lack the ability to wield our minds," he continued, "but we can at least wield a broom. We're to be friends, yes? In which case, permit me to help ye." He grinned at her. "If ye're amenable to calling me Hamish, that is."

He unwrapped the pie and she lowered her gaze. Her tongue flicked out and ran across her lips, rendering them moist and glistening.

"Ye'll not taste better in all the Highlands," he said. "I fancy a bite myself, if ye're willing to oblige."

Her eyes flared for a moment and his cock twitched at the flicker of desire in them. Did she understand his meaning? Then she blinked and the desire disappeared. But the ghost of a smile remained on her lips as she gestured to the broom.

"If we're to be on equal terms," she said, "you must first earn your pie."

He laughed again, and his soul let out a little sigh as her lips curved into a smile.

"I've not seen ye smile much, lass," he said. "But I take the blame for that. I hope I'll see ye smile many more times before ye leave us."

Her smile slipped and he cursed himself once more. Why must he refer to their inevitable parting?

Then he checked himself.

Why did the notion of their parting bother him?

"Here," he said, "take the pie and let me help ye."

She nodded and reached for the pie. Their fingers brushed, and Hamish caught his breath at the tiny spark of desire deep inside his center at the feel of her warm, delicate little fingers on his. Her eyes widened and his cock swelled with want as she parted her lips in surprise.

Would those lips taste as sweet as they looked?

He curled his fingers around her hand and drew her close, his cock surging with delight as she gave no resistance. Then he inhaled, slowly, savoring the sweet, rich scent of her—of honey and innocence. What might it be like to dip into that innocence and claim her sweetness?

"Lass," he breathed.

She flushed a delectable shade of rose, a sweet pinkness that gave a promise of pleasurable pinkness elsewhere.

Her eyelids fluttered as she blinked and her eyes darkened, the pupils dilating as she exhaled and shifted closer. He had only to dip his head and claim those lips as his own, and he had only to lift those skirts to claim her sweet body…

Holy ballocks—what the fuck was he *doing*?

He jerked back, the heat rising in his cheeks at the bulge in his plaid where his cock pressed eagerly against the woolen material. A moment longer and he'd have tossed up her skirts and fucked her against the wall, his knees abraded by the harsh stone while he roared out his pleasure like a stag in rut, claiming his woman, biting her neck to mark her as his so that no other male could take her.

Mumbling an apology, he shoved the pie into her hands and retreated. She caught the pie and cradled it to her chest. Her body trembled with distress, her eyes glistening with moisture. Then, overcome by shame, he turned and fled.

CHAPTER FOURTEEN

"**P**OCKMARKED HAG!"

"Devil's spawn!"

Harsh voices engulfed Mia's mind, against her senses, while her head throbbed with pain.

"Burn the witch!"

Hands clawed at her, circling her arms like ropes, cutting into the flesh. The stench of oil and smoke filled her nostrils. Then came the crackle of burning wood, followed by a low, steady rumble that increased to a roar as demons danced around her twisted, deformed body…

Mouth open in an airless scream, Mia sat up. The darkness dissolved and light flooded the world around her. Tears stung her eyes and she wiped them, blinking to let them adjust to the light.

Where am I?

She glanced about, but there was no sign of a pyre, nor the demons. She was in a chamber, filled with sunlight, surrounded by stone walls that glistened as if they contained tiny diamonds.

Mia lowered her gaze to the blanket covering her body—the thick woolen fabric woven into the pattern of a plaid, with shades of green and blue accented by flashes of red. She ran her hand over the wool, then recoiled at the memory of yesterday—the plaid in the same pattern worn by the man who had paid her a visit.

The man who found her so disgusting that he couldn't endure more than ten minutes of her company.

Mia slipped out of the bed and approached the washbowl that she'd filled from the river last night. She dipped her hands into the water, ran her fingertips over the skin roughened by pockmarks, then sighed.

No wonder she disgusted him.

After drying her hands, she made her way to the kitchen. There was still plenty to do—sweep the floor and clear out the fireplace, which was filled with soot and ash that bore the footprints of some kind of animal.

A deer, perhaps? She'd woken up earlier to the sound of something moving about outside, but when she peered through the window there was nothing to see save the river glistening in the first light of the dawn. Perhaps old Mrs. MacLennan had come to absorb her sins.

Her gaze fell on the remains of the pie that Hamish had brought over. He'd been right in that it was the best pie she had ever tasted—flavorsome meat balanced with sharp berries in crisp pastry—but he hadn't wanted to share it with her.

"Still," she said to herself, forcing brightness into her voice, "all the more for me."

Once she'd managed to get a fire going, she could accompany her breakfast with a hot drink. Mrs. Bron had given her a jar of tea and promised to ask the cook to set aside a jug of milk for her daily. Perhaps after she cleaned the kitchen she could venture over to the castle, provided she didn't encounter—

Mia startled as she heard a knock. She made her way to the main entrance and the door opened to reveal a woman carrying a basket.

The woman was a beauty. Dressed in a bright-blue gown, she looked out of place compared to her surroundings. Though the material of the gown was a little threadbare at the hem, the woman reminded Mia of a hothouse orchid in a dull garden, or a bird of paradise escaped from an aviary that found itself in a chicken coop.

The woman cast her gaze over Mia's form and Mia shifted from one foot to the other, aware of her disheveled appearance, her dull-gray gown with the stain on the skirts, and her pock-marked skin. But rather than superiority or judgment, Mia only saw casual disinterest in the woman's gaze, as if she cared nothing for looks.

The woman reached into her basket, retrieved a posy of purple flowers, and held it out.

Mia stared at the posy, and a flicker of hurt crossed the woman's expression.

"I take it ye've already heard of me," she said.

Mia shook her head. "Are you related to my husb—to the MacLennans?"

"Dinnae let Hamish MacLennan hear that or his head will burst. I'm Maisie. Maisie MacLennan."

"So you *are* related."

"Och no, ma'am—ye'll find most of us hereabouts take the name MacLennan whether we're related to the family or not."

"Forgive me if you're come to visit, Maisie," Mia said. "The cottage is still very dirty."

"Of course it is, seeing as nobody's been here since Old Ma MacLennan passed—save the odd deer or two. But that's why I'm come. To give ye a hand if ye want it." Maisie nodded to the posy. "And these, of course, if ye've got something to put them in. I heard ye'd left the castle for Riverview Cottage."

"Were you at"—Mia paused—"the wedding?"

"The likes of *me* wouldnae be welcome there," came the reply, "but Murdoch told me about ye. Well, he grumbled about ye being here, bad-tempered arse that he is. Have ye met him yet?"

"I might have," Mia replied. "But there are plenty of people unhappy about my being here."

Including my husband.

"Och, pay no attention to them! If they give ye trouble, just come to me and I'll deal with them, seein' as I warm most of their beds."

"So you're a..." Mia's voice trailed away.

The woman's laughter died. "I'm sorry," she said. "I'll be going. I ought to have known that a lady from London wouldnae want to associate with the likes of—"

"Stay," Mia said. "Please. It's just that I..." She gestured to the woman. "I-I've not met a... I mean... I know there are plenty in London and elsewhere, but I've not met a woman who earns a living from..." Her cheeks warmed with embarrassment. "Forgive me, Maisie, I meant no offense. Please, come in— though the cottage isn't fit for visitors."

"Not even the local hure?"

Oh, so that's *what the word means. Whore.*

Maisie frowned, and Mia cursed herself—she must have voiced that thought aloud. Then Maisie resumed her smile and gestured inside.

"Show me what I can do to help," she said. "I've brought oatcakes, freshly baked this morning." She let out a laugh. "Even hures need to know how to cook. Do ye have something to put these in?" She nodded to the posy.

"I-I think there are some jars in the kitchen," Mia said. "Is that heather?"

"Aye, I picked it fresh. Do ye know the tradition?"

Mia shook her head.

"It's said that if the first gift a newcomer receives is a posy of heather, then they'll be protected from evil spirits and will live a long and happy life on MacLennan land. And, if that gift is accepted, then the giver and receiver will become lifelong friends."

Mia couldn't manage anything more than "oh" as she stared at the posy. How would she possibly live a long and happy life here, given that she was destined to leave?

"Forgive me, ma'am," Maisie said. "I see I was too forward. Perhaps ye have friends already."

"I have few friends," Mia replied, "and they're all in England."

Maisie nodded. "I understand."

Her eyes flickered with an emotion Mia recognized, for she had seen it in the mirror.

The pain of rejection.

"But it would be good to have a friend here," Mia continued, "though I'd prefer not to be called 'ma'am.' Or 'Lady MacLennan.'"

"May I ask what yer name might be?"

"Euphramia," Mia said, offering her hand. "Euphramia Lucas."

"Not MacLennan?"

"Only in name, and not for long."

Maisie opened her mouth to reply, then closed it again as her gaze fell on Mia's hand. Then she took her hand and clasped it, her fingers brushing over Mia's pockmarks.

"My friends call me Mia."

"Then I'm pleased to know ye, Miss Lucas. And may I say it's a shame ye've had to leave the castle. Murdoch said Master Hamish threw ye out, but I said to him that Master Hamish wouldnae do anything so cruel. He's a good man, if a little stern at times. But then, he carries the cares of the clan on his shoulders—broad shoulders that they are…"

Maisie rattled on, a flare of lust in her eyes, and Mia tempered the little spike of resentment.

Perhaps that was why Hamish had been so eager to leave yesterday—to spend the night with a woman he could stomach looking at.

"It was my choice to leave the castle," Mia said. "Lord MacLennan and I have come to an arrangement. I will live here until I leave Glenblath, then we'll no longer be married. It won't be for some months, but I'll use the time as best I can to repay him for his hospitality."

"By living on yer own?"

"I wish to become a doctor," Mia said. "And by permitting me to leave, Lord MacLennan will be helping me to further that aim. While I'm here, I can tend to the sick."

Maisie's eyes widened.

"Lord MacLennan agreed to it," Mia added, "and Lady MacLennan approves."

"*Ye're* Lady MacLennan."

"No," Mia said. "I'm not—and I was never meant to be."

"Hamish married ye."

"Only because he thought I wouldn't…" Mia lowered her gaze to her marked hands. She had no wish for the world to think ill of Hamish. It was she who'd set her lawyer the task of finding a husband in the belief that she'd not survive more than a day beyond the marriage. And Hamish had agreed to return her fortune. Most men would have turned her out, penniless—or worse, kept her shackled in an unhappy marriage while they took other women to bed.

To Mia's shame, understanding flickered in Maisie's gaze.

"Well now!" Maisie said, her voice overly bright. She brushed past Mia to the kitchen and placed her basket on the table. Then she fished out an apron and tied it around her waist. "There's much to do to make the place good and tidy, but two pairs of hands will make light work of it." She picked up the broom that Mia had propped against the wall last night and let out a huff. "That Mrs. Bron could have given ye something better than *this*. It's lost almost all its bristles. Never mind, it'll do."

She paused and fixed her clear gaze on Mia.

"I take it ye dinnae mind my being here? Ye only need say the word and I'll go. Ask anyone hereabouts and they'll say that Maisie never outstays her welcome."

The little creases around Maisie's eyes spoke of pain and rejection. This woman, the doxy whom men used to satisfy their physical needs, who most likely warmed their beds at night, then left as soon as the men had taken their pleasure so that her presence might not taint their lives…

As a doxy rather than a wife, Maisie had freedom, but with that freedom came loneliness, for she had nobody to love her.

Perhaps she and I are more alike than any other.

Maisie paused, the ghost of a plea in her eyes.

"Very well," Mia said. "But I must insist on one thing."

Maisie's smile faded and she curled her fingers around the broom handle. "Of course, ma'am."

"I insist you call me Mia."

The doxy's smile broadened and she nodded. "Well! It'll be good to have a friend hereabouts. How about we get a fire going first? I've brought a tinderbox, as I doubt Old Ma MacLennan would have left one about the place, and even if she did, those lads would have pilfered it months ago—especially that Billy. He's a right one. That's Murdoch's lad, ye know. Takes after his da, he does."

She rattled on, and Mia found herself smiling at the woman's easy chatter. "I'd better go and find some firewood," she said. "I suppose a benefit of being surrounded by trees is that I'll never be short of it."

"There's plenty in yer log store, and some peat. I'll help ye carry it through."

"The store's empty," Mia said.

"It was full when I arrived," Maisie replied. "Perhaps ye missed it. I'll show ye."

She led Mia outside, to the lean-to shelter with the rickety roof that Mia had noticed yesterday on her arrival.

Mia let out a low cry. One half was filled with logs in a neat pile and the other half contained what looked like lumps of dark brown earth in the shape of bricks.

"There!" Maisie said. "The logs look well seasoned, but the peat will need to dry a bit more by the looks of it, or it'll smoke out the place."

"Did you bring these?" Mia said. "They weren't here yester-day."

"Not I. Perhaps it was Rory. It's the sort of thing he'd do— ever so kind, he is."

Was it Mia's imagination, or had Maisie's voice grown a little lower, and her cheeks a little pinker?

"Rory? Is he your husband?"

"Heavens, no!" Maisie laughed. "What man would want to marry a hure? He's Master Hamish's ghillie."

"Ghillie?" What the devil was *that*?

"Rory's da was ghillie to the old Laird MacLennan, and his grandda before him. His family have been at Glenblath for centuries—fought alongside the laird against Longshanks, they did. His ancestor was killed in the uprisings, but he already had a son—and since then, every first son has been called Rory, and has served as ghillie here." She let out a sigh. "Rory ought to see about getting himself a wife, or the line will stop with him. A lucky lass, she'll be, for he's a skilled man in the—" Maisie broke off. "Begging yer pardon, ma'am, for speaking out of turn."

"There's nothing to apologize for," Mia said. "And it's Mia, not ma'am, remember? Are you fond of Rory?"

Maisie plucked an armful of logs from the store. "I warm his bed, that's all. But I'll not take payment from him."

Her response told Mia all she needed to know.

She took two logs from the store, inhaling the scent of pine.

"Perhaps Old Ma MacLennan left them here during the night," Maisie said.

"Does her spirit carry logs as well as absorb the sins of others?" Mia said.

Maisie let out a laugh as they returned inside the cottage. "Old Ma MacLennan's spirit does what she likes," she said. "She might absorb *yer* sins, though I doubt ye've sinned in yer life. But a hure like me? Not even a thousand Ma MacLennans could absorb my sins, seeing as I'm the greatest sinner in the valley."

"I see no sinner," Mia said. "You've been the first person here to offer me friendship—save Lady MacLennan."

"Ah, she's a rare one," Maisie said. "She sometimes visits me—when she's up to the walk, that is—bringing a slice of pie, or a loaf or two. She's always asking me to come to the house, but of course I cannae be seen there, except when…"

She colored, and Mia nodded in understanding. Except when Maisie was sent for to warm a man's bed.

"He's a good man," Maisie said softly, as if she'd read Mia's mind. "Take it from one who knows more about a man than even his ma."

"You do?"

"Aye," came the reply. "Men only reveal their true selves in bed—when they're rutting or sleeping. And most men are boys needing a bit of love. Save Murdoch, that is. Murdoch is..." She shook her head. "Never mind him. I must work for my coin, same as others. I'm sure Rory disnae like being up on the slopes of Beinn Blath in a storm, or Master Hamish disnae like having to listen to the disputes among the tenants. But we must all take the less palatable parts of our lives, otherwise we'd not appreciate the pleasurable. For every Murdoch, there's a Rory, and a Master Hamish..."

Maisie trailed off and her color deepened as she met Mia's gaze. Doubtless she had warmed Hamish's bed several times and knew him more intimately than Mia ever would. Men were not expected to keep themselves chaste for the marriage bed. As soon as they reached adulthood, they took mistresses and entered brothels. Hamish would have done the same.

Why, then, did a little needle of pain stab Mia's heart at the notion?

"He's not called me to his bed since he went to London," Maisie said, again as if she'd read Mia's mind. "He was different when he returned—quieter, more serious, as if he carried a burden. And though he turned me away even when I offered a tumble for free, he took me into his arms and..." She shook her head. "No matter. Too many men hide their hearts in an attempt to be strong. But strength lies in listening to our hearts and responding to them." She turned to Mia and gave her a bright smile. "If I can give them a little strength by letting them speak to their hearts at night, then I'll die a happy woman."

And a lonely one.

"Perhaps we're not so different," Mia said.

"How could ye be likened to a hure?"

"We both wish to ease the pain of others," Mia said. "Perhaps a doctor is no different to a…a lady of the night."

"Lady of the night? Ha!" Maisie let out a peal of laughter. "I've never been called that before, But I like it. Maisie MacLennan, *Lady of the Night*." She straightened her stance, then dipped into a curtsy. "Lady of the Night, at yer service, Lady MacLennan."

Mia allowed herself a laugh, then startled as a knock came on the door. A male voice called out, but the flicker of hope in her heart died almost as soon as it flared. The voice was deeper and rougher than the voice she'd been longing to hear.

"Is anyone there?"

Maisie's eyes gleamed with delight. She patted her hair, then ran her hands over her skirts as if to smooth them, before she untied the apron and dropped it on the table.

There was no need to ask to whom the voice belonged.

Mia called out, and a man appeared. He was enormous—his thick-set frame filled the doorway—and he had to bend his head to fit into the frame.

"Do come in," Mia said.

He nodded and entered. He had an unruly mop of dark-red hair tamed only a little by his hat, and a thick beard that brushed against his chest. A pair of bright sapphire eyes settled first on Maisie, then he shifted his gaze to Mia. His lips curled into a grin, then with his free hand he removed his hat.

"Rory MacLennan, at yer service, Yer Ladyship. I hope I'm not intruding, though I see ye're not in want of company if ye've got the lovely Maisie."

"Be off with ye, Rory, and take yer nonsense with ye," Maisie said.

"You're very welcome, Mr. MacLennan," Mia replied.

"Call me Rory, lass, or ye'll be up to yer armpits in MacLennans." He lifted his left hand. "I've brought ye these."

Suspended from his hand was a dead bird, its feathers a rich reddish-brown color flecked with flashes of green and blue, and a fish, with silver-gray skin and a pink tone to its underbelly. The fish seemed to stare at Mia, its eyes bright and clear, as if it were still alive. And perhaps it had been moments earlier.

"Ye'll need to hang the grouse for a day or two before ye can eat it, but the fish ye can eat anytime. I caught it this morning."

"What do you mean—hang?" Mia said.

"Och, Rory," Maisie said. "Ladies from London aren't used to such things. Mia, can ye cook?"

"Yes, but I've never had to hang something before I cook it."

"I'll see to it, lass, if ye'd permit me," Rory said. "Old Ma MacLennan used to hang her game out by the back door. Best place for it, as it'll get ripe if ye hang it inside, and few can weather the stench."

"It doesn't sound very appealing," Mia said.

"Ye cannae beat the flavor of a well-hung grouse, lass. Have ye not eaten grouse?"

Mia shook her head.

"Then ye're in for a rare treat, isn't she, Maisie?" Rory said. "And there's none so fine as Glenblath salmon, but ye must treat it with respect and cook it properly."

"Rory!" Maisie said. "Dinnae speak to the lass so. She's not used to ye."

"Ah, Maisie, will ye admonish me later, as only ye know how?"

Maisie's blush deepened and she swatted Rory on the arm.

"Forgive me, Yer Ladyship," he said. "I'll hang this grouse up then I'll be going."

"Och no ye dinnae," Maisie said. "We've a house to clean and we're in need of a big brute to help us."

"Someone strong in the arm and thick in the head, aye?" Rory said good-naturedly. "Ye like me strong and thick." Maisie swatted him again, and he blushed and nodded to Mia. "Forgive me, lass," he said, glancing about the room. "This is a very comfortable cottage. Are ye intending to live here?"

"Until I return to England, yes," Mia said.

"Aye, that's a rare shame," he said. "I told Master Hamish—" He broke off as Maisie frowned. "Well, we'll make it comfortable for ye. It'll be good and quiet, tucked away. What do ye intend to do here, if ye dinnae mind my asking?"

"I have some understanding of medicine," Mia said. "I can treat the sick and injured. Before I fell ill myself, I'd hoped I might train to become a doctor."

"Were ye sick?" Rory asked.

"Rory!" Maisie nudged him again, and he shifted from one foot to the other in the manner of an admonished child.

"Och, forgive me, lass. Of course ye were ill," he said. "I was at the wedding. I-I'm sorry for ye, but it's a good thing ye survived, aye?"

"Not everyone here agrees with you," Mia said.

"Ye needn't take notice of them," Rory replied with a smile, "and if ye intend to heal the sick, ye'd be welcome. We've no doctor here, though Maisie has some skill, dinnae ye Maisie, lass?"

Mia looked at her new friend. "Do you?"

"Only a little," Maisie said. "I can tie a bandage and have helped to deliver a bairn…well, for folk that'll let me near them."

"Maisie could assist ye, ma'am," Rory said. "She's better doing that than…" Maisie again frowned at him and he shook his head. "Never mind, Maisie, love. Ye can do what ye wish."

"I could do with some help," Mia said. "I've much to do to get everything ready. I brought some medicines with me that Dr. McIver was kind enough to let me have, but as to ointments and lotions, I'll need to begin again, assuming the herbs I'd need grow here. I think I saw some calendula flowers yesterday."

"Calendula?" Rory said. "I've not heard the name."

"They're like large gold daisies," Mia said.

"Do ye perhaps mean Mary's Gold?" Maisie said.

Mia nodded.

"There's plenty in the gardens around the castle," Maisie

continued. "I think Mrs. McBride uses them in her soups. I'm sure she'd let ye take some. Do ye use them for a tea?"

"Yes, and a salve," Mia said. "I could show you how to make it if you wanted to help?"

"Ye'd like that, wouldnae ye, Maisie?" Rory said. "Haven't I always said that—"

"Ye say too much, Rory MacLennan," Maisie hissed. "Is this what ye want? To tell me what to do all the time?"

Rory glanced at Mia. "No, lass, but perhaps ye could learn a thing or two from Her Ladyship. Then ye could consider—"

"Rory, *please*," Maisie said. "Ye dinnae own me and ye never will."

"Aye," Rory said. "Ye belong to all the—"

"I belong to *nobody*," Maisie said, the moisture in her eyes belying the hardness in her voice.

Rory colored and nodded to the bird. "Best get this hung," he said. "I'll cook yer fish for supper when we're done. I can show ye how to gut it, if ye'd like."

"Thank you, that would be most kind," Mia said.

He nodded, then linked his arm through Maisie's. "Och, Maisie love, ye know my tongue runs away with me sometimes. What say I give ye a kiss to make up for it?"

"What say I give ye a kick up the arse?" Maisie said, though there was laughter in her voice again.

"My arse is not half so fine as yers, hen," Rory said, patting Maisie's behind. Then he disappeared into the kitchen, whistling.

Maisie folded her arms. "A great big fool, is Rory," she said, but Mia could hear the longing in her voice—the yearning of one who battled with herself not to love another because she believed that she could never be worthy of him.

When Rory returned, Maisie's bright demeanor had resumed and the three of them set about cleaning the rest of the cottage, Rory fetching water from the river while Mia and Maisie washed the rest of the windows, swept the floors, and brushed away the cobwebs. When Mia took the rug from the parlor outside to beat it, a thick cloud of dust exploded at the first stroke, and they dissolved into a coughing fit that ended up in peals of laughter, their mirth echoing across the landscape. Mia paused, mid-laughter, and glanced about the place she'd be calling home for a short while.

She stiffened as she saw a shape moving between the trees. Then she blinked and it disappeared. A deer, perhaps? Rory had pointed out the different footprints in the earth, identifying each animal that had made them, and said that deer in fawn often ventured down from the hillside in the late spring and summer. It would be something to look forward to next year…

Provided she'd not left Glenblath by then.

As the sun slipped toward the horizon, casting a soft pink haze across the sky, they retired inside to eat the fish that Rory had shown Mia how to gut and roast on a spit. Mia sat with her new companions, eating the freshly roasted fish with her fingers, the fire casting a warm orange glow on their faces, and listening to Rory's tales of the spirits and pagan gods who lived on the mountain—Beinn Blath.

When had she ever been so free as she was today? Not beholden to a father, or a husband, or social convention—but simply living, enjoying the fruits of a day's work with companions whom she could laugh with, who did not recoil in horror at her appearance, but took pleasure from her company.

She blinked and cast her gaze over Rory's features—the strong forehead, and the wide, square jaw…and the eyes that reflected the firelight and flared with longing as he looked at Maisie. It was not the base desire that a man showed toward a woman, but a deeper connection, a call of the soul.

Rory loved Maisie, though he couldn't admit it, even to himself.

What might it be like to be loved by such a man? To indulge in the simple pleasure of sharing a meal they'd cooked together? And to think, the ladies of London Society—an institution that Mia's father had tried desperately to ingratiate himself with—

would call these people savages. Far better to be a happy savage than a miserable Society wife.

And to be the wife of a Highlander…

I am the wife of a Highlander.

Mia shushed the little voice in her mind. She would soon be wife to no one.

Perhaps she and Maisie weren't so different. No matter how they might wish for a loving partnership with another, they would never be accepted and loved, openly, for what, and who, they were.

CHAPTER FIFTEEN

"I DINNAE UNDERSTAND why ye've not been to see yer wife. She's been at Riverview Cottage almost a fortnight, and she's had few visitors. The poor lass must be lonely."

Hamish glanced up from his ledgers and eyed his mother. She sat, in her usual chair, her knitting on her lap. Monarch lay on the hearthrug at her feet and lifted his head at the sound of her voice, before yawning, stretching out his front legs, then tucking them in again with a satisfied grunt.

So, this was why Ma had insisted he spend the morning in her chambers—not to keep a lonely widow company, but to be lectured. She'd not even offered him a glass of whisky—he could smell it as soon as he'd entered the chamber, though there was no sign of the bottle.

"Ye've invited her to dine with us every day," Hamish replied. "If she disnae wish to come, ye cannae expect me to drag her here by the hair."

For a moment, the image crossed his mind—him, the pagan beast, catching his woman and tossing her over his shoulder to claim her in his cave. His cock hardened almost instantly, and he drew in a sharp breath.

Devil's ballocks, where had that notion come from?

Perhaps Murdoch was right—he needed a good, hard rutting to ease the lust simmering in his body. Fisting himself at night could never completely rid him of the itch that lay deep in his center. But though he'd enjoyed women before, particularly Maisie with her skillful touch and welcoming curves, he couldn't bring himself to touch another since he'd pledged to be faithful to *her*.

Ye're a weak fool, son.

His father's ghost whispered in Hamish's mind, but he need only look at his mother to understand the consequences of infidelity. Ma had loved and been betrayed. Hamish would be damned if he'd ever be responsible for the slow erosion of a woman's soul.

"Perhaps ye should look to yerself when asking why Mia's not accepted my invitations," Ma said. "I understand ye'll be turning the lass out as soon as ye can afford it, but there's no need to pretend she disnae exist."

There was no danger of that, seeing as she was always in his mind, simmering away during the day, and coming forth at night to admonish him with her soulful hazel eyes.

"I daresay ye've even forgotten what she looks like," Ma continued.

There was no danger of *that*, either. He'd never forget how sweet the sound of her laughter was.

Or how the spike of envy had poked at his soul when he'd seen the ease with which she'd shared a moment of mirth with Maisie and Rory. He'd watched—like the outsider she thought herself to be—concealed between the trees, while she laughed with the ghillie and the whore.

Unable to stop himself, he had ventured toward her cottage to watch her every day since, taking a small speck of joy at the sight of smoke rising from the chimney, indulging in the sight as she busied herself with whatever it was she did—venturing to the river and back, setting off on her own, to return later with a basketful of greenery. Occasionally she'd pause, as if she knew she were being watched, and a hunted expression would darken her eyes, like a deer sensing a predator.

"No, Ma," he said. "I know what she looks like."

"Aye," his mother huffed. "Pity ye cannae see beyond the marks on her skin. They're fading, ye know."

"Are they?" he said, unable to temper the hope in his voice. The brave lass didn't deserve to be censured for her looks.

His mother shook her head, disgust in her eyes. "Perhaps ye'll soon be able to look at her without flinching. Ye disappoint me. I thought I'd raised ye to be a better man. I expect that sort of behavior from the likes of Murdoch and Robbie, but to see it in my own son..."

"Murdoch and Robbie?" Hamish said. "Have they been giving the lass trouble?"

"No more than ye'd expect," Ma said. "I spotted them when I visited her. Maisie saw them off—she's never short of a word or two when she needs it. She's visited the lass almost every day."

"Aye, that she has."

"So ye *have* been to see her?"

"N-no, Ma," Hamish said, cursing himself. Ma stared at him, her sharp-eyed gaze unsettling him as it always did when she'd caught him fibbing as a lad. "I know how kind Maisie is," he continued. "She always takes on the stray dog that nobody else wants."

"Och, son, must ye disappoint me further, likening yer wife to a stray dog?"

Bloody ballocks, couldn't he say, or do, anything right in Ma's eyes?

But his mother was right. Maisie had befriended Euphramia—openly and without prompting. Whereas he...

He let out a sigh. What were a few armfuls of logs, handed over in secrecy under cover of the night in case anyone saw him? A true act of friendship shouldn't necessitate secrecy for fear of discovery. A true friend defended another from the censure of those around her. A true friend was happy to declare that friendship and weather the contempt of others.

"Ye make me quite ashamed," he said.

"That'll be yer conscience," she replied. "Perhaps ye should heed that more rather than Murdoch and the like. If ye fear what others think of ye for doing the right thing, then ye're behaving as a coward, not a laird. The laird should lead by example and not be afraid to do what he knows in his heart is right. If ye stand up for the lass, others will follow." She took his hand. "What happened to my brave wee boy? He's grown into a better man than his father. But ye could be the best of men if ye just—"

"Ma, she wants this annulment as much as I do," he said. "More so."

"Aye, and I'll not quarrel with ye on that if yer mind's set on it. But that's no reason not to show her kindness for the brief time she's here. Give her fond memories of Glenblath—of *us*. Is that too much to ask, given what she did for ye when she had no need to?"

He opened his mouth to argue that despite Euphramia's gifting him her fortune, he was now required to pay it back. Then he closed it again.

"Perhaps I'll visit her," he said.

"Good lad. Why not take a slice of that cheese? And Mrs. McBride has a loaf fresh from the oven this morning doing nothing. When ye go, tell the lass I'll be seeing her later, as usual."

"As usual?"

"Och, dinnae try to fool me, son." Ma resumed knitting and curved her lips into a smile. "She looked well when I visited her yesterday, did she not?"

The needles clack-clacked against each other as Ma's hands moved with more deftness than Hamish had seen in a long while.

"Aren't ye in pain?" he said, gesturing toward her hands.

"Only a little." She paused and raised her left hand. The joints were as swollen as they'd always been, but had lost a little of their redness.

He leaned closer to get a better look, and she curled her fingers into a fist, her eyes narrowing in discomfort.

"Better, aye?" she said. "I've not been able to do that for some time."

Hamish inhaled and caught a raw scent in his nostrils. "Yer hands stink of whisky, Ma."

"It's the lass's liniment, which I apply every day. It's eased the pain a little."

"But—*whisky*?"

"The whisky's only to draw out the medicine," Ma said. "It's the heather that eases the pain, so the lass said. To think! Something we have in abundance, that I've only ever thought of as a pretty flower, is easing my pain."

"Are ye sure she's not playing ye false?"

"Ask her yerself," she said, resuming her knitting, "or are ye content to skulk in the woods and watch her from afar?"

Devil's cock, how *did* she know?

He opened his mouth to deny it. His mother paused and fixed him with a hard stare, then continued knitting, the steady click-click of the needles grating on his senses.

"Very well," he said. "I'll visit the lass if ye wish it."

"Yer visit only has value if *ye* wish it," Ma said. "I'll not have ye go under sufferance."

"It's not sufferance, Ma."

He rose and kissed her on both cheeks, then made his way to the kitchen, where Mrs. McBride had already set aside a thick slice of cheese and a loaf, in a basket. He inhaled the aroma of freshly baked bread. The cook, who was dusting the table with flour, let out a huff.

"Mind ye dinnae eat all that yerself," she said. "It's for Miss Lucas."

"Miss Lucas?"

She cocked her head to one side. "I take it ye'd prefer I address her as such, seein' as she'll not be Lady MacLennan for long."

"Did ye conspire with my ma to—"

"Och, be off with ye!" the cook said, placing a ball of pastry onto the floured table. "I've supper to prepare and no time for ye getting under my feet. Tell the lass that if she keeps the cheese wrapped in the cloth to prevent the mold getting to it, it'll last up to a fortnight."

Before Hamish could reply, she picked up a rolling pin and waved it at him. He grabbed the basket and she shooed him out of the kitchen. Her laughter, like that of a cackling crone, could be heard echoing along the passageway as he approached the main doors, and he could swear he still heard it as he reached the path to Riverview Cottage.

Smoke rose from the chimney in an almost straight line, evidence of the stillness of the day. The cottage was in a sheltered spot where the land formed a hollow, protecting it from the worst of the frosts. If she were still at Glenblath when the winter set in, would she weather the cold? Fine ladies from London weren't expected to toil in the harsh Highland winters. But then, fine ladies from London weren't expected to be able to light their own fires, or roast haunches of venison.

As he approached the cottage, he caught the faint sound of singing. Not an accomplished voice, but the tune was a merry air. He paused at the threshold and lifted his hand to knock on the door. Would she welcome the intrusion?

Would she welcome *him*?

Before he could retreat, the singing stopped.

"Who's there?" she said.

He paused, hands in midair as he heard footsteps.

"Is that you, Rory? Maisie's not with me today, so you might wish to—Oh!"

The door opened to reveal his wife, and she let out a cry.

"Forgive me…" He hesitated. What the devil was he supposed to call her? He held up the basket. "Mrs. McBride set aside this for ye," he said, his cheeks warming as if he were a nervous lad not yet out of boyhood. "A loaf of bread and some cheese."

She wiped her hands on her apron. "Would you like to bring them inside? And perhaps"—she gestured behind her—"you might wish to see what I've done here. With Maisie and Rory's help."

When he didn't respond, her smile slipped. "Of course, there's no obligation. I'm sure you must have many things to attend to."

"Nothing that cannae wait, Miss…I mean, lass…" He hesitated again.

"Why don't you call me Euphramia? Miss Lucas is overly formal."

"Euphramia?"

"It *is* my name. You said it once, though, of course, at the time you hadn't expected to speak it again."

Fuck. Could she make him feel even guiltier?

Then she laughed, and he caught his breath at the mirth in her eyes that rendered them quite beautiful, gleaming with myriad colors in the sunlight. Gone was the broken creature he'd rejected. Standing at the threshold of a cottage she'd made into a home, she looked freer than he'd ever seen her. Perhaps the prospect of dissolving their union had given her a sense of hope— enabled her to blossom and breathe.

"May I stay?" he said. "For a while, at least. I'd like to see what ye've made of the place."

"A laird's inspection?"

Ballocks, could he not say the right thing?

"No…Euphramia," he said. "I only want to make sure that ye're comfortable here."

His heart warmed to see the smile on her lips.

"I'm very comfortable," she said. "Shall I make tea? There's a pot on the boil, so it'd be no trouble—unless you take sugar. I have none here."

"Tea without sugar would be perfect, I thank ye."

She ushered him inside, then led him into the parlor. It had been transformed from the last time he saw it. Gone was the broken chair. Instead, there were two armchairs beside the fireplace, each covered in a plaid blanket. A table, covered in what looked like a pile of rags, was in the center of the room, with a chair at each end, and a chest of drawers had been placed in the corner. One wall was now covered in shelves containing an array of jars and bottles. The threadbare rug was still there, but the pattern seemed a little brighter. And the smell of must and damp had gone. The air was now filled with the warm scent of peat and pine, together with an exotic aroma of herbs and spices. A fire crackled in the fireplace with an iron kettle suspended over the center.

"I recall ye saying this was where ye'd treat yer patients," Hamish said.

"And receive guests," she replied. "Sit, please, and I'll make the tea."

He placed his basket on the table, then took the chair she indicated. Then she exited the parlor, returning shortly afterward with a tray bearing two mismatched cups and an earthenware teapot with a crack in the spout. Using a cloth, she lifted the kettle from the fire, then poured water into the pot, giving it a stir before replacing the lid. She began to fold the rags on the table, placing each one in the chest of drawers.

"You don't mind if I continue with this, do you?" she said. "I've so much to do before your mother visits."

"Of course not—are ye wanting help?"

"You're my guest, Lord MacLennan."

"Hamish, please."

"Hamish."

His name on her lips, though barely a whisper, sent a little thrill through his body. What might it be like to hear her crying his name while she begged him to take her?

Tempering the little pulse of lust, he crossed his legs and gestured to the furniture.

"Where did all this come from?"

"Rory, mostly," she said. "He brought the table over, and secured the shelves." She indicated the chairs. "Maisie gave me those, and the blankets were a gift from your mother. I've promised to return everything before I leave."

"Ye should keep the blankets if Ma gave them to ye," he said, "to remind ye of Glenblath."

She colored and looked away.

"And," he continued, "all this?" He motioned toward the items on the shelves.

"Bounty from your estate," she said, winding a strip of linen around her hand before slipping it off and placing it in a drawer. "Save a few things I brought with me." She plucked a jar from the lower shelf and held it up. "This is heather liniment," she said. "It's what I've been using to treat your mother's condition."

"Her...condition?" he said. "She's merely old, is she not? Dr. Chisholm said that she was suffering from...what did he say? Ah yes, *a rapid onset of decrepitude, giving rise to sensations of acute discomfort in the upper appendages.*" She snorted, and Hamish tempered his annoyance. "Do ye take offense at the diagnosis of a renowned doctor from Edinburgh?"

"I do when he talks nonsense," she replied. "What you said isn't a diagnosis, but a description of the symptoms, using an unintelligible language, no doubt to secure a higher fee."

"And ye know this because...?"

"Because," she said quietly, "and may the Almighty forgive me for speaking out of turn...because it's what my father used to do—and many like him. They gave unintelligible names to descriptions of symptoms, then prescribed a generic cure, usually a leech applied to the affected part of the body. Your Dr. Chisholm's diagnosis is something any fool could make, given that, in essence, all he's saying is that your mother is ageing and experiencing pain in her hands."

"So, what is my mother suffering from if it's not merely her age?"

"It's a swelling of the joints," she said. "I cannot recall the precise name for it—but Dr. McIver taught me a little about it, which he learned when he studied in France for a while, at the Salpêtrière Hospital."

She raised her eyebrows expectantly, then let out a sigh as he shook his head.

"She's also experiencing the effects of a lack of sunlight," she said. "I understand your Dr. Chisholm advised her not to take milk in her tea and avoid cheese, when, in fact, an absence of each will exacerbate the symptoms."

He stared at her. Was she a clever charlatan, trying to fill his mind with nonsense, or, as her confident manner suggested, did she actually have some understanding of medicine?

"Don't you believe me, Lord MacLennan?" she said, her voice hardening.

So much for Hamish.

She let out a sigh and replaced the jar on the shelf. "A woman always has less credibility in the eyes of the world when her opinion contradicts that of a man."

"So ye assume Dr. Chisholm is a man, not a woman?" Hamish teased, then he regretted his words as the determination in her expression faded, as if she surrendered the debate, knowing that her opponent did not deserve to hear her arguments.

"There are few women doctors," she said, "and, even if Edinburgh were awash with them, *you* would never employ one."

"Why not?"

She rolled her eyes. "In the short time since I arrived here, Lord MacLennan, I've learned enough about you to know that you'd never listen to anything a woman said, let alone employ one as a doctor. In your eyes, my sex is fit to fulfill only three functions—providing a man with a dowry, bearing him sons, and pouring the tea. Of course, in my case, I'm only good for one."

She picked up the teapot and poured a measure into each cup.

"I trust I've dispatched my one viable function to your satisfaction, sir."

Fuck.

Why did he always have to make such an arse of himself?

"I'm sorry…Euphramia," he said. "If ye're helping ease Ma's pain, then I ought to be thanking ye, not teasing ye. Tell me more about what ye have here." He gestured to a large iron pot at the end of the lower shelf. "What's that?"

"Calendula salve," she said. "Or, at least, it will be when it cools. It's for preventing putrefaction of wounds."

"Do ye have a salve for preventing a man from making an arse of himself?" he said. "Better still, a potion to make a woman forget a man's foolish words that he did not mean?"

She met his gaze and the corner of her mouth lifted. Then she reached for a small glass bottle on the top shelf with a yellowing label.

"Laudanum," she said. "Enough of this will render a man unconscious, so at least I'm not required to listen to his foolish words for an hour or so."

"And ye found that here?"

"I brought this with me. There's only a little left, but Dr. McIver told me I could always write and ask him to send me anything I needed."

"Dr. McIver—that's the man ye studied with?"

She nodded.

"Will ye write to him?"

"That depends on your generosity. I've no paper to write on, and no money for postage."

"I'll bring some next time I visit," he said, "or..." He paused at an uncomfortable sense of shyness.

"Or?" she said, returning the bottle to the shelf and picking up the milk jug. She raised her eyebrows, and when he nodded, she poured a splash into each teacup.

"Ye could take dinner at the castle with us tonight and I can give ye some paper then."

She paused and parted her lips.

To delay her refusal, he added, "And a pen, and some ink."

Then she smiled and a flicker of pleasure illuminated her eyes, like the sun peeking out from behind a cloud.

"Well, if you're offering a pen and ink as well, how can I refuse?"

She passed a teacup to him and her eyes widened as his fingers brushed against hers. Then she picked up the remaining cup and approached the other chair beside the fire.

He sipped his tea and watched her as she settled into her seat. Her body relaxed, and she closed her eyes, her nostrils flaring slightly as she inhaled. Then she opened her eyes again and regarded him.

Silence fell, save for the crackling of the fire. Perhaps he should fill the void with a remark on the weather, or how pretty her gown was—ladies were supposed to enjoy such conversations. But the woman sitting opposite, her face glowing in the firelight, had no need for such inanities. She was no ordinary Society lady. She was intelligent and independent, and not afraid to speak her mind on a subject about which she was passionate. Yet she was also comfortable in the silence, not feeling the need to fill it with meaningless remarks.

Then he smiled to himself. How many times had he dreamed of this moment—of the simple pleasure of spending an afternoon beside the fireplace, in silence, with his wife?

And here he was—spending an afternoon beside a fireplace. In silence.

With his wife.

He met her gaze and lifted her teacup to her lips, and he caught a shy smile. When he mirrored the gesture, lifting his own cup, he realized that the tea had grown cold.

He set his cup aside and leaned forward, and a flare of hope flickered in her eyes. But before he could speak, the door was knocked upon and she startled, her cup rattling on its saucer. She rose and smoothed down the front of her gown.

"That will be Lady MacLennan."

She exited the parlor and returned with his mother.

"Would you like some tea"—Euphramia glanced at Hamish—"Your Ladyship?"

"There's no need to stand on ceremony before my boy," Ma said. "I've told ye to call me Eilidh, lass, and I insist on ye complying. And yes, I would like some tea, but perhaps later?"

"Of course, Eilidh," Euphramia said. "How are your hands today?"

"My right hand is less swollen, I believe, but the left was giving me some pain last night."

"Let me see."

Euphramia gestured to the seat she'd vacated and Hamish's mother took it. Then she kneeled beside Ma, took both her hands in hers, and inspected them.

"Yes, the joints on the left hand look redder than they did on your last visit. Have you been doing anything unusual?"

Ma shook her head. "Only a little knitting. I confess I spent a little more time at it than I'd anticipated, but it's the first time I've been able to knit without pain."

Euphramia nodded. "I see. Do you still have enough of the heather liniment?"

Ma nodded.

"Good, well, keep applying that." Euphramia turned her hazel eyes to Hamish. "Will you make sure your mother applies it three times a day?"

"I can apply it myself, lass," Ma said, smiling.

Euphramia continued to inspect Ma's hands, running her fingertips along the joints. "I have some willow bark for the pain," she said, "if Mrs. McBride can make a tea with it. But I'd like to get hold of some ginger root. Its warming properties are excellent for easing joint pain, if you don't mind your hands smelling of ginger. Does Mrs. McBride have any?"

Ma shook her head. "I've never known her to have any. Isn't it terribly expensive?"

"I could write and ask Dr. McIver for some," Euphramia said.

Hamish glanced up at the shelves. "What about the laudanum?" he said.

"I wouldn't recommend it," Euphramia replied. "Your mother's condition is chronic, and laudanum is not appropriate for long-term treatment because it gives rise to dependency."

"But—"

"Och, let the lass do her job, will ye, Hamish?" Ma said with a huff. "Ye wouldnae interrupt Dr. Chisholm, would ye?"

"No, but—"

"No, but *what?*" Ma said. "Because he's a man? Mia here has done more to ease my pain in a fortnight than Dr. Chisholm did over three years—and at no expense. Ye're making the place look untidy, sitting there with that witless expression on yer face. Haven't ye got wood to chop or tenants to shout at?"

Why did she have to speak to him as if he were a wayward child—and in front of Euphramia?

Hamish heard a sound that resembled a snort. He looked up to see Euphramia trying to hide a smile.

He rose and bowed. "Very well," he said. "A man knows when he's not wanted."

Euphramia narrowed her eyes and looked away.

Curse it! He'd done it again.

But, as he'd watched her, happy to kneel on the floor unlike any lady he'd met, and the tender care with which she treated his mother, he'd come to realize that she was not unwanted.

"I'll leave ye in peace," he said. "But Ma…"

"Aye?" his mother said sharply, fixing her gaze on him.

"Would ye be so kind as to bring my wife back with ye, when ye're finished? She's agreed to dine with us."

My wife…

He heard a small intake of breath and looked at Euphramia to see her staring at him, lips parted. She exchanged a glance with his mother, then rose to her feet, brushing dust off her skirts.

"I-I think perhaps it's best if I remain here," she said. "I still have some venison left, and it may not last another day. And Maisie said she might pay me a visit. Yes—that's it, Maisie's visiting. I've no wish to disappoint her."

Hamish's mother took her hand. "Are ye sure, lass?"

Euphramia glanced at Hamish, then nodded. The light in her eyes had gone.

"B-but," she said, a tremor in her voice, "I should like to call on you tomorrow, that is, if you're still amenable to letting me have some paper and a pen."

"Of course, lass," Hamish said, "but—"

"And," she continued, fixing her gaze at Hamish's feet, "I should like to write to Dr. McIver as soon as possible. He's unaware that I'll be leaving here, and I wish to continue my studies with him when I return home."

Hamish flinched inwardly.

Home. She did not think of Glenblath as her home—not even the little cottage that she'd taken such pains to make so comfortable and welcoming.

"Surely there's no need for—" his mother began, but Euphramia interrupted, her voice tight.

"I think there's every need, Eilidh," she said, her voice wavering. "I must think of my future."

Hamish opened his mouth to protest and his mother frowned at him and shook her head. Then she patted Euphramia's hand.

"Of course, my dear. We'll do anything ye want. Won't we, Hamish?"

Hamish couldn't do anything but nod. What had caused Euphramia's transformation?

"Now, leave us, son, so Mia can treat me," Ma said.

Euphramia tidied up the teacups and took the tray into the kitchen.

"Go!" his mother snapped. "Go before ye upset her further."

"What have I done?"

"Keep yer voice down!" she whispered harshly. "Men! Ye can never say or do what is right."

"I invited her to dine with us, Ma—what more did ye want?"

"Aye, but did ye have to refer to her as yer wife?"

Fuck. Was *that* it?

"Did I?" he whispered.

"Just then, when ye invited her to dine."

"Well—*isn't* she my wife?"

"Aye," she said. "The wife ye dinnae want. The wife ye're intending to turn away as soon as ye can afford to rid yerself of her."

He shook his head. "I cannae understand ye, Ma. First ye want me to call her my wife, then ye admonish me for doing so."

"If ye cannae work it out for yerself, then ye dinnae deserve an explanation," Ma said. "Hush! She's coming back."

The door opened and Euphramia appeared, a pile of blankets and a pillow in her arms. What the devil was she going to do with those?

"Hurry along, son," his mother said, rising. "I've no wish for ye to intrude on this."

He eyed the blanket and pillow, but said nothing. Then he bowed to Euphramia. "Thank ye for the tea."

"You're welcome," she said stiffly. Then she set the blankets on the chest of drawers, plucked one from the top of the pile, and laid it out on the table.

"Go!" Ma said, shooing him as she might a particularly persistent and annoying cockerel.

Considering himself thoroughly dismissed, Hamish exited the cottage, closing the door behind him. But he couldn't resist peering through the window to watch the women unobserved. Euphramia was placing a pillow at one end of the table on top of the blanket she'd covered it with. Then she led his mother toward the table and helped her to climb on top.

What in the name of the devil's tits was she *doing*?

When she began to undo the buttons securing Ma's gown at the back, he let out a low cry of surprise. Euphramia stiffened and turned toward the window.

Shit.

Hamish slipped sideways and crouched low, his heart thumping in his ears. He glanced up to see the soft orange glow from the window that stretched across the air, forming a pattern in the ground. Then a shadow appeared and he held his breath. Would she berate him for spying? But she merely drew the curtains, shutting out the light save for a thin sliver of orange broken by the ferns on the ground. After waiting a few heartbeats, he retreated to the path and made his way back to the castle.

Chapter Sixteen

Her basket over her arm, Mia pulled her shawl tight around her shoulders and continued along the path, which was becoming steeper the higher she climbed. The smooth surface underfoot had long since become treacherous, loose stones and rocks ready to entrap unsuspecting ankles. Twice already she'd slipped and fallen with a jolt as a stone shifted under her feet.

Perhaps they were right. The Highlands was no place for a Sassenach. Eilidh had been kind enough to lend her a sturdy pair of boots, though they were too big for her and her heels already carried the telltale soreness of blisters.

She spotted a flat rock ahead and picked her way over the rocks until she reached it. Then she climbed onto it and surveyed her surroundings.

From her vantage point she could see the castle, with its turrets at either end, surrounded by the lush green gardens, and whitewashed outbuildings and other dwellings dotted about. The road curved in an arc from the building, before disappearing into the dark green forest, only to appear again farther away, and fade into the distance. Along the skyline, mountains formed a jagged ridge that dipped and rose into sharp, white-topped peaks. Shielding her eyes from the sunlight, she let her gaze wander over the land until she spotted the river, gleaming like a giant silver snake, winding around the contours of the land. She followed the line of the river to the cluster of pine trees and smiled to herself as she caught sight of a building near the river's edge. Riverview Cottage. Her home.

Only it wasn't her home, though she'd been here almost a month. She was merely a passerby, stopping briefly on her path to achieving her dream.

When Hamish had last visited, he'd referred to her as *my wife*. In the eyes of the law she was his wife, but to hear it on his lips brought forth a rush of hope that had taken the air from her lungs, and she'd almost lost her composure. But he was only being polite to placate his mother. Mia would have preferred his censure—preferred it if he doled out the taunts that other men made when she'd come across them while collecting the calendula flowers. Murdoch, the older man's name was, and she recalled him from the day she'd arrived. His companion, Robbie, had seemed more congenial until he laughed as she'd stood to face them and lost her balance, spilling the orange flowers on the pathway. Only Maisie and her threats to "rip yer cocks out of yer breeches" had sent them on their way.

Even if Hamish had wanted her to stay—even if she herself had wished it—the people living in Glenblath would never accept her. Only Eilidh, Maisie, and a handful of the servants at the castle looked upon her with anything other than hostility.

And Rory.

Higher up along the path, just before the grass and heather disappeared and the rocks took over, Mia could discern a small stone building nestled among a handful of pine trees, their trunks glowing a pinkish brown in the sunlight. A wisp of smoke rose from the building, swirling in the wind before dissolving into the air higher up.

Would Rory welcome a visit, or would he see it as an intrusion, particularly if Maisie were with him? And would it be wise to continue climbing? Mia's foot was already sore, and Dr. McIver had always said that if one could already feel the soreness in one's feet, then the blister was inevitable. Perhaps it was also true of the heart—when a soul felt the first seeds of longing, then heartbreak was an unavoidable certainty.

But now was not a time to dwell on regrets. It was a time to relish the joy of being alone on a mountainside. Resuming her attention on the valley below, Mia pulled out the remains of the bread from her basket and nibbled on it while she gazed at the view, setting aside all notions of how she would have come to love that view forever had life taken a different turn. Then she dipped her hand into her bounty, the pink flowers she'd spotted on the path, nestling among the rocks on her way up. She pinched one between her thumb and forefinger, relishing the aroma—sweet and woody, with an undertone of mint. When brewed as a tea, it would help ease the symptoms of coughs and colds.

If anyone came to her for treatment, that was. Since her arrival, she'd had only two visitors for treatment—Elspeth for a cut to her finger, and Eilidh. But even if the whole estate shunned her, it mattered not if she could ease one person's suffering. The joy in Eilidh's eyes when she spoke of her pain having eased enough for her to undertake the ordinary tasks that others took for granted, such as pouring a cup of tea or knitting a scarf—it was enough to make Mia feel as if she had some value in the world.

Would she find solace when she returned to England? Or would the people there shun her as well, her face rendering her a pariah until the day she died?

Don't be such an ungrateful fool!

Her conscience chided her, reminding her that she had much to be thankful for. Such as the view before her now—a view she could happily sit and watch until the sun slipped below the horizon.

But Rory had warned her of the dangers of remaining out on the mountainside for too long. Not only did the cold take a grip on a person's body, seeping into their bones before they realized it, but darkness fell quickly after sundown, catching many an unwary soul on the slopes, where grown men had been known to die from the cold. The land here might be beautiful and wild, but it was also unforgiving.

With a sigh, she climbed off the rock and began her journey back to the cottage. Beinn Blath would not be going anywhere, and she would have plenty of opportunities to enjoy an hour or two's solitude on the slopes before she left Glenblath forever.

As she descended toward the valley, Mia spotted another clump of tiny purple flowers peeking out from between the rocks. She stooped to pluck a handful, then she stiffened as she heard a sharp cry.

Mia looked up, her gaze moving over the pale-blue sky. But there was no sign of the eagle or his mate. She stood up, rubbed her lower back, then resumed her descent, picking her way through the rocks and moving slowly so as not to exacerbate the blisters forming on her heels.

The scream came again, this time much closer, and a thin, high voice cried out.

"No! Leave me be!"

Then she heard laughter—not the merry laughter born of mirth, but the sharp taunts of those who sought to make sport of another for the gratification of their cruelty.

The path curved to the left around the side of the hill. As Mia approached the turn in the path, the ground below came into view, sloping steeply downward and dotted with huge rocks. Standing atop one rock were three figures, pointing toward the ground and laughing.

Then she heard the scream again, like an animal in pain.

"Ha-ha!" a voice cried. "Stupid girl! Stop yer bellyaching and get up or it'll be the worse for ye."

"I cannae! It hurts!

"You there!" Mia cried. "What's happening?"

The figures turned, and as Mia approached, taking care not to stumble as she descended the slope, she saw that they were boys. One she recognized from the day she had first arrived at Glenblath—he'd been clinging to his father's hand and staring at her wide-eyed.

"What's it to *ye*?" the largest boy sneered. "Pockmarked hure, that's what ye are!"

The middle boy let out a laugh, while the smallest shifted from one foot to another. "That's enough, Billy," he said. "Do ye want a thrashing from yer da?"

"I'm only saying what my da says, Jamie," the larger boy said. "He says she's a witch."

"Then best be quiet, or she'll cast a spell on ye," the second boy said. "She'll turn ye into a newt."

"Shut yer mouth, Calum, ye weak-bellied fool!" Billy said. "And *ye* can stop yer mewling as well!" he added, gesturing to the ground.

"Is someone hurt?" Mia said.

"It's none of yer business!" Billy said.

"But Billy," the smaller boy, Jamie, pleaded, "she hurt herself when ye pushed—"

"I said shut yer mouth!" Billy interrupted. "*All* girls cry. It's what they do. They're sniveling little wretches. That's what my da says."

Evidently Billy had learned much from his father.

"Has a *girl* been hurt?" Mia said. She approached the boys.

"Go away, witch!" Billy taunted her.

"Be quiet," Mia said, "or I'll cast a spell on you."

The boy's eyes widened with the fear that all bullies harbored when faced with an opponent they believed to be stronger. Then his companion nudged him.

"Come along, Billy. Yer da will give ye a thrashing if ye're late."

The larger boy cringed, then the boldness returned and he stuck out his tongue at Mia.

The crying had stopped. Were they playing a trick of some sort?

Then, as Mia drew near, she saw it—the crumpled form of a child, a girl, limbs akimbo, with a mass of ebony curls, her white face turned toward the sky. Eyes closed, her forehead furrowed into a frown of pain, lips parted as if she were screaming.

But no sound came.

"Dear God!"

Mia sprinted over to the child, almost stumbling on the uneven ground, then kneeled beside the girl's prone form. She placed her hand on the girl's chest, and relief washed over her as she caught the faint thrum of a heartbeat.

The child was alive, but unconscious.

She glanced up at the boys. "Help me, please," she said. "We need to take her home."

"I'm not helping a Sassenach witch!" Billy said. "Come on, Calum." His companion hesitated, then Billy caught his hand and tugged at it.

"Please!" Mia cried.

"No!" Billy said, tugging at Calum's arm again. The two boys turned their backs and picked their way toward the path. Mia turned to the third, who stood, white-faced, on the rock.

"Will you abandon your friend also?"

"Ada's not my friend," he said. "Billy and Calum are my friends."

"And do you think friends would abandon an injured girl?" Mia said. "Or worse—push her off a rock and endanger her life?"

The boy shook his head and whimpered. "H-he didnae mean to push her! She was just being a stupid girl and wouldnae jump!"

"So he pushed her, yes?"

He nodded.

"Then I'd say he *did* mean it," Mia said. She gestured to the girl. "This child's hurt, and those two boys have abandoned her. What do you think would happen if she were left out here?"

The boy said nothing, and Mia's temper rose.

"She might die, you foolish child! Is that what you want?"

"Of course not!"

The girl let out a soft moan and Mia placed a hand on her cheek. *Sweet Lord!* Her skin was freezing.

"Hush, sweetheart," she said. "Can you tell me your name?"

The girl's eyelids fluttered, then she let out a whimper.

"I must get her inside," Mia said. "It's too cold out here to do anything, and she'll catch a chill if she remains out here any longer." She shivered, her breath misting in the air. Then she placed her hands on the girl's body and ran them along her form. Her stomach clenched as she reached the girl's shoulders. The child's arms were twisted at an unusual angle, and when Mia touched her shoulder, she let out a cry. "I'm sorry, little one," Mia said. "But you'll be safe, as soon as I get you inside."

"Ada," a voice said, and Mia glanced up to see that the boy had climbed off the rock and was standing a few feet away, hands thrust into his pockets. "Her name's Ada."

"And you're Jamie, is that right?"

The boy nodded. "Aye. Jamie Sutherland."

"Sutherland?" Mia said. "Not MacLennan?"

"Aye, the minister's my da."

"Then, Jamie Sutherland, would you like to be a brave, strong boy, unlike your friends, and help me with Ada?"

The boy sniffed, then nodded.

"Come here, then," Mia said. "Ada's been hurt, but it's too cold for me to tend to her here. I must carry her to Riverside Cottage. Would you help me pick her up?"

The boy approached. Bright blue eyes glistened as they stared at the girl and a tear splashed onto his cheek.

"Here," Mia said crisply, adopting the tone that Dr. McIver said spurred onlookers into action, "I need you to help lift Ada into my arms, then I can carry her. You lift her there, under the knees."

"What if I hurt her?"

"Her legs aren't broken," Mia said, "so it shouldn't hurt. But I think she's injured her shoulder, so she may cry out as we lift her, but you mustn't stop. Can you be brave?"

Jamie nodded.

"Say it."

"Y-yes, ma'am. I can be brave."

"Good lad." Mia smiled encouragement, and the boy stopped sniffing and gave her a watery smile in return. Then, as she directed, he tucked his arms under the girl's knees as Mia slipped an arm under her torso, and together they lifted her until she was in Mia's arms.

Mia made her way back toward the path. The child weighed little more than a laden basket, but Mia's pace was hampered by the uneven ground. Footsteps followed, and she turned to see the boy carrying her basket.

"Sh-shall I come with ye, ma'am?"

Mia nodded, then continued along the path. Though the ache in her arms increased with each step, she maintained the pace until, at last, Riverview Cottage came into view. The little girl in her arms stirred occasionally, and let out a low groan each time Mia stumbled, but she did not open her eyes.

"Is that where ye live?" Jamie said, pointing to the cottage.

"Yes."

"That's the witch's house. She used to fly over the moors at night. Billy says she'll eat ye if she catches ye out on the moors on yer own."

"Do you believe everything Billy tells you?"

"Billy says that he's the biggest and the eldest of us, so we have to believe him."

"You can't think for yourself?"

The boy hesitated, and transferred Mia's basket from one arm to the other.

"This basket's heavy, ma'am."

"And would you believe Billy if he told you it weighed nothing at all?"

Jamie's eyes glistened with tears.

"Forgive me," Mia said. "Come inside and I can give you something to eat for your trouble. That is, if you think it's safe to enter a witch's house."

"I-I dinnae think ye're a witch."

"No matter what Billy says?"

"Aye."

Mia carried the girl inside and set her on the table in the parlor.

"Put the basket on the chest of drawers you see over there, Jamie," she said. "Once I've tended to your friend, I can get you something to eat. I take it Ada is your friend."

"C-can I do anything to help, ma'am?"

"That's very kind," Mia said. "Would you bring me two blankets from the cabinet in the corner? We need to make sure Ada's warm and comfortable before I take a proper look at her. I'm afraid the fire's gone out."

The boy approached the pile of blankets on the cabinet and plucked two from the top. Then he glanced at the fireplace. "I can lay and light a fire, ma'am, if Ada needs to be warm."

"You can?"

The boy puffed out his chest with pride. "My da showed me how, and I'm only six. Billy says I cannae light a fire, but I *can*."

"Then," Mia said, "perhaps you should listen to your own judgment, not what Billy says. The most important lesson a young man can learn in life is understanding the difference between right and wrong. And often you're the best judge of that—not those who profess to be your friends."

Jamie's eyes widened. "That's just what my da says."

"He sounds very sensible. But he might not approve of my letting you light a fire. Fire can be very dangerous."

"*Please.*"

Mia glanced at the little boy and saw earnestness and remorse in his eyes.

"I want to help Ada," he said. "I-I'm sorry for not helping her before. I knew Billy was going to push her, and I didnae stop him."

"Very well," Mia said. "Why don't you sweep out the fireplace then lay the fire while I take a look at Ada? But don't light it, mind. We can light it together. There's a broom in the kitchen to sweep the ash, and a log store to the side of the house."

The boy smiled, then disappeared into the kitchen, returning with the broom.

Mia turned her attention to her patient. The girl's pallor seemed to have worsened, her skin chalk white, save for the dark-purple semicircles beneath her eyes. Mia folded one blanket and tucked it beneath the girl's head, then placed the second blanket over her lower body. Then she began to inspect the girl's upper body, running her fingertips along each arm, recalling Dr. McIver's instructions on bones of the body—the lower and upper arm bones, the shoulder blade, and the collarbone…

That was it! The collarbone, which should run perpendicular to the breastbone, was distended, forming a lump near the center of the girl's chest. As Mia ran her fingertips over it, the girl let out a cry.

"Try to stay calm, sweetheart," Mia said, placing a hand on the girl's shoulder, but the child shifted position in an attempt to break free. "No," Mia said firmly. "You'll only hurt yourself more if you try to move."

"Who are ye?" the girl cried. "Where am I? I want my ma!"

"Ada!" Jamie approached the table and took the girl's hand. "Ada, ye're safe."

"J-Jamie?"

"This lady's here to help ye, Ada," Jamie said. "Ye're in her house—she carried ye all the way here!"

The girl lifted her head, then fell back with a cry.

"Och, Ada, I'm sorry!" the boy said. "I didnae want Billy to push ye."

"Then why did ye not stop him?"

"I…" He glanced at Mia. "I was afraid."

"I-I thought ye were my *friend*." The girl started to cry, her body shaking, then let out a whimper. "It hurts so much!"

"Keep still," Mia said. "Let me give you something for the pain, then I can make you better. You've hurt your collarbone."

"M-my what?"

Mia placed a light hand on the distended bone and the girl winced. "This is it," she said. "It's in the wrong place—brought about by your fall. I must move it back."

The girl's sobs increased and Jamie took her hand.

"Dinnae cry, Ada," he said. "This lady will make ye better." He turned to Mia. "Ye will, won't ye?"

"I'll do everything I can," Mia said. "Keep holding Ada's hand, and I'll fetch something for the pain."

The boy nodded, and Mia approached the shelves and reached for a jar containing long, thin shavings. She picked one out of the jar and held it up before the girl.

"Chew on this, Ada," she said.

"Wh-what is it?"

"Willow bark. It tastes bitter, but it'll help with the pain and the swelling."

"I-I dinnae know…"

"Go on, Ada," Jamie said. "If ye do, I'll not let Billy push ye again."

"Promise?"

Hope flared in the little girl's eyes despite the pain she must be feeling, then she opened her mouth and Mia placed the sliver of bark on her tongue.

"Eugh! It tastes horrid!"

"I'll make you some sweet tea afterward," Mia said, smiling. "Now, keep chewing, and try to stay still. Will you do that for me?"

Jamie squeezed Ada's hand. "Hold my hand," he said. "Squeeze it ever so tight when it hurts." He glanced at Mia. "That's right, isn't it?"

Before Mia could reply, she heard a loud knock on the door.

"Ada!" a deep voice cried. "Where are ye, lass?"

"Da!" Ada sat up, then let out a scream. The door burst open and a man entered. His eyes widened as he caught sight of the child on the table, and dark-blue eyes flashed with fury at Mia.

"What the fuck do ye think ye're doing with my child?"

CHAPTER SEVENTEEN

"A LLAN!" ANOTHER VOICE cried, and a woman appeared.

"Ma!" Ada sobbed. "It hurts!"

"Sir, madam," Mia began, "your daughter is—Oh!"

She let out a cry as the man gripped her arm and pulled her away from the child on the table.

"What witchcraft are ye weaving, woman?"

"N-nothing, sir, I assure you," Mia said, wincing as he tightened his grip. "Your daughter had an accident."

"Aye—I heard," the man growled.

"Allan, please," the woman said, "why dinnae ye hear what this woman has to say?"

"But that young Calum said—"

"And ye listen to that wee terror? This woman's no witch, for all that she's English."

Dear Lord! As if the marks on Mia's face weren't enough to engender prejudice, did these people hate her because of the country of her birth?

"Then what's that in Ada's mouth?" The man snatched the willow shaving from the girl's lips and threw it on the floor. "Do ye taint my bairn with yer poisons?"

Mia wrenched herself free. "Sweet heaven, will you listen to yourselves? Do you really think I'd pick up an injured child and carry her all the way back here just to…to what? Chant an incantation or two and turn her into a salmon?" She gestured to the girl on the table. "She's hurt—look at her shoulder! I was trying to alleviate her pain with that piece of willow bark that you saw fit to throw onto the floor."

"But…" the man began, and Mia folded her hands and glared at him.

"But *what?*" she said. "Have you believed the rumors about the pockmarked whore rather than formed your own opinion? By all means, take your daughter home—that is, if you wish her to continue to suffer and risk being maimed for life. After all, men care nothing for daughters, do they?"

"M-maimed?" the woman said, her voice wavering, and she rushed to her daughter's side and took her hand.

"Not if I can help it," Mia replied. "I don't know what you've been told, but this poor girl was injured by others, not by me."

The man turned to Jamie. "Is that true, lad?"

Jamie nodded, his eyes bright. "B-but we didnae mean to!" he said. "It's just that Billy—"

"Och, I might have known Billy had something to do with it," the woman said. "He probably sent Calum to tell us because he was too much of a coward to come himself. What happened, Jamie, lad?"

"I-I dinnae know…"

"Ye'll not be in any trouble for telling the truth. My Allan will see to that, won't ye, Allan? Ye'll have a word with Billy's da."

"Aye," Allan said, after a pause.

"It was Billy," Jamie said. "He pushed Ada down the hill and she fell. But I"—he glanced at Mia—"I did nothing to stop him."

"But you stayed behind for Ada, didn't you?" Mia said. "You're the only one who helped her."

"And ye," the boy said. He turned to the man. "This lady carried Ada all the way here, even though it was a long way, and she nearly fell twice. But I stopped her from falling."

The man patted Jamie's head. "Good lad," he said. He gestured to the piece of bark on the floor. "Willow bark, eh?"

"It helps to relieve pain," the woman said. "Dinnae ye remember my telling ye about it at school, Jamie, lad?"

The boy nodded.

"Och, lass, if ye were helping our Ada, then Allan's sorry for what he did, aren't ye, Allan?"

The man grunted and shrugged. His wife flashed him a look of irritation, but Mia knew that for a man, an apology was often considered a declaration of his lack of manhood. A grunt and a shrug were, in all likelihood, the most profuse declaration of regret that she was ever likely to witness from these Highlanders.

As she returned her attention to the little girl on the table, footsteps approached and another man appeared in the doorway. Her stomach gave a flutter as she recognized Hamish.

"Laird MacLennan!" The woman dipped into a curtsy and the man inclined his head.

Hamish stepped forward, his brow furrowed into a frown. "What's happened here?"

"It's our Ada!"

His frown deepened and he stared at Mia. "What has she done?"

"Oh, for pity's sake!" Mia cried. "Why must you all assume that I'm trying to harm the poor child? Is this what Highlanders think of women? Or just Englishwomen?"

Hamish's eyes widened and he shook his head.

"Or," Mia continued, gritting her teeth as she gestured to her face, "just pockmarked Englishwomen?"

He stepped forward and reached toward her. "I only meant—"

Mia slapped his hand away. "I care not what you meant," she said. "And I care not what any of you think. All I care about is this child. And if none of you will help me, then why don't you go to the devil and let me take care of my patient?"

"Fuck," Hamish muttered, and the woman drew in a sharp breath.

"Fuck!" Jamie echoed.

"Enough of that, lad," Ada's father said, clipping him around the ear. "Yer da would beat ye black and blue if he heard ye cursing."

Ada let out another wail and Mia took another shard of willow from the jar. "Here, sweetheart, take this," she said. "And if anyone tries to take it from you, I'll cast a spell on them, turn them into a worm, then feed them to the salmon in the river."

"What's wrong with the lass?" Hamish said, approaching the table.

"It's her collarbone," Mia said. "It's out of place and I must move it back. But"—she lowered her voice, lest the child hear—"it's going to hurt. A lot. So Ada needs to be kept still, and I need no distractions."

"Then let me help."

She let out a snort and he took her hand. She caught her breath at the fizz of heat in her blood, but when she tried to break free, he pulled her close.

"Please."

His emerald eyes shimmered with the soft plea, and, at length, she nodded.

"Very well," she said. "Will you do as I tell you? I know a man finds it hard to take instructions from a woman."

"Ma'am, can ye help my Ada?" the woman said.

"Of course she can, Mrs. MacLennan," Hamish said. "Trust her—as I do. Why dinnae ye hold yer daughter's hand while I help Lady MacLennan tend to her."

Lady MacLennan…

"Jamie, lad," Hamish continued, "do ye think Ada might like some wildflowers to cheer her up? I saw some by the river outside."

"B-but the lady said I could lay the fire. And I want to help Ada."

"Why don't you go and find the flowers?" Mia said. "You can lay the fire when you come back."

"There!" Hamish said, crouching to take the boy's hand. "Do as the lady says."

"Yes, sir." Jamie dipped his head, then exited the parlor.

"Allan, I think ye should go with him," Hamish said. "Keep

him outside until we call ye."

The man glanced at Mia. "Do ye trust her, laird?"

"Aye," Hamish said. "I'd trust her with my life."

The man nodded, then as soon as he left, closing the door behind him, Hamish touched Mia's arm.

"What must I do?"

"Hold Ada's shoulders to prevent her from moving," Mia said. "Don't press them too hard, or it'll hurt. Just hold them still."

He nodded, moved to the end of the table, and leaned over Ada's head. "Now, young Ada, lass, will ye be a brave girl for yer ma?"

Ada nodded, her eyes glazed with pain. Then Hamish met Mia's gaze and gave her a smile.

"On ye go, Mia, love."

Mia, love…

Tempering the traitorous pulse of hope, Mia turned her attention to the child. She placed her hand on the girl's chest where the distended bone protruded. The skin stretched over the bone, darkening in color where a bruise was already beginning to form. With her fingertips she explored the ridge of the bone, determining the exact position. She'd seen Dr. McIver perform the procedure only once before, but he was an experienced surgeon. Performing the task herself was not the same as watching and taking a few notes. But it needed to be done.

Remember, lass—swift and firm. A sound bone always wants to sit in its rightful place. Ye only need help it on its way.

Ready? she mouthed, placing her hand over the bone.

Hamish nodded.

Mia closed her eyes, then focused on her breathing to temper the tremors in her body.

On the count of three… One, two…

Three!

She pushed against the bone, inward and upward. It gave way and, with a dull crack, moved forward. Ada let out a scream, the piece of bark falling from her lips, but Hamish held her firm while she fought to break free. Then, a heartbeat later, she lay still.

The girl's mother sobbed and clung to her hand. Shortly after, Ada's eyes fluttered open and she drew in a shuddering breath.

"Ma!"

"I'm here, wee one," her mother said.

Mia ran her fingertips over the girl's chest, lightening her touch as she traced the line of the collarbone. Hamish raised his eyebrows, beads of sweat glistening on his forehead, and she nodded.

"It's worked," she said. "How are you feeling, Ada?"

The girl inhaled then let out a sigh. "I-it's hurting, b-but not as much as before." She tried to move, then cried out.

"Careful, sweet one," Mia said. "Your shoulder will be sore for a while. I'll need to bind it to let it heal. Mrs. MacLennan, your husband can come back in now."

The woman nodded and slipped outside. She returned so quickly with her husband and Jamie that they must have been listening outside—a conclusion that was confirmed when Mia saw the boy's stricken face. Jamie curled his fingers around the white blooms in his hand.

"Ada…" he cried, and Hamish placed a hand on his shoulder.

"She's well, Jamie, lad." He turned to Mia. "Have ye bandages?"

"Top drawer in the cabinet."

He nodded and fetched a roll of bandages from the drawer, then he helped Ada to sit and turned her little body so her legs were swinging over the edge of the table. Mia wound the bandage around the child's chest and shoulder, then she fashioned another strip of linen into a sling and looped it over Ada's body, fixing her arm in place.

"You'll need to rest your arm for a fortnight," she said. "Keep it in this position when you're not in bed."

"A fortnight?" the girl's mother said. "Oh my, I—"

"I can send Elspeth to help ye in the house, Mrs. MacLennan, if ye need it," Hamish said.

"No, *I* can do that," Mia said. "I'll need to visit Ada to make sure she's recovering, and I can give you a tea to brew to help with the pain, Mrs. MacLennan. She might experience some swelling around the joint, but that's to be expected. The tea will help."

"Och no, I cannae afford—"

"There's no charge," Mia said.

"But if ye're a physician…"

"I've agreed with"—Mia glanced at Hamish—"with Lord MacLennan that as long as I'm here, I shan't charge anyone needing medicine or treatment."

"Really? Why's that?"

Mia opened her mouth to reply then closed it again and caught a glimmer of guilt in Hamish's eyes.

"That's right," he said. "There's no need to concern yerself with payment. Just make sure yer lass is well again. And I'll still send Elspeth to tend to yer lass while ye're teaching at the school."

"Do you teach the children?" Mia said.

The woman nodded.

"But if that Billy's responsible for what happened to my Ada, I'll not want him in the school," Allan said. "What he needs is a damned good leathering on that hide of his, and if Murdoch won't do it, then I will."

"But what will that teach him?" Mia said. "Bullies never learn through being struck. Better to teach him the consequences of what he's done."

"Aye—a sore arse."

"Lady MacLennan's right," Ada's mother said. "I wonder…" she began, then she shook her head. "No, I cannae ask it."

"Ask anything," Mia said. "If it's in my power, I'll help."

The woman curled her arms around her daughter and rocked her to and fro. "I wouldnae have known what to do for my Ada, ma'am. Would ye show me? And…I can show the children at school. Perhaps if Billy learned the consequences of hurting my lass, he'd not do it again."

"I still think he needs a good leathering, Aileen, love."

"Well, with Murdoch as his da, the lad already gets plenty of those," Hamish said.

"Which perhaps explains why the boy bullies those he deems weaker than himself," Mia said.

"That's his da's choice and there's nothing a lass can do about it," Allan said.

"Other than teach him a better way," she replied, her temper rising. Why was it that a man was given free rein to beat his children merely because of his sex?

She turned to the woman and took her hand. "Mrs. MacLennan, I'd be delighted to show the schoolchildren something about medicine. Perhaps we can discuss it tomorrow."

"Tomorrow?"

"When I visit Ada to see how she's doing," Mia said. "Which reminds me…" She placed a light hand on Ada's head. "Did I not say I was going to find something special for a brave girl?"

Ada's eyes flared with delight. "Ooh, yes!"

"Are you fond of shortbread? I didn't bake it myself—Mrs. McBride is to be thanked for that. But I think you've earned a slice. Or perhaps two. What do you say?"

"Can I, Ma?" The girl turned to her mother, hope gleaming in her eyes.

"Just this once, Ada, lass," came the reply. "If ye're sure, Lady MacLennan?"

Mia made her way to the kitchen, took three pieces of shortbread, then returned. "I've brought a piece for you, Jamie, for being such a gallant young man."

The boy blushed and lowered his gaze.

"What do ye say, Jamie, lad?" Ada's mother said.

"Thank ye, Lady MacLennan."

"Good lad. The minister's brought ye up right. Ye'd better run along now in case he's wondering where ye are. If he asks, tell him ye've been helping the laird and he's to come to me if he disnae believe ye."

"Aye, Mrs. MacLennan."

The boy reached toward Mia, offering the flowers. When Mia took them, he wrapped his arms around her waist.

"That's enough of that, lad," Allan said. "Ye dinnae go mauling the lady of—"

"It's all right," Mia said, embracing the little boy. "Today's been an ordeal for you, hasn't it, young man?"

Jamie nodded his head against Mia's body.

"Poor wee soul," Ada's mother said. Then she lowered her voice. "His ma was taken when he came into the world. But he's a good boy for his da, aren't ye, Jamie?"

"I'm going to be minister when I grow up to be a man."

Mia smiled, then suppressed a yawn.

"I think ye should all leave"—Hamish glanced at Mia—"Lady MacLennan in peace now. She's tired and needs her rest. Mrs. MacLennan, I'll send Elspeth over to ye after breakfast tomorrow."

"Come along then, Ada," Allan said as he lifted the girl into his arms. Then he nodded toward Mia. "It's a good deed ye did, ma'am. I'll tell folk hereabouts to come to ye if they're in need of a doctor."

"Come along, Jamie, lad—I'll walk ye home," Mrs. MacLennan said, and they exited the cottage, leaving Mia alone with her husband.

She rolled up the unused bandages and placed them in the drawer. Then, as she turned, she felt a solid wall against her back. No—not a wall, a living, breathing man. A pair of arms circled her waist and drew her to him, and she felt his muscular body against her back—the broad chest, the taut thighs, and, in between...

...his length, hardening against her back.

Then he dipped his head and she felt his warm breath in her hair. Her skin tightened with want and she suppressed a cry. He splayed out his hand on her stomach and shifted it higher until his fingers reached the underside of her breasts. A ripple threaded through her as she felt her skin tighten, and when she looked down, she blushed at the sight of two little peaks poking needily at the fabric of her gown.

A low growl rumbled in his chest, which reverberated through her bones, and she held her breath, willing his hand to move higher. Then it did, and she let out a low cry as his hand cupped a breast, warm and welcoming, his fingers caressing, squeezing.

"Oh!" A cry escaped her lips and she tilted her head back, offering her throat to him. A thick warmth pulsed in her center and she shifted her legs, the heat rising as she felt the slickness between them.

"Oh, Mia…" he whispered.

Mia…

How she'd longed to hear him say her name!

"Hamish," she breathed, parting her thighs and pressing herself against his hardness.

He let out a low curse, then released her. Cold rippled across her back and she jerked free, swallowing her shame at her wantonness.

Pockmarked whore, they called her—and here she was, pockmarked and whoring herself to the man who didn't want her.

"Mia, forgive me, I—"

"It's Euphramia," she said, unable to disguise the bitterness in her voice. "Or Miss Lucas—seeing as that's what I'll be called soon, and you'll be glad of it."

"No, I—"

"Just go!" she cried. "I'm tired."

"Then get some sleep. I'll return tomorrow."

"No! I'm tired of *this*!" She gestured to the air between them. "Tired of not being wanted, tired of being a burden, and tired of the suspicion of people who know nothing about me, merely because of my sex, my face, and because I'm English. I take it you're making progress in raising the funds to return my dowry, because I cannot wait to leave!"

He jerked back, a flare of anger in his eyes. Then he sighed and nodded.

"Very well, I'll leave ye in peace. But first, shall I light the fire for ye?"

"I can do that myself," she said. "After all, I cannot rely on anyone else, can I?"

He opened his mouth to reply, then shook his head. "Forgive me, lass."

"What for?"

He let out a sigh and wiped his forehead. "For not deserving ye."

He bowed and exited the cottage, closing the door behind him. After a moment, Mia approached the window and looked out. Through the trees she could see the outline of the castle against the sky, a turret peeking out above the tree line. Then she closed the curtains and entered her bedchamber. Suppressing the tears, she drew the plaid blanket about her body and lay on the bed—alone—waiting for sleep to come.

CHAPTER EIGHTEEN

EVIL'S BALLOCKS—HOW COULD he have been so damned *foolish?*

As he strode toward the castle, Hamish aimed a kick at a large stone on the path. He missed, lost his balance, and stumbled to the ground.

"Fuck!"

After struggling to his feet, he winced and inspected his hands. Two small stones were embedded in his left palm and he plucked them out. A droplet of blood swelled on the flesh and he sucked at it to clean the grime off, grimacing at the metallic taste.

He glanced back at the cottage, where a sliver of light was visible in the window. Perhaps if he returned, and asked her to tend to it…

"Mia…"

He glanced about, as if he risked condemnation from the Almighty for speaking her name in so intimate a manner.

Then he recalled how he'd moaned her name as he palmed her breast. The lovely, ripe, round teat was everything he'd dreamed it might be—soft and warm, with the delicious pip at the center that hardened needily against his palm.

He let out a sharp breath at the surge in his manhood.

Devil take him—would he need to dive into the river to cool his ardor? Or would the ghost of Old Ma MacLennan claim him to absorb his sins?

And he *had* sinned. Not in deed, for he'd pulled himself back from the brink of destruction. But in thought, and wish…

He closed his eyes, surrendering to the image of his wife, bent over that table, her mouth open as she cried his name while he mounted her from behind and claimed her like any beast. But she was not a woman to be claimed. Rather than a submissive female, eager to please her man—the kind of woman that he'd thought most suitable for a wife—Mia had commanded him, and everyone else in the room, taking charge efficiently and firmly to administer treatment to the young lass.

And he had never in his life been so aroused.

What might it be like to have such a woman? To spar with her during the day, then witness her sweet surrender as he took her in bed, nipping her neck and rutting her like a stag, roaring with triumph to declare to the world that she was his…

But she didn't belong to him. She would be claimed by another—some lucky bastard.

"Been visiting yer wife, brother?" a voice sneered.

Iona emerged from the darkness.

"What if I am?" he replied. "I should be more concerned with what *ye're* doing, wandering about the place on yer own like a savage."

"Devil take yer cock!"

He caught her arm. "Why must ye disgrace the name of MacLennan, talking like a common hure?"

"*I'm* not the hure," she said. "Are ye fucking her? Does she spread her legs for ye and moan yer name like a bitch in heat?"

Hamish released her arm, and she drew back her hand and struck him across the cheek.

What the devil was *that* for?

He lifted his hand to rub his cheek, and his sister flinched. Though her eyes sparkled with defiance, he saw fear in them. But, even if she might infuriate him, he'd never hit her—nor any woman. Didn't she realize that? Or perhaps she was seeing how far she might push him with her taunts and wild behavior.

"Are ye angry with me, brother?" she said, a tight laugh in her tone. "Angry that I caught ye rutting?"

He tilted his head to one side. "Ma always told me that when a person is overly eager to accuse another of a sin, it means that the accuser has committed that sin themselves and they're pushing their own shame onto another."

She frowned. "What are ye saying, Hamish?"

"I'm saying that perhaps I ought to ask whether *ye've* been rutting—which would explain why ye're often out at night, like a stray cat in heat."

"How dare ye!"

She raised her fists, but he caught her wrists.

"Why dinnae ye beat me, then, brother, if ye think I'm a hure?"

"What purpose would that serve?" he said. "Would ye learn anything from it? Far better to let ye reflect on yer actions and those who might be affected by it."

Was it his imagination, or could he see guilt in her eyes?

"Brodie's a good lad," he said. "I wouldnae want to see him hurt."

"Brodie's a mere boy," she sneered. "He wouldnae know what to do with his cock even if it were stuffed inside a hure."

"Then who are ye carrying on with?"

"Are ye trying to pretend that ye care?"

"Does he have a wife?"

"What if he does?" she said. "Ye're happy for Maisie to spread her legs for everyone. Murdoch says she's the best hure in the Highlands, and ye're not against rutting her, either. Does that pockmarked wife of yers know that the cock that makes her scream also dips into—"

"Devil's breeches, will ye desist?" Hamish roared. "With that vile tongue of yers, I'll never find a husband willing to take ye on, and I have no wish to be saddled with ye forever!"

"I wouldnae take a man from here if ye paid me," she said. "They're all flea-ridden dogs, and their wives weak-bellied worms." A sly smile spread across her face. "That Evie's the weakest of them all—running after her man even when he's rutting another, doing his bidding after he's beaten her. Do ye think I want to be like *her*?"

Devil's cock—did that mean...

"Are ye carrying on with *Murdoch*?"

"I'm carrying on with no one!"

"Ye seem a little too eager to deny it."

"What does it matter what I say if ye'll never believe me?" she said. "I'm..."

She drew in a sharp breath and clamped her hand over her mouth. Hamish took her arms.

"What ails ye, sister? Ye've not been well for weeks. And despite what I might say, I love ye, and—"

"No, ye dinnae," she snarled, pulling free. "Ye're too busy loving yerself—and now ye're too busy rutting that Sassenach."

"I'm not rutting her," he said. "She's my wife in name only. Soon she'll be gone forever, and..." He paused, suppressing the pang of regret.

"So ye dinnae love her?"

He shook his head.

"I'll not believe ye if ye won't say it."

"For fuck's sake, Iona!" he cried. "I dinnae love her—is that enough to satisfy ye?"

"Ye seem a little too eager to deny it."

He opened his mouth to respond, then checked himself.

Devil's...

"Ha!" Iona let out a laugh. "Look to yer own sins before accusing me."

He continued along the path while she followed, issuing taunts, and he fisted his hands to control his temper. Then he stopped and turned to look at her.

"What were ye doing on this path, Iona?" he said. "It only leads to Riverside Cottage. Were ye going to see Euphramia?"

She colored, then shook her head. "Of course not. Why

would I want to see that pockmarked—"

He raised his hand. "I've heard enough! If all ye're going to speak is evil, I'd rather ye didnae speak at all."

Triumph glittered in her eyes. "Are ye angry enough to strike me?"

"No," he said. "Though ye may try yer damnedest, I'll never be truly angry with ye—only disappointed."

His softly spoken words, said with the weariness he felt, did more to deflate her than anger ever could. She opened her mouth to reply, then her lip wobbled and she closed it again. Her eyes glistened with tears, then, with a sob, she fled. He watched her retreating back until she turned a corner and disappeared.

What the devil was he going to do with Iona? She needed a firm hand that was also caring, nurturing, and efficient. And there was only one soul in the whole of Glenblath who had those qualities.

What a pity, then, that she was destined to leave.

CHAPTER NINETEEN

AS MIA FINISHED her luncheon, she heard a knock on the front door.

"Is that you, Maisie? I wasn't expecting you until later, but you can have a…"

Her voice trailed away as she opened the door to reveal a young man. She recognized him from the day she'd arrived at Glenblath, though she hadn't seen him since. Only a handful of souls had visited Mia in the weeks she'd resided at Glenblath. Murdoch had come to issue taunts. Maisie had shooed him away the first time and he'd only returned once, though he fled when he saw Rory approach.

Had this young man come to taunt her? Perhaps Murdoch had sent him. Bullies often persuaded others to taunt their victims—poor Jamie was under the influence of that lad Billy, who, unsurprisingly, was Murdoch's son.

Murdoch had a lot to answer for.

Mia folded her arms and met the young man's gaze. "Is there something I can do for you, Mr.…?" She inclined her head and waited.

"B-Brodie, ma'am. Brodie MacLennan. I…I was wondering if ye'd take a look at my arm. Mrs. MacLennan said ye might be able to help."

"Mrs. MacLennan?"

"Aileen MacLennan, her that teaches at the school. Her

lass…Ada…comes to visit the horses. She said ye'd helped Ada after she hurt her shoulder. So I-I thought ye maybe might want to help me."

"You look after the horses?"

"I'm head groom, ma'am."

Mia ushered him inside.

"Oh," he said, eyeing her half-eaten meal. "I-I'll come back if ye're busy."

"Not before you've shown me your arm," Mia said. "Does it pain you?" He hesitated, and Mia raised her eyebrows. "I see pain in your eyes, Brodie. There's no harm in wanting to ease it. May I see?"

He pulled back his sleeve. The lower half of his arm was covered in a bandage that was yellowing around the edges and dotted with dark brown stains. Slowly he unwound the bandage, his forehead furrowing, then dropped it on the table.

A deep gash ran along his forearm, about which the skin was swollen and red. Mia wrinkled her nose at the faintly sweet aroma, then moved her hand toward the wound. The boy let out a whimper.

"Keep still," Mia said. "I'll not touch it." She held her hand just above the wound, but could feel the heat on her palm.

No wonder tiny beads of sweat glistened on his forehead. The poor boy must be in agony.

"What happened?" Mia asked.

"I slipped and fell when unshackling the plough from the horses."

"When?"

"Three…no, four days ago."

"Four days? Why didn't you come and see me at the time?"

"I-I didnae think…" He hesitated. "I mean, the others said…"

"That I'm a witch more likely to cast a spell on you than tend to your wound?"

He averted his gaze. "No one knows I've hurt myself, ma'am… I-I dinnae want to lose my position. It was my fault. I was careless. Murdoch says that a careless man is no man at all, and Iona already thinks I'm more mouse than man. I bandaged it myself, and it didnae hurt much after it happened. But now…"

"But now it hurts and is hot to the touch—and, I suspect, you feel as if you're coming down with a fever?"

"H-how do ye know?"

"I've seen, and tended to, many wounds like yours," Mia said. She gestured to a chair at the table. "If you wait there, I'll fetch what I need to treat it."

Brodie nodded, and his feverish gaze followed Mia as she bustled about the room, setting a pot of water over the fire, gathering bandages, and plucking a jar of salve from the shelf. When she drew out a knife from the cabinet, he let out a low cry.

"No! Dinnae do it!"

"Do what?"

He gestured to the knife. "Do ye mean to chop my arm off?"

"Why in the world would you think that?"

"Iona says that's what doctors do—they'd just as soon chop yer arms and legs off."

Mia raised her hands in a gesture of appeasement. "You have my word that I'll not remove your arm. Your wound isn't so bad to necessitate such an action. But it has festered, and I need to remove the putrefaction so it can heal cleanly."

He glanced at his wound and rose.

"If I don't treat your wound, it will only get worse," she said. "And then…"

Brodie's eyes widened and a tear splashed onto his cheek.

"It's a simple procedure." Mia kept her tone neutral and gestured to the wound. "I won't ask you to trust me, because I know I must earn that trust—but perhaps…"

"Och, I trust ye, ma'am," he said, his cheeks flushing. "B-but I'm…"

Afraid.

"I understand," Mia said. "You're a little apprehensive because you don't know what I intend to do. I can explain as I go along so there's no unpleasant surprises. I can also give you something for the pain. You're in pain, aren't you, though you're being very brave not to show it. Wouldn't you like that pain to stop?"

He nodded, and resumed his seat. "Wh-what must I do?"

"Keep your arm still. Can you do that?"

Brodie nodded.

"Good," Mia said. "Place it on the table, then I'll begin once the water's heated."

He hesitated, as if to gather his courage, then nodded and placed his arm on the table.

To his credit, the young man only cried out once, at the first cut of the knife. Then he gritted his teeth, the beads of sweat swelling on his brow while Mia cleaned the wound in hot water. When she applied the salve, he swayed sideways as if he were going to faint. But he heeded her instruction to tell her about the horses he tended to while she wound a fresh bandage around his arm and secured it with a knot. When Mia finished, she placed a light hand on his arm.

"Bravo," she said. "I commend your courage."

Brodie shook his head, his cheeks flaming, and exhaled sharply. "I wasnae brave, ma'am. I've never been so fearful in my life. Murdoch already thinks me a coward. He'll—"

"I think we can ignore what Murdoch thinks," Mia said. "You confess that you were afraid, yet still you came, and weathered my treatment without a word."

"B-but I cried."

"At the first cut, then you were silent. Do you have any idea how many men screamed and cried for their mothers for far less when I treated them at the hospital?"

"Ye worked in a hospital?"

"I assisted a doctor in London. Dr. McIver—one of your countrymen."

"Then ye're not..." He colored and lowered his gaze.

"Not a witch?" Mia said, unable to disguise the bitterness in her voice. "Or a charlatan? Perhaps, Brodie, you should discover the truth for yourself rather than listen to tattle."

His color heightened and his lip wobbled as another tear splashed onto his cheek.

"Forgive me, that was unkind," she said. "You're in pain and a doctor should always put her patients first. Shall I make us some tea?"

"Oh, I dinnae know if I should…"

"It's a tea to help with your pain. I'll brew it for you now, then you can take some with you to brew yourself—or perhaps ask Mrs. McBride at the castle to help. But I'd like to see you again tomorrow, to see how you're healing. Now, take a seat by the fire."

Cradling his arm, he complied, and as Mia rose to make the tea, she heard another knock—a faint scratch, almost imperceptible—and went to the door.

A thin woman stood in the doorway. Her skin was so pale it was almost translucent, and she looked as if she might dissolve into the air at the slightest breath of the wind. Her eyes were dark, almost black against the pallor of her skin.

Mia's stomach fluttered with apprehension. Was it a ghost?

Then the woman spoke.

"F-forgive me"—she glanced over her shoulder, her eyes widening with fear—"Y-Yer Ladyship, but I thought I might…"

"Evie!" Brodie cried, and he appeared at Mia's side. Then he peered out of the door. "Are ye on yer own?"

"Aye," the woman said, in a thin, reedy voice. "Murdoch's out cutting peat and Billy's at school all day, so I thought"—she resumed her gaze on Mia—"I-I thought…" She stepped back. "F-forgive me. I shouldn't have come."

"Nonsense," Brodie said. "Ye should come in, seeing as ye've come all the way here. Murdoch needn't know where ye've been."

The woman frowned and stared at Mia.

"This is my cousin Evie," Brodie said. "She's Ailsa and Billy's ma. She's not been well, have ye, Evie?"

"Would you like to come in?" Mia said, offering her hand. "There's no need to be afraid. Despite what you may have heard, I'm no witch."

"Och, I ken that, Yer Ladyship," Evie said, "but if my Murdoch hears I've been—"

"Did you know, Evie, that all doctors pledge an oath of confidentiality to their patients?" Mia said. "I am duty bound not to utter a word of what passes between me and those who seek treatment. Not even to those who believe that they have ownership of another person. You'll be quite safe here. Brodie won't say anything, will you, Brodie?"

"Evie knows I wouldnae, dinnae ye, lass?"

"Come in, then," Mia said. "I've just finished making some tea, if you'd like a cup."

She ushered Evie into the parlor and settled her into a chair by the fire. On impulse, she reached for a blanket and draped it over the woman's knees. Evie clung to it, her thin, bony fingers curling into the fabric.

Brodie kneeled at Evie's feet and took her hands. "How are ye?" he said. "I've not seen ye for a fortnight."

Evie glanced at Mia, and Mia left the cousins while she made the tea. When she returned, Brodie was still at Evie's feet. They stopped talking and watched her, unease in their eyes as she set the tray on the table.

"Here's *your* tea, Brodie," Mia said. "It's made from willow bark with a spoon of honey to alleviate the bitterness. It'll help with your pain." Then she handed a cup to Evie, who cradled it in her hands before taking a sip. "How can I help you, Evie?"

"Och, it's nothing, ma'am. I'll just be on my way once I've had my tea."

"Evie, tell her," Brodie said. "There's no need for shame, for all that Murdoch says."

Mia let out a huff. Murdoch, it seemed, had a lot to answer for. "And what does Murdoch say?"

Evie colored, and Brodie took her hand and nodded. "Go on."

"I-I cannae give my husband another child," she said. "Not since…"

She glanced at Brodie, her eyes glistening with moisture.

"Evie lost a child last winter," Brodie said. "A boy. Stillborn—after her pains came early. She's not been strong since."

"And did anything happen to make your pains come early?" Mia said.

"I fell," Evie said. "I'm not strong enough to…" She curled her fingers around the blanket, then lifted her gaze to Mia, and Mia's heart broke at the plea in her eyes. "I-I was wondering if ye had something to make me strong, so I could give my husband another child."

Mia tempered the anger boiling in her gut, and fear flickered in Evie's eyes.

"Oh, forgive me, ma'am—I know it's sinful to speak of such things, a-and I'm not speaking against my husband, b-but I'm not a good wife to him, and I w-want…" Her voice wavered and Mia took her hand.

"If you want my opinion, I think it's Murdoch who's not being a good husband to you."

"B-but I love him. I vowed to obey him."

As, no doubt, Murdoch had vowed to honor and cherish his wife. But the rules of society and the church were intended to perpetuate the advantages of men and maintain the distinction between them and the women those men believed they had ownership of. And nobody could help with whom they fell in love—even if the object of their love would never return it.

Mia glanced over the young woman—the pallor of her cheeks, and the dark rings beneath her eyes.

"Do you tire easily?" she asked.

"Aye, ma'am."

"And sometimes feel faint when you stand?"

Evie nodded. "H-how did ye know?"

"I suspect you have anemia."

Evie's eyes widened with fear. "Am I going to die?"

"No," Mia said. "It's easy to treat and doesn't require medicine. Do you eat much meat?"

"I'm always cooking a bit of venison, though Murdoch likes to take his share. But he's a man, so he needs it."

"So do you," Mia said. "You should take more for yourself—set some aside when he's not looking?"

"Och, I dinnae know if I could…"

"Think of it as your way of ensuring that you get better. Murdoch wants you better, doesn't he?"

Mia could still see uncertainty in the other woman's eyes, so she plucked a jar from her shelf filled with dried leaves.

"These will help," she said, "either taken as a tea, or you could add them to a stew. And"—she hesitated, unwilling to cross the boundary between patient and friend, particularly if she was to leave Glenblath—"you can visit me any time for tea—or luncheon, on a day like today when your husband and son are not…in need of you."

"I-I dinnae know, ma'am. I've no money to pay ye."

"There's no need for payment," Mia said, and Evie's mouth creased into a grimace.

"I dinnae need charity."

"I'm not offering it," Mia said. "I made an agreement with Hamish that while I remain here, I'll treat anyone who needs me at no cost."

"Aye," Brodie said. "I heard Master Hamish say that myself."

At length, Evie nodded. "Thank ye, ma'am."

"And you promise to visit me when you can?" Mia said.

"Aye."

"Make sure ye do, cousin," Brodie said. "Ye can always tell Murdoch ye're visiting me."

Mia took a handful of leaves from the jar and wrapped them in a cloth. "Here you go," she said. "There are plenty growing hereabouts. I'll point them out next time you come if you'd like to gather them for yourself."

"I-I'd like that," Evie replied, then, as the clock over the mantelshelf struck six, she rose to her feet and teetered to one side, and Brodie caught her arm. "Oh!" she cried. "Murdoch will be home soon."

"Come along, cousin," Brodie said, offering his arm. "I'll take ye."

He steered her to the door, Mia following. As they stepped outside, Mia caught sight of a figure approaching the cottage. The figure stopped and Mia called out, "Who's there?"

It was Hamish's sister.

"Iona? Is that you?" Mia said.

Brodie drew in a sharp breath.

"What's it to *ye?*" Iona sneered.

"Iona—" Brodie began, but the girl let out a laugh.

"What are ye doing here, Brodie?" she said. "Wanting a potion to turn ye into a man? I doubt even *she'd* have something for that."

"Iona, there's no need—" Evie began, her voice carrying an undertone of steel in defense of Brodie, but Iona merely laughed.

"There's nothing for ye here, Evie MacLennan—I thought ye knew better than to visit the Sassenach witch. Does Murdoch know ye're here?"

"No—please…"

"Iona, that's *enough!*" Mia said. "Insult me all you like, but you've no right to insult others merely for wanting a little help."

"I'll say what I like!" Iona cried, her voice tight with emotion as if she were about to burst into tears. Then she turned and fled, and Mia could swear she heard sobbing.

"Brodie…" Evie said, but he shushed her.

"There's naught to worry about," he said. "Iona won't say anything to Murdoch."

"What if she does?"

Brodie let out a sigh. "She's a little wild, that's all—and she's wild because she's unhappy. But there's not a wicked bone in her body. She's like an animal cornered in a trap, begging to be free, who says more than she means. Isn't that right, ma'am?"

"Yes," Mia said. "She's an unhappy girl. I wonder why?"

"I wish I knew," Brodie said, a sigh in his voice that betrayed his own emotions.

Yes—nobody could help with whom they fell in love, whether it were a brute, a wild young girl…

…or a husband who wished for an annulment.

CHAPTER TWENTY

A s Hamish crossed the courtyard, he caught the echo of a familiar voice.

Her voice.

Last night she'd visited him again in his dreams, whispering words of desire—then she had dissolved into the dawn light while he woke with an erection fit to burst and his hands around his cock. His need for release increased with each passing day. But though their marriage was a mere formality and soon to end, he couldn't bring himself to touch another woman—not even Maisie, who, with her pliant body and expert hands, tempted a man merely by being within twenty feet of him.

Heaven help him if Euphramia was plaguing his mind during the day also.

Then he heard it again, and she appeared at the edge of the stable yard, carrying a package, Brodie at her side.

Hamish gritted his teeth to temper the pulse of envy as she tilted her head back and laughed. What had that young pup done to merit such a reward?

Then she paused, as if she sensed him, and turned. His manhood surged as she met his gaze and her eyes widened. Devil's breeches—did she know he had a cockstand as hard as granite beneath his plaid?

"Master Hamish, sir." Brodie raised his arm in greeting, which was bandaged from wrist to elbow.

"Did ye hurt yerself, lad?" Hamish said.

"Aye, but it's almost healed."

"Thanks to *ye*, I'll wager," Hamish said, nodding to Euphramia.

"It was nothing, really," she said. "I merely—"

"Och, dinnae talk nonsense—beggin' yer pardon, Yer Ladyship," Brodie said. "If it weren't for ye, I might have lost my arm. It's about time folk around here appreciated what ye could do for them—like ye've done for Evie, when no one else will help her."

She gave a shy smile that only served to harden Hamish's cock further. He shifted position, willing the surge of desire to subside.

"And there's Reverend Sutherland—ye've cured his cough, and—"

"Brodie, really!" She laughed. "It's the least I can do before I return to England."

Must she always remind everyone that she was to leave Glenblath?

Hamish gestured to the package in her hand. "Is that a gift from a grateful patient?" he said, wincing at the resentment in his tone.

"No," she said, an edge to her voice. "From a beloved friend."

Jealousy surged, and Hamish glared at Brodie. Then Euphramia held up the package.

"It's from Dr. McIver."

"What news from the good doctor?"

Fuck—he sounded like a petulant child.

"He's sent some ginger root for your mother and has written to tell me about an outbreak of smallpox in Hammersmith."

"Is he in danger?"

She shook her head. "Both Dr. and Mrs. McIver took the vaccine. He's setting up a vaccination scheme in the area. It's something I'd like to do here, with your consent."

"Surely there's no need for that?" Hamish said. "Isn't smallpox mostly confined to cities?"

"Mostly."

"In which case I see little need for it. I doubt folk here would want to take part. Not to mention the cost, when the estate cannae afford it due to my having to…" His voice trailed away and she nodded, understanding his meaning.

"I-I could forgo part of the repayment."

"Repayment?" Brodie said, raising his eyebrows.

"We should discuss this later, Euphramia," Hamish said. "Over supper, perhaps?"

He offered his arm, and she stared at it. "Tonight?"

"Aye."

She opened her mouth, as if to refuse. Then, after a pause, she sighed and placed her hand on his arm. Hamish suppressed the fizz of desire as she curled her fingers around his sleeve.

"Very well," she said. "I wanted to speak to Eilidh, in any case."

"I'll take ye to her."

Hamish dismissed Brodie, then led Mia inside the castle to his mother's parlor. His heart ached at the delight in Ma's expression when she saw her daughter-in-law.

"Has my son finally persuaded ye to dine with us?" Ma said.

Euphramia nodded, and Hamish steered her to a seat, then approached the door.

"Yet he sees fit to abandon ye as soon as he's brought ye to me," Ma huffed. "Where are yer manners, son?"

"I've errands to run," Hamish said, "but I'll see ye both at supper."

A smile curved his mother's lips. Then she kissed Mia on both cheeks.

"Ye're looking well, lass. The Highland air's good for ye—but ye're still too thin. That cottage is no place for ye when ye've a home right here at Glenblath Castle. I'll not press the matter, seeing as ye're such a determined lass, but I long to see more of ye when I have such little congenial company."

She glanced at Hamish, and he suppressed a smile. Ma had

always been the kindest soul to walk on the earth, always seeing the good in folk. But she harbored a different feeling for Mia—a feeling that shone from her eyes.

Love.

On impulse, Hamish took Euphramia's hand and lifted it to his lips.

"I'll see ye at supper—Mia."

She parted her lips and, unable to resist the temptation, Hamish brushed his mouth against hers. She let out a sharp sigh and retreated, and he swallowed the sense of loss. Though he'd caught the sweet, honeyed taste of her lips, his body craved more. But under his mother's watchful gaze, he couldn't do what he yearned to do—seize her like any self-respecting husband would and crush her mouth with his, plundering that sweetness until he'd had his fill.

Instead, he bowed and took his leave, pausing outside his mother's chamber to draw breath and temper his ardor. Though he craved to touch Mia, to taste her, he did not want to frighten her off like a spooked filly. As any horseman knew, the surest way to tame a mare was to let her come to him.

◆◆◆

"WELL, I'M RIGHT glad ye've seen fit to dine with Master Hamish, ma'am," Mrs. McBride said as she carried a pot of stew into the dining room. "It's not right for a lass like yerself to be on her own so much."

The cook leveled a stern gaze at Hamish as she placed the pot on the table.

"I don't mind the solitude, Mrs. McBride," Mia said. She smiled at the cook, her face glowing in the candlelight. "The stew smells delicious. You must write down the method so I can make it myself."

"Och, I dinnae write anything down, lass," the cook said,

tapping her head. "It's in here—passed from mother to daughter over generations. But then, perhaps I ought to write it down, seeing as I've not been blessed with children. Or I could pass it to young Iona here."

Hamish's sister—who, to his relief, had been mostly silent during the meal—smiled at the cook. "Thank ye, Mrs. McBride."

"Och, ye're a good lass," the cook said, patting Iona's shoulder, "even if ye were a terror when ye were wee. Bless me! I remember once when ye threw my roast goose out of the window to see if it could fly!"

Hamish's heart soared as he heard Mia's soft laugh. "And did it?" she asked.

"Of course it didnae!" Iona snapped. "Didnae ye know food cannae fly? Or are ye too fine a lady to—"

"That's enough!" Hamish said, and Iona pulled a face.

"Ye shouldn't say such things about Mistress Euphramia, Iona lass," Mrs. McBride said. "Of course she knows food disnae fly—and she's working very hard to make her cottage comfortable. I've seen it meself."

"Ye've been there?" Iona said.

"When I had that cough. Reverend Sutherland said she'd done wonders for his cough, with that syrup of honey and... What was it, lass?"

"Thyme," Mia said. "It grows on the mountain. My supply has almost run out. Perhaps, Iona, you could help me find more? You'll know better than I where to look."

"I've better things to do than—"

"*Iona,*" Hamish growled.

"It doesn't matter," Mia said, her tone a little less bright. "Your sister's not obliged to do anything she has no wish to."

Iona opened her mouth to reply, but Ma interjected.

"Ye must tell Hamish about the smallpox vaccine, Mia, lass."

"I've already said we cannae afford it, Ma," Hamish said.

"Ah, but we've been discussing it," Ma said, "and the expense will not be prohibitive. All yer wife"—Iona drew in a sharp breath at Ma's reference to Hamish's married status—"all yer wife requires is passage for herself and one other to Glasgow and back. I'm sure ye can spare the carriage for *that*."

"What about the cost of the vaccine itself?" Hamish said.

"Dr. McIver assured Mia in his letter that his colleague in Glasgow would be willing to forgo any fee," Ma said, "and even if he isn't, would ye want to risk the lives of those hereabouts who depend on us? I'm sure ye wouldnae want anyone here catching smallpox." She turned to Iona. "Would *ye* want to catch the pox?"

Iona shook her head. "I wouldnae want to look like *her*."

"Iona, I've warned ye—" Hamish began, but Mia interrupted.

"Your sister's right." She gave a smile that did not reach her eyes. "Who, of sound mind, would want to look like me? And that's the lesser evil, given how many people die from the disease."

"If I had to look like ye, I'd rather—" Iona began, but Hamish banged his fist on the table and his sister startled, her eyes widening.

"Better pockmarked on the outside than rotten on the inside," he said.

Iona opened her mouth to reply, then her lip wobbled and she closed it again, her eyes glistening as she picked at her meal.

"If you let me go to Glasgow, Hamish, I promise that you'll not have to pay toward the cost," Euphramia said. "Dr. McIver has also written to say that he's willing to give me a home and a position as his assistant."

She met his gaze, determination in her eyes.

"Did ye write to tell him about..." Hamish began, then his voice trailed off as he caught his sister watching him, intensity in her expression.

"That our marriage is to be annulled and I am to leave for England?" Mia said. "Why would I not? He's a dear friend in whom I can confide." She leaned forward. "Don't you see? This means that I can leave sooner than intended, for I'll not need my whole fortune returned. I can—"

Hamish raised his hand. "I've no wish to discuss yer leaving us when ye're our guest for dinner."

Or at all.

"Very well," she replied, smiling, and this time a gleam of mirth shone in her eyes. "Perhaps we should restrict our conversation to the weather."

"Or the school," Ma said. "Have ye told Hamish that ye're teaching at the school tomorrow?"

Euphramia gave a shy smile and a delicate bloom spread across her cheeks, making her look quite beautiful.

"Are ye?" Hamish said.

She nodded. "Just the rudiments of tying a bandage, dressing a wound, and so forth. I thought I might show them the ginger root Dr. McIver sent me."

Dr. bloody McIver! Why was she always singing his praises? He was a mortal man, not a bloody saint.

Hamish focused on his meal to temper his envy, then he glanced up to see Iona staring at him, understanding in her eyes. But other than curl her lips in a sneer, she said nothing.

"Ye'll need to watch out for Billy," Hamish said.

"I'm sure Mia can handle one wee boy if she can handle a great big brute like yerself," Ma said, "though that poor lass Evie has a great deal to put up with, what with her Murdoch."

"There's naught wrong with Murdoch, Ma," Hamish said. "He just expects his wife to honor the vows she made."

Mia let out a snort that ended in a fit of coughing.

"Are ye well, lass?" Ma said.

"Quite so," Mia replied, reaching for her wine glass. "But I've often wondered why the marriage vows are written as such, and why the bride's adherence to the vows is expected by the world when the groom may often do what he pleases."

"Not all men break their marriage vows, surely?" Hamish said.

"I'm sure a man exists somewhere who abides by the principle of the vows he's uttered," she said. "But where a man does not—and I think we can safely say that *most* do not—he won't suffer the vilification that a woman suffers on breaking her vows. Even if a woman is merely under suspicion of breaking her vows, she is assumed to be guilty and subject to gossip."

"For example?" Hamish said.

She took a mouthful of wine and straightened, as if readying herself for the challenge.

"Such as the vows of fidelity."

Hamish glanced at his sister, who was watching Mia, mouth open.

"As you are no doubt aware, excepting Eilidh here," Mia continued, "the only true friend I have made at Glenblath is Maisie, who is vilified by most for how she earns her living—vilified by the very men who break their marriage vows and purchase her services."

Iona drew in a sharp breath while Ma remained silent.

"Euphramia," Hamish said, glancing at his sister, "this is hardly an appropriate subject for…"

Iona let out a chuckle, which she silenced as Hamish shot her a look of fury.

"Perhaps it ought to be," Ma said. "After all, haven't ye—"

"Ma!" Hamish cried, and Iona laughed again.

"If I'd known she'd be so entertaining, I'd have insisted ye invite her for dinner sooner, brother," Iona said. "Her conversation makes up for having to look at her face." She turned to Mia and grinned, showing even white teeth. "Well…almost."

"Iona, for fu—"

"No, Hamish," Mia interrupted. "You're right. It was inappropriate of me to mention it when I'm a guest in your home." She turned to Ma and inclined her head. "Eilidh, forgive me."

"There's naught to forgive," Ma said. "We've been having very fine weather, have we not?"

The two women exchanged a smile that only served to heighten the jealousy needling at Hamish, and supper continued with them chatting amiably to each other while Iona watched, mouth turned down, her gaze flicking from one to the other. Occasionally she glanced at Hamish, pulled a face, then resumed her attention on the plate in front of her.

When the meal concluded, Mia leaned back, a smile of contentment on her lips as Mrs. McBride cleared the plates.

"Thank you, Mrs. McBride," she said.

"Ye're welcome, lass," the cook replied. "It's not often I get a bit of appreciation here."

"We all appreciate ye, Mrs. McBride," Hamish said, rising. "Euphramia, would ye like a nip of whisky?"

Mia glanced at the longcase clock in the corner and shook her head. "Forgive me, but I must get back. I have much to prepare before I visit the school tomorrow."

"But it's begun to rain," Ma said. "Why dinnae ye stay a while?"

"I can weather a little rain."

"Then would ye at least permit me to escort ye back to Riverview?" Hamish said.

She hesitated, then nodded. "I'd like that. Thank you, Eilidh…and Iona…for your company tonight."

Ma smiled in approval. Iona raised her eyebrows but had the good sense to say nothing. Then Hamish escorted Mia out of the dining room.

The rain had begun to fall more heavily as he accompanied his wife on the path toward the river. He placed his arm about her shoulders, and, rather than the rejection he'd expected, she smiled and they continued in silence—the companionable silence that a husband and wife shared when there was no need to express their contentment with words.

What could be more pleasurable than a man taking a nighttime stroll with his wife? But, rather than enjoying a pleasant walk with the prospect of a night in each other's arms, he was taking her to her lonely cottage, then would return to his lonelier bed.

As the silhouette of riverside cottage came into view, she let out a small sigh.

"Are ye happy, Mia?"

At first, she said nothing. They approached the door, and he opened his mouth to repeat the question.

"I am content," she said.

"Only content?"

"Content with the prospect of happiness on the horizon."

"I would have ye happy, Mia."

She tilted her face up, her eyes gleaming in the moonlight. "And I you, Hamish."

Then he lowered his mouth to hers.

At first, she stiffened, then her body relaxed as he pulled her close, enveloping her in his arms, relishing the feel of her softness against him. She gave a low whimper as he slid his tongue along the seam of her lips. Her fingers curled around his arms and he slipped his tongue inside, relishing the unspoken invitation. With hungry, insistent strokes, he swept his tongue across every corner of her mouth, claiming, tasting her. But it was not enough—he wanted to devour her until she was quivering and boneless, begging for release.

His cock stiffened as a little mewl escaped her lips. Such a sweet sound—the surest indication of female need as she readied herself to surrender her body to the male, like the deer presenting herself before the stag, to be mounted…

She let out a low groan and he withdrew.

Devil's ballocks, had he hurt her?

But no—eyes closed, face flushed, she was ready and eager. He took her hand, interlocked their fingers, and lifted it to his lips.

"Mia."

She opened her eyes, and he caught his breath at the raw need in them. They were so dark that they were almost black, save for the gleams of silver in their depths, like tiny stars pulsing with raw desire.

She blinked and pushed open the door, then paused at the threshold, and he held his breath in anticipation. Was she inviting him in? Dare he ask, knowing that he'd not be able to control himself if she did?

Then she opened the door fully, stepped over the threshold, and let out a cry.

He followed her in and froze.

The cottage had been ransacked. A chair lay in pieces on the floor. The shelves were empty, with the jars and bottles littered about, some intact, others smashed, shards of glass gleaming in the moonlight, their contents strewn over the floor. The drawer in the cabinet had been pulled out and their contents emptied over the table.

"Devil's ballocks!" Hamish cried. "Who would do such a thing? And *why*?"

"I can answer why," she said, her voice uneven. "As to who— it could be any number of people."

She crossed the floor, picking her way over the mess, and went through the door leading to the rest of the cottage. When she returned, her jaw was set in a hard line as if she gritted her teeth.

"Have they been everywhere?" he asked.

She shook her head. "No, just this room. How *kind* of them."

"I'm sorry."

She let out a snort. "I should have known better than to dine with you. Did you ask some of your friends to visit while I was at the castle?"

"Good God, Mia, surely ye didnae think I'd—"

"I don't know what to think!" she cried. Then she laughed. "It was a foolish thing to do, was it not? It won't make me leave any quicker. You should have told your friends that I was intending to leave sooner anyway. I thank the Almighty that I have some friends, at least, even if I have none here."

"Mia, ye do have—" he began, but she interrupted.

"What do I have? A husband who cannot stand the sight of me and declared it to the world—a man who, unwilling to honor the promise of returning the dowry he squandered, wishes to drive me away by ransacking my home. No." She raised her hand as he opened his mouth to protest. "He's too much of a coward to do it himself, so he sends others to do his work for him."

Her words cut through his heart. Was that what she thought of him—that he'd stoop so low as to destroy the meager life she'd built for herself here?

But could he blame her for thinking it was his doing?

He was responsible. Perhaps not directly, but had he welcomed her as a husband ought, set aside his disappointment, and abided by the vows he'd made to her, she might have been happy here, not merely contented, living at Glenblath Castle, a loving daughter to Ma, a firm but kind sister to Iona, and…

…a future mother to his children.

He stooped to pick up a blanket.

"Stop that," she said. "I can do it myself. It's not as bad as it looks." She let out a bitter laugh. "Much like my face."

"But—"

"Just go!" she cried. "If you care for me"—she hesitated—"no, if you feel anything for me other than contempt, then leave." Her voice wavered and she wiped her forehead.

If he cared for her? Didn't she know that he—

He caught his breath.

No. Loving her was not something he could allow himself to do.

"Mia, I…"

"Please," she whispered. "I want to be alone."

She met his gaze—and his heart withered. The desire that had, moments ago, pulsed thickly in her eyes had gone, replaced by disappointment and betrayal. Unable to say anything to assuage his guilt or ease her pain, he bowed and left.

As he trudged back along the path, he turned at the corner before the cottage was out of sight. A stream of smoke was already rising from the chimney and he caught a soft orange glow from the window. An accomplished lass, she was, and a voice whispered in his mind that though his home might be Glenblath

Castle, his heart resided in the isolated little cottage, with the kindest, most capable, and most unappreciated woman he'd ever had the privilege to know.

CHAPTER TWENTY-ONE

M IA HAD ALMOST finished sweeping the floor when she heard voices.

"Mia, are ye there?"

"Of course she is, Rory, ye great fool! Didnae ye see the smoke from the chimney?"

She smiled at her friend's voice.

"Come in, Maisie," Mia called, wiping her hands on her apron. "You're here early…" The front door opened and Maisie entered, a basket over her arm. Rory's head appeared, peering around the doorframe. "Shall I make some tea?"

Rory nodded. "Aye, ye'd better, lass. I can see that young lad approaching, and he never says no to a cup." He turned away from the door and called to someone outside. "Hey, Brodie lad, get yer arse inside quickly—it's a cold one today and we dinnae want to keep this door open forever."

The young man appeared, stamping his feet. "It's right cold today, it is."

"Cold enough to freeze a man's cock off," Rory said. "Beggin' yer pardon, ma'am."

"To what do I owe the pleasure?" Mia said, unable to hide her smile. "It's early yet."

"We heard…I mean, we thought…ye'd appreciate a little help," Maisie said.

"And ye might appreciate these also," Rory added, raising his hand to reveal a brace of grouse, "seeing as ye've learned to pluck and cook Glenblath grouse to perfection."

"Courtesy of your excellent tutelage," Mia said. "But I couldn't accept *two* grouse. It's too generous. Perhaps you should give one to Evie instead?"

"And have that great lump of her husband eat it all?" Maisie laughed. "Nay—ye should accept it for Evie's sake, Mia. I know ye've been letting her have a bite or two each time she visits ye."

"Oh, no, she—"

"It's no bother, lass," Rory said with a wink. "I'll not tell Murdoch. Now, let me get these hanging for ye, then we can see about tidying the place up."

"Tidying up?" Mia said.

"Aye." He glanced about the parlor, eyes narrowing as his gaze wandered about the shelves on which half of the jars were now missing, Mia having swept up the broken shards last night. "It looks as if ye've tidied away the worst of it."

She felt her cheeks warming. News traveled fast.

"Is everyone talking about it?" she said. "Laughing at the pockmarked witch having been taught a lesson?"

"Of course not," Maisie said. "I dinnae think anyone knows, unless Master Hamish saw fit to tell them, and I doubt that."

"Why?" Mia said, unable to disguise the bitterness in her voice.

"Because he swore us to secrecy—said he'd toss Rory off the estate if he spoke as much of a word about what happened to ye."

"When was this?"

"He visited me last night," Rory said. "Foolish lad to climb halfway up the mountain! Got caught in the rainstorm. He said ye'd had a bit of bother and to visit ye in the morning to help."

"He did?"

"Aye," Maisie said. "Soaked to the bone, he were. But a dish of tea soon set him to rights."

"Och, Maisie, love," Rory chided, and Maisie let out a soft laugh.

"I think young Brodie here knows what I get up to most nights. Dinnae ye?" she said. "Why are ye here, lad?"

The young man blushed. "M-Master Hamish said that I was to visit Lady MacLennan to offer my services—he said it was only right, seein' as she'd been kind enough to treat my arm. But he said nothing about her being taught a lesson." He glanced about the parlor, his gaze settling on the half-empty shelves and the remnants of the smashed chair in the corner. "What happened?"

"A-an accident, nothing more," Mia said.

"Master Hamish said it was deliberate," Maisie said. "But there's no need for ye to bother. He'll soon find out who's to blame, and will bring them to justice. He disnae tolerate such unkindness."

Mia suppressed a snort and shook her head. "Not even against—" She broke off as Maisie took her hand.

"Surely ye dinnae think Master Hamish would tolerate any unkind treatment of ye?"

When Mia didn't respond, Maisie's expression darkened.

"Do ye think he had something to do with this?"

"Why?" Mia said. "Did he say anything to you?"

"No, lass," Rory said, "other than ye needed help, and though he wanted to give it, ye were too unhappy to accept his help. He said ye needed a friend—a friend that ye could trust." He took her other hand. "Lass, surely ye didnae think Master Hamish had anything to do with what happened, or"—he glanced at Maisie—"that ye cannae trust him? He's a good man."

"Aye, that he is," Maisie said.

"And kind," Brodie added. "The best master, or so my da used to say—kinder and fairer than the old laird. And he'd never do anything to hurt ye, ma'am."

"Then who?" Mia said.

Maisie set her basket on the table and pulled out several jars and bottles. "Will these replace what was broken?"

Mia nodded. "Yes, thank you, but I'll need to collect the herbs again, and what with winter coming, they'll be scarce. I count myself fortunate that the calendula salve was untouched, at least, as there won't be any more flowers until the spring, by which time I'll be gone."

"Perhaps, perhaps not," Maisie said, setting her basket aside. "Ye dinnae suppose it was Iona? Hamish once told me that she smashed six wine bottles when he told her she was too young to drink it. She said that if she couldn't have it, then neither could he."

"No," Mia said. "Iona may be willful, and she dislikes me, but I don't think she'd do anything like this. She might smash a jar or two in front of me, or in front of Hamish, to gain his attention, but I can't see her behaving in such an underhand manner as to destroy my belongings in secret."

"Cannae ye?" Maisie said.

Brodie's eyes widened. "No!" he cried. "I cannae believe Iona would do such a thing. Sh-she's unhappy, but she's not cruel."

"She's thrown plenty of cruel words yer way, Brodie," Maisie said. "But ye're too sweet on her to think her capable of any evil."

"I agree with Brodie, Maisie, lass," Rory said. "Iona's just a little wild, like all young lasses her age who grew up without the steadying hand of a father. What that lass needs is a husband to take her in hand and tame her wild ways." He let out a chuckle. "What about *ye*, Brodie, lad? Surely ye must be old enough to know that yer cock's not just for pissing."

Brodie went as red as fire and his lower lip wobbled.

"Rory!" Maisie cried, slapping the ghillie on his arm. "I've told ye before, ye shouldn't speak so in front of Mia. She's not used to our uncouth ways."

"I'm only saying what the rest of us are thinking, love."

Maisie's eyes widened at Rory's term of endearment, but she said nothing.

"There's plenty of lasses hereabouts who'd take Brodie in hand." He let out a chuckle. "There's Florrie—her who lives along the valley."

"What, Campbell's widow?" Maisie said. "She's forty if she's a day. She'd make mincemeat of young Brodie."

"But she'd teach him a thing or two," Rory said with a chuckle. "And if Brodie's needing a son, there's no sturdier pair of hips in the whole of Glenblath."

Maisie frowned and folded her arms. "And how would ye know, Rory MacLennan?"

He blushed and shrugged. "Campbell used to tell me how she used to—"

"I dinnae want to hear it!" Maisie huffed.

"Och, come here, Maisie, hen," Rory said, drawing her close for a kiss. "Ye know *I'd* never look twice at her. She's not as pretty as ye. But she'd do for Brodie—give him a son to take over as head groom." He turned to Mia. "Ye see, lass, that's the tradition here. The menfolk will hand their livelihoods over to their sons. Brodie's da was head groom before him, weren't he, lad?"

Brodie nodded, his color deepening.

"And what do they do with their daughters?" Mia said. "Or do daughters have no worth?"

"Och, they're worth a lot, lass," Rory said. "They become wives of the menfolk. Well...the *respectable* daughters become wives."

Maisie's hand slipped and her basket fell to the floor. Mia picked it up and handed it to her. The other woman's eyes were gleaming with moisture, and Mia caught a sheen of vulnerability that disappeared as soon as it came, as if, for a heartbeat, the armor protecting Maisie's heart had slipped—as Mia's armor had almost slipped last night.

"Maisie?" Mia said, taking her hand.

Maisie shook her head. "It's nothing." Then she turned to Rory and gave him a hard smile. "Well!" she said, a little too brightly. "It seems as if I'm not needed here. Mia, I'll come tomorrow and see how ye're getting on. I'm sure I spotted some wild thyme yesterday, and I can show ye where it is."

Rory raised his eyebrows. "Shall I come with ye, Maisie?"

"No," came the reply. "There's a bed needing warming and my empty pockets are in need of a coin or two."

Without waiting for a response, she took the basket and exited the parlor.

"What was that about?" Brodie said. "Did I say something amiss?"

"Och, I dinnae ken," Rory said with a sigh. "I'll never understand women. Begging yer pardon, Mistress Mia, but ye're an enigma to us. Master Hamish said just the same last night. Perhaps ye can tell me why my Maisie turns from being the happiest, most carefree lass in the world to a harridan?"

But a knock on the door spared Mia the need to reply as Aileen MacLennan arrived, ready to take her to the school.

Which was just as well—for there was nothing to gain from explaining to a man what love did to a woman.

CHAPTER TWENTY-TWO

As Hamish entered the schoolroom, a child sitting at the back turned to look at him. The boy colored, his eyes widening as he recognized his laird. Hamish placed his finger on his lips.

"Shh, Calum," he whispered. "Ye must listen to what ye hear in school if ye're to grow up to be a fine lad like yer da."

The boy nodded, then resumed his attention on the teacher who sat on a chair at the front of the schoolroom, her bandaged foot resting on another chair…

…and the woman standing beside her.

Hamish caught his breath as he watched Mia deftly bandage the teacher's foot.

"So, as you see, I've wound this tight enough to ensure that Mrs. MacLennan's ankle is supported, but not so tight as to—" She broke off as she caught sight of Hamish. He smiled encouragement, and, after a pause, she returned the smile and his heart swelled to see that the disgust in her eyes of last night had gone.

The class turned to stare at him, and whispers threaded through the room.

"Children!" the teacher said. "Ye know better than to chatter during a lesson. Now, it appears that we have another guest today. What do ye say to Laird MacLennan?"

"Good afternoon, Laird MacLennan!" the children chorused.

"Is there anything we can help ye with, Yer Lordship?" the

teacher asked.

"No, Mrs. MacLennan," Hamish replied. "I've come to learn about bandages. Please continue." He gestured to Mia. What ought he to call her in front of the children?

The teacher came to his rescue.

"Miss Lucas has been teaching us about more than bandages, sir."

Hamish winced.

Miss Lucas…

But then, that was what, no doubt, she'd be called when she embarked on her future life as a doctor.

"Is that so?" was all he could think of to say.

Mia blushed. "I've told the children a little about vaccination."

"Why are ye blushing, Miss Lucas?" one child said, and Mrs. MacLennan shushed the little girl.

"Sienna, lass, we dinnae ask questions about anything other than the lesson."

"Yes, Mrs. MacLennan," the girl said. "Sorry, Mrs. MacLennan."

"Please continue…Miss Lucas," Hamish said. "I have no wish to discompose ye. I can leave if ye wish it."

"No," Mia said. "Stay. Please."

Her soft words warmed his heart, and he leaned against the back wall and smiled. "Thank ye, lass." He felt his own cheeks warm as her smile reached her eyes. The little girl—Sienna—stared at him, then opened her mouth, and the teacher clapped her hands.

"Concentrate, children!" she said. "Do continue, Miss Lucas."

"Very well," Mia said. "Now, children, you've seen how I've tied a bandage on Mrs. MacLennan. Who would like to have their leg bandaged next?"

The children glanced at each other and the whispering resumed, then a young lass at the front of the class put her hand up.

Mia smiled. "Thank you, Ada," she said. "Come and exchange

places with your teacher."

She helped the little girl onto the chair then propped her leg up on the other.

"Now, who would like to tie the bandage on Ada's leg?"

More whispers, then a boy in the middle of the class let out a laugh.

"Is there something you wish to say, Billy?" Mia said.

"No," the boy said, his voice sulky.

"Do you find it amusing, the notion of bandaging Ada's leg?"

Billy folded his arms and stuck out his lower lip in defiance. "She's a *girl!*"

"Girls are the same as boys," Mia said. "They have arms and legs, just like you."

"Not everything they have is the same, is it?" Billy said. "We have something that the girls dinnae."

He let out a giggle, and some of the other boys laughed.

"Quite so," Mia said. "Boys are physically different to girls in many aspects. And to make up for the lack of'—she hesitated— "of what you are referring to, girls have larger brains, Billy, which heightens their capacity for intellect relative to their male counterparts."

Hamish suppressed a smile.

The girl who'd spoken earlier raised her hand. "Is that true, miss?"

"Of course, Sienna," Mia replied. "There have been numerous studies on the relative levels of intellect between men and women. The results don't tend to be widely recognized or published, given that most of the journals are owned by men. But we know better, girls, do we not?"

"Yes, miss!" the girls chorused.

Billy scowled and leaned back in his seat.

"But boys can be useful," Mia continued. "After all, many fine doctors are men. Perhaps Billy can show us what men are capable of if they apply their minds appropriately. Billy, would you like to apply a bandage to Ada's leg?"

He shook his head.

"It's only fair that you try," Mia said. "If a young man is prone to accidents—or is often present when accidents occur—he must know how to deal with any injuries sustained. With that in mind, I think you're the most appropriate person to bandage Ada's leg today."

Billy glanced about the room, his eyes shimmering with uncertainty.

"You want to be a capable man when you grow up, don't you, Billy? To look after your wife and children—and to look after your mother."

At the mention of his mother, Billy's lip wobbled.

"Go on, Billy," one of the boys said.

"Your mother's very kind," Mia said, her voice softening. "I'm sure she'd be very proud if you could show her how to tie a bandage."

The boy scraped his chair back and stood.

Mia held out her hand. Billy approached her and took it, and she leaned over him and whispered something in his ear. His color deepened, then he picked up a bandage.

"Remember what I said? You need to tie it tight enough so it won't work loose, but not too tight. You wouldn't want to hurt Ada, would you?"

He gave a slight shake to the head, and Ada flinched.

"Now, Ada, perhaps we might learn to trust Billy. You're not going to hurt Ada, are you, young man?" The steel had returned to Mia's voice.

"No, ma'am."

The boy held the bandage against Ada's leg, then, while Mia issued gentle instructions, he wound the bandage around her ankle and secured it with a knot.

"Is that comfortable, Ada?" he said.

The little girl's eyes widened and she nodded. "Aye. Thank ye for not hurting me."

Billy retreated.

"Not so fast," Mia said, catching his hand. She patted his shoulder, and Hamish caught her whispered words of praise: "Well done, young man. Your mother is fortunate to have such a capable son."

The boy flushed with pleasure.

"Class, I think Billy deserves a round of applause, don't you?" she said.

The children clapped as Billy resumed his seat.

"Well done, everyone," the teacher said, "especially ye, Billy and Ada. Now, it's almost the end of the day, so make sure yer desks are tidy. Miss Lucas, did ye have anything else to say?"

"I just have some questions for the children," Mia said. "Remember what I talked about at the beginning of the lesson? Who can tell me the name of the disease I caught in London that caused these marks?"

She gestured to her face, and a volley of hands shot up.

"Yes, Calum?" she said.

"Smallpox?"

"That's right. And what do we call the process that doctors follow to ensure you're protected from diseases like smallpox?"

Several hands went down, until there were two left aloft.

"Billy—and Jamie," Euphramia said. "Who would like to answer?"

"Vack..." Billy began, then frowned.

"Vaccine!" Jamie said. "Billy, dinnae ye know *anything*?"

"I know how to tie a bandage better than *ye*, Jamie Sutherland."

"And I think, on that note, we'll bring the class to a conclusion," the teacher said. "What do we say?"

"Thank ye, Miss Lucas!" the children chorused.

"Very good. Tidy yer desks, then ye're free to go."

The children busied themselves arranging books and papers, then filed out of the schoolroom. Mia chatted to the teacher while she tidied the bandages and jars on the table at the front and placed them in a basket. She glanced up as Hamish approached.

"That was well done," he said.

"It was nothing," she replied. "I used to help at a school near the hospital in London. Most children want to learn, and the younger ones can apply themselves to the basics of what I teach them without the need to read and write. Your praise should be directed to Aileen here." She gestured to the teacher. "A guest in a school is someone new, a change from their routine, which will always excite interest. The real skill in teaching is being able to maintain a child's interest over a sustained period."

"Ye shouldn't talk yerself down, ma'am," Aileen said. "Ye did well today." She glanced toward the few children remaining in the classroom and lowered her voice. "And ye handled young Billy, though he cursed something awful. He can be a handful— most folk hereabouts would strip his hide for the way he behaves, and I confess to wanting to give him a leathering after what happened to my Ada. But he cannae help having Murdoch for his da. Whereas his ma…" She hesitated and looked up. "Evie! What are ye doing here?"

Hamish turned to see Murdoch's diminutive wife in the doorway.

"Ma!" Billy rushed toward his mother and flung his arms around her waist.

"Careful, lad," Hamish said. "Ye'll knock yer ma over."

Evie placed a kiss on the top of her son's head. "I fancied a walk on my way to see Ailsa," she said, "and I wanted to meet Billy at school. I hope he's been behaving, Aileen."

"I *have*, Ma!" Billy said. "Just like ye told me."

"Aye, that's right," the teacher said. "He showed everyone how to tie a bandage on Ada's leg."

"Ada?"

The boy put his thumb in his mouth and nodded, leaning against his mother.

"You're looking well, Evie," Mia said. "I trust you're still visiting me tomorrow for luncheon? I've some more of that nettle soup you love so much."

Evie wrinkled her nose then let out a soft laugh. Hamish stared at her. When had he last seen Murdoch's wife smile, much less laugh?

Mia joined in her laughter. "Dr. McIver always says that the more disgusting something tastes, the more it's likely to be good for us."

Dr. bloody McIver again!

As if she'd heard his thoughts, Mia glanced at Hamish, frowned, then resumed her attention on Evie.

"I'll have a bowl with you," she said. "If I dish out the medicine, I must be prepared to take it myself."

"Nettle soup?" Billy said. "Does it sting yer tongue?"

"No," Mia said, laughing. "Once it's cooked, it's safe to eat."

"Ma, we learned about vack…" Billy said. "Vack-seen? Is that it?"

"Yes, vaccines," Mia said. "A medicine to protect against diseases," she added as Evie raised her eyebrows in inquiry. "I'm hoping to set up a procedure here at Glenblath to vaccinate everyone against smallpox."

"Can we have the vack-seen, Ma?" Billy said.

"I'll have to ask yer father," Evie replied.

"Will ye ask him tonight?"

"I-I'll need to find the right time, Billy, lad. Dinnae ye go saying anything until I've spoken to him. Ye know how he—" She broke off, blushing.

"Ask him in your own time," Mia said. "Perhaps Hamish might help persuade him? After all, he's the laird."

Hamish opened his mouth to say that a laird ought not to interfere in how a husband ruled his home—and Murdoch, more than others, wouldn't appreciate being told how to manage his wife. Then he closed it as he caught the plea in Mia's eyes.

"I'll see if I can speak to him," he said. "That is, if ye're determined to go ahead with the vaccine?"

She set her mouth in the determined little line that always threatened to undo his resolve, then nodded.

"Ye're a kind woman," Evie said. "I'm so glad ye're here with us at Glenblath."

"As am I," Hamish said, before he could stop himself.

Mia glanced at him, and her lips parted as she drew in a sharp breath. Evie glanced from Hamish to Mia and back again. Then she patted Billy's hand.

"Come along, lad. I've a hundred things to do before I set to making yer da's supper, and standing about here won't get them done, will it?"

"I ought to be going also," Mia said with a grin. "I've nettles to pick."

Evie let out another laugh and led her son out of the classroom. After bidding farewell to the teacher, Mia followed, her basket over her arm, Hamish in her wake. As they stepped outside, he reached for her basket.

"Let me."

"It's not necessary," she said. "I carried it here, so I can carry it back."

"Och, I know that, lass, but will ye indulge me and let me do something for ye, to make up for being such an arse last night?"

"I rather think I was the"—she paused—"the *arse* last night."

He suppressed a smile at the way her tongue curled over the profanity. "Then yer penance shall be to let me carry yer basket."

Smiling, she handed it over.

"I ought not to have blamed you for smashing my things when I know you could never have done it," she said. "It was uncivil of me to turn you away when you offered help. Thank you for sending my friends over this morning. I didn't deserve such kindness."

"Ye *do*," he said. "There's much to admire in ye—and Mrs. MacLennan's right about the way ye handled that young Billy."

She gestured to the retreating backs of Evie and her son, who clung to his mother's hand.

"He's not a bad boy at heart, though he's done bad things," she said. "It's obvious that he's learned many of his ways from his father. But I believe that his love for his mother will be his salvation."

"Aye," Hamish said. "The true test of a man's goodness is how he treats his ma. And"—he turned his gaze to her, his heart flickering at the expression in her hazel eyes—"and how he treats his wife."

He offered his free arm. "Now," he said, summoning the mettle to voice his wish despite the fear of rejection, "I'd like to escort ye back to Riverview."

"But it's out of your way."

"That matters not," he said. "What matters is that here, and now, ye're my wife, and I'm glad of it. I wish to escort my wife home."

She blinked, the color of her eyes deepening, and the flicker of rejection in them threatened to cleave his heart in too.

"Please dinnae deny me, Mia," he whispered, his voice catching.

After a pause, she nodded.

"Very well, husband," she whispered. "You may escort me home."

The flare of joy in his heart was tempered by the realization of what it signified...

...that he was in danger of falling in love with his wife.

CHAPTER TWENTY-THREE

RIVERVIEW COTTAGE CAME into view and Mia froze as she saw movement inside. Had whoever ransacked her home returned for more?

Hamish took her hand. "There's nothing to fear, lass. It's only Lachlan."

"How do you know?"

"H-he had a mind to visit ye."

The front door and opened and Lachlan appeared. "Ma'am," he said, before bowing to Hamish. "Master Hamish."

"Is there anything I can help you with, Lachlan?" Mia said.

The young man shook his head. "No, thank ye, ma'am. Master Hamish, there was no trouble. Maisie came with a basketful of nettles—we've washed them and left them drying on the kitchen table. I kept the fire going, as ye can see, and I went outside regular to check the woods, like ye said."

"Hamish?" Mia said. "What's been going on?"

"Master Hamish asked me to watch over the cottage for ye, seein' as ye'd had some trouble," Lachlan said, despite Hamish's frowning at him.

"That's enough, lad," Hamish growled. "Be off with ye, now. I'm sure Brodie's needing a hand with the horses."

The young man glanced at Mia, then nodded and set off. She turned to Hamish to see him smiling, a faint color on his cheeks.

He set her basket on the table in the parlor. "It was the least I could do," he said, "after..."

"After I accused you of ransacking my home?"

"Yer home will be safe now, lass, I assure ye."

"So you know who's responsible?"

He let out a sigh. "It's like ye said, *I'm* the one responsible because I'm the laird. But I've sent a message to every man and woman at Glenblath to tell them to leave ye be or face retribution. They'll listen to me."

"Will they?"

"Loyalty to the laird runs deep in the Highlands. Anyone—man, boy, or woman—disobeying their laird forfeits their right to live on his land."

His hand still on the handle of the basket, Hamish dipped his head. When he lifted it again, she saw regret in his eyes.

"I ought to have spoken to them before, lass."

"About what?"

"Had I told everyone, from the moment ye arrived, that ye were my wife and they must respect ye as such, this wouldnae have happened. Instead, I..." He shook his head. "Will ye forgive a man for behaving like a stag's arse? I may not have treated ye with the respect ye deserve—and as such, ye'll be well rid of me when the time comes. The least I can do before ye leave us is ensure that ye're safe."

She reached for the basket. Their hands touched, and she caught her breath at the fizz in her stomach. Then he released the basket and watched while she took it into the kitchen and placed it beside the pile of nettles.

"What must man do to be offered a cup of tea?"

Mia turned to see him smiling at her. "Would you like a cup of tea, Hamish?"

"Why, that's most gracious of you, fair lady," he said, in what Mia could only assume was an attempt at an English accent.

She suppressed a laugh as she filled the kettle and set it over the fire, then she took one of the chairs beside the fire and gestured to the other.

"Ha!" he said, taking a seat. "I knew I'd get ye to smile. Will I pass for an English gentleman?"

"No."

His smile disappeared and she placed a hand on his arm.

"I meant no disrespect," she said. "English gentlemen care only for a pretty face, a title, and a dowry. Whereas you…"

"Whereas I," he said, taking his hand, "only care for a dowry." He shook his head. "What must ye think of me?"

"I think you're very kind to walk me home."

Mia glanced at his hand, where fresh callouses adorned the skin of his fingers.

"You're hurt," she said, rising. "I've something that would ease the soreness in your skin."

She approached the shelves and picked up the jar of calendula salve, then she uncorked the jar and held it out.

"Smell it—it's a pleasant aroma."

He sniffed at the contents. "Is that what ye use on Ma? It disnae smell the same."

"No," she said, taking down another jar and uncorking it. "I use this for your mother."

He leaned over and inhaled, then jerked back, his eyes widening. "Devil's ballocks! What was *that*?"

"Do you not like it?"

He sniffed, more tentatively. "It's not unpleasant," he said, "but it's like nothing I've ever known."

"What is it like?"

"Warmth," he said. "And…freshness."

"Anything else?"

"I dinnae know how to say it without giving offense—but it reminds me of Mrs. McBride's mutton stew."

She smiled. "Does Mrs. McBride put rosemary in her stew?"

"Devil take me if I know, lass, but I think she has some in her garden."

"And it's the very same garden from which she permitted me to take a few sprigs," Mia said, corking the jar. "The other thing you can smell is the ginger root."

"The *what?*"

"Don't you recall the ginger that Dr. McIver sent me?"

She caught a flash of resentment in his eyes before the smile returned. "And ye asked him to send it to help Ma?"

She nodded. "The ginger has a warming property that soothes the skin, and the rosemary alleviates aching muscles. I use it when I'm giving your mother a massage."

He nodded. "Ma mentioned it—she said she's never felt such relief from the aches in her bones."

"She's very kind."

"No," he said. "*Ye're* the one who's kind. I wonder if…" He hesitated, his color rising. "I wonder if ye might show me what ye do with it?"

"Do you have an ache that needs soothing?"

His eyes flared with hunger.

"Aye," he whispered. "I have an ache, lass."

He rose and curled his fingers around hers.

"A-an ache?" she said, aware of the tightness in her voice. "Where?"

"I have several," he whispered, "but the one I'll tell ye about is in my back."

"And…have you been doing anything in particular to result in an ache in your back?"

"Chopping wood."

"Chopping wood?" She glanced at the fire. "Like the wood that heats my home? The logs that form the pile in my log store that never seems to decrease, no matter how many fires I light?"

His mouth twitched into a smile, and Mia's heart swelled at the shyness in his eyes.

"Would ye ease the ache for me, Mia?"

"Gladly." She gestured to the chair. "Turn so that your back is facing me, and…would you mind if I removed your shirt?"

"Not at all, lass."

He turned until his back faced her, his legs spread around the back of the chair. Then he shrugged off his jacket and unlaced his shirt. Mia's breath hitched at the first glimpse of skin. Then he lifted the shirt farther until, finally, he was naked from the waist up.

Sweet heaven! His body was more magnificent than she could have believed. As her gaze followed the curvature of his spine, from his neck to the base, she could see the planes of muscles toned through years of hard work, strong and sharp, as if he had been carved from marble. He was no gentleman—his frame lacked the athleticism of the Society fops who spent their time in idle indolence, indulging in the occasional promenade in the park or a ride on horseback. Instead, he was a savage, roughened through years of toil—a man who had no need to utter the niceties of London Society to get what he wanted because he simply took it.

Like a stag claiming the female during a rut.

Mia flicked her tongue out and ran it along her lower lip to stem the swell of hunger. Then she heard a soft laugh and looked up to see his gaze fixed on her.

"Like what ye see, lass?"

He turned, and she whimpered as his chest came to view in all its magnificent, primal glory.

Surely it was a sin for a man's body to be so…

So *beautiful.*

A slow smile curved his lips. "I dinnae ken if it's me, lass, but the air in here has grown hot all of a sudden."

His tongue flicked out and he licked his lips, and Mia let out a squeak as an unfathomable pulse throbbed inside her center. She shifted her legs to quell the rising ache and his eyes darkened, as if he recognized the wicked sensations in her body.

Mia curled her fingers around the jar.

"P-please lean forward," she said, aware of the tremor in her voice. "Relax over the back of the chair as much as possible, then I can begin."

"It's been a while since a woman asked me to lean over the

back of a chair."

Though she couldn't fathom his meaning, its wickedness was plain, given the mischief glowing in his eyes. Then he nodded.

"Forgive me, lass. I dinnae mean to tease ye."

He leaned over the chair, his back muscles rippling with the movement. Mia dipped her fingers into the jar and rubbed her hands together to spread the salve over her palms, relishing the scent of ginger and rosemary.

She placed her hands on his shoulders and he drew in a sharp breath.

"Hamish, are you well?"

"Aye, lass. I like having yer hands on my body."

He was right. The air had grown hot. But now was not the time to give in to sensations that she didn't—and might never—understand. Her duty was to take care of her patient.

And what a magnificent patient he is!

She let her hands glide along his skin, leaving a glistening trail of salve, feeling with her fingertips along each muscle, each tendon, as she searched for the telltale tautness.

As she reached his lower back, the tension in his muscles changed and she met a hard knot.

"Just relax," she said. "Let me know if it hurts."

He shook, and she froze.

Was he in pain?

Then he let out a chuckle.

"Is something amusing?" she said.

"Och, no, lass. It's just, in my experience, it's the man who tells the woman to relax and let him know if it hurts."

The heat in her cheeks increased. Diverting her mind from the wickedly delicious sensations in her body, Mia continued to massage his lower back, running her hands along the taut muscles until they began to soften and relax.

Then he let out a low growl—like the deep purr of a satisfied lion.

"Are you well?" she said.

"Och, lass, what ye're doing to me…! It's fit to make even a stone statue spend with want."

She stilled.

"N-no," he growled, his body vibrating beneath her hands. "Dinnae stop."

He curled his fingers over the back of the chair, and his knuckles whitened as Mia slid her fingers across his back. She blushed at the tiny noises of pleasure that escaped his lips as she continued to work on his muscles, increasing the pressure where they were the most knotted. At length, the tension eased and his murmurs of pleasure faded to a deep sigh. By the time Mia had wiped her hands of the salve, he had slumped over the chair, eyes closed, lips curved in a smile of satisfaction.

She placed her palm between his shoulder blades.

"Mmm…" he murmured, his chest expanding and contracting in a deep sigh. Then he sat up and yawned, stretching his arms out before he turned to face her.

"Did I ease the ache?" she said.

"Not really, lass," he replied, his voice a low rumble. "The ache in my bones has long gone, but I now suffer another ache."

"Where?" she asked, reaching for the jar of salve.

He shook his head and placed a hand over his heart.

"Here," he said, "though it may take more than yer salve to ease it. But there's one thing ye can do for me."

"Which is?"

Uncertainty darkened his eyes. "Perhaps it's wrong of me to ask."

Emboldened by his humility, she curled her fingers around his and smiled.

"Did you not say that I was your wife—for the moment, at least? If I recall, I pledged to obey, and while I trust you'd grant me the power of refusal if I deem any request you make to be unreasonable, I would also hope that I can trust you not to make such a request."

His eyelids fluttered, and Mia's heart ached at the gentle plea in his eyes.

"Then I ask…" He nodded to the jar of salve. "I only wish to ask…that ye permit me to return the favor."

"Th-the favor?"

"Aye." He pulled her close. "I'm sure ye have an ache in need of easing, and I should very much like to place my hands on yer skin to ease that ache."

He smiled at her low gasp.

"Are ye consenting, lass, and respecting yer man's wishes to tend to his woman?"

His woman…

How could such words, that spoke of base possessiveness, send such a thread of heat through her body?

"I see ye like my turn of phrase, lass."

He rose, his body glistening with salve. The firelight cast sharp shadows across his chest muscles, which were nestled together in pairs, and Mia's gaze wandered over them, taking in the soft, downy hair that grew thicker lower down. She suppressed a cry of disappointment as the view was rudely and cruelly curtailed by the belt at his waist, below which he bulged against his plaid.

"Perhaps ye like what ye see," he said.

Mia blinked, her cheeks warming with shame as she focused her gaze on the broad chest in front of her. Then he caught her chin with his fingertips and gently tilted her head until their eyes met.

"Do ye fear that I'd not be gentle with ye?"

"N-no, Hamish, I…"

"Do ye trust me, lass?" he whispered, his breath warm against her skin.

She lowered her gaze to his lips, then nodded.

"I do."

Her words were an echo from the day she'd uttered her vows to a stranger barely visible behind her shroud. But, unlike that day, when she had surrendered to her demise, he invited her to surrender to…

To what? Pleasure?

A shiver coursed through her at the notion of…*pleasure*. Not just the innocent enjoyment she took from a walk in the sunshine, a lungful of fresh air, or having completed a worthy task such as making a salve. No, the pleasure he promised was dark, sinful, lacking in chasteness.

But what was the harm in a simple massage?

He guided her to the chair and she sat, leaning against the back.

"Do ye not sit as I did, facing the back of the chair?" Hamish said.

"My ache is in my shoulders, not my lower back, therefore there is no need."

"Yer shoulders, aye?"

He moved behind her, and an uncomfortable heat bloomed in her body at the anticipation of his touch. When he placed a hand on her shoulder, she startled and he let out a soft chuckle, caressing the underside of her chin with his knuckle.

"Och, lass, there's no need to be as skittish as an untamed filly—or perhaps ye need to be tamed."

His words sent a deep curl through her belly, and she squeezed her thighs together.

"Close yer eyes, lass, while ye enjoy my touch," he whispered.

Suppressing a whimper, she obeyed, then relaxed against the back of the chair.

"There's my good lass."

She heard him exhale, slowly, then he tugged at the neckline of her gown, lowering it until her shoulders were exposed. When he next placed his hands on her shoulders, she suppressed a gasp at the prick of pleasure at his touch. He squeezed, gently, then ran the tips of his thumbs along her skin, the movement slick with salve, yet the little spikes of friction from his callouses ignited a fire in her belly. Though his touch soothed the tautness in her shoulders, elsewhere in her body, strange, unfathomable tensions began to swell.

An ache sparked inside her center as he continued to rub with circular motions, each time deepening his touch. No novice was he. Unlike Mia's first attempt at a massage, when Dr. McIver had scolded her timidity and instructed her to press harder than she dared, Hamish took hold of her boldly, with a possessiveness that bordered on indecency.

A faint mewl escaped her lips.

"Do ye take delight at the touch of my hands?"

"Mmm…" she murmured, tilting her head back.

He continued to caress her, each hand making a gentle, sweeping motion, soothing her shoulders, then moving across her collarbone. Then he slid his palms along her throat until his fingers met the neckline of her gown, where her breasts, warm and heavy, seemed to strain against the fabric.

When his fingertips touched the laces at the front of her gown, she caught her breath as the fire in her belly flared. He leaned over her, and strands of his hair tickled the skin of her forehead before he placed a light kiss between her brows.

His fingers stilled against the knot in the laces, and remained there for several heartbeats. Then, with a swell in her soul, she understood.

He was awaiting her consent.

She nodded—an almost imperceptible gesture, but he must have recognized it for what it was. With a delicate touch that belied his huge frame, he unlaced the front of her gown and slid his palms over the soft skin of her breasts. The fire ignited once more as the warmth from the salve penetrated her sensitive skin while the scent of ginger filled the air, mingling with the aroma of rosemary and something else—a deep scent, sharp and sweet, with top notes of pleasure and base notes of wickedness.

He cupped a breast. "Och, lass—with the softest flesh in my hands, and the sweetest scent known to man in my nostrils, mayhap I've been transported to heaven."

Her skin tightened at his voice, which rasped like gravel. Then he ran the tip of his thumb over a nipple, which sent a bolt of fire through her body.

"Oh!" She opened her eyes to see him looking over her, his head framed by a halo of hair that glowed in the firelight like a sunset. His eyes were dark—the pupils dilated so they were almost black.

"Do ye like my hands on ye, lass?"

"Y-yes," she said, her body responding to his voice as she leaned into his touch. "Oh…" She drew in a lungful of air, the heady perfume thickening and swirling in her mind.

Oh, yes…

He dipped his head and brushed his lips against her cheek. Though she tilted her head up, offering her lips, he merely smiled, and she grimaced in frustration.

"Och, lass, will ye not await yer pleasure with patience?"

Boneless and pliant, she relaxed in the chair, acknowledging his mastery over her body.

"I would have ye give yer consent, lass, for I wouldnae want to—"

"You have it," she said, the urgency in her body overpowering her mind.

His eyes flared, savage hunger in them.

"Then close yer eyes, lass."

She obeyed, relishing the heightening of her other senses, the exotic cocktail of aromas in the air, the warmth of the fire on her skin, the heat swelling in her center and…

…and—oh my!—the roughness of the callouses on his hands was exquisite as he swept his palms over her breasts once more, pausing to flick her nipples and chuckling softly at her sharp gasp of pleasure. Then he shifted his palms lower, caressing her belly until his fingertips reached the curls at the juncture of her thighs, where a wicked dampness had begun to form.

Surely he wasn't going to touch her…*there*? What purpose would a man have to—

"Oh!" A burst of heat ignited in her center as he slipped his fingers inside her curls. She clamped her legs together, trapping his hand, ashamed to reveal the moisture that pooled in a place so intimate that it must be the very worst of sins to touch.

"Och, lass—did I not ask ye to trust me?" he whispered.

"B-but I—"

"Shh… Trust yer man."

My man…

Swallowing her shame, Mia fought to control the tremors coursing through her body as her heart hammered against her chest.

"There's my good lass."

What the devil was happening? The moisture in her center surged at his praise, and his mouth curved against her cheek as if he recognized it for what it was, though she remained ignorant of its meaning. But a thrill deep inside her body spoke of the promise of pleasure…if she were willing to surrender to it.

He brushed his lips against hers, then nuzzled her with the tip of his nose.

"Do ye trust me?"

"Y-yes…"

At the gentle insistence of his hand, she parted her thighs and inhaled as he dipped his fingers into her curls.

"Oh… Sweet lass, ye're as ready and willing as a man could ever hope for his woman to be."

"R-ready?" she whimpered. "I-I don't—Oh!"

He ran a fingertip across her flesh. Thick heat swelled at his touch, and she tilted her hips, chasing the pleasure. She surrendered to the needs of her body, which urged him on, willing him to delve deeper, to caress her with greater fervor. And, as if he knew what her body desired, he obliged, whispering words of praise while soft nickers of pleasure escaped her lips. When she gripped the sides of the chair and thrust her hips upward, a primal growl filled the air—that of the stag laying claim to his mate.

Then, with a sharp exhalation, he slipped his finger inside her and the world shattered. An explosion of pleasure rippled through Mia's body in wicked waves that battered her with the relentlessness of a stormy sea.

"Hamish!" she cried. "What's happ…" Her voice died as her body was gripped by another wave. "I-I don't know—Ahh!"

The wave crested and her body disintegrated. He continued to caress her while she shifted her legs, devouring the pleasure. Then, at last, the swell subsided, leaving her languorous and replete. When she opened her eyes, she saw him smiling at her, delight gleaming in those dark-green orbs. Then he lifted his hand, which glistened in the firelight, and slipped it into his mouth.

Sweet heaven! How *depraved* could a man be? Yet she couldn't deny the secret thrill in her own wicked little soul at the notion that her body had given him pleasure in return.

But a flare of want still glowed in his eyes, speaking of needs unmet. She turned to face him, and her cheeks warmed at the bulge between his thighs. She reached for it, then hesitated.

"Ye may touch him, lass," he said, his voice hoarse. "He'll give ye greater pleasure than ye can imagine."

"Y-you mean, even greater than…?" She gestured to her body, and he smiled.

"Aye, lass. I could have ye screaming my name so loud that the McTavishes will hear ye in the glen beyond the mountain, and ye'll come undone so hard that ye'll not be able to walk for a fortnight."

Wicked temptation urged her to take him.

Then she glanced up and caught sight of the jars on the shelves.

Medicine—that was where her future lay. Not as a wife destined to be cast aside. And ruination would shatter that future, for who'd pay a whore for services as a doctor?

The spell broken, Mia pulled the front of her gown together and fumbled at the laces to secure it.

She glanced up at him. Regret had replaced the desire in his eyes.

Mia forced a smile. "Thank you, Hamish," she said.

"What for, lass?"

"For not ruining me. I know enough of anatomy to understand that you have left me intact. Which is fortunate, given our plans to annul our marriage."

"Aye, lass," he said, his voice strained. "Most fortunate."

The tendons in his neck seemed to protrude as he gritted his teeth.

"If ye have no further need of me, I'll leave ye be," he said. "But if ye get any further trouble, let me know."

"I will."

She offered her hand, and he stared at it for a heartbeat, then shook it—as if they had just engaged in a business transaction. Then he withdrew his hand and almost fled out of the parlor, mumbling his apology as he let himself outside, closing the front door behind him.

Mia approached the door, then paused as she heard a long, low groan.

Was he in pain? She shifted to the window and drew back the curtain, peering outside, and saw him silhouetted against the moonlit reflections in the river, his body hunched. She caught movement, his arm at his groin, moving back and forth in a repetitive motion that increased in pace until he let out a hoarse cry and bent over. He remained still for a while before righting himself and wiping his hand on his plaid. Then he lifted his head and glanced toward the cottage.

Ashamed at the prospect of being caught witnessing such an...*intimate* activity, Mia shrank back, her cheeks on fire.

By the time she'd composed herself and looked out of the window again, he was gone.

CHAPTER TWENTY-FOUR

THE FOLLOWING WEEK, Mia attended the school again and, with the teacher's permission, described the process of the smallpox vaccination. A letter had arrived from a Dr. Nimmo in Glasgow that morning, expressing his delight at being able to grant a favor to his friend and colleague Dr. McIver and administer the vaccine. In fact, in his letter the doctor said that he *would be more than willing to supervise while you administer it yourself, given Dr. McIver's assurances that you're a capable young woman with bright prospects of becoming a doctor.* Her pride at such praise of her abilities buoyed her joy, and she'd almost skipped to the school.

Joy had been absent since Hamish escorted her home a week ago. The glow of pleasure at his touch had lasted only moments after he'd left, dissolving into the ashes of shame.

On her return to Riverview Cottage, Mia paused as she caught sight of a flash of red hair between the trees.

Was it him?

Her cheeks warmed with a cocktail of desire and shame. But what did she have to feel shame for? She'd taken nothing but a small scrap of pleasure at the touch of his hand that had left her intact in body, if not in mind. She was still a respectable woman—a maiden—with the prospect of becoming a doctor, facilitated by a true friend and his colleague. Let *him* feel shame for having taken advantage of her need, and for the base act he'd committed outside her window…

She caught her breath at the memory—the grunts of pleasure that he'd taken at his own hand because he would not take pleasure from her. Then she chastised herself. Why would he take pleasure from the wife he didn't want?

The path turned a corner, and Mia's visitor came into view. But it wasn't the man she called husband. Instead, she saw the pale face and vivid green eyes of Hamish's sister.

Surely Iona hadn't been responsible for ransacking the cottage before? But why else would she be here with such guilt in her eyes?

The young woman clasped her hands together and her gaze darted about as if, like a deer on the moor, she sensed a predator.

"Iona, how pleasant you're come to visit," Mia said with a smile. "Is there anything you need?"

The girl frowned and tilted her head to one side, as if she were trying to make Mia out.

"I'm not here to visit ye," she said at last.

"Nevertheless, I find you near my door," Mia replied. "Perhaps you wandered here by mistake. I'm always getting lost about the place, as it's so expansive."

"What a foolish thing to say!" Iona said. "I never get lost. I've lived here all my life. Ye keep getting lost because ye're an outsider."

"That I am," Mia said. "But often when I'm deep in contemplation, my mind can drift into the unknown, and before I realize it, I'm no longer on the path I intended." She approached the front door, her back to the girl. "You're welcome to something to eat. I've some bread and cheese—enough to share."

"I dinnae want anything from ye."

"You must suit yourself, of course. The cheese was a gift from Mrs. McBride—but the bread I baked myself, so you may wish to refuse that."

Leaving the front door open, Mia entered the parlor and braced herself for evidence of tampering. But the room was untouched, the shelves neatly stacked and her unfinished mending on the table in the same attitude she'd left it that morning. She took her basket into the kitchen then inspected the rest of the cottage, but there were no signs of interference. When she returned to the parlor, she saw Iona standing in the center of the room, her gaze wandering over the shelves and their contents.

Mia motioned to a chair, but the girl made no move to sit, so Mia took the tinderbox from the mantelshelf and set about lighting the fire she'd laid that morning. When the first flames began to curl around the logs, she turned and saw that Iona had taken a chair and was rocking back and forth, her eyes gleaming in the firelight.

"Do ye think I did it?" she said, gesturing to the shelves.

Mia raised her eyebrows.

"B-breaking yer things," Iona added. "Hamish threatened to beat me. But not out of any liking for *ye*."

Mia exited the parlor to fill a pot with water, then returned and suspended it over the fire, aware of the girl's gaze on her. Then she set about preparing her luncheon, placing the food on the table together with two plates and two cups.

Iona watched as Mia settled herself in the chair at the other side of the fireplace and waited. After a pause, she spoke again.

"He's very strict."

"His duty as laird is to be strict," Mia replied.

"Aye, but I cannae—" Iona broke off and sighed.

"Your brother has to maintain the safety and order of the household to protect those who are dependent on him," Mia said. "He rarely has the luxury of indulgence."

"Is that how it must be?"

"It's how it *is*," Mia said. "It doesn't mean that he's incapable of love—only that he cannot show it in a manner that gives immediate comfort. Brothers, fathers, and…husbands don't love any less merely because they cannot show it. So the responsibility of giving comfort and counsel often falls to mothers and sisters."

"I have no sisters, and I cannae tell Ma what…" Iona shook

her head and the sneer returned to her lips. "Ye're talking nonsense," she said. "Sassenach nonsense."

Mia let out a laugh. "I suspect I am, seeing as I have no father or mother living, nor have ever had siblings. As to a husband"—she paused to maintain her composure—"in every sense that matters, I don't have a husband either. Now, how's that water coming along?" She leaned over the pot. "Only a few minutes more, then we can have tea."

"I dinnae want *tea*."

"Well, I do," Mia said crisply. "I might as well make two cups as one."

Iona said nothing to that. As the first hiss of steam rose from the pot, she rose and approached the shelves, her gaze wandering over every jar, every pot, as if searching for something.

"In answer to your question," Mia said, "no. I don't."

"Ye dinnae what?"

"I don't think you were the one who broke my things."

"Why not?"

"You may be an angry young woman—even unhappy…" Mia began.

"I'm not unhappy."

"But you're not cruel, or unkind."

"I've called ye a pockmarked hure."

"Excepting your mother and a handful of others, who in the whole of Glenblath can say they've not called me such?" Mia replied. "Does that mean every soul here is cruel? There's a difference between saying something unkind and *being* unkind. You're clever enough to understand that."

"Are ye trying to flatter me?" Iona asked.

"What would be the point of that? An advantage of having a face like mine is that I'm not bound by the need to flatter others. An ogre has the freedom to speak the truth without fear of being judged, given that she's already judged by all she meets."

"Ye're not an ogre."

Iona's words were so soft, Mia could have believed she'd

imagined them.

Then Iona gestured to the jars and bottles. "Are ye as clever as ye say in treating ailments?"

"I know a little about the healing properties of different herbs."

The curiosity in the girl's expression intensified. Was she perhaps suffering from something that might explain the unhappiness that always sat in the depths of her eyes?

Mia indicated the calendula salve. "This helps to prevent putrefaction of wounds. I used it on Brodie after he cut his arm. And"—she pointed to the jar containing the strips of willow bark—"this was to ease his pain."

Iona's eyes widened. "B-Brodie? Was he hurt?"

"He was in a lot of pain when he came to me, but I've never known a young man to be so brave when I tended to him."

"How brave?"

"As brave as any soldier," Mia said. "I once assisted Dr. McIver in the removal of a soldier's leg after he'd fought at Waterloo. Captain Broom, his name was. The bravest man I'd met—until Brodie."

"Was Brodie in danger of…"

Iona's throat bobbed as she swallowed. Mia placed a hand on the young woman's arm, but Iona jerked free.

"Brodie's injury was severe because it had been left to fester," Mia said. "But it's cured now. I've used the salve for smaller injuries also, such as Evie MacLennan when she grazed her arm, and Rory when he cut his hand."

"Do ye have anything to *prevent* sickness or injury?"

"To prevent injury, no, other than counsel to take care," Mia said. "But sickness—if you're referring to the vaccination scheme, I'll be able to prevent the onset of smallpox."

"And…other ailments?"

"Such as?"

"Och, I dinnae ken." Iona shrugged. "Maisie comes here a lot, and everyone knows a hure needs medicine to prevent her from getting"—she brushed a hand over her belly—"f-from getting caught."

Her blush deepened as Mia met her gaze.

"Some doctors claim to have medicines to prevent a pregnancy," Mia said, "but I'm not aware of anything that's been proven by credible research."

"A-and"—Iona lowered her gaze and clasped her hands together—"if it's too…too…"

"Too late to prevent, for it has already occurred?"

Iona nodded.

"Some doctors claim to have medicines to put an end to…" Mia paused, unwilling to voice such a claim. "But the danger is such that I wouldn't recommend their usage. I could never advocate such suffering."

The girl whimpered. "S-suffering?"

Mia nodded. "More often than not, taking such medicines results in death. I've seen young women, desperate to save themselves from falling into ruin, suffer agonizing deaths while the men who brought about that ruination live their lives unencumbered. I wouldn't wish such a fate on anyone—not a friend, a sister, nor even a young girl who professes hatred for me."

Iona placed both hands on her belly, but Mia focused her attention on the jars in front of her.

"There are medicines to give a woman comfort in her confinement," she said. "I hadn't expected to remain at Glenblath long enough to necessitate their use, but I can prepare some and leave them behind for when I'm gone."

"Ye wouldnae take them with ye?"

"Not if anyone here was in need of it."

Mia plucked a jar from the shelf, formed of clear glass, containing the remnants of a knobbly root covered in silvery skin.

"Do you know what this is?"

Iona shook her head.

"It's ginger root," Mia said. "You'll not find it growing hereabouts. I was sent this."

"What do ye use it for?"

"When crushed, the root can be used to make a salve that warms the skin and eases pain—I use it on your mother. But it has other uses. For example, when a slice is steeped in water to make a tea, it can soothe the sickness that women experience in pregnancy." Iona frowned, and Mia continued. "Of course, anyone can drink it—the taste is not unpleasant. I can use it for our tea today if you'd like to try it—purely for the taste, of course."

"For the taste only?" Iona said.

Mia nodded and, when the girl made no objection, cut two slices from the root, placed one in each cup, then poured hot water over them.

"If you like the taste, I'll give you some to take back to the castle." She cut several more slices and placed them on the table.

"Och, no!" Iona cried, eyeing the small pile. "I cannae have anyone finding out—especially not Hamish."

Mia began to reach for Iona's hand, then withdrew. Behind the veneer of resolve in the girl's eyes, Mia saw a lost soul. But Iona would never trust her if she forced apart that resolve. Instead, Mia relaxed back in her chair and sipped her tea.

"Perhaps you should speak to your brother."

"Och, no, he'd be so angry. I fear he'd give me a beating, and—" Iona broke off, closing her eyes. When they opened again, the resolve had once more settled in place.

"I meant about the vaccination program," Mia said. "I'll be very busy when it takes place, even with Maisie's help, and would welcome another pair of hands. Hamish might like it if you—"

"No, he wouldnae," Iona said. "He disnae think I can do anything. Besides"—she lifted her lip in the familiar sneer—"I'm a laird's daughter and shouldn't be expected to do work best suited to servants."

"I understand," Mia said. "But I'd still counsel you to talk to him. Tell him how you're...how unwell you're feeling. He's a kind man and would want to help you."

"He's not kind," Iona replied. "How can ye say so when he cannae wait to send ye away so that he can take a richer and prettier bride?"

A tear splashed onto Iona's cheek.

"I-I must be going," she said. "He'll be angry if I'm not back soon."

"Of course," Mia said. "Thank you for visiting me. It's been a pleasure."

Iona opened her mouth to reply and Mia braced herself for another insult, but she merely mumbled her thanks, then fled. Mia watched the girl's thin frame toil along the path, then she returned to the parlor and cut herself a slice of bread. As she cast her gaze over the table, she noticed that the slices of ginger had gone.

CHAPTER TWENTY-FIVE

THE DOOR TO Hamish's study opened and Brodie appeared.

"Master Hamish, Her Ladyship's asking whether ye wish to join her and Mistress Euphramia, and"—the lad colored—"Miss Maisie."

Hamish suppressed a smile. Brodie had yet to discover what his cock was for. To him, a sensual creature such as Maisie, with her experience of cocks, and men, of all shapes and sizes was a goddess to be both desired and feared.

Two words that also described Maisie's fellow guest.

Mia.

Since Hamish had last seen her—when he'd almost rutted her over that chair in her cottage—Mia had tortured his mind, inviting him in his dreams to bury himself between those hot, damp curls. Each morning he'd woken with a cockstand fit to burst and fisted his pleasure into his bedsheets just like he had fisted himself on her doorstep, shame engulfing him at his inability to step more than five yards away from her door without spending.

How disgusted she must be! He'd behaved like a beast.

Was it because she was forbidden to him? Not by the law, nor the Almighty—but forbidden by his conscience. It was easy to tell his rational self that she was the last woman he wanted for a wife. But the unconscious self—his soul—knew different. In truth, he'd almost forgotten that her face was pockmarked. Instead, he saw only the soft brown curls with a glimmer of chestnut when they caught the sunlight, that pert little nose, the stubborn mouth that spoke of strength of character, and those brilliant hazel eyes that glimmered with a sharp intelligence, then softened with kindness before they darkened with desire.

But if he saw her now, those eyes would only look at him with disgust.

He was the scarred one, with ugly marks on his soul. And he'd almost ruined her out of nothing more than a need for base gratification.

But what pleasure that gratification would have brought!

"Be silent," he spat out through gritted teeth, as the voice of temptation whispered in his ear.

"Master Hamish?"

He glanced up to see Brodie looking at him.

"What shall I tell Her Ladyship?"

"Nothing," Hamish said. "I'll join her directly."

He rose and made his way to his mother's chambers, where he found her sitting beside the fireplace as usual and Monarch—the treacherous cur—curled up at her feet. Her guests rose on his arrival. But the dog, other than opening a single yellow eye then closing it again, didn't deign to acknowledge his presence.

Unable to meet his wife's gaze, Hamish first looked at Maisie, whose eyes betrayed a discomfort to rival his own. Though she had warmed Hamish's bed in the past, Maisie had never yet been invited into Ma's chambers. What laird's wife would be seen entertaining the local whore?

"M-Master Hamish," Maisie stammered, "forgive me for being here. I didnae intend—"

"Now, my dear, there's no need for *that*," Hamish's mother said. "Ye're here on business as my guest, is she not, Mia?"

Hamish let his gaze drift toward his wife, expecting contempt, but all he saw was an easy, open smile.

She inclined her head. "Maisie and I have you to thank, Hamish, for agreeing to the use of your carriage for our journey."

"J-journey?" he said, a knot of apprehension in his stomach. "Ye're leaving Glenblath already?"

"Mia's going to Glasgow," his mother said. "She's been telling us all about the vaccination process. It sounds fascinating, if not a little daunting. It almost put me off my tea."

"I'm sorry for that, Eilidh," Mia said, resuming her seat and gesturing for Maisie to do likewise.

"Och, ye needn't worry, lass. I've given birth to two children"—Ma eyed Hamish with a wry smile—"one of whom was a great, lumbering giant of a lad who fair split me in two. I can weather a description of a little bloodletting. Maisie's the brave one, to take the first cut."

"Cut?"

Hamish glanced at Maisie. Perhaps her discomfort was to do with what was to happen to her in Glasgow.

Ma let out a laugh. "Och, *men*! They think us the weaker sex, yet they'll pass out at the first sight of blood. Did yer Dr. Nimmo administer the vaccine without crying for his ma? As for yer Dr. McIver, I cannae believe that he was able to saw a man's leg off and retain his wits afterward."

"Saw a man's leg off?" Hamish said. "Devil's ballocks, what does the vaccination process entail?"

Maisie giggled and Mia turned away to hide her smile.

"Och, dinnae be a fool, lad," Ma said. "And ye're making my chamber look untidy standing there. Pour yerself a cup of tea and sit, for the love of the Almighty, or I'll turn ye out."

Hamish did as he was bidden. It was often easier to obey Ma without question when she was in a determined frame of mind.

"Yer limbs are safe, Hamish," she said, once he'd sat. "But it's good to know that Mia here could perform surgery if needed, with a stout heart and skilled hands."

"Eilidh…" Mia began, but Ma raised her hand.

"Iona told me all about it, lass."

"Iona?" Hamish said. "What does *she* know?"

"A great deal," Ma said. "I'll thank ye not to speak badly of yer sister. She's been making friends with Mia, hasn't she, lass?"

"Well…" Discomfort filled Mia's eyes. "She asked me a little about medicine and some of the operations I've assisted with."

Hamish shook his head. "Iona wouldnae hold out the hand of friendship unless she wanted to bite it off ye."

"Och, ye're too harsh on the lass," Ma said.

"Ye must admit, Ma, she's been too wild of late. I…"

Hamish's voice trailed away as the door opened and Iona appeared. Her eyes widened as she saw him.

"Come in," Ma said. "Do ye want something?"

"Only to get away from that Brodie. He's been following me about again. I dinnae like it."

"Get in and close the door," Hamish said. "Ye're letting the heat out."

Iona scowled, then Mia rose and offered her hand.

"Why don't you sit next to me?" she said. "I've brought some ginger for your mother to take in her tea. Will you try some?"

Hamish braced himself for an insult, but his sister closed the door and took the seat next to Mia.

"Ginger?" Hamish said. "I thought ye used it for rubbing on…" His cheeks warmed at the memory of smoothing the salve over Mia's body, the soft skin of her breasts with the precious little pearls in the center, the delicately curved stomach, and those welcoming curls hiding the promise of pleasure…

"Ye dinnae look well, brother," Iona sneered. "Is it because ye're taking tea in the same chamber as yer mother, yer sister, yer wife, and yer hure?"

Maisie drew in a sharp breath.

Hamish leaped to his feet, hands fisted, and Iona shrank back, the defiance in her eyes diminishing.

"I thought I'd raised ye to be better than that, child," their mother said quietly. "Ye must always be welcoming to guests."

"What if the guest has no right to be here?" Iona said. "Or if the guest is unkind, or uncivil?"

"It matters not," Mia replied. "If a guest is kind enough to favor us with their company then it's our duty to make them feel welcome—is that not right, Iona?"

Hamish's sister turned to Mia, and the two women stared at each other, as if sharing a silent communication. Then Iona looked away.

"F-forgive me, Maisie," she stammered.

Maisie grinned. "I cannae take offense, Miss Iona. I've heard every insult known to man—and woman. I'm immune to them, as I'll soon be immune to smallpox."

"Ye have my thanks, lass, on behalf of all of us at Glenblath," Ma said, "even if others are incapable of thanking ye properly for taking the first cut."

There that phrase was again. "What are ye talking of—*the first cut?*" Hamish said.

Ma raised her eyebrows at Mia. "Tell him about the vaccine, lass."

"The vaccine's administered into the blood," Mia said. "A cut is made, usually in the patient's arm. Then a small amount of…fluid is dabbed into the cut."

"Fluid?" Hamish swallowed the ripple of nausea in his throat.

"Aye," Maisie said, her eyes gleaming. "Pus gathered from sores."

Devil's ballocks! Hamish gripped the back of a chair. He heard a low cry and glanced up to see Iona placing her hand over her mouth. His sister rose and sprinted outside.

"Miss Iona?" a voice said from the passageway. "Are ye well?"

"Devil take ye, Brodie!" Iona cried, then her footsteps faded into the distance.

"Do ye want some air also, Hamish?" Ma said. "Ye're looking a little green."

"Aye," Maisie added, "as green as the mold on Rory's old cheese."

"Is it safe, what ye plan to do, Mia?" Hamish asked.

His wife nodded. "Quite safe, I assure you. Maisie will feel unwell for a day or so—no more than eight and forty hours. Then

I can pass the vaccine around."

"How?"

"By taking the fluid from the sores that arise on Maisie's skin and administering it to the next patient, then the next, and so forth, until it's been passed to everyone. It's like a chain. As soon as the fluid forms, it can be passed to the next patient, but once it clears up, the chain is broken, so I must act quickly. If I can administer the fluid from Maisie's arm to five souls, then each of those five to another five, and so forth, we could have the whole estate protected from smallpox within a fortnight."

Hamish shook his head. "I doubt folk will be willing to be cut."

"It's a small incision and, provided I keep my knife clean, the risk is minimal."

"And if nobody is willing?"

"I hope to persuade them using reason," Mia said. "Or, at the very least, the sight of my face and the opportunity to remove the chances of their suffering the same fate might be sufficient. If not, then there's little I can do."

"When do ye leave for Glasgow?"

"In three days. Dr. Nimmo is expecting us three days after that. We should be back within a fortnight."

"Ye're going unaccompanied?"

"Brodie has agreed to attend us," Mia said. "I may need a second patient to ensure the chain is not broken."

"He's agreed?" Hamish asked.

"He offered," his mother said. "He said he owed Mia a favor after she saved his arm."

"Eilidh, I didn't really save—" Mia began, but Ma interrupted.

"Ye did, lass. When will ye stop talking yerself down? Ye've done so much for us here, and are about to do even more. I dinnae ken what we'll do if ye ever leave us."

Mia colored, then rose to her feet. "Forgive me, I must be going. There's much to do before we leave."

"Can ye stay not for a while more, lass?"

"Forgive me, Eilidh, but I must make up another jar of your ointment before I go—there's not enough left to last you while I'm away."

Mia exited the chamber. Maisie rose too, but Ma caught her hand.

"There's no need for ye to leave, lass. I promised ye a slice of cake."

She gave a pointed look toward Hamish, who followed Mia out. Monarch rose, his claws clicking against the stone floor, to trot at his side.

Hamish caught up with his wife at the main doors. *Heavens!* For a lass, she could shift quickly on those legs of hers when she wanted to.

"Mia."

She froze, then turned. But what could he say to atone for his behavior?

After a pause, he offered his hand. She hesitated at first, then took it.

"I'm sorry," he said.

"What for?"

"Ye must think me a beast."

She smiled, her eyes glowing in the light of the setting sun that streamed through the high, arched window. Then she stooped to scratch the top of Monarch's head. The deerhound let out a soft grunt of pleasure and thumped his tail against Hamish's leg.

"Not all the time," she replied softly. "And no different to any man."

"Am I the same as any man?"

She ran her fingertips over the callouses on his hands.

"I have little experience of men, but from what I've seen, you're as different to the rest of your sex as Monarch here is different to a litter of pugs."

"What—I'm hairy, unkempt, and savage?"

She laughed. "Aye—at least compared to the ninnies of London Society."

"*Aye?*" he said. "Are ye beginning to use our language, like a true Highland lass?"

"A token of speech, nothing more," she said. "A Sassenach can never be a true Highlander—so I've been told."

Iona had said as much to Mia's face.

"Forgive my sister," he said. "I dinnae understand her anymore."

Mia hesitated, and her eyes narrowed, as if she were contemplating something.

"Iona's not a bad person," she eventually said. "Like any soul, she craves freedom."

"How do ye know?"

"We're both women," she said, giving him the indulgent smile a schoolmistress bestows upon a particularly dim-witted child. "You're a man, and as such, will never truly experience the restrictions placed upon our sex. But more than freedom, Iona craves love—yours in particular."

He let out a snort. "Then why does she continually test my patience?"

"She craves your love so much that she tests it—in an attempt to find the limit of your love," Mia said. "She'd rather have your anger than your indifference. But show her that you love her— that she can trust you—and she'll love and trust you in return."

"What must I show *ye?*" he whispered, holding his breath in anticipation of her response.

She met his gaze. Tones of green and blue shimmered in her eyes with flecks of gold and brown, and the world seemed to grow still, dissolving into the air until they were the only two creatures in existence—two souls reaching out across a chasm, linked by an invisible, indelible thread.

Then she blinked and the thread snapped.

"That way, madness lies," she whispered, as if to herself, and moisture gleamed in her eyes.

Then she blinked again and the moisture had gone.

"It matters not," she said, her tone once more that of the businesslike doctor lecturing a belligerent patient. "I'll be leaving soon. We can part as friends and place the memory of any…*indiscretions* into a vault, where they belong, to fade over time, like footprints in the snow that disappear when the snow melts."

The deerhound let out another whine and Mia's smile returned as she stooped, once more, to rub the dog's head.

"Beautiful boy, aren't you?"

Then she straightened, bade Hamish farewell, and left the building, stopping beside the stables to speak to Brodie. The jealousy that had sparked in Hamish's heart when she made a fuss of his dog burst into flame as he caught her laughter while she chatted to the lad.

Hamish leaned on the doorframe, his gaze fixed on the path long after she'd disappeared.

Did she honestly believe that he would forget her as easily as she might forget him?

CHAPTER TWENTY-SIX

M IA HAD TO admit that, even in winter when the cold air rendered her face almost numb, there was no better place in the world than the Highlands. Beinn Blath—Maisie and Rory still laughed at Mia's attempts to pronounce the mountain—stood over the estate like a benevolent sentinel, or a pagan god watching over the people who went about their business, scraping a living from the land.

Unlike London, where they looked bare and forlorn in winter, the trees that clothed the slopes of the mountain had come alive, their solid forms glowing pink in the cold winter light, a splash of color against the backdrop of the landscape dusted by snow and frost.

And the scent! The smoky, woody scent of pine, so unlike the pine forests she'd ventured into in England—it was richer, deeper, more...

More primal.

Mia paused by the river's edge on her return to the cottage, to absorb the music, tilting her head toward the winter sun.

Then she opened her eyes and sighed. Pausing to indulge in her surroundings would only increase the regret that she was to leave. And there was work to do. Over a hundred souls had already given their consent to take part in the vaccination scheme, and she needed to set out a schedule to ensure that the chain did not break. And there was the stew to warm up for luncheon for Evie's visit.

So much to do! She'd never been so occupied.

And she loved it.

Further occupation awaited her in the future, both the immediate, with her departure for Glasgow tomorrow, and thereafter.

Mia heard the crunch of a footstep on frost and turned.

"Who's there?"

The only response was a rush of the breeze in the treetops and the ever-present backdrop of the water.

"Evie, is that you?"

Her call was met with silence, and she unlocked the door, placed her basket on the parlor table, and made her way to the kitchen to fetch a pot. Then she went back outside to fill it from the river. A further crunch of footsteps made her turn, and she called out.

"Is someone there? Do you need help?"

But there was no response. Mia returned to the cottage, set the pot beside the fireplace, and gathered an armful of logs from the basket to lay the fire.

The door slammed behind her and she startled, dropping the logs.

Standing in front of the door was a man.

"Wh-who are you?" Mia stammered.

He stepped forward.

"Murdoch?" Mia said, as his face came into the light, eyes glittering with loathing, lips curled into a sneer.

"Aye."

"I-is Evie unwell? D-do you want me to visit her?"

"My wife's nothing to do with ye, woman. I dinnae want ye to do anything other than leave her be."

"But she—"

"She disnae need a woman such as ye."

"What?" Mia said. "An Englishwoman? Or a pockmarked whore?"

"Witch!" he snarled. "Ye should be whipped for that foul tongue of yers."

"Why?" Mia said, her tone expressing more boldness than she felt. "It's what you call me."

"Ye're a woman and must do as ye're told or face the consequences."

"Is that what you tell your wife?" she said, folding her arms. "Do you make *her* face the consequences of speaking for herself?"

"She's my *wife!*" he roared. "And she's a fool for listening to yer poison. If I were yer husband I'd have ye whipped raw. In fact…"

He paused, and his mouth curled into a cold smile that did more to heighten her fear than his anger.

"I know just what ye need."

He reached for the door, and Mia's stomach churned in horror as she heard the key turn in the lock. Then he advanced. She glanced about, and her gaze fell on a candlestick. She moved toward it, and he lunged forward and grasped her wrist.

"Let me go!" she said. "You're hurting—"

He pulled her hard against his body, then gripped her arms, and she let out a groan as his thick fingers dug into her flesh.

"Meddling hure!" he snarled. "Ye need teaching a lesson."

"And you're the man to do it?" she said. "Is this how you've cowed Evie into submission such that she's too frightened to ask for help when she's unwell? I—Oh!"

He shook her roughly, then pushed her back until she slammed against the wall. She tried to wrench free, but he only gripped her more tightly, causing her to groan in pain.

"Hamish should have turned ye out the day ye darkened Glenblath with yer poisonous ways," he growled. "And now ye're going to spread yer poison across the clan, tricking the foolish into believing that ye're saving us? Just like the witches of old, ye are, and ye need to be stopped."

"I'm trying to help the people here," Mia said.

"Quiet, hag!"

Mia kicked out and connected with his shin. He loosened his grip, enabling her to pull free, then backhanded her across the face. Mia stumbled backward with a scream, her vision blurred with tears of pain.

"Foolish lass!" Murdoch snarled. "There's none to help ye, and many who'll thank me for giving ye a thrashing. Ye're a—"

He broke off as there was a knock at the door.

"Get ye gone!" he cried.

"No!" Mia screamed. "Please—help me!"

The knocking came again, this time harder, then it stopped and Murdoch let out a laugh.

"See?" he said. "We all want ye gone."

"Murdoch, please," she said. "Don't do anything you might regret."

"I'll not regret putting a woman in her place. I only regret I didnae do it sooner. I—"

A splintering crash filled the air as the door burst open. A huge man barreled through the doorway, stumbled on the floor, then righted himself. With a roar, he sprinted toward them. Mia raised her hands to defend herself against further assault, but none came. Instead, Murdoch was pulled off her and thrown to the side.

"How dare ye!" a deep voice bellowed.

Hamish…

His hair gleaming in the fading sunlight, eyes glowering with fury, he advanced on Murdoch. "Take yer filthy hands off my wife!" he roared. "Nobody touches my woman."

"But Hamish, she—"

"Be silent before yer laird! Speak again and I'll have ye banished from Glenblath. Touch my wife again and I'll sever yer hands from yer body then feed them to the swine."

Mia scrambled to her feet and backed away from the two men who were circling each other like stags in rut.

Indignation coursed through her veins. She was no female beast to be fought over and taken by the strongest—not when the man she'd married had no claim to her at all because he'd forsaken her. But she couldn't suppress the primal pulse that swelled low in her belly at the thought of being claimed by a man who, in his flame-haired, broad-chested fury, was bestial, potent, and utterly masculine.

"Ye've been bewitched by a hure, Hamish," Murdoch said. "I'll—"

He broke off as Hamish slammed his fist into his jaw. As Murdoch staggered backward, Hamish caught his hand, then drew out a knife.

"Did ye touch her with this hand, Murdoch?"

The other man nodded, the arrogance in his expression replaced by fear.

"Then this hand is forfeit."

Horror curled in Mia's heart at the determined expression in Hamish's dark eyes.

"I shall not take it today, Murdoch, but henceforth, this hand belongs to me. If it offends me, I'll take it. Do ye understand?"

Murdoch glanced at Mia.

"Ye dinnae have the right to even *look* at her!" Hamish roared. "Or do ye wish to forfeit yer eyes also?"

He grasped Murdoch by the lapels, pushed him toward the door, then tossed him outside as if he weighed no more than a child.

"Begone!" Hamish cried as Murdoch stumbled backward. "If I hear ye've come within sight of this cottage, I'll have ye turned out of Glenblath with one hand less."

He slammed the door then turned to face Mia.

The expression in his eyes changed into an emotion more primal, more intense than the fury it replaced.

Raw, base desire.

He fisted his hands, shaking as if he fought to control the intensity. Then he pulled Mia hard against his body and crushed her mouth with his. A groan of pure need reverberated through him, feeding the desire that swelled deep within Mia. His tongue pressed insistently against her mouth, and as she parted her lips to welcome him, he shuddered, a low growl filling the air—as the dominant stag claimed his mate. He lifted her up and carried her backward until they collided with the chest of drawers. She wrapped her legs around his waist, desperate to ease the ache between her thighs. As if he understood her need, he slipped his hand between them, moving toward the source of her heat.

Mia let out a cry as a fizz of pleasure sparked, and she parted her legs wider to chase the sensation, pressing her center against his fingers. Ignoring the shame at her wantonness, she surrendered to the need, letting her body plead for what she could not ask in words.

"Do ye want me?" a low voice growled.

She nodded against him, her breathing ragged.

With a savage grunt, he thrust forward. Mia bit her lip, tasting blood as she felt a tight pinch in her center. She clung to him, trembling, then he shifted position and thrust once more with a sharp exhalation. She cried out as the ache swelled, but her body relished the sensation as it came alive with each movement, pleasure flaring in the pit of her stomach. He thrust again, increasing the pace as the sounds he made grew in urgency, the low, primal grunts heightening in pitch to needy groans and cries. Then, at last, with a roar, he buried himself in her one final time. Her body burst and waves of pleasure battered at her—deeper and more intense than the pleasure she'd taken at his hands. Unable to withstand such exquisite ecstasy, Mia tilted her head back and screamed his name.

"Oh, woman! Oh!" The man inside her let out a cry, his voice filling her mind, spiraling in the air until the world dissolved, leaving nothing but him. Her man. The beast who'd fought for, then mounted, his mate.

When his voice grew hoarse, he pulled her to him, enveloping her body in his arms. He continued to shift inside her, his movements weaker, while she arched her back to draw him deeper inside.

Then, at last, they grew still, bodies trembling, hearts beating in unison.

As the fog of desire faded, Mia opened her eyes. Shame returned to conquer the pleasure at what she saw—herself, clinging to the man who had just debauched her against the cabinet, her thighs widespread, the flesh rosy with lust, skirts bunched to the waist, her hands clinging to him, urging him to mount her—a mare in heat. With a cry she pushed him back. Ignoring the sense of loss as he slipped outside of her, she lowered her skirts.

She met his gaze, searching for a shame to match hers, but all she saw was primal possession. For him, she was nothing but a conquest. But for her—she was now ruined, her dream of freedom and a future gone.

"What have I done?"

CHAPTER TWENTY-SEVEN

HAMISH'S SEMIHARD COCK still twitched with need, as if his body could never get enough of the woman he'd claimed.

And how delicious had been the claiming! All the more for his having waited so long.

Then she pushed him away, as if his touch disgusted her. The fog of lust that throbbed with every heartbeat dissipated as he heard her cry.

"What have I done?"

He blinked and met her gaze.

Horror and disgust glowed in her hazel eyes. She lowered her skirts and slid off the cabinet. Then she backed away, fisting the material of her gown and rubbing at her legs as if to remove the very essence of him. He caught the sharp scent of rutting.

"Unclean…" she whispered, tears filling her eyes. "Lord save me—I'm ruined. All hope is gone."

He pulled out a drawer and retrieved a cloth, which he handed to her. Wide-eyed, she stared at it.

"Wh-what are you doing?"

"It's to clean yerself with, lass—to wipe my seed from yer legs."

"Your…seed?"

"I can smell it on ye."

"Dear God!" she wailed. Then she snatched the cloth and backed away, colliding with the wall.

Why couldn't he think of the right thing to say? She looked like an injured deer in a trap, almost mad with terror. But the way to calm a deer—grasp it by the back legs and pull it free—wouldn't work on the terrified woman standing before him.

"Did I hurt ye, lass?"

She narrowed her eyes, and he recalled her sharp cry as he entered her before her body had pulsed with life around his cock and she'd screamed her pleasure.

"Hurt me?"

He gestured toward her skirts. "A woman's first time is painful, and I'm not a small man."

She wrinkled her nose in distaste, and though he relished how the fear faded from her eyes, the cold contempt that replaced it stabbed at his heart.

"You think I know nothing of the act between a man and a woman?" she said, her voice tight. "I have studied anatomy and am well aware of the functions of the human body. And, I might add, the variation in size among men."

Fuck.

He almost preferred the fear to the contempt.

She lowered her gaze to his groin, where his cock still twitched with need as if, now he'd had a taste of the finest venison, nothing else would satisfy his appetite.

"It's a myth," she said. "But given that you're a man and therefore incapable of rational thought, I daresay you'll continue to believe in it."

"What myth?"

"That the size of a man's"—she paused, her color heightening—"appendage is directly proportional to his virility. But it matters not. Yours was not so large compared to others."

"I've not had any complaints before."

He regretted the words almost before he uttered them, but rather than show hurt, she laughed.

"Have ye been with other men?" he said.

"You've stated it to be impossible, having recognized that this was my first time. But *you've* been with other women. Why, then, must I follow a higher standard than you?"

Jealousy surged and he stepped forward. *"Have* ye?"

She let out a snort. "What do you think I am, Hamish—your whore?"

"No!" he roared. "Ye're my wife."

She fisted her hands, and for a heartbeat he thought she might burst into tears. Then she spoke, coldly and calmly.

"I am not, and never will be, your *wife*," she said. "You reject-ed me the moment I arrived, if you recall."

"But it's different now we have…now I have…"

"Now you've what?" she said. "Fucked me against the wall to mark your triumph over another man?"

"Devil's ballocks, woman! Ye've an evil tongue on ye."

"Better than a blackened soul," she snarled. "Did you think I wanted this?"

"Ye screamed my name loud enough for Ma to hear it in the castle while I fucked ye."

"And I shall regret that until the day I die!" she said. "Is this how you seek vengeance on me, by destroying my dreams?"

He wiped his forehead, but the ache behind his eyes still hammered at his skull.

"No, lass, I have no wish to destroy yer dreams. But now the marriage is consummated, we must—"

"No!" she cried, her eyes widening with fear once more.

Sweet devil's cock—did the thought of being married to him strike such terror in her heart?

"No, please!" she said. "You want this marriage even less than I. You gave me hope, Hamish—hope that I could leave here with my fortune and pursue my dreams. Do you hate me so much that you wish to destroy that hope?"

"I dinnae hate ye, lass."

"Then we must proceed as planned," she said. "Nobody need know what happened here today."

"But Murdoch—"

"You vowed him to silence. A-and he wasn't to know that you'd force yourself on me as soon as you threw him out." She clasped her hands together. "Yes," she said. "I just need to clean myself, remove all trace of you. The river. I-I'll go in the river…"

"Ye cannae, lass. Ye'll freeze to yer death."

"Better that than remain here."

He caught his breath at the stab of hurt. Did she hate him that much?

"I'll proceed with the vaccination plan," she said, as if to herself. "That will remove me from here for a while, then I can make arrangements to go when I return."

"But yer fortune, Mia—I've yet to raise the full amount."

"I cannot stay here a moment longer!" she said. "Surely you must see that? We should proceed with the annulment as soon as possible. You must write to your solicitor tonight."

"But what will ye do?" he said. "If ye decide to marry again, yer next husband will know—"

"I'll *never* marry," she said. "But if I do, I-I'll tell him I was raped."

Her words struck him as surely as if she'd slapped him across the face.

"Surely ye cannae—"

"It happens more often than people care to believe," she said, coldly, "both in wedlock and outside. Of course, in wedlock, the man believes himself entitled to take his wife unwilling, but outside the law there is a higher principle."

"Which is?" he said, the weight of defeat pressing on him.

"That of right and wrong."

She spoke so quietly that her voice was almost a whisper, as if the cloak of despair covered her like a shroud. He met her gaze, and though she tilted her head up, as proud as a queen—or a laird's wife—the sorrow in her eyes broke his heart.

"Then, lass," he said, "if that's how ye feel, I'll leave ye be."

"Please do," she said. "I have no wish to set eyes on you again."

"Mia, I—"

"It's *Miss Lucas* to you, Lord MacLennan," she said. "I trust you'll respect my wishes, even if you were incapable of respecting my person."

Defeated, Hamish bowed his head then exited the cottage, taking his leave with a promise that he'd send Rory to repair the door. Then he retreated along the path and stopped in the shadow of the fir trees. After a moment, she emerged from the cottage, and his soul ached at the soft crying—not the tears a woman sheds when she wishes to manipulate her man into giving her what she wants, but the subdued tears of despair when a woman has been betrayed by the man who gave her hope, then took it away.

She stumbled toward the river's edge and Hamish tensed. If he tried to prevent her, she'd only reject him, but he couldn't leave her while she might be in danger. So he watched, a silent sentinel, as he'd watched over her at the cottage unobserved so many times before, to ensure that she was left unmolested.

She lowered herself into the water and he heard her sharp cry. Then she proceeded to scrub her legs, rubbing them with a frenzied motion. At length, she rose from the water, her gown clinging to her form, revealing every curve. He caught his breath at the sight of the dark nipples and delectable triangle of curls between her thighs where he'd buried himself only moments before.

She paused and looked in his direction, and he shrank back into the shadows. Then she returned to the cottage. He continued to wait until, at length, the soft orange glow of the fire glimmered from the window and a thin trail of smoke rose from the chimney. Then, overcome with shame at what he had lost— or, perhaps, she had never been his to lose—he made his way back to the castle.

It seemed as if the one act that should have sealed their union forever had driven them apart irrevocably, at the very moment when he understood how much he loved her. And now, he had a chance to prove his love—by honoring her wish and letting her go.

CHAPTER TWENTY-EIGHT

"IT'S A PLEASURE to meet you at last, Miss Lucas."

Dr. Nimmo, a neatly attired man with hair graying at the temples, a trimmed mustache, and the faintest of Scottish burrs, rose from his desk as Mia entered his study. She found her hand enveloped in a warm, welcoming handshake.

"I hadn't expected to see you," she said. "I understood from the hospital secretary that you delegate the vaccination work to junior staff."

"That wouldn't do, would it?" he said, gesturing to a seat. "McIver told me to take particular care of you and to oversee the process personally. And I admit to curiosity. It's not often I encounter a *woman* wishing to administer the procedure. But, as I've always said to Mrs. Nimmo, not all women are delicate orchids wishing to be preserved in hothouses all their lives."

"Does Mrs. Nimmo agree with you, sir?" Mia asked as she sat.

He leaned over the desk and lowered his voice. "Mrs. Nimmo says it herself. Now, I assume that, as a survivor of smallpox yourself, you're not to be the first patient to receive the vaccine."

"How did you..." Mia began, then trailed off. Her pockmarks may have faded, but they were visible enough to have not spared her from stares and whispers during the journey to Glasgow—the perpetrators being told, smartly, by Maisie, to "gawp at something worth gawping at or I'll have yer arses."

The doctor smiled. "Your face is testimony to your bravery,

Miss Lucas. Now, have you brought the patient with you? Given the length of your journey back to the Highlands, I'd advise delaying the application until the moment before you depart, so as not to break the chain."

"I have two patients with me to ensure the chain is not broken, sir."

"And where are they?"

"One is outside—the other's waiting in the carriage. I intend to leave as soon as I've administered the vaccine to the first patient, then, if necessary, administer the second during our journey home."

The doctor steepled his fingers together, then leaned back in his chair.

"McIver was right about you."

"What did he say?"

The doctor tilted his head to one side. "Come now, surely you don't expect me to resort to flattery?"

Mia's cheeks warmed and she lowered her gaze. "Forgive me, Dr. Nimmo. I meant no offense."

He let out a soft laugh. "I fear it's I who should beg forgiveness. Dr. McIver merely said that you were one of the most remarkable young women of his acquaintance, and that the world would be poorer if your skills were not put to proper use."

"Dr. McIver is too kind."

"I'll be the judge of that, though I'll admit that the praise of my good friend and colleague is enough to introduce a little prejudice in your favor. Now, you say the first patient is outside?"

"Yes, sir. Sh-she wouldn't come in."

"Why ever not?"

"She wasn't sure whether you'd be willing to admit her. You see, she's a..." Mia hesitated.

"A what? A servant? A milkmaid? I'm not discriminatory when it comes to my patients. And you'll understand that, given the nature of the vaccine, most patients I use as a source are milkmaids."

"Of course, sir," Mia said. "I've read Dr. Jenner's paper on the subject. But Maisie is a…"

She paused. Ought she be honest and risk expulsion, or tell a falsehood for the greater objective?

"Ah."

One little word—not even a word, really, but it conveyed the doctor's understanding. He regarded Mia with his frank gaze.

"You fear that I'd refuse to treat a woman whose profession renders her objectionable in the eyes of many—including those who purchase her services?" he said.

Mia nodded.

"An understandable assumption to make," he continued, "but I take my oath of service in the spirit in which it was written. Every soul deserves to be treated, and I'd never refuse to admit a brave woman willing to help her kinsmen by taking the vaccine to them."

He lifted a small brass bell from the desk and rang it. Shortly after, the clerk who'd ushered Mia in appeared.

"Ah, Jonas. Please send Miss…?"

"Maisie MacLennan," Mia said.

"…Miss MacLennan in. Tell her that I particularly wish to see her. And send for young Ginny."

"Aye, Dr. Nimmo, sir."

The clerk bowed and disappeared, then returned shortly after with Maisie. The doctor gazed at her, taking in, no doubt, the painted face, the too-bright but shabby attire, and Maisie's evident discomfort at being a whore who'd passed through the front door of one of the finest medical establishments in the country. But his expression showed none of the lust that glimmered in the eyes of almost every man who looked upon Maisie. Instead, they showed appreciation and respect.

"Do come in, Miss MacLennan."

"But sir, I've no right to—"

"You're my guest, come to receive the vaccine, which gives you every right to be here."

Maisie took the seat next to Mia.

"I applaud your bravery, Miss MacLennan," Dr. Nimmo said.

"Thank ye, sir."

"Shall we proceed, or do you wish me to explain the process first?"

"No thank ye, sir… I mean, yes, we may proceed," Maisie said. "Mia has already explained the process."

"And are you equipped, Miss Lucas?"

Mia opened her valise and took out a knife wrapped in a cloth, a small pouch containing her needles, and a candle.

"My dear," the doctor said, "you come better prepared than most of my students, but a woman knows the benefits of preparation more than a man, as I always say."

Or, Mia suspected, as *Mrs.* Nimmo always said.

"I have a candle," he said. "Save yours for your journey in case you have need of it."

He retrieved a candle from a drawer, set it in a candlestick, then handed it to Mia with a nod. She rose and lit it from the fireplace, then, as she returned to the desk, the door opened and a young woman entered.

"Ah, Ginny," the doctor said. "Our benefactress. How are you today, child?"

"I'm well, thank ye, Dr. Nimmo, sir."

"Though not *completely* recovered from cowpox, I trust?" he said, nodding to the girl's arm. "Sit, please."

The girl gave a shy smile, then took a seat and lifted her sleeve to expose a cluster of blisters on her forearm.

Maisie's eyes widened, but she lifted her own sleeve.

"Are you certain, Maisie?" Mia said.

"Aye."

Mia picked up her knife and held the blade in the candle flame for a heartbeat. She paused to let it cool, then held it against Maisie's arm.

"Good—very good," the doctor said. "Now, just a small incision."

Mia drew the knife across Maisie's skin. A droplet of red began to swell, but Maisie nodded to continue.

Mia set the knife aside and picked up her needle, again, holding it into the flame. She held it against Ginny's arm and raised her eyebrows in inquiry.

"Go on, miss," the girl said. "It won't hurt. Ye're the fourth doctor to see me today."

"I'm not a doctor."

"Not *yet*," Dr. Nimmo said with a smile. "Go on. A small droplet is all you need."

Holding her breath, Mia slid the tip of the needle into the blister, waited for a small bead of yellow liquid to form, then drew it out again. Slowly, she moved the needle toward Maisie's wound, then placed the tip in the center.

"Excellent," the doctor said. "Have you a bandage?"

Mia drew a strip of cloth from her valise and wound it around Maisie's arm.

"Not too tight," Dr. Nimmo said. "It's just to stop any bleeding. You should be able to remove it in an hour or so. Brave lass, Miss MacLennan," he added, nodding to Maisie. "And thank you, Ginny." He fished a coin out of his pocket. "A shilling for your trouble, child."

"Let *me* see to that," Mia said, fishing out a coin from her valise and handing it to the young girl, whose eyes widened.

"Half a crown? Thank ye, miss."

"It's you whom *I* should be thanking," Mia said. "For attending today and for subjecting yourself to the hands of a woman."

"Och, ye were gentler than…" The girl blushed as she glanced at Dr. Nimmo. "Beggin' yer pardon, sir."

"You're quite right, Ginny," the doctor said, mirth in his voice. "I fear that even my brightest student is not so deft as this young woman here. Well, my dear," he added, rising and extending his hand to Mia, "if you are adamant about leaving as soon as possible, I'll not keep you. I trust we shall meet again when I might have the privilege of addressing you as Dr. Lucas."

Mia took his hand, then the clerk escorted her and Maisie out to where the carriage was waiting.

Brodie's face appeared at the window. "Is it done, ma'am?"

Mia nodded as she helped Maisie into the carriage, then they set off.

"Did it hurt?" Brodie asked.

"Not at all," Maisie said. "A slight sting when Mia made the… What was it called?"

"Incision," Mia replied.

"And how do ye feel?" Brodie asked.

"I'm well. At least, for now."

"You may have a slight fever later tonight," Mia said, "or tomorrow. Let me know the moment you see blisters forming on your arm like Ginny's."

Maisie nodded, then relaxed into her seat. Mia turned her attention to the view from the window, the gray stone buildings of the city set against the darkening sky. When they thinned out to open countryside, she leaned back and closed her eyes. But sleep eluded her as the memory of her last encounter with Hamish pushed to the forefront of her mind—the sensations that had torn through her body as he'd claimed her like a beast, followed by the cold, harsh reality of ruination at the hands of a man who could never love her.

At all costs, she must keep their encounter a secret—not only to the rest of the world, but to herself. Were she to recognize the delicious wickedness that she'd savored as her body had opened itself to pure pleasure…

No!

"Mia?"

She glanced up to see Maisie staring at her.

"What ails ye?"

"Nothing," Mia said. "It's you we should be concerned about."

"Och, I'm well," Maisie said. "But something ails ye. I can see it."

"Nonsense."

"Do ye think I'm a…" Maisie glanced toward Brodie, whose head lolled to one side as he slept, emitting tiny snores. "Do ye think I'm a whore for nothing? I can tell when a person is deep in thought—or deep in sorrow." She folded her arms and tilted her head to one side. "Does it have something to do with why ye had that doctor address ye as Miss Lucas, not Lady MacLennan?"

When Mia didn't respond, Maisie took her hand.

"Something's happened, hasn't it?" she said. "Ye were quiet on the journey here. Even young Brodie noticed it. Is it Master Hamish?"

Mia's heart fluttered at the mention of his name.

"Aye." Maisie nodded. "I knew it would be something to do with the master, seein' as he didnae come to wave ye off. But I did see him."

"Did you?" Mia asked.

Maisie gave a knowing smile. "Aye. At the window of his study, watching as ye climbed in. He continued to watch as we traveled along the drive, and when I looked out of the window before we turned the corner, he was still there."

"Oh."

Mia cursed herself. Was that all she could manage to say while feigning nonchalance?

"Ye've lain with him, haven't ye?"

"Maisie!" Mia whispered, glancing at Brodie.

"Och, that lad will sleep through anything—if Glenblath castle were to crumble into dust, it wouldnae rouse him from a doze."

Mia opened her mouth to deny it, then closed it again.

"I saw a fire in yer eyes two or three days before we left," Maisie said, "but it was dulled by something else. As if…" She sighed, then shook her head.

"As if what?" Mia said, unable to conquer her curiosity.

"As if yer body had been awoken to pleasure and had found its home—but yer soul had been crushed."

"Sweet heaven! How can you—"

Maisie patted Mia's hand. "It's the skills of my trade—understanding the needs and desires of men and women. I saw it in his *eyes*, also."

"Saw what?"

"A physical need met, but a soul unsatisfied," Maisie said. "Master Hamish is afraid. I've never seen him afraid before."

"I doubt if a man such as Hamish has been afraid of anything," Mia said.

"Och, not of toil, or disease, or an opponent stronger than he," Maisie replied, "but of his heart. And the stronger the man, the more potent the fear."

Mia shook her head. "There is no fear in his heart. He made that perfectly clear after we..." Her cheeks flared with heat. "It matters not. Both he and I have different paths to take to fulfil our dreams—mine of becoming a doctor, and his..." She hesitated, willing the tears pricking at her eyelids to remain confined. "His ambition is to secure himself a prettier, wealthier bride as soon as our marriage is annulled."

"And is that what *ye* want?"

No! Mia's soul cried out with yearning. *I want to be loved.*

She glanced at her friend—a friend to whom she owed absolute honesty. But an admission of her heart would unlock the floodgates of despair that she might never be able to stem once opened.

"Yes," Mia said quietly. "It's what I want."

The fact that she had lied thickened in the air. But rather than wrench a confession from her, Maisie lifted Mia's hand to her lips. Then she drew her close and held her in the comforting embrace of a friend—a friend who recognized that her heart was broken.

CHAPTER TWENTY-NINE

"TELL ME, HAMISH Alastair Jamie MacLennan, why have ye not been to see yer wife?"

I'm in trouble.

Hamish glanced up from his ledgers to see his mother embroidering a cushion, the needle flying in and out with a smooth, unstrained motion. But rather than tight-lipped anger, the expression on her face displayed calmness, and serenity, as if she were merely commenting on the weather.

But, as he had learned over the years, serenity of expression in his ma was likely to hide a turmoil of fury. It was how she'd survived a lifetime with his da, after all.

She cut the dark-green thread she'd been working with then picked up a skein of pale-purple silk, threaded her needle, and resumed her work.

"What are ye doing?" he asked.

"Embroidering a cushion."

"I can see that."

"Then why ask if ye knew the answer?"

"Perhaps I was making conversation."

"Och, ye're many things, son, but a conversationalist isn't one of them. Besides, if ye wished to make a conversation, why didnae ye answer my question? Were ye waiting for me to answer it for ye?"

"Of course not."

"Then perhaps ye already know the answer, and are afraid to admit it to yer ma. Ye're even afraid to admit it to yerself."

She paused and met his gaze.

Devil's cock! The stare of a formidable matriarch was usually enough to crack open a mussel at twenty paces, but the look in Ma's eyes now was enough to cleave Beinn Blath in two.

"I dinnae ken what ye're on about."

She continued to stare at him, as she had done when she caught him as a boy after he let the chickens loose and his da's dog had killed almost the entire flock. Da thrashed him so hard he'd had a sore arse for a week. But it was Ma's silent disapproval that had cut him more deeply. Da had cared only for Hamish's failure to conform to parental rules. Ma had cared for the consequences of his recklessness—the lives needlessly lost through a thoughtless act of a boy who cared little for others.

And that thoughtless boy had grown into a thoughtless man.

But how could he tell his mother that he'd shunned Mia since her return from Glasgow for *her* sake, because she had asked him to and because he could no longer trust himself? He had ruined her body, violated her like a rutting animal.

"Och, son, have I not raised ye to be a better man than yer da?"

"She disnae want to see me, Ma."

"Did she say that?"

"She said she had no wish to set eyes on me again." Hamish winced at the note of petulance in his voice. But his attempt at gaining sympathy from his mother failed.

She arched an eyebrow. "What did ye do to make the poor lass say *that*?" He paused, and her expression darkened. "Perhaps it's best if ye dinnae tell me, for I fear I shan't like the answer. Ye're my son and I love ye—I have no wish to have that love put to the test."

She continued her work, then spoke again after a pause.

"I hear the vaccination scheme is progressing well."

"Has she treated ye?"

"Aye, and Iona. Mia insisted yer sister be one of the first."

"And Iona agreed? I thought she disliked Mia."

Ma's lips curved into a smile. "Iona's been assisting her. She's been every day at Riverview Cottage—save yesterday, when she was unwell. It was Iona who persuaded the household to take the vaccine. They've all taken it, except young Ailsa."

"Ailsa?"

"Murdoch's lass." Ma flicked her gaze to Hamish. "I saw him shortly before Mia left for Glasgow," she said. "He was having words with Ailsa in the garden as she was fetching water."

"Were ye spying?"

Her cheeks flushed a delicate shade of pink.

Ha! Not so perfect, are ye, Ma?

She shot him a look that silenced the little voice of triumph in his head.

"Can I not take a walk in my own gardens?" She drove the needle into her work with a little more force, each motion sending a prick of apprehension through Hamish, as if she were imagining driving the needle into his flesh. "His face was black and blue," she continued. "He said he'd been sparring with Robbie."

"Well, there ye have it."

"Only Robbie's not much of a fighter. Murdoch's been our Games champion for the past four years, and ye cannae forget how he wrestled the MacDouglases' eldest to the ground at their Games. There's not a man alive who can best him…"

She paused, and he was assaulted by the full force of her gaze.

"…save one."

Devil's ballocks, did all mothers possess the ability to read their son's minds? Or just *his* mother?

"Och, son, ye may think me a fool, but I'm not blind. I know ye care for her. Even if ye cannae admit it to yer ma, ye should admit it yerself."

Oh, fuck it—there was little point in trying to deceive her.

"I cannae intrude on her again," he said. "She hates me—she

almost said as much."

Rather than show distress, his mother smiled again.

"Then there's hope for ye yet."

"Hope!" he scoffed, then resumed reading his ledgers, though he was unable to focus on the words.

"If a man, or woman, harbors hatred," she said, "it means that their heart is alive—with passion, fury, and life. Do ye believe that hate is the opposite of love?"

"Isn't it?" Hamish said. "I always thought—" He broke off, unable to disguise the hoarseness in his throat.

She leaned forward and placed her hand over his. He glanced at it, taking in the smooth skin and the knuckles, which, though still swollen, no longer bore the raw redness of pain. A faint aroma reached his nostrils—the salve that Mia used to treat his mother's hands.

"The opposite of hate is not love, Hamish," she said softly. "It's indifference. And Mia could never be indifferent to ye. She was asking, only yesterday, whether ye'd be taking the vaccine."

Hope flared in his soul.

"She's been trying to teach Iona to administer it," his mother said, "but yer sister's too afraid to cut ye."

"Oh."

"Can ye not go to her, lad?"

"But she said—"

"Och, are ye a man or a worm? The vaccine's a small cut to the arm, nothing more. Ye hardly feel it, she's so gentle, and ye're only sick for a day afterward."

"I can weather a cut to the arm, Ma."

She rolled her eyes. "If ye're man enough to beat the hide off Murdoch for her, then ye're man enough to face her for a few moments. She may not wish to see ye, but that won't stop her from doing what she knows is right. So why is it stopping ye? Are ye afraid of her?" She tilted her head to one side. "Or are ye afraid of yerself? I've seen the way ye look at her."

"I cannae," he said.

"So ye'll risk catching the pox for the sake of yer pride?" She shook her head. "That's not courage, son, it's cowardice. Did ye not hear that there's been an outbreak on MacDouglas land? They're in the next glen but one."

"It's just a rumor."

"It's not. Young Donald—the lad who helps Rory with the fences—is courting a MacDouglas lass. Rory told Maisie, who told me that—"

"Do ye listen to whores' gossip now?"

"A whore ye were content to bed, if I recall," she retorted. "I dinnae ken what to do with ye when ye're content to put lives at risk."

"Only my own life."

"Foolish lad!" she cried. "There's many hereabouts who aren't taking the vaccine. Folk here follow yer lead. Have ye not stopped to think why so many at Glenblath cannae accept her— why so many have refused to take the vaccine?"

"Such as?"

"Murdoch, for one. He's refused it for himself as well as Evie and their bairns. Then there's Robbie and Shona and their wee lad, and Gordon and his brothers. Twenty families in all, I reckon." She shook her head, disappointment in her eyes. "When ye rejected that poor lass the day she arrived, ye set yerself, and many others, on a path of prejudice and misunderstanding. She's borne that prejudice with fortitude and kindness, striving to protect the folk who look to ye for that protection rather than her."

"I protect the clan," Hamish growled. "Everything I do is for them. Dinnae ye understand that's why I married for a dowry, not for love—for the sake of the clan!"

"The qualities needed in a laird's wife are not a pretty face for ye to admire and a fortune for ye to spend. She must hold the clan in her heart so that it runs through the blood in her veins."

"Ye mean she must be a Highland lass?"

"No, son, I mean that she must be willing to embrace her

responsibility to the souls at Glenblath with pleasure, not duty. Neither birth nor fortune will dictate whether she can do that."

"Then what will?"

"The Almighty," she said. "Have ye never asked why He chose to spare Mia and send her here to Glenblath—to us—rather than take her for Himself?"

Yes. He had wondered.

At first, he'd roared with rage at Fate for shackling him to a woman he'd not wanted. But, for many weeks now, he'd roared with considerably more rage at himself for not appreciating the gift he'd been given.

And what had he done? Violated that gift, placing a chasm between himself and Mia.

He snapped the ledger shut and placed it on a nearby table.

Ma nodded at the book. "I take it ye're almost in a position to repay her dowry."

"We should have most of it by next quarter day," he said. "Eight hundred, perhaps more. But if the poor weather holds, the Candlemas rents may not be sufficient. Tenants have less cash to spare after a harsh winter."

"Mia will understand."

"I doubt she'll accept eight hundred in cash and twenty head of cattle."

"She will if she's as eager to annul yer marriage as ye. The prospect of freedom will make it so."

Her voice was toneless—neither encouraging nor judging, merely her stating a fact.

He nodded, not trusting himself to speak.

"Son?"

He glanced up at her crystal-clear eyes.

"I'll not tell ye what to do about yer wife. Ye must look to yer own conscience. But there's one thing I will ask of ye."

He braced himself. "What is it, Ma?"

"Take the vaccine," she said. "If I must lose my daughter-in-law, I shall at least take comfort in knowing that she'll succeed wherever she goes. But I couldn't bear to lose my son."

But the expression in her eyes told him that she wouldn't be able to bear losing Mia, the daughter-in-law who had secured a place in her heart.

And neither would he.

But I've already lost her.

He curled his fingers around hers, then nodded.

"Aye," he said, "I will."

CHAPTER THIRTY

"THERE!" MIA SAID, rolling down the little girl's sleeve. "Well done for being such a brave girl."

"Ma said it wouldnae hurt," Ada said. "And it didnae—not at all."

Mia raised an eyebrow.

"Well, maybe a wee bit," Ada said, "but not as much as when ye treated my shoulder. Thank ye, ma'am."

"Ye should be thanking *me*, Ada. It was me who passed the special medicine on."

Ada turned to the boy who'd just spoken, who sat on the edge of Mia's table, swinging his legs.

"Thank ye, Jamie." Blushing, Ada leaned over to kiss the boy on the cheek.

"Bleurgh!" Jamie shrank back, but he made no attempt to wipe his cheek, and his face turned a similar shade to Ada's.

Mia exchanged a smile with Ada's mother. "Your daughter shouldn't feel any worse than you did after your vaccination," she said. "Being a child, she should recover more quickly. But keep her home for at least two days. I'll give you some willow bark should you need it, but if you have any concerns, send for me and I'll come directly."

"Did I do right by not bringing Ada sooner?" Aileen said. "She's not been well. I kept her away from school, as she'd taken a chill and I didnae want to take her out until she'd recovered."

"That was the sensible thing to do," Mia said, placing a hand on the woman's arm. "It's best to take the vaccine while healthy to avoid being overwhelmed. I'd only advocate taking it when unwell if there was an outbreak of smallpox, when the risk of taking the vaccine is minimal compared to the alternative."

The kitchen door opened and Iona appeared. "Shall I make tea?"

"Och, no need to bother, lass," Aileen said. "We mustn't take up any more of yer time. Ada, lass, let's get ye home and tucked up in front of a fire. Do ye want to come with us, Jamie, lad? That is, if Miss Lucas isn't expecting any more patients today?"

Iona's eyes narrowed at Aileen's address.

Mia shook her head. "No one else is coming today."

"If they do, they can come back tomorrow," Iona said. "Ye must be exhausted, Mia. How many folk have ye treated today? Ten?"

"Eleven, counting Ada," Mia said.

"Then it's time we left ye in peace," Aileen said. "Come along, Ada. Ye too, Jamie."

"Wait," Iona said. "I've a piece of shortbread for each of ye brave children. Ye can take a piece also if ye wish, Aileen."

"That's very kind, thank ye."

Iona smiled and disappeared into the kitchen.

"She's in good spirits," Aileen whispered. "I'm glad she has a friend in ye. She was always a little..." She made a random gesture as her voice trailed off. "Not that I wish to offend anyone, but she's always been a bit of a handful. The old laird was always too harsh with her."

"Iona's been a great help with the vaccinations," Mia said. "She was the first to take it after I returned from Glasgow, and though I was concerned about her health, she made a quick recovery."

"Her health? Is she sickening for something?"

Mia cursed her folly. Iona's secret would not be such for long. Though she had taken to wearing multiple shawls, her thickening waist wouldn't be easily concealable for much longer. But it wasn't Mia's secret to tell.

"I'm concerned about the health of every patient I treat," she said, as Iona reappeared. "Ah! Here's the shortbread. Who deserves a slice?"

"Me!" the children chorused.

Iona held out a package, which Ada grasped, her eyes wide as she inhaled the sweet scent of freshly baked biscuits.

"Mind ye dinnae eat yer ma's slice," Iona said. "If ye're good, I'll let ye have two slices next time ye visit. Or I could ask Mrs. McBride to show ye how to make it at the castle. What do ye say to that?"

"Ooh, yes!" Ada said, trembling with excitement.

"Good lass. Now, mind ye tell all yer friends to come and take the vaccine. There's plenty of folk hereabouts who haven't."

"Is that so?" Aileen said. "Tell me who they are and I'll speak to them."

"They'll come if they want," Mia said.

"Aye, but sometimes they need a good kick up the arse," Aileen said. "It's not the women, it's the men, who think they rule the world. Take poor Evie—she wants to take the vaccine, and give it to her bairns, but that fool Murdoch won't let her."

"Och, Murdoch won't listen to anyone but himself," Iona said. "I thought he'd listen to me, but he said I was…" She shook her head. "It disnae matter what he said. He's an arse."

"Ma," Ada said, "what's an—"

"That's enough, Ada!" Aileen said.

Iona blushed. "Forgive me for cursing in front of yer bairn."

"No matter, lass. Ada hears worse from my Allan."

"Couldn't yer Allan persuade Murdoch to take the vaccine?" Iona said.

Aileen shook her head. "He wouldnae hear a word from Allan on the matter—not even when Allan told him about young Donald's sweetheart."

"Donald?" Mia said, flicking through the papers on her table.

She ran her thumb along the list of names. "Ah, there he is—I thought I recognized the name. He came for the vaccine a fortnight ago. What's his sweetheart's name?"

"She's not one of *us*. She's a MacDouglas. Donald said she's had to stay at home to take care of her grandma, who fell ill a day after her ma. He said she's not expected to last long, but she's an old 'un. Eighty summers, they say she's seen. My ma only lasted seventy, and she was as hale as the best of them."

"Perhaps I should visit the MacDouglases," Mia said.

"Ye dinnae want to do that, lass. Folk there are unwelcoming toward outsiders—Sassenachs in particular."

"Folk here aren't too welcoming either," Mia said before she could stop herself. "Oh, forgive me, Aileen, I didn't mean *you*."

Iona colored and picked up Mia's papers, shuffling through them. Her gaze wandered over the list of names, then stilled, and her mouth set in a firm line. Moisture glittered in her eyes.

"Well, I'll leave ye two in peace," Aileen said. "Shall I send Allan over with a leg of mutton for yer supper?"

"That's kind, but not necessary," Mia said. "I don't expect payment for my services."

"What about a gift from a grateful friend?"

Mia caught her breath as her heart swelled. "Only if you can spare it."

"Och, just bring it, Aileen!" Iona said. "Do ye have such an abundance of friends, Mia, that ye dinnae wish for one more?"

Jamie sidled up to Ada and offered his hand. "Come on!" he said brightly. "Ye'll need help getting home, won't ye?"

After they left, Mia closed the door and leaned against it.

"Why dinnae ye rest while I make tea?" Iona said.

"It's you who should be resting."

Iona's hand drifted to her belly. Then she glanced at the list of names on the table and blushed.

"Has..." Mia hesitated, unwilling to broach the subject that had been left unspoken since she'd learned of Iona's condition. "Has your child's father said..."

"He disnae want me," Iona said, "so I dinnae want him. He only wanted to tell his friends he'd put his cock in the laird's sister. Then he called me a hure, saying he'd tell Hamish that I've been spreading my legs around the clan like Maisie, and anyone could be the father."

Mia raised her hands in supplication. "Forgive me. I won't mention it again. But people will find out eventually. At the very least, you should tell Hamish."

"Why? He disnae care about me."

"I think you'll find he cares about you very much, even if he cannot show it."

Iona pushed out her bottom lip and folded her arms.

"Very well, what about your mother?" Mia said. "Eilidh was the first one here to welcome me without judgment, when others were all too ready to…"

Her voice trailed off as Iona's eyes filled with tears.

"Well, that's all in the past." She took Iona's hand. "But you need a friend. I might not be here when you enter your confinement."

Iona sniffed, then lifted her hand to her mouth and swayed sideways.

"I knew you'd been overtaxing yourself today," Mia said. "Take a seat and *I'll* make tea. I'll give you a moment to yourself while I fetch the water."

She retrieved a pan from the kitchen, then exited the cottage and made her way to the river. Her breath misted in the cold air, but as she turned her head to the sky, the sun bathed her face with a gentle warmth.

She smiled to herself—if anyone had asked her a year ago if she'd be able to survive a life in the cold, unforgiving environment of the Highlands, without the comforts of a London home, she'd have laughed. But here she was, in a land where the air was as fresh as the sweetest grass, where even the frost that gripped the land, making it iron hard, held a particular beauty, glimmering like diamonds in the winter sunlight.

The river brought forth its own style of beauty. Though the water moved too rapidly to freeze compared to the Thames in London, ice crystals had formed on the edge of the river, sprouting like tiny shoots, their silvery-white tendrils stretching out where the water lapped against the shore.

Mia crouched beside the water's edge and traced a tendril with her fingertip. Soft footsteps approached and she smiled.

"I thought you were going to take a rest, Iona."

"How did ye know it was me?"

Mia turned to see the girl staring at her, her brilliant-green eyes wide in her pale face. In her woolen gown that stretched over her swollen belly, her frame thin and delicate, she was the most vulnerable-looking creature Mia had ever seen. She rose, suppressing the urge to take the girl in her arms.

Who would protect Iona when she was gone?

A twig snapped in the distance and Mia glanced up. Then she caught the familiar white flash of a deer disappearing through the trees into the density of the forest. Rory had said that the harsh weather would drive the deer off the higher slopes, and he'd been right. Since the frosts had begun, Mia had been gifted most mornings with a visit from the gentle brown creatures, some of which were bold enough to come within reach and let her stroke their soft fur before skittering away, like children playing a game of dare.

"If I promise to tell Ma," Iona said, "will ye make me a promise in return?"

Mia opened her mouth to say that it depended on the promise, but the plea in the girl's eyes cut through her heart.

She nodded. "Of course."

"And ye'll keep yer promise?"

Mia rose and extended her hand. "Yes," she said, approaching Iona, who took her hand, curling her thin fingers around Mia's in a grip that was tight with desperation.

"I-I'm afraid of my confinement," she said. "Evie almost died when she had young Billy, though that Shona is robust enough to birth over a hundred bairns. Will ye promise not to leave Glenblath until after I've had my baby?"

Another twig snapped, then a deep voice roared, "Until ye've had yer *what?*"

Mia turned toward the voice to see its owner emerging from behind a tree, hands fisted at his sides, his face contorted in pure rage.

It was Hamish.

CHAPTER THIRTY-ONE

S WEET SWIVING HEAVEN! Surely his ears deceived him?

But when his sister turned, Hamish saw the evidence in the form of her swollen belly.

"What the fuck is *that*?" he cried, striding out of his hiding place and gesturing to the evidence of his sister's whoring.

Iona stepped back, her eyes gleaming with fear. Then the defiance returned.

"What do ye think, brother?" she sneered. "Surely even ye must know, given the amount of rutting ye get up to, what happens when a man sticks his cock in—"

"Iona."

Though Hamish's wife spoke softly, Iona paused.

"Try not to distress yourself," Mia said. "As for you"—she turned to Hamish—"I thought you and I had agreed to remain apart. What are you doing here?"

Ignoring her question, he gestured toward his sister. "How long have ye known about this, Mia?"

"For some weeks, though I fail to understand what business it is of yours."

"She's my sister—and she's unwed. Devil take ye, Iona, have ye no shame?"

"Oh, and I suppose the *man* had nothing to do with it," Iona scoffed, folding her arms.

"Bloody Murdoch," Hamish said with a huff. "I knew he was

carrying on, but I didnae know he'd be so foolish as to succumb to *yer* advances."

"Hamish, you don't know—" Mia began, but he interrupted.

"Och, I do! Iona's been wandering about at night like a stray cat in heat—been seen at all hours with Murdoch—but I didnae think she'd be so foolish as to spread her—"

"*Stop!*" Mia said. "It takes two people to make a baby. Your sister's about to be a mother, yet the child will have a father, also."

Iona let out a groan.

"Devil's ballocks," Hamish muttered. "I'll have to speak to him."

"No!" Iona cried. "Ye'll do nothing of the sort. The fa..."—she wrinkled her nose—"the man who sired my child disnae want me. He called me a hure and said that any man could be the father."

Fuck. It was worse than he'd thought. Was there a man in the whole cursed clan whom she'd *not* parted her thighs for?

But when Hamish saw the distress in his sister's eyes, he silenced the voice of condemnation in his head. There'd be plenty of time to admonish her when she'd grown calmer.

As for his wife...

"Did ye not think to tell me about my sister's..." He paused before he added the word *whoring*.

Mia arched an eyebrow, her eyes hardening.

"Her...condition," he said. "I'm her brother and her laird."

"It's her body, Hamish," Mia replied. "It's not my tale to tell. Though I do regret one thing."

"Which is?"

"I urged Iona to tell you that she was expecting a child. In my folly, I believed you'd show her kindness and understanding rather than condemnation. I thought you loved her."

"I do," he said. "But even ye must understand how this will look—the laird's sister, with child, and unmarried. Fuck, Iona, I'll be a laughingstock."

"Why?" Mia said. "For not keeping under control the women you think you own? We're not cattle to be tethered and penned when we don't follow our master's commands. Yet you have nothing to say against the man who sired Iona's baby. Doubtless you'll applaud his virility and ignore his infidelity."

"So he is married?"

Iona tilted her chin up, cheeks reddening, eyes bright.

"His wife won't care," she said. "She spreads her favors around more than Maisie. Which means she's a fool, seeing as Maisie at least gets a coin when she parts her thighs. A shilling a time, if it's a quick rutting—isn't that right, brother? Ye've done it often enough."

"Surely ye dinnae think—"

"Enough!" Iona cried, placing her hands over her ears. "I cannae bear to hear any more!"

Before Hamish could respond, his sister picked up her skirts and ran along the path toward the castle, sobbing. Her crying could still be heard after she'd turned a corner and disappeared.

"That was well done," Mia said, picking up the pot at her feet.

"What, my sister's behavior?"

She rolled her eyes, then set off toward the cottage.

"Wait!" he called, following her.

She turned at the door and sighed. "You should go after her. She needs you."

"She needs a thrashing."

Mia's eyes widened, and Hamish shook his head, his initial fury already dissipating.

"Och, no, she disnae. But ye must agree that some of the blame lies with her."

"She's barely older than a child herself."

"She's a year older than Ma was when she married," Hamish said. "If she's old enough to spread her thighs and bear the fruits of her debauchery, then she's no longer a child."

"I don't mean her age," Mia said. "I meant her character. Any fool can see that Iona's a wild spirit—she acts on impulse. Perhaps when she's older she may settle, but before she does…"

"Before she does, I should expect her to continue to behave like an animal? And Ma…" He paused, his gut twisting with horror. "Devil's ballocks, does Ma know?"

"I don't think anyone does."

"I find it hard to believe that, given how brazen she's been."

"She's not brazen. She just wants you to notice her."

"Then she's more of a fool than I thought," he said, tamping down his anger. "Does she *want* to be thrashed?"

"Would you thrash her?"

"Of course not. But…" He hesitated, tempering the sorrow that lay in his mind, barely concealed by the anger. "I-I dinnae want to fail her, and I have failed her. And Ma will be heartbroken."

"Iona will tell your mother when she's ready," Mia said.

"Why did she tell ye?"

Mia pushed open the cottage door, and he followed her inside. "She didn't exactly tell me," she said. "But she told me nonetheless."

"Do ye talk in riddles?"

Her lips twitched—the precursor, he hoped, to a smile.

"She wanted me to find out, but couldn't bring herself to tell me, so she asked the right questions."

"Aye," he said, almost to himself. "Ye *do* talk in riddles."

Mia twisted her mouth, as if to prevent her smile from widening. "Imagine a wife is thirsty and she wants her husband to bring her a pot of tea," she said. "What would she say to him?"

"I suppose she'd say, 'Fetch me a pot of tea, husband.'"

"Spoken like a man," she said. "And what would the husband say? What would Murdoch say if Evie said such a thing?"

He shrugged. "Any self-respecting husband would tell her to fetch it herself because it's women's work."

"Very well," she said. "Now imagine I've come to visit you at the castle. If I were shivering by the fire and told you that I was terribly thirsty and my body was aching with the cold, what might you say?"

"I'd offer ye a cup of tea."

"And you'd wait for me to fetch it?"

"No, lass, I'd…" His voice trailed away as she burst into laughter, and his heart soared. Anything was better than her contempt.

"You'd make the tea?"

"Och, no, but I'd go to the kitchen and ask Mrs. McBride to make it for ye."

"What a shockingly *modern* individual you are for your sex," she said, and he winced at the edge in her voice. Then she sighed. "I've no wish to argue with you, Hamish."

"But ye've still not answered my question. Why did Iona tell ye? She's hardly shown any liking for ye. In fact, she and Murdoch—"

"Perhaps the less we say about Iona and Murdoch in the same breath, the better. I don't know for certain who the father is. I believe she was happy for me to know about her condition because I'm soon to leave Glenblath. And whom can we trust more with our most intimate secrets than a stranger? After all, I shan't be the one staring at her with judgmental eyes after the baby is born."

"Will ye stay until then?"

"Yes," she said. "I made a promise. And I keep my promises."

All except one.

But Hamish refused to voice the riposte. After all, the dissolution of their marriage was at his insistence. Or, at least, it had been.

"You didn't answer my question," she said. "What *are* you doing here? I thought we'd agreed to remain apart after…" She colored and looked away.

"I came to take the vaccination," he said.

"For yourself?"

"Aye, and for the benefit of others. How many families haven't taken it?"

"Twenty or so, if Maisie's list of names is accurate. I've not been able to persuade them. But I didn't have much hope of Murdoch agreeing. Nor Robbie. Reverend Sutherland took the vaccine last week. I had hoped that the minister taking the vaccine might persuade others to follow."

"Their laird taking it might persuade more," Hamish said. "Ma said I ought to show an example for the sake of the clan."

"So you're here on your mother's insistence—and for no other reason?"

"Aye."

Her smile slipped. "I'm afraid you're too late."

"Too late? But ye can administer it now, cannae ye?"

"I need another patient to pass the vaccine on. There's only young Jamie Sutherland who has the blisters. He's coming tomorrow, so you could return then."

"Aren't ye going to offer me a pot of tea, seein' as it's women's work?"

His feeble little joke did nothing to restore the light that had gone from her eyes.

"You should go after your sister," she said. "She needs you more than I ever could."

Her words sliced through his heart. But Mia was right—she didn't need him. What had he ever done to prove himself worthy of her?

"Iona needs *ye* also, Mia," he said. "I'm glad she could tell ye."

"She'll need you when I am gone, unless…"

"Unless what?"

"Unless she comes with me. I've said she can if she wishes it." She gave a wistful smile. "She's proving to be an adept helpmate and would make a competent nurse."

"Ye—and *Iona*?" He shook his head. "She's never succeeded at anything other than irking her brother."

"Perhaps that's why she asked if I might consider taking her with me when I leave Glenblath," Mia said. "A rejected wife and a rejected sister—ruined woman and unwed mother. We can be misfits together."

"Och, ye're not a ruined…" His voice trailed off as her expression hardened. "Forgive me, Mia," he whispered.

"There's nothing to forgive," she replied. "I ruined myself. It was my mistake. But in a short while, it will not matter."

"No, it won't," he said, unable to disguise the bitterness in his voice. "Come Candlemas, ye'll be free of us."

"Candlemas?"

"The next quarter day. I hope to have raised sufficient funds to meet yer demands, though if the tenants are unable to provide the cash ye seek, ye might have to do with a few head of cattle in lieu of the rest."

Her mouth settled into a straight, firm line. "I'll take what you have to give if it grants my freedom."

"In which case, I'll write to my lawyer in Edinburgh to proceed with the annulment."

"Very good," she said, rising. "I'll see you tomorrow for your vaccination, then we needn't meet again unless to discuss the settlement."

Had he imagined it, or was there a tremor in her voice? But the expression in her eyes was shuttered.

Considering himself dismissed, and unable to think of what to say that didn't make him look even more of a fool, Hamish bowed and saw himself out. Only by the time he arrived at the castle had his mind formulated an appropriate response: a wish that they might remain friends, perhaps write to each other so that he might hear of her successes—and successes they'd undoubtedly be—on her road to becoming a doctor.

But it was too late. Why could he never think of the right thing to say to her when he'd had no trouble conversing with women before—or enticing them into his bed?

Perhaps it was because, for the first time in his life, he feared saying the wrong thing. He cared what Mia thought of him. The depth of his feelings for her had lain dormant in a corner of his soul, where it had been given the spark of life the day he'd first met her in that sorrowful little London parlor. But now, his soul was filled with it.

The castle doors opened to reveal Hamish's mother, her face contorted with distress.

Fuck.

So Iona had told her. Or, more likely, in her cowardice she'd merely revealed her swollen belly.

"Och, Hamish!" Ma reached toward him.

He took her in his arms and pulled her close. "Dinnae distress yerself," he said. "I'm not angry. I was at first, but I'm resigned to it now."

"Resigned?" she cried. "How can ye be so cruel when ye've seen the evidence?" She shook her head. "What shall we do? We must tell Mia—she'll know how to ensure we survive."

"Ma, aren't ye being a little overexcited?" he said. Then he smiled inwardly at Mia's remonstration. "Come inside and I'll make ye a pot of tea."

"Tea? Is that what ye think will save us when there's so many lives at risk?"

"What the devil are ye talking about? Iona will be well."

"Not *Iona*, son—i-it's Ailsa. She spent her Sunday afternoon off with that MacDouglas lad—ye know, young Taran, who's undergardener at MacDouglas Castle—and she's been taken ever so bad this morning, shaking, feverish, and the marks on her face... Och!" She covered her face with her hands. "I've never seen anything the like. Ye must fetch Mia, for she'll know what to do. But son, so many souls here haven't taken the vaccine—what are we to do?"

Vaccine?

Dear God, no...

Tears ran down her cheeks—the woman who had birthed him, survived an abusive marriage, influenza, and several harsh winters that would have seen off the hardiest of folk succumbed to despair at the notion of the suffering of the people who depended on her.

Hamish drew her into his arms and uttered a silent prayer to the Almighty that He would spare every soul whose life was at risk when faced with the inevitable.

Smallpox had come to Glenblath.

CHAPTER THIRTY-TWO

WHEN MIA ARRIVED at Glenblath Castle, Eilidh ushered her inside. The older woman looked as if she'd aged ten years since Mia had last seen her. Her face pale, forehead lined with distress, eyes glistening with unshed tears, she stood in the doorway, swaying from side to side as if she might faint any moment.

"Forgive me for sending for ye so late, Mia. Has my son told ye the news?"

Mia glanced at the huge Highlander who'd returned to her doorstep a broken man, not half an hour after they'd parted. Then she placed a hand on the older woman's arm.

"You should rest, Eilidh. Take some sweet tea. I can see to the girl. It's Ailsa, isn't it?"

"I'll take ye to her," Hamish said. "She's in the maids' chamber on the top floor."

He led her along the stone passageway, then up a series of winding staircases until they stood before an arched wooden door, which Hamish knocked on, then opened to reveal a chamber with three beds. The bed beside the window was occupied, and beside it sat a thin, gray-haired woman.

"Elspeth?" Mia entered the room, removing her shawl. "What's happened here?"

"It's young Ailsa, ma'am," the maid said. "She wasnae feeling good last night, so I sent her to bed early."

Mia approached the bed and suppressed a cry. The young maid's face was flushed with fever, her forehead glistened with moisture, and her hair clung to her face in damp curls. With each inhalation, she shuddered.

There was no doubt as to her ailment. Her face and neck were dotted with angry red sores that stared mockingly at Mia to remind her of the sores she'd first seen on her father's face, and then in the mirror—marks to herald the onset of a siege from the Grim Reaper himself.

"It's smallpox, isn't it?" Elspeth asked. "I can see it in yer eyes."

Mia took Ailsa's hand, which lay limply in hers. "I'm afraid so."

"Devil's ballocks!" Hamish cried, his expression filled with horror.

"You need to leave," Mia told him.

"But the lass is my responsibility. I'm her laird and it's my duty to take care of everyone. And ye'll need help. I should stay for her sake."

"You must leave for *your* sake," Mia said, tempering the swell of fear as she met his gaze. "You've not had the vaccine. You're not safe."

"Th-then what…?"

Mia's heart almost broke at the desolation in his eyes, and she took his hand.

"The best thing you can do for her—and for everyone—is to keep yourself safe," she said. "Go to your chamber, or your study. Remain there until I can be certain that there are no more infections. Mrs. McBride can send you food, and when I've treated Ailsa here, I can vaccinate you. Everyone who hasn't taken vaccine is at risk."

"Then I must warn them," he said. "Sweet Lord Almighty, why did I not order them as laird to take the vaccine? I have failed them—and I've failed ye."

"Protect yourself, Hamish, and you will not have failed anyone."

He lowered his gaze to her hand where she'd taken his.

"I'll do as ye say," he said. "Elspeth, I command every soul under this roof to obey my wife's commands, without question. She's the only one who can save us."

"Aye, Master Hamish."

He squeezed Mia's hand and released it. Then he placed his hand over his heart.

"Elspeth," Mia said, "tell me what happened to Ailsa."

"Aren't ye going to treat her?"

"Yes, but the most urgent task is to understand how she caught the disease and from whom, so we can ensure it doesn't spread."

Elspeth nodded. "She took ill last night. I sent her to her chamber, but when I came up later, she was quiet, and I didnae think to check on her. Och—it's my fault!"

"It's nobody's fault," Mia said. "If she was already infected, there's nothing you could have done."

"I could have sent for ye."

"I'm here now, and I'll do everything I can. Now, where did she go before last night? Did she meet anyone?"

"She had her Sunday afternoon off with the young lad who's courting her."

"Who?"

"One of the MacDouglases. She said his ma had been taken ill."

"And Ailsa came straight here afterward?"

"She'll have visited her family first," Elspeth said. "Ailsa might be a flighty lass, but she's fond of her ma and her wee brother, even if her da's a big brute."

"Evie…" Mia whispered, ice-cold fingers of fear clawing at her stomach. "We must send a message to Murdoch—tell him to keep his family at home until I can visit them."

"Let *me*," Hamish said. "Murdoch's a stubborn fool, but he'll not ignore an order from his laird."

"Very well," she said. "And you must send messages to every

family that has not taken the vaccine and tell them to do the same. I have a list at the cottage."

He nodded. "Aye, I saw it. I'll go myself."

"No!" Mia said. "You must remain inside."

"Then I'll send Brodie and Lachlan. I saw them outside earlier." He approached the door, then paused. "What if anyone's showing signs of sickening?"

"Have them brought to me at Riverview Cottage," Mia said. "I'll use my parlor as a hospital."

"Och, no, lass, ye can have a chamber here. Ye'll need all the help ye can get. Elspeth, see to it, will ye?"

The maidservant glanced at Ailsa, then rose and bobbed a curtsy before exiting the chamber.

"Do ye need anything?" Hamish asked.

"Some water and clean cloths," Mia said. "I've brought everything else I need."

"I'll bring ye some."

"No, you cannot return." Mia gestured to the sick girl in the bed. "It's not safe for you."

"Tomorrow, then? Will it be safe tomorrow?"

She shook her head. "If we can contain the infection, it might be safe in a few days. But if it's spread, it could take weeks, given how many people hereabouts are not vaccinated. That's why it's important to isolate not only the sick, but those who are not protected."

He took her hand, then lifted it to his lips.

"Mia, forgive me for not taking the vaccine sooner—and for not persuading others to do so."

"There's nothing to forgive," she said. "You love the people here in your care. I'm sorry if I ever implied otherwise."

"I'm a fortunate man to have ye. I lo—" He hesitated, then nodded. "Thank ye," he whispered. "I'm glad ye're here. I'm proud to call ye wife, even if I'll soon no longer be able to do so."

She curled her fingers around his, and his nostrils flared. But before she could respond, the door opened and Elspeth returned.

"Mrs. Bron is organizing the great hall for ye, ma'am," she said. "She's asked if ye'll be wanting to stay here at the castle while ye treat the sick."

Mia turned to Hamish, and saw nothing but the most intense need in his eyes.

"Please," he whispered. "We need ye—*I* need ye,"

At length, she nodded, and her heart swelled at the flicker of hope in his eyes.

"Mrs. Bron says we're all to be at yer disposal for as long as ye need us," Elspeth added.

"Thank you," Mia said. "I pray it shall not be for long."

CHAPTER THIRTY-THREE

Hamish couldn't remember a time he felt so impotent, so inconsequential, as he did during the month following Ailsa's falling ill. More than thirty souls were brought to Glenblath Castle with signs of infection, a steady stream arriving the first week, which trailed off as the days passed. His wife greeted each arrival with compassion, optimism, and a determination to assuage their fears.

No wonder those doctors had praised her so much! Hamish could only feel shame at the resentment he'd harbored at Mia having the admiration of other men. It had been a resentment born of male pride and a sense of ownership over the woman who belonged to him in the eyes of the law and the Church. But in the eyes of the Almighty, the higher power, she was a woman in her own right—independent and intelligent. She ran the makeshift hospital better than any man, with the efficiency of a trained doctor and the kindness of a woman, nurturing each patient, tending to their pains, holding their hands, and soothing them to sleep at night while they coughed and groaned.

As for his sister…

Iona, despite her condition, had insisted on nursing the sick alongside Mia. At first Hamish had assumed she'd grow weary of the drudgery of issuing medicine, wiping foreheads, bathing sores, and fetching and carrying, but she obeyed Mia's orders with an enthusiasm and compassion that never waned, not once complaining about the aches in her back and feet—aches that were apparent when he saw her collapse into a seat at each day's end, rubbing her back and placing a protective hand over her swollen belly.

As for the disgrace to his family—Hamish couldn't be more proud of his sister. She was a warrior, a future mother protecting herself and the child she carried, weathering the taunts, even those that came from the lips of those she tended to. The worst offender was Murdoch. Even in the throes of fever he called her a hure, yet she held her tongue and cared for both him and his frail little wife.

Clearly, despite Reverend Sutherand's preachings—which Hamish had listened to with more care now that death hung over Glenblath—some men were irredeemable.

Was Hamish also irredeemable?

He glanced at the scar on his arm where Mia had administered the vaccine to him over a fortnight ago, and to others whom she'd managed to treat before they succumbed to the smallpox.

"Are ye proud of her, son?"

Hamish turned to see his mother standing beside him, leaning over the gallery at the activity below.

"My sister?" he said. "Or my wife?"

When she did not respond, he nodded.

"I'm proud of both," he said, watching his wife weave her way through the beds to tend to Shona. Robbie's wife had been one of the first to insist that Mia be banished for the marks on her face, yet Mia had cared for Shona with compassion, soothing her when she cried at night after Robbie had abandoned her at their doorstep, saying he had no wish for a pockmarked wife—then, a few days later, consoling her when the Almighty had seen fit to claim Robbie for His own.

"She'll make a fine mother," Ma said. "Perhaps, one day, a fine wife also."

"I thought ye'd be angry when ye discovered Iona was with child."

"I'd suspected it for some time. My Iona was never afraid of how she looked, never cared for modesty or propriety. Then she started covering herself with shawls as if she had something to hide. Only a numbskull would fail to see what she was hiding."

"I thank ye for putting yer numbskull son in his place."

She smiled. "Ye're a *man*, son. Men are the last to notice what really matters."

"Ye're not angry with her?"

"Not as angry as ye were, from what Iona told me." She sighed, then gestured to the activity below. "Compared to all this, where lives are being lost, what right have I to be angry at her for bringing a life into the world? But I confess I was disappointed at first. I wanted my daughter to make a respectable match, perhaps as a laird's wife, as befits her status. But I shouldn't measure her happiness by what I believed would make me happy at her age. Iona's my child and I love her no matter what. Besides—as Mia told me, when a woman is with child, there's also a man involved. If I should direct my disappointment at anyone, it should be him, whomever he might be."

Hamish resumed his attention on the makeshift hospital. Mia had risen from tending to her patient and was now issuing instructions to Mrs. Bron and Maisie.

"Perhaps *she'll* make a fine mother one day also," Ma said. "She's already a fine wife. Mrs. Bron has nothing but good to speak of her."

"Och, Ma…"

"Dinnae 'och, Ma' me, lad," she said. "If ye won't listen to me, then listen to yer heart. *I'll* tell ye if no one else will. Ye love her. And, if ye think love's not enough, ye *need* her."

"Aye," he said, sighing. "But *she* disnae need *me*."

The dog at his feet let out a whine, and Ma took Hamish's hand, curling her thin fingers around his.

"Ye're talking nonsense, lad," she said. "Even Monarch knows it, dinnae ye, boy?"

The dog—treacherous beastie—thumped his tail on the floor,

then let out another whine.

"Do ye wish to go for a walk, boy?" Hamish said.

The tail thumped again, this time with more enthusiasm.

"Should ye be going outside?" Ma said.

"Mia said that once I was recovered from the effects of the vaccine, it was safe for me to wander about—and the fresh air would do me good."

"Perhaps she might join ye."

"Dinnae disturb her, Ma."

"Then ye should consult with yer conscience, son, seeing as he'll be yer only companion, save Monarch."

Hamish bowed. Leaving her standing at the balustrade, he made his way outside, Monarch trotting at his heels.

Night had long since fallen. The moon cast a soft blue glow on the horizon, illuminating the snow-capped peak of Beinn Blath. But even the mountain seemed to frown at him, the rock formations near the summit reminding him of an angry pagan god demanding that he listen to his conscience.

But Hamish had no need to hear his conscience. He already knew that he'd wronged her. Mia—the woman he'd fallen in love with. Not even a walk on the mountain slopes would clear away the doubts in his mind that had long since been shattered.

He loved her. He had always loved her, even though he'd fought against it and broken her heart while doing so. But she neither loved nor needed him. It was his mother, or Iona, or Maisie that she turned to, rather than him. By fulfilling his wish of keeping her, he would stifle her soul. The greatest act he could commit to prove his love would be to let her go.

By the time he returned, the activity in the great hall had abated. The candles extinguished, the only light was the glow from the fireplace, which Brodie had taken upon himself to feed faithfully in between running errands for Mia and following Iona about with his tongue hanging out like a lovesick puppy.

A steady hush had descended over the castle, punctuated by the clicking of Monarch's claws against the stone floor, the crackling of the fire, and the occasional cough from the hall. Hamish entered, moving along the lines of makeshift beds, exchanging a word or two with the patients. Then his gut twisted with horror as he came to Murdoch's bed.

It was empty.

Then he heard the distant sound of a woman crying—quiet, brokenhearted sobs.

His heart tightened, tugging at his soul, as if an invisible thread linked him to the owner of the voice.

It was Mia.

Where was she?

He followed the passageway, passing Freydis carrying a bundle of bedsheets. The young maid bobbed a curtsy, her face streaked with tears.

"What's the matter?" Hamish said. Freydis merely burst into tears and scuttled off.

His stomach churning with unease, Hamish followed the sound until he came to a thick oak door. He knocked and the sobbing stopped. When he opened it, he saw Mia rising from a chair next to an unlit fireplace. Her companion rose also, his back to Hamish. Then he turned and Hamish exhaled in a sigh of relief.

"Murdoch," he said. "When I saw yer empty bed, I feared the worst. But ye're recovered, thank the Almighty!"

Murdoch shook his head. His dominant stance—the arrogance that shimmered about his bulky frame—was absent. Then he spoke, his voice a hoarse whisper.

"I cannae thank the Almighty," he said. "Not when He's forsaken me as punishment for my sins. I—"

He broke off, coughing, and covered his mouth with his hands.

"M-Murdoch, you should get some rest," Mia said, her voice hoarse and strained. "Why don't—"

"I deserve no rest," Murdoch said quietly.

"What the devil's happened?" Hamish said.

Murdoch shook his head, and Monarch let out a whine and approached the burly Highlander, leaning against his leg. Murdoch, who rarely showed affection for any living soul, lowered his hand and caressed the dog's head.

"Mia?" Hamish said, stepping toward her.

"I-it's Evie," she said, her eyes glistening. "Sh-she..." She glanced at Murdoch, who cringed, his shoulders hunching, as if burdened by a great weight. "She succumbed an hour ago. I-I thought she was getting better—she took a little of Mrs. McBride's broth and said she was looking forward to seeing Billy again. Then she..."

She shook her head. "The next time I saw her, she'd gone. I wasn't even there—she had nobody with her when she—" She broke off, her chest rising and falling. "I'm sorry," she whispered. "So, so sorry."

Hamish extended his hand toward her. She stared at it, trembling with the effort to keep the tears at bay.

Then she took his hand and met his gaze. He didn't know what was more heartbreaking—the glimmer of despair deep in her eyes, or the stoicism with which she tried so valiantly to conquer her despair to give comfort to Murdoch, a man who had never deserved such a sweet wife.

"Hush, my love," he whispered, drawing her close. "Ye've nothing to be sorry for. Ye were a good friend to Evie, and she knew it. She's at peace now, with the angels, and feels no more pain."

He placed a kiss on her head and she softened in his arms, as if he'd unlocked her sorrow. Clinging to him, she parted her lips and sobbed, her tears soaking into his shirt.

She began to shiver. How long had she been sitting in this freezing chamber? Hamish moved to summon someone to light the fire, but his wife only tightened her grip.

"Hamish, please..."

She closed her eyes and buried her head in his chest.

Perhaps he ought to have been glad that, at that moment, she needed him. But to see her despair was more than he could bear. And to acknowledge that he'd willingly throw himself into the pits of hell to ease her pain was to understand that he loved her— more than life itself.

"Please don't go," she whispered. "Hold me for a while longer."

"But…"

"Do as she says, Hamish," Murdoch said, his voice a low growl. "Ye should give that woman of yers everything and anything she wants. Had I listened to her, my bairns might not be marked with the pox—and my Evie…" He curled his hands into fists. "My sweet wee woman might still be here with me—to tend to my bairns, to warm my bed, and to fill my heart. I—"

He broke off, shaking, and Hamish's heart ached to see the strongest, most brutish of men broken by sorrow.

"I know ye didnae think I loved that woman," Murdoch said. "I see the judgment in yer eyes. But Evie was my heart. I wanted to be strong for her—rule my family with a firm hand to protect them from what I believed had been brought among us to bring them harm, for my Billy to grow up to be a strong lad, and my Ailsa to be an honest young lass. Isn't that what every husband and father wants? Isn't that what it means to be a man?"

He gestured to Mia, his eyes darkening with rage. Hamish held her closer as if to protect her.

"Murdoch, I ken ye're angry, but—"

"Och, Hamish, do ye think my anger is at *her*?" Murdoch shook his head. "I'm angry at myself—and every man who seeks to judge an outsider, who's incapable of looking beyond his doubts and fears to see her goodness. I hated yer wife for being a Sassenach, and marked by the pox. I called her hure and encouraged others to do so, and ye did naught to stop me."

In his arms, Mia stiffened, and Hamish caressed her hair, as if soothing a frightened filly, until she grew still once more.

"I've been repaid for my folly," Murdoch said, his voice hoarse. "Dinnae make the same mistake I did."

"Ye cannae blame yerself."

"But I *do*," Murdoch said. "I must face my bairns and tell them that their ma is no more. That will be my true punishment—to look into their eyes and know that I'm the cause of their grief."

"Just as I will have to look into the eyes of every soul at Glenblath and know that I'm to blame for the loss of the lives of so many good people," Hamish said.

And for breaking the heart of the woman I love.

Mia leaned against him, slipping. He caught her and lifted her into his arms.

"Yer wife's exhausted," Murdoch said. "I dinnae think she's slept more than a few minutes while caring for us. Perhaps it's time someone cared for her."

"But I dinnae deserve her."

"Aye, ye do," Murdoch said, his voice quiet. "Or at least, unlike me, ye still have the chance to prove that ye do." He thrust his hands into his pockets, then straightened his stance. "And now, I must try to do right by Ailsa and Billy," he said. "I wouldnae have them hear from anyone other than me that their ma's with the angels."

He wiped his eyes, then exited the chamber, leaving Hamish alone with his wife. But Mia had succumbed to exhaustion. His conscience berating him for relishing the feel of her in his arms—and the knowledge that, in that moment, she needed him, if only for a little while—he carried his unconscious wife to her chamber.

CHAPTER THIRTY-FOUR

THE MINISTER FINISHED the final prayer. Then he closed his Bible and bowed his head. Silence descended over the company in the churchyard as the trio who stood apart from the main group shuffled toward the open grave.

Murdoch, with his children Ailsa and Billy.

The huge Highlander unfolded a piece of paper in his hand. Then Ailsa linked her arm with his, tilted her head to meet her father's gaze, and nodded while Billy clung to his hand.

A baby cried, quickly silenced, then Murdoch spoke.

"May we hear her in the breath of the Highland wind.
May we see her in the light of the winter sun.
May we feel her warmth by the hearth of our home.
We will remember her when the day is done."

Mia blinked, her eyes stinging with the tears she fought to keep at bay. A hand touched her shoulder and she reached for it, running her fingertips over the roughened skin.

"Hamish…"

"Aye, Mia, I know."

She leaned against him, succumbing to her need for his strength. He dipped his head and she felt his warm lips brush the top of her head.

"Come, lass," he whispered. "Let them say their last goodbye to Evie. We have our duty to be strong for our clan."

Our clan…

He paused, and when she whispered her consent, he linked his arm through hers. He turned and nodded to Reverend Sutherland, who began reciting a prayer. Then he led her through the company, who parted and bowed their heads. Eilidh followed, Iona by her side. Then the rest of the clan lined up behind them, forming a procession toward the castle building.

The great hall, no longer a makeshift hospital, had been transformed. Long tables lined the perimeter, laden with pies, soups, and roasts. A feast to honor the departed—ten souls in all, of whom Evie was the last to be buried.

Mia caught her breath as she recalled the last time she'd seen the great hall ready for a feast—the wedding feast that her arrival had interrupted. The man beside her now, the disappointed bridegroom, paused, as if recalling the same memory.

"Forgive me, Mia," he whispered, his eyes glistening.

Were his tears for Evie, for his clan…or for her?

"What for?"

"For everything," he said. "For not taking the vaccine—which brought about deaths that will lie heavy on my soul—and for causing so much work for ye while my people suffered. But most of all…" His voice cracked and he closed his eyes, his nostrils flaring as he inhaled. When he opened them again, moisture pooled in the corners. "Most of all, for not being the husband ye deserve. For not loving ye as ye deserve."

Mia's heart clenched.

He had said it. Though he begged forgiveness—his humble plea only making her love him more—in the same breath he admitted that he didn't love her. She would have borne it better had he been a cruel man. But he was not. He was a man of honor, loyal to his clan and the people who depended on him. And to *not* be loved by such a man…

"There's nothing to forgive," she said. "And if there were, you'd have my forgiveness without needing to ask."

He led her toward the high table at the far end, seated her in the center, then sat beside her. The company followed, pausing before them to nod in greeting before taking their seats—first Eilidh and Iona, who took the seats either side of Mia and Hamish, then the rest of the clan. When Murdoch approached, he paused and bowed his head.

"Laird MacLennan, Lady MacLennan…"

Mia opened her mouth to protest, and Hamish squeezed her hand.

"Please, Mia," he whispered. "Today, ye're my wife and Lady of Glenblath, even if ye wish ye weren't."

She glanced at him, but his face was in profile and she couldn't see his full expression. But she caught a glimmer of moisture in his eyes. Then he blinked and it was gone.

After the company was seated, the feast began, to honor the lost souls and give thanks for those who had survived. Amid the backdrop of soft music, the company ate, their conversation muted, the deep tones reminiscent of the sounds of the river.

How she would miss them—the servants and tenants who now looked upon her with affection and gratitude. The handful who still made their dislike clear—Shona, and one or two others—could not lessen her sense of belonging. But she would be leaving, once Iona's child arrived. Hamish had raised funds to repay most of her dowry, and a letter had arrived from Portia offering Mia a home and expressing her desire to see her again.

A light hand touched hers and Mia turned to see Eilidh watching her, compassion in her clear green eyes.

"Are ye well, lass?"

Mia nodded, unable to speak lest her sorrow betray her.

"Today's not a day to be unhappy, lass. Evie wouldnae have wished it."

"I-I know, Eilidh. She's at peace now."

"Och, lass, I wasnae referring to yer sorrow over Evie's passing. I was referring to yerself, and how ye're soon to be leaving us once Iona's had her bairn."

The man beside Mia stiffened.

"Has young Brodie been giving ye satisfaction?" Eilidh continued, then she glanced at Hamish as his knife slipped to the floor and fell with a clatter.

He turned his gaze to her, his expression hardening. Eilidh merely smiled and nodded to him.

"Brodie's been so helpful, son," she said. "Not content with fetching and carrying for yer sister, even though she's perfectly capable of fending for herself, Brodie's been helping Mia pack her belongings for when she leaves Glenblath."

"Is that so?" Hamish said, his voice a low growl as his gaze settled on the young groom sitting beside Ailsa. Brodie glanced up and his eyes widened. Then he colored and resumed his attention on the plate in front of him.

On Hamish's other side, Iona sat, staring at Brodie across the hall as she pushed her food around her plate.

"Are ye going to eat that, sister," Hamish said, "or play the fool with it?"

Iona leaned back in her seat. "I'm not hungry."

"Are you well?" Mia said. "Your cheeks are red."

"I'm hot, that's all," Iona said, narrowing her eyes, a flicker of pain in their expression.

"You look uncomfortable."

"A slight ache in my back," Iona said. "I rose too quickly this morning and hurt myself. But it's better now." She took a bite of meat as if to prove her point. "Brodie's just as bad as ye—asking if I'm well twenty times a day."

"Och, yes," Eilidh said, her lips curving into a smile. "He's such a kind lad. He's been writing a catalogue of all Mia's medicines for her to take with her. I remarked on the excellence of his penmanship, did I not, Mia?"

"You did," Mia said.

"But I swear," Eilidh continued, "I've never seen penmanship as exquisite as Lady Portia's."

"Who the devil is *Lady Portia*?" Hamish growled.

"Mia's particular friend," Eilidh said. "She's invited Mia to stay with her. Would ye credit it, she's the sister of a duke—the Duke of Foxton!"

"So ye prefer a duke to a laird?" Hamish said, fixing his gaze on Mia, and she caught a flash of frenzy in his eyes—the look of a stag when faced with a rival.

"I doubt I'll see Portia's brother when I visit her," Mia said.

"That must be a misfortune for ye," he muttered, before taking a bite of venison, his jaw bulging as he chewed.

"Besides," Mia continued, "Portia's brother is a rake who thinks too highly of himself. Countless women—young and old— pine over him in the hopes that he might bestow them a scrap of his attention, but he's too devoted to self-gratification to notice, except when congratulating himself on adding another shattered heart to his tally."

"And did he shatter *yer* heart?" Hamish said. "Is that how ye became friends with this Lady Portia?"

"Och, no, son!" Eilidh said. "Mia treated Lady Portia for a bullet wound."

"A *what*? How does a lady sustain a bullet wound?"

"In a duel," Mia said.

"Hellion!" Hamish grunted, resuming eating.

"But I will confess," Mia said, "her brother is very hand-some."

"The swiving fucker."

His voice was barely a whisper—so faint that she might have imagined it, save for the flash in his eyes, the reflection from the fire in the hearth giving them a reddish glow.

An uncomfortable silence descended, where he seemed to bristle with annoyance, his body tense, like a hunting dog poised to pounce, hackles raised, ears erect and alert. Each time Mia spoke to Eilidh, he shifted closer, as if straining to hear her words, while the conversation around the hall grew noisier as the guests imbibed wine.

But when the feast was over and he stood to deliver a speech, the compassionate man returned as he honored the fallen and gave thanks for the survivors. Then he turned to Mia and offered his hand. With several pairs of eyes on her, she took it and stood. Was he about to declare that they would soon be rid of her?

"And now," Hamish said, after the whispering abated, "I wish to honor one among us who did more for our clan than any other. My wife, Euphramia Mary MacLennan, Lady of Glenblath!"

The scraping of chairs filled the hall as the company rose and lifted their glasses.

"Lady of Glenblath!" they chorused.

Mia blinked back tears and sipped her wine. Then Hamish lifted her hand to his lips and declared the feast to be over. The party filed out, save for the servants, who left their seats and began to clear the plates. Mia picked up her plate and reached for Hamish's, but he caught her hand.

"No, lass," he said. "The Lady of Glenblath has earned her rest."

"But I'm not—"

He dipped his head and silenced her with a swift kiss. Then he rose and steered her out of the great hall. Monarch, who had been sleeping in front of the fire, leaped to his feet and trotted after them. But Hamish didn't steer Mia toward her chamber—where Eilidh had insisted she remain until she left Glenblath for good, and, in her weakness, she'd agreed. Instead, he led her around the castle building, along the corridors and passageways that she'd come to know. Perhaps he intended for her to say goodbye to every stone that formed the building—every wall and tapestry, every soul that resided there…

By the time they reached Mia's chamber, a fire was already crackling in the hearth, courtesy of Ailsa, who was poking at the base as Hamish pushed the door open.

"Ailsa, there's no need to do that when you're mourning your mother," Mia said.

The girl rose and dipped into a curtsy. "It's what Ma would

have wanted, Yer Ladyship," she said. She touched her face where the pockmarks, still fresh, had yet to fade. "I-I'm sorry I weren't more—"

She broke off as Mia stepped forward and pulled her into her arms.

"It's forgotten," she said. "What matters now is that you're alive—and your mother lives on in you. I know that she'll be looking down, so proud of the lovely young woman you are."

Ailsa sniffed and wiped her nose.

"Be off with ye now, lass," Hamish said, his voice gentle. "Tell Mrs. McBride that ye're not to do any work this afternoon. Murdoch and wee Billy need ye more than Lady MacLennan and me."

The girl curtsied once more then slipped out of the chamber, leaving Mia alone with her husband.

They stood, staring at each other, the warmth and crackle of the fire filling the gulf between them. Then he held out his hand, uncertainty in his eyes.

"Mia… Mia, I want—"

He broke off as a scream came from outside.

"Lady MacLennan!"

Hamish sprinted to the door and pulled it open to reveal a young maidservant.

"Freydis? Has my mother been taken ill?"

"N-no, Master Hamish. I-I meant Lady Euphramia. We need her. It's Iona—her pains have come."

Mia took the young girl's hand. "It's nothing to fear," she said. "Let me fetch my things. Meanwhile, I'll need plenty of hot water, if you could run and ask Mrs. McBride."

"N-no—Elspeth said to bring ye right away," Freydis sobbed. "I-it's the baby. There's something wrong."

"What's wrong?" Mia said, a knot of dread tightening in her gut.

"The baby's not turned—that's what Elspeth said. A-and it's already coming! Elspeth said that Mistress Iona could die. I've seen it before, Yer Ladyship—young Davinia, her who used to live in the croft near the school. She lost her child, and the Almighty took her the next day."

"Davinia was a sickly girl," Hamish said. "She always had been. My sister has a hearty constitution. She'll be well, won't she, Mia?"

His voice carried an undercurrent of despair. Mia took his hand and he curled his fingers around hers, tightening the grip until Mia groaned with pain.

"Davinia died screaming in agony, Master Hamish," Freydis said, tears rolling down her cheeks. "Elspeth said that if Iona's baby hasn't turned, it'll die and take the mother with it. She said—"

"Dear God!" Hamish cried. "Won't ye stop? Bring the hot water, and cease yer prattling."

Freydis ran off, still sobbing, and Hamish turned to Mia, his eyes glazed with fear.

"Is there anything ye can do?"

Mia's heart urged her to reassure him, but a voice inside her head spoke of the fate that most likely awaited Hamish's sister.

She squeezed his hand.

"I can try," she said. "I'll do everything I can."

As MIA ENTERED Iona's chamber, her confidence waned, along with her hope. Elspeth's tear-stained face was that of a woman already in mourning. As for the young woman on the bed…

Iona lay on her back, legs akimbo, her arms splayed out as if she'd been frozen in the throes of agony. Her face, creased and contorted, was a deep shade of red with an unnatural sheen of moisture on her skin. Eyes closed, lips drawn back to reveal her teeth, she moved her head weakly from side to side, soft moans escaping her mouth.

Elspeth glanced up.

"I-I dinnae know what to do for her, Yer Ladyship. I found her at the foot of the stairs, bleeding and in pain. She… Dear God Almighty!"

Elspeth let out a cry as the woman on the bed came to life, her back arching as she seemed to strain toward the heavens, seeking respite from the pain. She opened her mouth wide and wailed, and Mia's skin tightened in terror.

"Shall I send for yer mother, Master Hamish?" Elspeth said.

"Not yet," he said, placing a gentle hand on the small of Mia's back. "Let my wife tend to her first."

"But—"

"I *said*, not yet!" he cried, his voice growing in strength. "Mia, what can ye do for her?"

Mia glanced at him as the shroud of fear threatened to envelop her. "I-I don't know…"

He took her hand. "Yes ye do, my love. Go to her. She needs ye. *I* need ye."

Mia approached the bed and touched Iona's arm. The young woman turned her gaze toward Mia, her green eyes dulled to a dark gray, almost as if she'd already succumbed.

"Iona," she whispered, "I'm here."

"Mia?"

Thin, bony hands curled around Mia's wrist, then tightened as Iona stiffened once more.

"Help me!" she cried.

Mia uncurled Iona's fingers from her wrist, then approached the foot of the bed. She peered between Iona's parted thighs and stifled a gasp.

"The baby's coming," she said, pushing up her sleeves.

"Shouldn't ye wash yer hands first, Yer Ladyship?" Elspeth said.

"There's no time. The child's coming. I must act now, or…"
Or both mother and child will die.

Hamish drew in a sharp breath, as if he'd heard the voice in

Mia's mind.

Iona let out another wail and terror clawed at Mia's heart. What if her intervention caused more harm? Dr. McIver had said that most mothers did not survive a birthing if the baby had not turned—and new mothers almost not at all, unless with the help of a skilled surgeon, and someone with the ability to remain calm under pressure.

And she was neither.

"Mia, dinnae be afraid," Hamish said. "Ye're Iona's best hope."

"What if I cannot save her?"

"Ye won't save her if ye dinnae try, my love."

My love...

Mia closed her eyes, recalling Dr. McIver's notes. Then she reached forward and placed her hand on the emerging child.

"Hamish!" Iona cried. "Where are ye?"

"I'm here, sister," he said.

"Will I die today? Mia! Tell me if I'll die today."

Hamish exchanged a glance with Mia, his eyes narrowing as he recognized her fear. Then he mouthed, *Be strong for her, lass.*

Mia nodded.

"Not if I can help it," she said. "Now, I want you to listen to my voice and do as I say. You must try not to push even though you'll feel that you need to. Can you do that for me?"

"Y-yes, I—Oh!"

Iona let out another cry as Mia felt the child's body, cupping the tiny form as its legs emerged—first one, then the other, then the lower torso.

"Thank the Lord!" Elspeth exclaimed. "It's a girl!"

"It's not over yet," Mia said. "There's still a risk that..." She glanced toward Iona's face, contorted in agony, and lowered her voice. "The risk to the child is at its greatest unless I can turn her around."

"What can I do?" Hamish said, and placed a hand on Mia's arm. "Let me help ye."

"I-I don't know," she said. "I read about this in Dr. McIver's notes, but I've not even seen him undertake the procedure, much less do it myself. What if I fail?"

"Then ye'll at least have tried," he said. "There's none other with whom I'd trust my sister's life, or my own."

Mia's heart swelled as she swallowed the rising terror. Dr. McIver had always said that while caution was a quality essential in a physician, fear was the doctor's most powerful foe.

And the man beside her, supporting her—the man who called her *my love*—strove to conquer her fear on her behalf. She owed it to him to show that his trust was not misguided.

"Very well," she said. "Hold the child in position. Firmly, but gently—yes, like that. Now, the next time Iona moves, the child will want to come farther out, but you must keep her there while I try to free her arms."

"Aye, I understand."

Iona let out another wail and Mia froze. Hamish met her gaze.

"I trust ye, lass," he said. "Ye've saved countless lives already and we're so much in yer debt—ye can save two more today. My clever, brave wee wife."

He smiled encouragement, and Mia slipped her hand along the tiny form until she felt a shoulder. Then, carefully, she rotated the baby.

"The next time Iona moves, pull—but gently," she whispered.

He nodded, then, as Iona stiffened once more, the child slipped farther out, releasing her arms.

"Stop!" Mia cried. "I must protect the baby's head. Wait until I say."

With her fingertips, she found the chin and slipped her hand up to cup the delicate little head. Then she closed her eyes and uttered a prayer before gently easing the head out. Iona let out a wail as the child finally slipped from her body, then collapsed back on the bed, eyes closed.

"See to Iona, Elspeth," Mia said.

"What about the child, Yer Ladyship?"

Mia glanced at the tiny form. Fear morphed into dread as the child's lips darkened in color until they were almost purple. She placed a hand on the baby's chest and held her breath. Then the little girl tilted her head back, opened her mouth, and let out a long, low wail. Her chest expanded as she inhaled, and her cheeks reddened as she screamed at the world to herald her entry into it.

Tears stung Mia's eyes as she pulled a blanket around the little form and held the child in her arms—the child she had brought into the world.

Then she heard a long, low sob and looked up to see her husband, his eyes red-rimmed and glistening, tears falling onto his cheeks.

"You have a niece," she whispered.

"Aye," he said. "*We* have a niece."

"Is...my baby alive?" a soft voice asked.

"Aye, Mistress Iona," Elspeth said. "And she's beautiful, just like her ma. Would ye like to meet her?"

The old maidservant approached Mia, arms outstretched. For a moment, Mia felt a rush of loss as she handed the child over and closed her eyes, unwilling for others to see the ugly ball of resentment and envy that curled in her gut.

Then a large, warm hand cupped her chin. She opened her eyes to see her husband watching her, his expression filled with pride and love.

"My beautiful wife," he breathed. "How did I survive—how did any of us survive—without ye?"

He lifted his hand and traced a line around her face with his fingertip, caressing her forehead, then following a trail along her cheek toward her mouth, where he placed his fingertip against her lips.

How could a man so brawny, with the body of a beast, touch her with such tenderness? A tear swelled in his eye, then splashed onto his cheek. She placed her hand on his face and brushed away the tear with her thumb.

"There's no shame in shedding a tear, Hamish," she said. "A new life has entered the world, a beautiful little girl for you to love and cherish. How can anyone express their joy at such a gift other than to shed a tear?"

He took her hand. "I vow, on this day, that I shall ever again shed a tear, until"—he hesitated, a flicker of shyness in his eyes—"until I have cause to."

"Cause?"

"Aye," he said. "The next tear I shed shall be on the day that my own firstborn child is placed into my arms."

His words broke the spell.

Was he, even now, looking to the day that her replacement might give him an heir? Now Iona's baby had come, Mia had no reason to stay at Glenblath—no promise to keep her here.

The door burst open and Eilidh appeared, Freydis at her side.

"Daughter!" she cried. "I heard ye were—"

"I'm well, Ma," Iona said. "Would ye like to meet yer grand-daughter?"

"Och, Iona!" Eilidh said, embracing her daughter. "My clever wee lass!"

"I should leave you to get acquainted," Mia said, stemming the tide of tears, and before anyone responded, she exited the chamber. As soon as she'd shut the door behind her, she leaned against the wall and succumbed to sobs. The beginning of a new life had heralded the end of Mia's life at Glenblath—a life away from the people, the family, and the man she had come to love.

CHAPTER THIRTY-FIVE

STEEL FINGERS GRIPPED at Hamish's heart as he saw his wife slip away. Today marked the end of her commitment to stay.

"Och, for the love of the devil's fat, round arse!" his mother cried. She turned to Iona and placed her hands on her hips. "I'm glad yer bairn's a girl, lass. At least she'll grow up with *some* intelligence."

"Unlike her numbskull of an uncle," Iona said, rising from the bed.

"Ye shouldn't be getting up, sister," Hamish said.

"And ye shouldn't be such a bloody arse, brother," she huffed, grimacing. "*Shite!* It feels like my cunny's been turned inside out."

"Iona!" he said. "Dinnae curse in front of the bairn—or yer laird."

"She'll hear a great deal worse from *ye*, I'll warrant, brother."

"And ye *are* an arse," his mother said, lifting the baby into her arms. "Do ye love yer wife?"

"Of course I bloody do!"

"Then tell her."

"Better still, *show* her," Iona said, her breathing labored as she limped toward a chair by the fireplace. "Och, that hurts."

"That'll teach ye to go carrying on with men such as Murdoch," Hamish said. "And now yer bairn's here, I must take him to task—make him face his responsibility, whether he's in mourning or not."

"Murdoch?" Iona let out a snort. "Ye think it was *Murdoch?*"

"Then who was it?"

"It was Robbie, wasnae it, lass?" Ma said quietly, as she rocked the baby in her arms. "I saw the way he looked at ye—heard how ye spoke of his Shona carrying on with others, and Shona never liked ye. Did ye love him, lass?"

Iona bit her lip, then shook her head. "I thought I did, but then he called me a hure when I said I was expecting a bairn—said it could be anyone's brat."

She reached toward Ma, who passed the baby back to her. Then she dipped her head and placed a kiss on the child's cheek.

"She's nobody's but *mine*," Iona whispered. "My wee Mairi."

Mairi—it meant *beloved*.

"Aye, she'll be beloved, with ye as her ma," Hamish said. He opened the door and saw his wife's retreating back at the far end of the passageway. "Mia!"

She stopped and turned, her face streaked with tears, and he held out his hand.

"Do ye not want to see yer niece?"

For a moment, he thought she'd refuse. Then she wiped her eyes and returned, each step seeming to take an age as he waited to touch her again. As she drew near, he took her hand.

"Iona!" she said. "You shouldn't be up after such a difficult confinement."

His sister let out a laugh. "We MacLennans are hardy lasses. And I have my doctor to take care of me, do I not?"

"Who?"

"*Ye*, of course!" Iona laughed.

Hamish's heart swelled and, to his shame, his groin tightened at his wife's smile.

Devil's sweet, hairy arse—how beautiful she looked!

"Ye must come and meet the bairn properly, lass," he said. "Ye're not just a doctor who delivers a child and leaves. Ye're her family. Wee Mairi will love ye as much as the rest of us—save one, whose love for ye nobody can surpass."

Mia's eyes flared with hope as if she wished, but could not trust, to understand his meaning. Then she nodded.

"Of course. I'm sorry, Iona, for leaving."

She approached the fireplace and Iona handed the child over. Hamish held his breath, then his heart began to sing as joy illuminated Mia's warm hazel eyes.

"Hello, little one," she said. "Forgive me for being so uncivil as to not greet you properly. I'm Mia, and I am..." She paused and lifted her gaze.

"This is yer aunt, wee Mairi," Hamish said. "She brought ye into the world and ye owe her yer life—as so many of us do."

"And this," Iona said, "is Mairi." She met Mia's gaze. "Mairi Euphramia MacLennan."

Mia drew in a sharp breath, her eyes widening. "Iona, I don't deserve such—"

"Aye, ye do," Iona said. "Ye saved her life, so ye're responsible for her as much as I. I'll need ye to teach her to be strong, good, and kind—to be a better person than her ma." She cast a saucy glance at Hamish. "And better than her uncle, though *that* won't be difficult."

Iona tilted her head to one side and regarded Hamish with her clear green eyes, and he smiled at the determined expression in them—and the firm set to her jaw. If wee Mairi took after her ma, she'd be a handful.

Then he saw it once more—the intensity of longing in his wife's eyes as she smiled down at the little soul in her arms. How might she smile at her own child?

He blinked and his eyes blurred with moisture as she handed the baby back to Iona. When his vision cleared he saw his mother staring at him, and her lips moved as she mouthed something.

Show her, ye great big arse.

"Mia, would ye come with me?" he said, offering his hand. She stared at it, then, at length, placed her hand in his. He steered her out of the chamber.

"About fecking time," Iona grumbled as she pulled a face. "Ye great big fool!"

He led his wife down a flight of stairs, then along the passageway toward the back of the castle building until they reached a thick, arched oak door engraved with Celtic knots. There he paused, tempering an onset of shyness.

What if she didn't like it?

"What's this?" Mia asked.

Unable to respond, his throat tight, Hamish opened the door and led her inside.

The room had been cleaned from floor to ceiling, the stones almost gleaming in the light of the sun that caught the walls, picking out the crystals in the granite. One wall was covered with shelves that contained an array of jars, arranged in order of size, and a large wooden chest almost filled the opposite wall—each drawer Hamish knew to be filled with freshly laundered sheets and bandages. The fireplace, which had gone unused since his da's passing, was swept and laid, ready for lighting, with a pile of logs stacked to one side. An iron pot, which Hamish had polished yesterday until he could almost see his face in it, was suspended over the fireplace, and a thick wooden table dominated the center of the room.

The chamber was as close as Hamish could get to replicating Mia's parlor at Riverview Cottage.

"Take a look," he said, pulling her farther into the room. "What do ye think?"

Mia glanced at him, a slight frown furrowing her forehead.

He gestured to the shelves. "Rory helped me with those, and Maisie cleaned the jars all ready for ye to use."

She approached the shelves and ran her fingertips over the jars.

"The cabinet came from the old log store," he said. "But it's cleaned up well and only needed minor repairs. Open the drawers!"

She glanced up, and he cursed his eagerness. *Devil's ballocks,* he sounded like a wee lad desperate to earn his ma's praise. And he *was* desperate—for a sign of approval from the woman he loved.

Was this how the eagle felt when he'd built an eyrie for his mate, collecting twigs and branches to make it sound and feathers and heather to keep it warm, then perching himself on the edge, tempering his pride at his handiwork while he waited for her judgment—not only of the nest he'd built for her, but of his suitability as a mate?

Mia approached the cabinet and pulled open the top drawer, where rolls of bandages were stacked in a neat pattern.

"Maisie made the bandages. She knows how ye like them. She said I ought to…"

His voice trailed off as she turned her gaze on him, and he held his breath.

Would she reject him, or think him too forward?

"O-of course, ye're under no obligation," he said, rushing the words out to avoid her disapproval if she thought he sought to imprison her. "I know ye can be a doctor anywhere. But ye can also be a doctor *here*, among people who care for ye, who need ye. Y-ye can still leave, if ye wish it, b-but if ye wish to stay a little longer, this room is yers."

"And—my medicines?"

"They're still in yer chamber. But there's room for them here, see?"

He pointed to the empty spaces on the shelves.

"It's *yer* choice, Mia. I didnae wish to choose for ye. It's a gift, this room. For ye. Whether ye accept it will not change how much I love ye. We can still use what's here—Iona's learned much from ye, and Maisie's offered to help her. Well, what she said was that if I was so foolish as to let ye go, she'll use it to the best of her abilities. Rory told her she shouldn't speak to her laird so, but I said to Rory that she had every right to, seein' as she's been such a friend to ye. And perhaps wee Mairi might want to learn about medicines and herbs when she grows up. Of course, I want ye to be here to teach her, but if ye're not, I…"

He paused, his heart hammering against his chest as she raised her hand.

Had he said too much? Was she angry—or the room not to her liking?

"What did you say, Hamish?" she said quietly.

"Och, I know she's a wee bairn, but Mairi will be a bright lass, I'm sure of it, with Iona as her ma, and I'm sure she'd want to—"

"No," she said. "What did you say *before* that?"

A light flickered in the depths of her eyes, the soft hazel deepening into shades of green and brown. Dare he believe that her eyes showed a hope to match his own?

"I said that I love ye, Mia."

He took her hand and ran his fingertips over her skin, which was dotted with callouses on the underside—the marks of her toil and dedication—and pockmarks on the back—the marks of her bravery.

Then he placed his hand on her face. Her chest rose and fell in a sigh and she closed her eyes, leaning into his touch. He ran his thumb over the marks on her skin and moisture pricked his eyes.

How could anyone think her scars distasteful? He had long since seen them as marks of her beauty—that he loved as much as the rest of her.

She opened her eyes and doubt clouded their expression, as if she still felt shame. She moved to withdraw, but he drew her close and placed a kiss on her cheek, his lips brushing against her scars.

"Ye're beautiful, Mia."

"But I'm—"

"Ye're *beautiful*," he repeated, his voice firm. "I'll cut the ballocks off anyone who says otherwise."

Unable to stand before the goddess he wished to worship, he lowered himself to his knees.

"Hamish, you shouldn't—"

"Hush, wife, and hear what I have to say. Ye promised to obey me, didnae ye?"

Her eyes flared with defiance, and his cock—that treacherous part of him that yearned to be buried in her once more—stirred at the prospect of taming that defiance in his bed.

And perhaps elsewhere, such as against the wall, over the table, or among the heather on the slopes of Beinn Blath…

"Stay," he said. "Not for obligation or duty, but for love. I *love* ye, and I need ye like the fish in the river need water, like the trees need the light and the air, like the sinner's soul needs redemption."

He bowed his head and brushed his lips against her hand. Then he flicked his tongue against her fingers and was rewarded with a little gasp of pleasure.

"Ye're a strong lass," he said. "Strong enough to rule Glenblath by my side, and in my stead. We need ye—*I* need ye. And though ye may never need me, I am yours if ye'll accept me—ready, and here. For ye. All for ye."

He bowed his head, uttering a silent prayer to the Almighty.

Silence fell, which, though it might only have been a few heartbeats, was, to him, an eternity of agony. Then she slid her fingers against his, until they interlocked.

"You're wrong, Hamish," she said quietly. His stomach clenched with apprehension and he opened his eyes to see her smiling at him, her eyes gleaming with tears.

"Wr-wrong?"

"Aye," she whispered, her lips curving into a smile. "I do need you—and I love you. I loved you from the moment I realized it was you who brought me the logs—that it was you who watched over me, unseen, to make sure I was safe."

"Then I win," he said, "for I believe I loved ye from the first moment I saw ye—the ghost whose final act was born of generosity and kindness. And I thank the Almighty that He brought ye back to life and into my arms. It now only remains for me to ask ye one question. Will ye consent to be my wife—not for convenience, nor an act of kindness to a stranger. But as a woman, willingly cleaving herself to the man who loves her?"

He almost wept at the joy that flared in her eyes. A tear splashed onto her cheek and she nodded.

"Yes," she said. "Yes, I will marry you—not as a dying woman wanting to help a stranger, but as a woman, utterly, completely, and devotedly in love."

He rose to his feet, lifted his head, and let out a roar of joy. Then he circled his arms around her waist and spun her around.

"Hamish!" she said, laughing. "Let me go!"

"No, lass," he said. "That is something I shall never do. Ye're my beloved wife, and I'll never let ye go again."

CHAPTER THIRTY-SIX

"A TOAST, TO Mairi Euphramia MacLennan!"

"Mairi Euphramia MacLennan!"

The company lifted their glasses as Iona stood beside Brodie, who cradled the baby in his arms.

"Not like *that*, Brodie," Iona snapped. "Ye mustn't let her head fall back. Mia said so. Here—like this."

"*Ye* show me, then, Iona."

Iona rolled her eyes, then placed her hand over Brodie's. The two of them colored, and Mia exchanged a smile with Hamish as the lovesick young man tended to baby Mairi as if she were his own.

And perhaps, one day, she would be.

Rory rose to his feet, Maisie at his side, her face flushed with wine and pleasure. "And a toast to Laird and Lady MacLennan, who affirmed their vows today!"

"Laird and Lady MacLennan!"

A cheer rose as Mia found herself swept into her husband's arms.

"Hamish, what are you—"

"Och, woman, surely ye ken what I'm about on the night we celebrate our union? Do ye want me to toss ye over my shoulder like the beast that I am and claim me in my lair?"

Sweet heaven! His words, crude and base though they were, stirred such unholy sensations in her belly as to be most scandal-

317

ous. But as she turned to glance at the minister, she saw Reverend Sutherland, wine glass in hand, grinning from ear to ear.

"He'll not mind," her husband said. "Did ye not hear him preach about the duties of a husband and wife and how the sanctity of marriage must be celebrated and worshipped? I cannae think of a better way to worship ye than to spread those pretty thighs and—"

"Hamish!" Mia cried, as Rory let out a deep belly laugh.

"Och, Master Hamish, I'll wager ye'll hear yer name coming from yer woman's lips as she's coming apart in yer bed."

"Rory!" Maisie said, slapping his arm. "Ye shouldnae say such things to Master Hamish."

"Och, lass, dinnae worry—ye'll be getting the same attention from yer man tonight." Rory turned to the minister. "Beggin' yer pardon, Reverend Sutherland, but when a man's about to wed this fine creature here, it's a sin to leave her be before I make an honest woman of her."

"Ye mean when I make an honest man of *ye*, Rory," Maisie said.

Amid the cheers, Mia's husband carried her out of the great hall, then he broke into a run as he made his way to their bedchamber. As soon as he set her on the bed, he shed his plaid while she unlaced her gown until he stood before her, his naked form gleaming in the light of the fire. Her gaze wandered over the planes of his muscles, the arms and legs that looked as if they had been sculpted from marble, the soft, downy chest hair that grew denser lower down—and his thick manhood, ready and eager for her, that bobbed as he approached the bed.

Since he'd declared his love, Hamish had brought her to pleasure with his hands and mouth almost every night—and several afternoons, when he'd slipped into her parlor to pleasure her against the wall, taken her against a tree in the forest, eliciting all manner of sensations as she writhed at his touch, the bark digging into her back. Last night he'd parted her thighs at the dining table at supper to slip his accomplished fingers inside her while she tried—in vain—not to spill her stew. Then he'd lifted her onto the table, swept the stew aside, and feasted on her. But tonight…

Tonight he would give her his all—the part of him that beckoned to her as she licked her lips in anticipation of tasting him as he had tasted her.

"Does my wife like what she sees?" he teased.

"Yes."

"And does she forgive me for being a rutting beast?"

"I find I relish having such a man for a husband."

"I can be gentle also, lass," he said, "though I fear tonight I'll not be able to restrain the wild stag within me. I've been hungry all day—hungry to bury myself inside ye."

"Then claim your female," Mia said, parting her thighs. The brief pulse of shame at her wantonness dispersed as she caught the exultation in his eyes. What could be more glorious than to give pleasure to her man, whom she loved above all?

He crawled onto the bed, his muscles rippling, and the familiar sensation of heat pooled in her center. Then, with a swift movement that belied his big body, he speared her with a single, hard thrust.

"Oh!" Mia cried out as her mind shattered with pleasure. Then her body followed, rippling through her center, sending waves of ecstasy through her. So unlike the pleasure at his touch, the pleasure from having him deep inside her was almost unbearable in its deliciousness. "Hamish!"

At her cry, he came to pleasure, her name on his lips, and writhed on top of her, claiming her mouth as thoroughly as he claimed her body while she wrapped her legs about his waist to draw him deeper in.

At length, he grew quiet, still inside her, then he brushed his lips against her breasts, pausing to kiss each nipple, igniting a tiny fizz of pleasure. He placed his head on her chest and let out a deep sigh.

"If only I could spend the rest of my life here," he whispered, "with ye in my bed, and my cock inside ye, where he can serve ye best."

Her body pulsed and he smiled.

"Ah, my woman enjoys it when I speak like a beast. I can feel ye're eager to take him again."

"Am I such a wanton, Hamish?"

"Ye're *my* wanton. And I wouldnae have ye any other way. Ye'd have been wasted had ye returned to yer Sassenach dandies. Would they have given ye such pleasure as I can?"

He began to withdraw and she arched her back, her body recognizing, instinctively, its need for him. His eyes gleamed with wickedness and he slipped inside her once more.

"I'll take that as a no, lass—as a confession that only I can give ye the pleasure ye deserve."

They lay together listening to the crackle of the fireplace and the distant sound of merriment as the company continued to celebrate their union—a union they had forged as strangers then reaffirmed as unlikeliest of lovers—the Highland Beast and the Ghost of the Ton.

About the Author

Emily Royal grew up in Sussex, England, and has devoured romantic novels for as long as she can remember. A mathematician at heart, Emily has worked in financial services for over twenty years. She indulged in her love of writing after she moved to Scotland, where she lives with her husband, teenage daughters, and menagerie of rescue pets—including Twinkle, an attention-seeking boa constrictor.

She has a passion for both reading and writing romance with a weakness for Regency rakes, Highland heroes, and Medieval knights. *Persuasion* is one of her all-time favorite novels, which she reads several times each year, and she is fortunate enough to live within sight of a Medieval palace.

When not writing, Emily enjoys playing the piano, baking, and painting landscapes, particularly of the Highlands. One of her ambitions is to paint, as well as climb, every mountain in Scotland.

Follow Emily Royal

Newsletter Signup: subscribepage.io / RKBvRE
Facebook: facebook.com / eroyalauthor
Bookbub: bookbub.com / authors / emily-royal
Instagram: instagram.com / eroyalauthor
Amazon: amazon.com / stores / Emily-Royal / author / B07NCBKJZ4
Website: www.emroyal.com
Goodreads: goodreads.com / author / show / 14834886.Emily_Royal
Twitter: @eroyalauthor

www.ingramcontent.com/pod-product-compliance
Lightning Source LLC
Chambersburg PA
CBHW051235050726
47594CB00001B/183